COLLECTED STORIES

DJUNA BARNES

Collected Stories

Edited with an Introduction
by Phillip Herring

SUN &
MOON

CLASSICS

110

LOS ANGELES
SUN & MOON PRESS
1996

Sun & Moon Press
A Program of The Contemporary Arts Educational Project, Inc.
a nonprofit corporation
6026 Wilshire Boulevard, Los Angeles, California 90036

This edition first published in 1996 by Sun & Moon Press
10 9 8 7 6 5 4 3 2 1
FIRST EDITION
©1996 by The Estate of Djuna Barnes
Editing and revisions ©1996 by Douglas Messerli
Introduction ©1996 by Phillip Herring
Biographical material ©1996 by Sun & Moon Press
All rights reserved

This book was made possible, in part, through an operational grant from
the Andrew W. Mellon Foundation, through a matching grant from
the National Endowment for the Arts, and through contributions to
The Contemporary Arts Educational Project, Inc.,
a nonprofit corporation

Cover: untitled drawing by Djuna Barnes
Design: Katie Messborn
Typography: Guy Bennett

LIBRARY OF CONGRESS CATALOGING IN PUBLICATION DATA
Barnes, Djuna [1892–1982]
[Short Stories]
Collected Stories of Djuna Barnes
p. cm — (Sun & Moon Classics: 110)
ISBN: 1-55713-226-7
I. Manners and customs—Fiction. II. Title.
PS3503.A614A6 1996
813'.52—dc20
96-2107
CIP

Printed in the United States of America on acid-free paper.

Contents

The Stories of Djuna Barnes[1]

Her parents newly divorced, desperate for employment, Djuna Barnes (1892–1982) took the most prudent course and followed the career path of her grandmother Zadel into journalism. Zadel had taught her writing, but to add another skill Djuna had gone to art school for life drawing and illustration. This was to be her only formal education. She then free-lanced for nearly every English-language newspaper in New York and quickly rose to become a highly-paid journalist; she gave the Sunday magazine readers what they wanted—a bit of melodrama, a glimpse at the idle rich, and a hint of decadence. Of this work Barnes was not proud, but it did pay the bills; stories she wished to be known eventually appeared in literary magazines such as *The Little Review* and *The Transatlantic Review*, and were collected in volumes of overlapping contents. Now, for the first time, Sun & Moon Press has collected all of the known stories of Djuna Barnes into a single volume.

There is a quality of strangeness in a typical Barnesean story that lingers in the mind long after the details have begun to fade. Baroness Elsa von Freytag Loringhoven, the derelict artist who made her eccentric costumes from discarded junk, and once slugged an inattentive William

Carlos Williams, expressed a familiar judgment: "I cannot read your stories, Djuna Barnes...I don't know where your characters come from. You make them fly on magic carpets—what is worse, you try to make pigs fly."[2] Though there are no flying pigs or magic carpets in these stories, one knows what the Baroness meant, for Djuna Barnes's own sense of privacy seemed paradoxically to affect her ability or willingness to reveal the psychological motivation of her characters. Although many of them seem to have been infected by depression bordering on psychosis, or seem to be the victims of life's cruelest jokes, they are largely opaque to our scrutiny.

The odd mental states, sexual repression, and inexplicable behavior of Barnes's walking wounded often recall the atmosphere of Sherwood Anderson's *Winesburg, Ohio* (1919), transported to the European scene which Barnes knew so much better than small-town life in America. The best of her stories rival in quality those of *Winesburg*—no mean achievement—but the psychologies of her most interesting characters go a step beyond Anderson's in frustration; they are human volcanos awaiting to erupt at odd moments in surprising ways, for reasons that often elude us.

Despite Djuna Barnes's skill at portraying the agony which she herself felt, few American writers of the century could be described as less politically correct or more insensitive to the nuances of racial stereotyping than Djuna Barnes, but this was a function more of ignorance than mean-spiritedness.

Although most of the characters in Barnes's stories are originally from Europe, in the early years she really didn't know much about the languages or cultures of her subjects; in fact, often their names do not reflect their national origins at all, or reveal no specific ethnicity: Madeleonette, Clochette, Du Berry, Zelka Fenken, Varra Kolveed, Monsieur Ampee, his wife Lyda and rival Fago, Pilaat Korb, Freda Buckler, Julie and Paytor Anspacher.

Other characters are identifiably ethnic though most of their names would be quite odd in their countries of origin: Una and Lena (Polish), Skirl Pavet (Polish), Theeg Pontos (Polish), Kurt Anders (Polish), Trenchard the Baker and his wife Jennie (French), Gaya (Italian), Amietiev (Armenian), Addie (Italian), and Otto and Katrina Silverstaff (in the earlier version he is German-Jewish and she Russian). The insisted-upon ethnicity of these characters is the shakiest part of their characterization. Sometimes the names are simply strange: in "Who Is this Tom Scarlett?" one finds six satellites around Tom: Tash, Spave, Glaub, Freece, Umbas, and Race.

Sometimes the characters in Barnes's stories are Russians living in France: Moydia, Erling von Bartmann, and Vanka. The transplanted Polish sisters in "The Earth" are rivals for the strong, dumb Swede. In "Smoke," Misha replenishes lost iron in the family blood line by marrying a Swedish woman, broad in the beam. Jews are represented by Silverstaff in "The Doctors"; Nicholas Golwein in "The Robin's House" is "half Tartar, half Jew," (p. 310), while Oliver Kahn is the "hot, melancholy" Jew (p. 310)

Introduction

of "Oscar." Several characters are not specifically named as Jewish, but are portrayed as such, among them the pawnbroker named Lydia Passova in "Mother." Of course, Passova as a Jewish surname is quite ludicrous.

Like some writers of her time, Barnes was often indelicate about race. For instance, "The Hatmaker" portrays "Black May, Madam's 'nigger' maid, devoted and simple, [who] would stand in the middle of the [room] gasping" about how spoiled her mistress was. Another story is frankly entitled "The Nigger," and details the death of a particularly obnoxious Southern white man whose black nursemaid does what she can to comfort him in his last hours, submissively bearing his insults, her hunger, and the general horror of the situation. After his death, she is hardly inclined to mourn.

The prize for insensitivity might go to "The Head of Babylon," where the quadriplegic Theeg celebrates her wedding day. The daughter of Polish farmers on Long Island (Babylon is just south of Huntington, where Barnes had lived), our "head" orates rather like Oscar Wilde's John the Baptist (Jokanaan), who loses his head for loudly proclaiming judgment. Barnes's early interest in Wilde, whom her father and grandmother Zadel had known, is seen again in "What Do You See, Madam?" (1915). There Mamie Saloam had always wanted to dance Salomé and to kiss the lips of the decapitated John the Baptist, but it is Billy the willing stagehand (acting the part of the saint) who keeps his head long enough to get a kiss.

Besides foreigners, the group which interested Barnes

the most in her stories and journalism were people of aristocratic breeding, wealth, and good taste, which was convenient since readers of journals like *Vanity Fair* were fascinated by a class which had the wealth and freedom to do as it liked.

As with European ethnicity, no matter how Barnes pretended to aristocratic taste and connections, beginning in the 1920s she experienced only brief glimpses of that world, and much of what she described sprang from a fertile imagination. Reflecting on "Aller et Retour" and "The Passion," the stories Barnes judged to be her best, Natalie Barney said that Djuna Barnes had the "extraordinary capacity...to capture social circles which she had every reason not to know," bringing "back to life...an entire civilization in which she has not participated."[3]

Many of the newspaper stories included in the posthumous volume *Smoke* were probably written in just a few days, to meet an editor's deadline at the *New York Morning Telegraph Sunday Magazine*. They were stories meant for the wider readership of newspapers and popular magazines, while the ones Barnes wrote later in life are generally more complex, ponderous, and morose, intended for readers of a more discriminatingly morbid taste. These vignettes preview, and enable us to make sense of, the "petites histoires" of *Nightwood*: Hedvig Volkbein, who dances a "tactical manoeuvre"(*N* 4), the Duchess of Broadback (Frau Mann), "whose coquetries were muscular and localized" (*N* 12), Nikka the Nigger, the tattooed exhibitionist (*N* 16–17), and the legless Mademoiselle Basquette ($\mathcal{N}$ 26), who rolls around the Pyrenees on a sort of skateboard. We might sample here a few of the more important stories, early and late.

A strange early story is called "Fate—the Pacemaker" (1917), later renamed "No-Man's-Mare." It is about Pauvla Agrippa, who dies and is bound with a fishing net to a wild horse who thinks she is a hearse. On the way to the cemetery, for no apparent reason, the horse-hearse lunges into the sea and swims out to a watery grave. History does not give us many instances of horses committing suicide, but this one seems determined to make a splash even if it kills her, or perhaps a mourner had addled her brain by whispering that *mare* was "sea" in Latin. In any case, the startled mourners need only wait for the wave which will bring "No-Man's-Mare" and Pauvla ashore again, but in the meantime they can look for two hearses. This newspaper story, from Barnes's time of apprenticeship, is comically inept.

"The Earth" (1917) is about two Polish-American sisters, Una and Lena, farm women who also remind the narrator of mares—work horses this time—and these are content to stay on land. As in "Prize Ticket 177," the women become rivals for a man, here a Swedish farmhand, but when Lena is cheated in a land deal by her older sister Una, she elopes with the Swede whom she felt that by protocol Una would have merited. Honesty and youth win out over age and cynicism because one of the sisters was more "spirited" and the other would not say her neigh.

A variation on "The Head of Babylon" is "Smoke" (1917), in which a family's genetic lineage is diluted when gentle, civilized, affluent partners are chosen over hard-as-steel ones more suitable to the laboring life. The Fenkens are "healthy," "potent," "unconquerable," and people call them the "Bullets." "'We Fenkens...have iron in our veins,'" Zelka says to her husband, "'in yours I fear there's a little blood'." Their son has less iron, and his daughter Lief, who dies in childbirth, even less. Lief's husband Misha, apparently agreeing with his sister that the Fenkens had "lived themselves thin," goes on to marry a broad, healthy Swedish woman.

These early newspaper stories were collected in *Smoke*. Those Barnes prized more were included in the bound volumes of her work, though it must be said that her taste was fallible. For instance, "The Earth," "The Head of Babylon," "Smoke," and "The Terrorists" are conceived in clarity and executed with convincing strokes, which cannot be said of some later stories.

"The Rabbit" (1917) tells the story of a simple, gentle farmer from Armenia, Rugo Amietiev, who is blissfully content with the pastoral life. From an uncle he inherits a small tailor shop in Manhattan and dutifully leaves his homeland for a dreary life of sewing clothes in the city. Symptomatic of the callousness of this new dead life is a butcher across the street who slaughters and displays the animals Amietiev loves.

The tailor has the misfortune to become involved with Addie, a fierce Italian girl who deprecates him as "a poor sort of man" (p. 201), but who invites him to prove worthy of her through some unnamed daring act. Left to his own imagination, Amietiev steals a rabbit from the butcher shop and strangles it, hoping this presumably heroic deed might suffice to prove his worth as a mate. Instead, it seems to kill in him all feeling, perhaps all innocence, ironically making him more suited to the unnatural life he now must lead. Whether or not Addie will be part of that life is an open question. As well as any work by Barnes, "The Rabbit" appears to mirror its author's gloomy pessimism regarding the human enterprise.

"Indian Summer" (1917), one of Barnes's better stories, is about an unlovely woman, Madame Boliver, who, at fifty-three, suddenly blossoms into a gorgeous young woman who attracts suitors in great numbers. Madame might have been the next Helena Rubenstein, but instead she opens a salon and entertains the bright, rich, and famous. Finally she agrees to marry the unlikeliest suitor, a poor Russian of thirty named Petkoff. Their courtship is intense, and Madame becomes steadily more beautiful with a ripeness now grown suspect. After a brief illness, she dies, and the story ends oddly with the puzzled Petkoff smoking a cigarette, saying "damn it," as he paces beside the bier. Perhaps "Indian Summer" was inspired by Oscar Wilde's *The Picture of Dorian Gray*.

A volume of Barnes's literary work was named after her story "A Night Among the Horses" (1918), a confidence well placed, for it is surely one of her best stories. Barnes told Sven Åhman that she wrote it after reading August Strindberg's play *Miss Julie*.[4] "A Night Among the Horses" shares a value system with "The Rabbit": here again we have a simple country fellow, a horse trainer, who has the opportunity to improve his station through marriage to a socially ambitious landowner, Freda Buckler. But John knows that it is wrong to pretend to be what he is not. Attuned to the earth, he feels at one with its motion, though not with the tuxedo in which he crawls at dusk, presumably after drinking too much at Freda's party. Unsteady on his feet, he falls, "striking his head on a stump" (p. 248). For some reason his horses are racing around the country lanes; they fail to recognize him in his tuxedo, and he is trampled to death by them. Social climbing can be a dangerous business.

"Spillway," originally entitled "Beyond the End" (1919), is in subject and descriptive power one of Barnes's most successful stories, except that it evokes a metaphysical complexity that remains murky at the end. Julie Anspacher returns home to her country estate after five years in a sanatorium, and with her is her daughter Ann, about whom her husband Paytor has never known. Mother and child are still afflicted by tuberculosis. Angry and nervous, Julie offers only sharp retorts as Paytor attempts to welcome her home.

At the sanatorium Julie has had a love affair. Assuming that she and her lover would both die in a month or so, and nothing would be known of her liaison, she thought of little beyond the pleasure of a romantic encounter. Now she feels guilty, for seizing the day has made Ann one of life's little ironies. Though they love each other, and in time Paytor might be able to forgive, Julie cannot forgive herself. Deeply distraught by the metaphysical and moral implications of what she has done, issues which seemed simple at the time of her infidelity (and are still far less complex than the story implies), she has returned in effect so that her husband can help her to confront these issues. But this he is unprepared to do. The story ends with a gunshot that signals either target practice or, more likely, the suicide of Paytor. Julie in moral crisis resembles Katrina Silverstaff, though the issue is different. Both could be figures in an Ibsen play.

"Mother," unlike Joyce's *Dubliners* story of the same name, seems at first oddly titled, for Lydia Passova the pawnbroker is neither a mother nor motherly. She does, however, have an unnamed English lover probably young enough to be her son. Basically a slice of life, the story is superior to many by Barnes because no murky metaphysical question rises to the surface to smile like a Cheshire cat. Tight-lipped, emotionless, obviously a hard bargainer, Lydia Passova reveals nothing about her past until one day, like her angora cat, she simply dies and that is that. What saves the story is its careful description.

"The Doctors," earlier called "Katrina Silverstaff," is perhaps the most horrifying of Djuna Barnes's stories. In the early version she is a former medical student: "the only woman in her class, the only one of the lot of them who smiled in a strange, hurt and sarcastic way when dissecting."[5] Her husband was the "typical Jewish intellectual."[6] In the later *Spillway* version, the couple had studied gynecology together in Freiburg and are not really described ethnically. There is love between them, and two children, but also estrangement. Katrina speaks Barnes obscurantese so that it is difficult to tell what her problem is, but it seems to have to do with vivisection and everything being "too arranged."

In her rage Katrina cooks up an especially ugly suicide, which will devastate all who love her. She decides to take the peddlar Rodkin as her lover for one night: "some people drink poison, some take the knife, others drown. I take you" (p. 325). Why Rodkin submits to this is unclear, but he seems to misunderstand her intentions. She wills her death, becomes catatonic, and dies. Rodkin, as it turns out, is such a nonentity that he imagines an affair with Katrina will make him "somebody," though in this he is wrong (p. 325). At the end Katrina is dead, the grieving family wonders what has happened, and Rodkin is now more of a nuisance than a nothing.

Katrina is in some sense a religious fanatic, for she says, "I dislike all spiritual decay" (p. 324), but she also seems to seek damnation as a sort of protest—one critic describes it as "spiritual vivisection."[7] One can only speculate about the nature of this protest, but it seems to be partly against life's predictability. Her choice of adultery with a random peddlar as a means to suicide is a parting shot at her gynecologist husband.

"Aller et Retour" (1924), a story with the true Barnes flavor, is about a Russian widow, Erling von Bartmann, now of Paris, who travels to Nice to see her seventeen-year-old daughter Richter, whom she hasn't seen in seven years. Sophisticated, world-weary, and cold, like other Barnes women of this type, she has come to see what can be made of Richter now that the girl's father is dead. Speaking in imperious tones of the rottenness of life, Madame von Bartmann has no idea of how to relate to her daughter, who is anxious to please but is finally offended by her mother's haughty arrogance.

Madame says, "Life is filthy; it is also frightful. There is everything in it: murder, pain, beauty, disease—death...You must know *everything*, and *then* begin. You must have a great understanding, or accomplish a fall.... Man is rotten from the start.... Think everything, good, bad, indifferent; everything, and *do* everything, *everything*! Try to know what you are before you die. And...come back to me a good woman" (p. 369–371).

The innocent Richter is, of course, horrified and now avoids her mother. Madame has assumed that Richter desires emancipation, and that her life journey will take her through every degradation, but, in fact, her daughter seems content to become the wife of a government clerk of "staid habits" (p. 372). She will be secure, have children, and lead the conventional life of a middle-class wife. When Madame Bartmann finally understands, she decides to approve this union. Happy to escape the daughter she scarcely knows, she realizes that her trip has been "unnecessary."

"Cassation" (1925), formerly entitled "A Little Girl

Tells a Story to a Lady," is set in Berlin (the café scene is in the Zelten, where Barnes had stayed in 1921) and draws on her recollections of that time and place. One of the stranger, murkier stories, it is told in retrospect by a Russian dancer, perhaps the one Robert McAlmon mentions in *Distinguished Air*, who takes cocaine.[8] She becomes involved with a local married woman of Italian background who invites her to live with her as a nanny to her idiot child, who makes no sound but a "buzzing cry" (p. 387). The married woman's behavior is obsessive, overbearing, and largely incomprehensible to the dancer (as to the reader), who eventually leaves for Paris. Barnes seems to have heard this story from a Paris friend, Tylia Perlmutter, who helped color illustrations in *Ladies' Almanack*. Tylia and Bronja were Polish-Jewish sisters. Barnes was anxious about the story in later years; in a letter to Rolf Ekner she denied that the story was about lesbians.[9]

"The Grande Malade" (1925), originally "The Little Girl Continues," may also be about the Perlmutter sisters. This time Bronja ("Moydia") is featured. In a short memoir Kay Boyle provided considerable insight into the story's origin:

> Moydia had borrowed a pair of high-heeled slippers from Laurence Vail's sister, Clotilde, to wear to the funeral of Monsieur x. The elegant shoes turned out to be too small for Moydia, so she carried them reverently in one hand as she walked

through the streets of Paris in the funeral proces-
sion of her young lover. I knew Monsieur x through
his second novel, *Le Diable au Corps*, which I had
translated for The Black Sun Press. His name was
Raymond Radiguet [1903–23], and he was barely
twenty when he died.[10]

Radiguet was a protégé of Jean Cocteau. In "The Grande
Malade," Moydia is fifteen, and so coquettish and theatrical that one suspects that her mourning lasted about as
long as her spectators' attention span.

"Dusie" (1927) is less a story than a descriptive narra-
tive centered on the Left Bank lesbian scene which Barnes
knew so well. Perhaps she also knew of Gabriele
D'Annunzio's liaison with the actress Elenora Duse.
Though of scant literary value, "Dusie" is interesting because it is unmistakably about Barnes's lover Thelma
Wood; the setting is Natalie Clifford Barney's house at 20
rue Jacob, where Barnes and Wood housesat in August
of 1924 when Barney and Romaine Brooks were on the
isle of Capri. "Dusie," published a year before *Ladies'
Almanack*, looks forward to that work, which satirizes the
Barney circle.

"Dusie" also previews the Robin of *Nightwood*, the
fictional counterpart of Thelma Wood, for Dusie is "very
young...tall, very big and beautiful, absent and so pale.
She wore big shoes, and her ankles and wrists were large,
and her legs beyond belief long. She used to sit in the
corner of the café, day after day, drinking, and she had a

bitter careless sort of ferocity with women" (p. 404). There is also the absent quality of Robin in *Nightwood*, and the same mystification about her person.

One often saw Dusie in the house of Madame K, "a splendid house, with footmen standing behind the great iron doors in white gloves" (p. 404). Madame K herself is "large, very full and blond" (p. 405), like Natalie Barney. Clarissa is probably Romaine Brooks: "it was as if everyone was her torment, as if she lived only because so many people had seen and spoken to her and of her" (p. 406). The barbs of *Ladies' Almanack* are previewed in "Dusie."

"The First of April" (1930) is one of Barnes's typical *Vanity Fair* stories of the aristocracy. Apparently readers did not tire of the romantic liaisons of barons and contessas. This one is about the Bavarian Baron Otto Lowenhaven and the Contessa Mafalda Beonetti, each of whom had married partners who, after thirty years of tolerating infidelity, persuade them that their rivals were now old enough to make such affairs ridiculous. Independently, the Baron and Contessa send telegrams canceling their Roman rendezvous of April first, but all comes right in the end and they renew their devotion.

Barnes's love story "Behind the Heart" celebrates her transitory passion for the young writer Charles Henri Ford. The touchingly romantic story describes their daily life in Paris during a week in the late summer of 1931, at a time when she was thirty-nine and he twenty-one. The story was not published during Barnes's lifetime. She lent the typescript to Ford to read, but, when their passion cooled, she may have had second thoughts about celebrating in public yet another relationship gone dead.

"The Perfect Murder," probably the last story Barnes wrote, is one of her most delightful. The subject is a dialectologist named Professor Anatol Profax, a very odd-looking (and odd-thinking) scholar who has a bald head with "cavernous" eye sockets and dresses in a frock coat.

Like Professor Henry Higgins of Shaw's *Pygmalion* or *My Fair Lady,* Profax obsessively classifies people according to their dialect, until one day he meets a real life trauma in the form of an extremely engaging young woman who bumps into him and soon proposes marriage. She has lived and died many times, always coming back as a different trauma. Profax is intrigued, especially since her way of speaking is so paradoxically unclassifiable: she is "lovable and offensive," abominates "false pride in violence," loves her "enemies and Mozart," "can't stand [her] friends," takes "solitude standing up" and so confuses the professor that he cuts her throat. Out of sight, the trauma disappears, only to appear again across from him staring out of a cab window.

A letter of 19 February 1923 from Djuna Barnes to her mother goes far to explain the mood in which many of her stories were written. She excuses herself for failing to show love, and for her "hurried, acrid, or caustic" manner of speaking: "To me, who am at best, a little melancholy—?having life is the greatest horror—I cannot think of it as a 'merry, gay & joyous thing, just to be alive'—it seems to me monstrous, obscene & still with the most obscene trick at the end..." Although she wrote these words in 1923, Djuna Barnes could just as well have written them at the end of her life, nearly sixty years later, for it remained a consistent view. And yet in her best work Djuna Barnes transformed bitterness into art; as Emily Coleman once wrote her, "You make horror beautiful—it is your greatest gift."[11]

—PHILLIP HERRING
University of Wisconsin

Notes

1   Stories by Barnes were collected in *A Book* (New York: Boni & Liveright, 1923), *A Night Among the Horses* (New York: Boni & Liveright, 1929), *Spillway* (London: Faber & Faber; New York: Farrar, Straus, 1962; Harper & Row, 1972), and the *Selected Works of Djuna Barnes* (New York: Farrar, Straus, & Cudahy, 1962). There is considerable overlap among these volumes. *Selected Works* seems to have preserved the stories Barnes believed to have been her best. In 1982, the year of her death, Sun & Moon Press published a collection of the earliest stories called *Smoke*.

   A Book contains six drawings not reproduced in the later volumes; *A Night* contains three stories not in *A Book*: "Aller et Retour," "A Little Girl Tells a Story to a Lady" (later called "Cassation"), and "The Passion." The *Spillway* volume, reproduced in *Selected Works*, contained only nine stories: "Aller et Retour," "Cassation," "The Grande Malade" (formerly "The Little Girl Continues"), "A Night Among the Horses," "The Valet," "The Rabbit," "The Doctors," "Spillway" (formerly "Beyond the End"), and "The Passion."

2   Margaret Anderson. *My Thirty Years War* (New York: Horizon, 1970), 182.

3   Natalie Clifford Barney, *Adventures of the Mind* (New York: New York University Press, 1992), 168.

4   *Dagens Nyheter*, 24 May 1959, 29.

5   *A Night Among the Horses*, 104–5.

6   *Ibid.*, 105.

7   Suzanne C. Ferguson "Djuna Barnes's Short Stories: An Estrangement of the Heart." *Southern Review*, 5 (Winter 1969), 39.

8   Robert McAlmon, *Distinguished Air*. n.p. 1925, 24.

9   Djuna Barnes to Rolf Ekner, 16 February 1960.

10 Kay Boyle, "Djuna Barnes: 1892–1982," *Proceedings of the American Academy and Institute of Arts and Letters*. 2nd Series, no. 34 (New York 1983), 79–82.

11 Emily Coleman to Djuna Barnes, 27 August 1935, 7.

A Note on the Texts

The stories included in this volume first appeared in newspapers, magazines, and books as noted below. We have included all the known stories of Djuna Barnes with the exception of one story, "The Murder in the Palm Room," originally published in *Vanity Fair* under the name Dobrujda. I listed this in my *Djuna Barnes: A Bibliography* because the drawing printed with this story appeared to be in Barnes's style; but there is no specific evidence that this story is actually by Djuna Barnes.

We have used the original versions of all stories except for those revised in *Spillway and Other Stories,* published in 1962 by Faber and Faber in England and included in *Selected Works of Djuna Barnes,* published the same year by Farrar, Straus and Cudahy in New York.

"The Terrible Peacock," *All-Story Cavalier Weekly,* xxxvii (October 24, 1914); reprinted in *Smoke and Other Early Stories* (Los Angeles: Sun & Moon Press, 1982).

"Paprika Johnson," *The Trend,* vii (January 1915); reprinted in *Smoke and Other Early Stories.*

"What Do You See, Madam?" *All-Story Cavalier Weekly,* xliii (March 27, 1915); reprinted in *Smoke and Other Early Stories.*

"Who Is This Tom Scarlett?" *New York Morning Telegraph Sunday Magazine,* March 11, 1917; reprinted in *Smoke and Other Early Stories.*

"The Jests of Jests," *New York Morning Telegraph Sunday Magazine,* April 1, 1917; reprinted in *Smoke and Other Early Stories.*

A Note

"Prize Ticket 177," *New York Morning Telegraph Sunday Magazine,* April 8, 1917; reprinted in *Smoke and Other Early Stories.*

"A Sprinkle of Comedy," *New York Morning Telegraph Sunday Magazine,* May 27, 1917; reprinted in *Smoke and Other Early Stories.*

"The Earth," *New York Morning Telegraph Sunday Magazine,* June 10, 1917; reprinted in *Smoke and Other Early Stories.*

"The Head of Babylon," *New York Morning Telegraph Sunday Magazine,* July 1, 1917; reprinted in *Smoke and Other Early Stories.*

"No-Man's-Mare," first published as "Fate—the Pacemaker," *New York Morning Telegraph Sunday Magazine,* July 22, 1917; reprinted as "No-Man's-Mare" in *A Book* (New York: Boni and Liveright, 1923); reprinted in *A Night Among the Horses* (New York: Horace Liveright, 1929).

"Smoke," *New York Morning Telegraph Sunday Magazine,* August 19, 1917; reprinted in *Sun & Moon: A Journal of Literature & Art,* no. 3 (Summer 1976) and in *Smoke and Other Early Stories.*

"The Coward," *New York Morning Telegraph Sunday Magazine,* August 26, 1917; reprinted in *Smoke and Other Early Stories.*

"Monsieur Ampee," *New York Morning Telegraph Sunday Magazine,* September 16, 1917; reprinted in *Smoke and Other Early Stories.*

"The Terrorists," *New York Morning Telegraph Sunday Magazine,* September 30, 1917; reprinted in *Smoke and Other Early Stories.*

"The Rabbit," *New York Morning Telegraph Sunday Magazine,* October 7, 1917; reprinted in *A Book, A Night Among the Horses,* and in a revised version in *Spillway* (London: Faber and Faber, 1962).

"Indian Summer," *New York Morning Telegraph Sunday Magazine,* October 14, 1917; reprinted in *A Book* and *A Night Among the Horses.*

"A Night in the Woods," *New York Morning Telegraph Sunday Magazine,* October 21, 1917; reprinted in *Smoke and Other Early Stories.*

"Finale," *Little Review,* v (June 1918).

"Renunciation," *Smart Set,* LVI (October 1918).

"A Night Among the Horses," *Little Review,* v (December 1918); reprinted in *A Book, A Night Among the Horses,* and, in a revised version, in *Spillway and Selected Works.*

"The Valet," *Little Review,* VI (May 1919); reprinted in *A Book, A Night Among the Horses,* and, in a revised version, in *Spillway and Selected Works.* The earlier version was also collected in *The Little Review Anthology,* ed. by Margaret Anderson (New York: Heritage House, 1953).

"Spillway," published orginally as "Beyond the End," *Little Review,* VI (December 1919); reprinted in *A Book, A Night Among the Horses,* and, in a revised version with the new title, in *Spillway and Selected Works.*

"Oscar," *Little Review,* VI (April 1920); reprinted in *A Book* and *A Night Among the Horses.*

"Mother," *Little Review,* VII (July–August 1920); reprinted in *A Book* and *A Night Among the Horses.*

"The Robin's House," *Little Review,* VII (September–October 1920); reprinted in *A Book* and *A Night Among the Horses.*

"The Doctors," published originally as "Katrina Silverstaff," *Little Review,* VII (January–March 1921); reprinted in *A Book* and *A Night Among the Horses,* in a revised version with the new title, in *Spillway and Selected Works.*

"The Diary of a Dangerous Child," [under the pseudonym Lydia Steptoe] *Vanity Fair,* XVIII (July 1922).

"The Diary of a Small Boy," [under the pseudonym Lydia Steptoe] *Shadowland,* IX (September 1923).

"A Boy Asks a Question," published originally as "A Boy Asks a Question of a Lady" in *A Book* (New York: Boni and Liveright, 1923); reprinted in *A Night Among the Horses* and, in a revised version under the new title, in *Spillway and Selected Works.*

A Note

"The Nigger," *A Book* (New York: Boni and Liveright, 1923); reprinted in *A Night Among the Horses.*

"Madame Grows Older: A Journal at the Dangerous Age," [under the pseudonym Lydia Steptoe], *Chicago Tribune Sunday Magazine,* March 9, 1924.

"Aller et Retour," *Transalantic Review,* I (April 1924); reprinted in *Transatlantic Stories,* ed. by Ford Madox Ford (New York: Dial, 1926), *A Night Among the Horses,* and, in a revised version, in *Spillway and Selected Works.*

"The Passion," *Transatlantic Review,* II (1924); reprinted in *Transatlantic Stories, A Night Among the Horses,* and, in a revised version, in *Spillway and Selected Works.*

"Cassation," published originally as "A Little Girl Tells a Story to a Lady," *Contact Collection of Contemporary Writers* (Paris: Three Mountains Press, 1925); reprinted in *A Night Among the Horses,* and, in a revised version with the new title, in *Spillway and Selected Works.*

"The Grande Malade," published originally as "The Little Girl Continues," *This Quarter,* I (1925); reprinted in a revised version with the new title in *Spillway and Selected Works.*

"Dusie," *America Esoterica* (New York: Macy–Masius, 1927).

"A Duel without Seconds," *Vanity Fair,* XXXIII (November 1929); reprinted in Cleveland Amory and Frederic Brandlee, eds., *Vanity Fair: Selections from America's Most Memorable Magazine: A Cavalcade of the 1920s and 1930* (New York: Viking, 1960).

"The Letter That Was Never Mailed," *Vanity Fair,* XXXIII (December 1929).

"The First of April," *Vanity Fair,* XXXIV (March 1930).

"The Perfect Murder," *Harvard Advocate,* CXXVIII (April 1942); reprinted in Jonathan D. Culler, ed., *Harvard Advocate Centennial Anthology* (Cambridge, Massachusetts: Schenkman Publishing, 1966).

28

"Behind the Heart," *The Library Chronicle of The University of Texas at Austin,* Summer 1993.

"Saturnalia," in Douglas Messerli, ed., *50: A Celebration of Sun & Moon Classics* (Los Angeles: Sun & Moon Press, 1995).

"The Hatmaker," previously unpublished.

—DOUGLAS MESSERLI

The Terrible Peacock

IT WAS DURING the dull season, when a subway accident looms as big as a Thaw getaway, that an unusual item was found loose in the coffee.

Nobody seemed to know whence it had come. It dealt with a woman, one greater, more dangerous than Cleopatra, thirty-nine times as alluring as sunlight on a gold eagle, and about as elusive.

She was a Peacock, said the item, which was not ill-written—a slinky female with electrifying green eyes and red hair, dressed in clinging green-and-blue silk, and she was very much observed as she moved languorously through the streets of Brooklyn. A Somebody—but who?

The city editor scratched his head and gave the item to Karl.

"Find out about her," he suggested.

"Better put a new guy on," said Karl. "Get the fresh angle. I got that Kinney case to look after today. What about Garvey?"

"All right," said the city editor, and selected a fresh piece of gum.

Garvey was duly impressed when Karl hove to alongside his desk and flung his leg after the item onto it, for Karl was the Star.

Rather a mysterious person in a way, was Karl. His residence was an inviolable secret. He was known to have accumulated money, despite the fact that he was a newspaperman. It was also known that he had married.

Otherwise, he was an emergency man—a first-rate reporter. When someone thought best to commit suicide and leave a little malicious note to a wife who raved three steps into the bathroom and three into the kitchen, hiccuping "Oh, my God!" with each step, it got into Karl's typewriter—and there was the birth of a front-page story.

"So you're to look her up," said Karl. "She's dashed beautiful, has cat eyes and Leslie Carter hair—a loose-jointed, ball-bearing Clytie, rigged out with a complexion like creamed coffee stood overnight. They say she claws more men into her hair than any siren living or dead."

"You've seen her?" breathed Garvey, staring.

Karl nodded briefly.

"Why don't *you* get her, then?"

"There are two things," said Karl judicially, "at which I am no good. One is subtraction, and the other is attraction. Go to it, son. The assignment is yours."

He strolled away, but not too late to see Garvey swelling visibly at the implied compliment and caressing his beautiful, lyric tie.

Garvey didn't altogether like the assignment, nonetheless. There was Lilac Jane, you see. He had a date with her for that very night, and Lilac Jane was exceedingly desirable.

He was at that age when devotion to one female of the species makes dalliance with any others nothing short of treason.

But—he had been allotted this work because of his fascinations for slinky green sirens! Garvey fingered the tie again and withdrew his lavender-scented handkerchief airily, as an altarboy swings a censer.

At the door he turned under the light and pushed back his cuff, and his fellow workers groaned. It was seven by his wristwatch.

Outside he paused on the corner near the chophouse. He looked up and down the gloomy street with its wilted florist-window displays and its spattering of gray housefronts, wishing there were someone with him who could be told of his feeling of competence in a world of competent men.

His eyes on the pavement, lost in perfervid dreams of Lilac Jane, he wandered on. The roaring of the bridge traffic disturbed him not, nor the shouts of bargemen through the dusk on the waterfront.

At last through the roseate visions loomed something green.

Shoes! Tiny shoes, trim and immaculate; above them a glimpse of thin green stockings on trimmer ankles.

There was a tinkle of laughter, and Garvey came to himself, red and perspiring, and raised his eyes past the slim, green-clad body to the eyes of the Peacock.

It was she beyond question. Her hair was terribly red, even in the darkness, and it gleamed a full eight inches above her forehead, piled higher than any hair Garvey had ever seen. The moon shone through it like butter through mosquito netting.

Her neck was long and white, her lips were redder than her hair, and her green eyes, with the close-fitting, silken dress that undulated like troubled, weed-filled water as she moved, completed the whole daring creation. The powers that be had gone in for poster effects when they made the Peacock.

She was handsome beyond belief, and she was amused at Garvey. Her silvery laugh tinkled out again as he stared at her, his pulse a hundred in the shade.

He tried to convince himself that this physiological effect was due to his newspaper instinct, but it is to be conjectured that Lilac Jane would have had her opinion of the Peacock had she been present.

"Well, young man?" she demanded, the wonderful eyes getting in their deadly work.

"I—I'm sorry—I didn't mean—" Garvey floundered hopelessly, but he did not try to escape.

"You were handing me bouquets by staring like that? That what you're trying to say?"

She laughed again, glided up to him and took his arm. "I like you, young man," she said.

"My nun-name is Garvey, and I'm on the—the Argus."

She started at that and looked at him sharply. "A reporter!"

But her tinkly laugh rang out again, and they walked on. "Well, why not?" she said gaily.

Then, with entire unexpectedness: "Do you tango?"

Garvey nodded dumbly, struggling to find his tongue.

"I love it!" declared the Peacock, taking a step or two of the dance beside him. "Want to take me somewheres so we can have a turn or two?"

Garvey swallowed hard and mentioned a well-known resort.

"Mercy!" cried the green-eyed siren, turning shocked orbs upon him. "I don't drink! Let's go to a tearoom—Poiret's." She called it "Poyrett's."

Garvey suffered himself to be led to the slaughter, and as they went she chattered lightly. He drew out his handkerchief and dabbed gently at his temples.

"Gracious!" she drawled. "You smell like an epidemic of swooning women."

Garvey was hurt, but deep within himself he decided suddenly that scent was out of place on a masculine cold-assuager.

They turned into a brightly lighted establishment where there were already a few girls and fewer men.

They found a table, and she ordered some tea and cakes, pressing her escort not to be bashful as far as himself was concerned. Garvey ordered obediently and lavishly.

Presently the music struck up, and he swung her out on the floor and into the fascinating dance.

Now, Garvey was really some dancer. But the Peacock!

She was light and sinuous as a wreath of green mist, yet solid bone and muscle in his arms.

She was the very poetry of motion, the spirit of the dance, the essence of grace and beauty.

And when the music stopped, Garvey could have cried with vexation, though he was considerably winded.

But the Peacock was not troubled at all. Indeed, she had talked on through all the dance.

Garvey had capitulated long ago. Lilac Jane? Bah! What were a thousand Lilac Janes to this glorious creature, this Venus Anadyomene—Aphrodite of the Sea- Foam?

In the bright light of the tearoom her green eyes were greener, her red hair redder, her white throat whiter. He would have given a Texas ranch for her, with the cattle thrown in.

He tried to tell her something of this, and she laughed delightfully.

"What is it about me that makes men go mad over me?" she demanded, dreamily sipping her tea.

"Do they?" He winced.

"Oh, shamelessly. They drop their jaws, propriety, and any bundles they may be carrying. Why?"

"It's the most natural thing in the world. You have hair and eyes that few women have, and a man desires the rare." He was getting eloquent.

"But—I'm not at all pretty—thinness isn't attractive, is it?"

"It is, in you," he said simply. The fact that he could say it simply was very bad indeed for Lilac Jane.

She dimpled at him and arose abruptly. "Now I've got to vanish. Oh, Lily!"

A girl, undeniably pretty, but just an ordinary girl, crossed over.

"This is Mr.—er—Garvey, Miss Jones. Keep him amused, will you? He dances very nicely." And as he struggled to his feet, attempting a protest: "Oh, I'm coming back again," and she was gone.

Garvey tried to think of some excuse to escape from the partner thus unceremoniously thrust upon him, but the girl blocked his feeble efforts by rising expectantly as the strains of "Too Much Mustard" floated on the ambient atmosphere.

There was nothing for it but to make good. And, after all, she was a nice dancer. He found himself asking what she would have at the end of the dance.

Anyhow, he reflected, he had still his assignment to cover. The Peacock was still as great a mystery as ever—more of a mystery. But she had said that she would return. So he waited and danced and ate and treated.

Half an hour later the Peacock *did* return—with another man.

To Garvey everything turned suddenly light purple. That was the result of his being green with jealousy and seeing red at the same time.

The newest victim of her lures (for such even Garvey recognized him to be) was an elderly business man, inclined to corpulency, with a free and roving eye. Garvey hated him with a bitter hatred.

The Peacock danced once with him, then abandoned him, gasping fishily, to another girl's tender mercies.

She stopped briefly at Garvey's table, gave him a smile and a whispered: "Here, tomorrow night," and vanished in a swirl of green silk—probably in search of more captives.

Garvey put in a bad night and a worse next day. Who was she? What was her little game? What would happen tomorrow night?

He didn't care. Lilac Jane was definitely deposed in favor of a green goddess whose lure quite possibly spelled destruction.

But he didn't care.

He told the city editor that the Peacock story would be available next day, and added the mental reservation, "if I haven't resigned." And he mooned through the work in a trance that made for serious errors in his "copy."

Yet he had no illusions about it, save an undefined and noble impulse to "rescue the Peacock from her degrading surroundings."

Somehow the phrase didn't quite apply, though.

Once he thought of Lilac Jane, with her warm, normal, womanly arms stretched out to him. He took her picture from his pocket and compared it with the mental picture he carried of the Peacock, then put the photograph back, face outward.

Thus Lilac Jane's flags were struck.

Directly afterward the brazen office-boy communicated to him in strident tones that a "skoit" wanted him on the phone.

For a second he thought of the Peacock; but no, Lilac Jane was due to call. Whereupon he fled ignominiously.

It may be deduced that he had not forgotten Lilac Jane after all, merely misplaced her.

Garvey fell into the elevator, the cosmic tail of the Peacock filling his existence. He threw quoits with the god of a greater wisdom, and came out of his reverie and the elevator with a pair of jet earrings dancing before him. They were the earrings of Lilac Jane.

But beneath them, as the periods beneath double exclamation points, floated a pair of green boots.

Moodily he ate, moodily he went to his room—apartment, I beg his pardon. And at six o'clock he was ready for eight.

He took out his watch and wound it until the hands quivered and it made noises inside as though it were in pain.

He stood before the mirror and motioned at his Adam's apple, prodding the lyric tie into shape and stretching his neck the while until it seemed about to snap and leave a blank space between his chin and his collar button.

A man in love ceases mentally. All his energy is devoted to his outward appearance.

If Napoleon had been in love while on the field of Austerlitz, he would not have rejoiced in his heart, but in his surtout and small clothes.

If Wellington had been so afflicted during the battle of Waterloo, the result might have been different.

Therefore, when Garvey was finally attired, he was like unto the lilies of the field that toil not, neither do they spin. He glanced at his watch when all was at last perfect, and all but sat down suddenly. It was midnight!

But then he saw that the poor watch was travelling at the rate of a mile a minute, trying to make up for that last winding. The alarm clock said seven-thirty.

Whereupon Garvey achieved the somewhat difficult feat of descending the stairs without bending his knees. Spoil the crease in his trousers? Never!

And shortly thereafter he was at the tango tearoom, looking around eagerly for the Peacock, his heart pounding harder than his watch.

The place was crowded, and the dancers were already busy to the sprightly strains of "Stop at Chattanooga."

For a space he looked in vain. Then his cardiac engine missed a stroke.

There she was—seated at a table in the far corner.

As fast as he reasonably could without danger to his immaculateness, Garvey headed Her-ward.

Yes, it was undoubtedly the Peacock. She was leaning her elbows on the table and talking earnestly—talking to—Karl!

Garvey was abreast of the table by now. He must have made some sort of a noise, for they both looked up.

The Peacock smiled sweetly, with a touch of defiance. Karl grinned amiably, with a touch of sheepishness. And both said: "Hello!"

Then said Karl: "Old man, allow me to present you to—my wife." Garvey choked and sat down speechless.

"Might as well 'fess it," said Karl. "Only please remember that the idea was solely mine."

"It was *not*!" said the Peacock sharply. "You wouldn't hear of it when I suggested it."

"Well, anyhow, I have all my money invested in this tearoom. But business has been mighty dull; it looked like bankruptcy.

"Then Mrs. Karl here—she was La Dancerita before she fell for me, you see, and—well, she's been drumming up patronage."

"It was fun!" declared La Dancerita-that-was. "I nearly got pinched once, though."

"I wrote that squib at the office that got you the assignment, thinking to help the game along a little." He smiled a deep, mahogany, wrinkled smile that disarmed when it reached the blue of his eyes. "So now you know all about the Peacock."

Garvey swallowed twice and sighed once. Then he took something from his breast pocket and put it back again.

"I—er know somebody that likes to tango," he said irrelevantly.

Paprika Johnson

EVERY SATURDAY, just as soon as she had slipped her
manila pay envelope down her neck, had done up her
handkerchiefs and watered the geraniums, Paprika
Johnson climbed onto the fire-escape and reached across
the strings of her pawnshop banjo.

Paprika Johnson played softly, and she sang softly too,
from a pepsin disinfected throat, and more than reverently she scattered the upper register into the flapping
white wash of the O'Briens.

Sitting there in the dusk, upon her little square of safety,
in a city of a million squares, she listened to the music of
the spheres and the frying of the onions in Daisy Mack's
back kitchen, and she sang a song to flawless summer,
while she watched Madge Darsey loosen her stays in the
tenement house opposite.

Below Paprika, straight as a plumb-bob would direct,
sat the patrons of Swingerhoger's Beer Garden, at small
brown tables that had once been green, perhaps, or blue.
Paprika, unconscious of the laws of state, the rules of San-
skrit, and of the third dimension, was also unaware of the
trade that waged below her; was unaware of the hoisting
of hops and of dilettanteism.

Also, in the beginning, she was unaware of the existence of the boy from Stroud's. This is beginning at the beginning.

Paprika had a bosom friend, in the days when roses found no hedge from her neck to her hair, when she allotted to them no design, save the generous and gentle smiling bow that was her mouth. And her bosom friend, like all bosom things, was necessary and uncomfortable.

She borrowed incessantly, did Leah, she borrowed Paprika's slippers out of bed, and her shifts into bed, and she borrowed her face powder, and her hair ribbons and her stockings. And she borrowed, most of all, Paprika's charm.

Leah was thin and pock-marked and colorless, and still, without the stiffness of a wall flower was one, and chose Gus to lean on.

It goes without saying that Gustav was blind, as blind as a man in a rage and as a man in love.

He listened to Paprika's soft voice, and not being able to estimate the distance that sound carries, put his arm about Leah's waist while Paprika sat upon the other side of the table.

Leah would have been just as well pleased to have had Gus in her own room, but that was impossible, as it was chaperonless.

Paprika was safe, because Paprika had a moribund mother under the counterpane, a chaperon who never spoke or moved, since she was paralyzed, but who was a pretty good one at that, being a white exclamation point this side of error. Therefore, Leah was hugged in Paprika's presence.

Gus thought he knew what he was doing, because on his trip to the back sink in the hall, he heard things about Paprika that were kind and good to listen to, and he thought they were said of the one he hugged. Therefore, he shaved and was happy.

Now, listen; I'll tell you something.

Gustav kept behind his ninety-eight-cent alarm clock, where he could not lose it, the address of an oculist who would cure him for a remuneration. No one is sending perfect cattle to heaven without pocket padding, so Gus waited until he could pay to see again, and in the meantime, toiled up to the eighth floor of evenings and sat with the girls. And Paprika being a bosom friend worth having, lent Leah her violet extract.

At night when she dug into bed, Paprika exchanged notes with Leah about their mutual work. Paprika typewrote and Leah pushed Sloe Gin Fizz toward erring youths, who drank with averted faces.

Which proves without my saying it, that Leah was all right on the inside—perhaps—but that her intentions were a lot better than her claims on beauty.

Yet, Leah realized and gave worship for the part that Paprika had played for her, she comprehended, and was almost humbled by the devotion of her friend, in keeping Gus's arms about her waist. She whispered her loyalty into Paprika's ear in the silence of the night, while Paprika pushed her gum into the leg of the bed.

Among other things, Leah said that she would do as much for her sometime, in another way—if she could, and lay back, knowing that the dark was doing as much for her as it was for the hole in the carpet.

Paprika was touched and bought a banjo.

So on evenings when she had talked Gustav's arm half-way round Leah's waist, she took her banjo out upon the fire escape, and practiced a complicated movement from Chopin.

Across the cliff she looked and watched the moon grope its way up the sky and over condensed milk signs and climb to the top of the Woolworth Building. And Paprika wondered if her time was soon coming and smiled, for she knew that she was as good to look upon as a yard of slick taffy, and twice as alluring.

Unconsciously, Paprika was the cabaret performer of the beer garden. The men about the tables put their hands into their shirt bosoms, and felt the ticking of the tolerably good clock their mother had given them. Or others felt into the breast pockets and felt the syncopated beat of the watch their father had given them (from frequenting just such a garden). And others, without any inherited momentum, looked wanly upon the open faces of dollar Ingersols, and sipped with slow, bated breath.

The combination of Paprika, beer and the moon got into the street and nudged the boy off his stool at the head of Stroud's donkeys stabled in lower Bleecker Street; edged him off, and after a while it was said that the boy from Stroud's was becoming a man in Swingerhoger's beer garden.

The boy from Stroud's was a tall blond wimpet who

had put his hands into his mother's hair and shaken it free of gold; a lad who had painted his cheeks from the palette of the tenderloin, the pink that descends from one member of a family to the other, quicksilver running down life's page. And the fact that at twenty the boy from Stroud's still had it, proved that he was his mother's only child. He also had great gray eyes, and an impassible mouth, a hand that was made for soft-brimmed hats and love notes, and a breaking voice like a ferryboat coming in from Staten Island.

He sat in the beer garden three nights before he dared follow up the music from above. When he looked, he decided that the perspective on Paprika made her very alluring. And so the boy from Stroud's, who had turned the donkeys around for supper, crowded down, into the portfolio of his soul, the pattern of P. Johnson.

And she, all oblivious and smelling of white roses and talcum, might have gone on indefinitely, but one night, stumbling up the stairs in the dark, came against a little packet. She picked it up and, woman-like, tried to read it in the hall. Failing, and being over-anxious to discover its contents, she tried again at the crack of light running along Daisy Mack's door, and on to the fifth floor, running up a little higher and balancing herself vertically over a vertical package at Eliza Farthingale's. But Eliza burned only one candle, and Paprika could make less of it than ever, and finally, having got to her room by a long stage of short runs, read it in the light from her open door, saw that the hand was a masculine one. And being Paprika and a woman, and thinking that she had nothing on her bosom friend, she sidled in backward and dropped it in among the bananas on the sideboard.

After supper she took it and the banjo out upon the fire-escape, and read it by the light of the moon.

The involuntary suicides in the beer garden sipped slowly and finally ceased altogether, and Swingerhoger, who had hopes of rolling up silk sleeves out of them, became uneasy at the sight of bricklayers whining over their brew. He did not know that all the trouble came of a silent banjo. Paprika wasn't playing, she was reading the note from the boy. Inside the note was a photograph taken side face with a soft look and collar; his fine Roman nose was enhanced by a dark background. What did it matter to her if he was turning the donkey around?

About this time Leah, who had lost part control of her hands, never being sure when she could use them—lost control of her one finger on the left hand altogether, it being weighed down by the weight of a diamond, purchased by Gus.

Paprika kissed her, and Leah went down upon her knees and thanked God for a willing sacrifice, and, by way of surety, prayed that Gus might remain forever in the dark. Then arising, she dusted her knees and inquired of Paprika if she looked well in curlpapers, and got into bed.

"My dear," said Paprika, wiggling her toes in the last effort to get comfortable, "don't let him know anything about it—ever—me, I mean. And if, after you are married

I can do anything, just whoop and I'll be there. By the way, are you going to start in, in Yonkers, where they have Gaby Deslys and cats, or in the Bronx, where you get commuter's grouch and new laid eggs?"

Leah answered from the depths of the bed and Paprika's warm arm. "Neither. You see, dear, Gus is a sort of cousin to Mr. Swingerhoger, and Swingerhoger is going to let Gus run a part of the business, and pay him a salary, and so we are not going to leave you, only to move in downstairs, into the second floor front. And I'm so glad."

"Why?" demanded Paprika, losing forever the vision and the hope of the second floor front.

"Because I'll be near you, dear—don't you understand?"

And Paprika, being a good bosom friend, understood.

Now, the boy from Stroud's, having gotten tired of picking straw out of the donkey's ears, decided to take a risk and pick a wife out of the sky.

He had seen Paprika from the beer garden, but Paprika was eight floors distant, and though his soul's eyes were extra keen, they were not keen enough to discover, with any directly satisfying accuracy, whether Paprika's petticoats were three or two, as he got her, a silhouette against Manhattan, enhanced as she was by the whole of the left side of the Hudson, he came to the conclusion that she was fit for a flat off Bleecker Street with eggs for breakfast.

And so it was that Paprika presently bought a yard of

baby blue ribbon and tied up a bunch of letters and put them beneath her chemises in the lower drawer.

She did not think that she was taking a risk. She had seen the picture of the boy, and he was a good cameo, so she allowed her heart to keep pace with him, as Dan Patch with his shadow. In her mind's eye she was already carrying the shaving soap into the dressing room.

In a flurry of hot ginger tea and white voile, Leah was married. For the last time, a single girl, without as yet the knowledge of the one-sided effect of a dresser with military brushes on one corner, and an automatic stop on the other. She hugged and kissed Paprika and cried a lot down her neck and felt that she was being parted by the whole of a geography and an isthmus. And after they carried her Swedish trunk and her bouquet down to the second floor front and she and Gus turned at the landing and threw kisses back to Paprika, who leaned over the banister.

Paprika hitched up her one-fifty "American Madame," patted her back hair and went and sat down upon the china chest.

She was grateful to circumstances that had made it possible to swap the boy for Leah. Also she sang as she played her banjo, and didn't care that the night got in front of the Municipal tower and shut out the million lights.

But the man in the beer garden, who was nobody in particular, spoke to Swingerhoger.

"Why haven't you discovered for yourself that the

drawing card here is that little girl who comes in about three beer time, and after pinning her handkerchiefs to the sash, yanks the strings of the banjo into the harmony of the human breast?"

Swingerhoger made a warp of his fingers to catch the woof of his gold seals, and looked worried.

"Are you perfectly sure that they come here to hear her play as much as for anything?"

"As much as for anything," answered the man, who was nobody in particular. "They think they have found the spring and the song, which has left the city altogether, and the cry of the birds and the plaint of a woman, the rarest things I know in little old New York."

"Perhaps you're right," said Swingerhoger. "Perhaps if I put it to her delicately, she will take it in the right way, which is, that it is a compliment and an honor to play to Swingerhoger guests, and she may put in more of her time at it."

The man who was nobody in particular looked a long while into the inherited vapid face of the garden owner, and he did not think of the arrangement of that gentleman's mind.

"You must pay her," he said.

"Pay her? What for?"

"To play and sing, my friend. She has a job somewhere in this lonesome city, and she must fill the hours. If you pay her she can play for you from, say, four to twelve p.m., and then you are already a wealthy man."

"But," said Swingerhoger, dropping his seals, "no other beer garden is doing this."

"And that," said the man who was nobody in particular, "is where you get in your start. When the thing gets winded all the gardens will take it up, and then you're done. But until then the chance is yours."

To Paprika, therefore, Swingerhoger took the proposition.

The man from nowhere, who was nobody in particular, got a free beer.

"Play for you?" queried Paprika, keeping him out by the chain on the door. "How can I? I have a stenographer's job to fill, in a silk office. I'm getting ten per, and it just keeps tapioca in mother's mouth and the pepsin in mine, and it hangs out a few starched things and a ride now and then on the cars."

"You don't understand. I pay you ten dollars just the same and all you got to do is lie in bed all day until four and then you play for me until midnight and hit the mattress again, see?"

"Gee!" gasped Paprika, "in bed all day. I'm dreamin', but say, I can't do it anyway, because," she blushed this time, "I'm leaving soon." She smiled, the last letter from the boy lay next her fifth rib.

"But," he protested, walking down backward, as she followed, "you don't understand. Nothing to do all day and then only play an easy tune now and again, between bites of the pralines and sips at the sherry lemonade. I'm getting rich on you, Miss Johnson. Think it over. Why, only today I gave my cousin Gus a bank account on you."

Paprika smiled again and shook her head. "I'm changing my tune anyway," she said, and added softly, "to a lullaby."

And so at last, though she had never seen the boy from Stroud's face to face, she put the chair over the rent in the carpet, the vase over the moth hole in the piano scarf, and the stain just back of the hat rack she covered with a picture of three pink gowned girls walking over a brittle paper stream.

Her heart beat terribly fast. She got that same sensation that Leah had gotten. She felt that nothing was going to be as it had been. She took a dose of soda water, but it was not the treatment for the trouble. Therefore, resigning herself to her best dress and a peach of a haircomb, she waited for the boy from Stroud's who was coming to see her.

The little hands on the clock came coquettishly in front of its gold face and parted suddenly as if saying, "Oh, all's well, I need not hide," with the pettish nonchalance of ninety-eight cent clocks.

Paprika fussed a bit with the position of her feet and decided, after all, that she looked better standing up, and had gotten a pose to suit every one, herself included, half drooping over moth-eaten geraniums, when Leah hurled herself into the room.

"Oh, my God!" she said, stumbling over to the mantlepiece, and stood there shaking.

"He got it from behind the clock," she wailed "and now the oculists have taken their last diagnosis, and they say that he can have the bandage removed, and I didn't understand and I'm done, I'm done." She took to shaking the mantle and its blue array of willowware and the peacock feathers sticking in the mucilage. Also she shook Paprika.

"What can I do?" asked Paprika, and Leah fell upon her.

"This once—this once—he would never get over the shock—and I can't, I can't!"

"You can't what?" demanded Paprika.

"It's Gus, you don't understand. The oculists have just left him and he can *see!*"

"*Well?*"

Leah took a step toward the girl who had been her bosom friend, and she heaved her forty-nine-cent belt up. "He mustn't see me—yet."

And so she stood. Leah, the friend who had got a husband in the dark, and now must stand before him in the light that had come to him with his prosperity, gotten by the playing of Paprika. And Paprika, realizing this, did not know what to do.

Leah came to her and took her arms in both her hands, nursing them between her palms with long frightened fingers, and looked at Paprika and could not speak.

Paprika had forgotten the boy from Stroud's. She had forgotten her best dress and the sense of backthrust feet, and she put her chin out.

"You want him to pin his eyes on *me*?"

And Leah nodded her thin head back and forth, and took her lip in between her teeth. "He won't be so sorry, after—when he gets used to it and me, when I come in later and you straighten things out. He will be too much a man to be a quitter."

And Paprika understood what it meant to a woman to be willing to keep her own at such a cost. Also Paprika thought she was overestimating Gus's sense of beauty.

So she said "all right," looked at the clock and thought, at a rough estimate, that she had time, and descended to the second floor front.

She stirred as she sat by Gus's bed at the step on the stair that halted a bit, and then went on up. She remembered that she had told nothing to Leah about his coming, and Leah was up there in the dusk—but Gus was taking the bandages off.

In the dim light, the boy from Stroud's took off his hat. He was breathing hard from the eight flights and a heart full of a sensation that was like being run over with molasses and crowned with chocolate meringue. In the corner he saw the dim shape of a woman. He never looked toward the bed where slept the perfect chaperon. He shut the door reverently and came a step in. The figure in the corner moved and moaned like a seal at twelve p.m., moved and moaned and put her hand to her unlovely hair and blinked at him from startled blue eyes with her mouth open.

The banjo leaning in the corner caught his eye as he

leaned forward, and he laughed suddenly, shortly, with a hard disillusioned break, and suddenly, without a word, caught up his hat and ran pantingly down the stairs. Heedless, he ran past the second story front on to the first, and fell into the murky light of Swingerhoger's beer garden, threw up his hands and cried something about "perspective and a picture plane" and darted out of the garden and disappeared in the direction of Bleecker Street.

Well, that's about all, excepting as we said, Paprika Johnson still holds the job as the first cabaret artist, at thirty years old. Still of evenings she sits upon the fire-escape and plays her banjo as her handkerchiefs dry, just as she did on that afternoon three minutes after Gus had taken the bandages off and she had come into the garden to get a pitcher of lemonade to celebrate, and leaning across the counter, she had said, "All right, I'll take that job."

Also she never told Leah that her chance "to do as much for her sometime, in a different way," had come and gone.

What Do You See, Madam?

MAMIE SALOAM was a dancer.

She had come from the lower stratum of the poor, who drape their shoulders with cotton, and their stomachs with gingham.

The Bowery, which is no place at all for virtue or duplicity, had seen Mamie try on her first fit of sulks and her first stay laces. They knew then that her pattern was Juno, her heritage Joseph, and her ambition jade. At the age of ten she had learned to interpret Oscar Wilde, when Oscar Wilde had gone in, rather extensively, for passion and the platter, and had parried off creation with a movement and a beard.

On that moonlit night, when she chucked Semco, the sailor, under the chin, and swiped one of the park lilacs for keeps, Mamie grew up.

Between his lips and hers she had learned competition. His was the greater kiss, his arms the greater strength, his voice the master voice.

Mamie became fire and felt hell where it burns low among the coals, and the street that sensed her homecoming on staccato heels, heard the wide-mouthed laughter she threw her mother as she rolled into bed.

Thereafter she swore that her life should be given to

portraying detached emotions, to placing love on the
boards. Her ambition was to kiss the lips of John the Baptist as they lay in plaster glory upon a little tin plate.

When a subaltern puts his head under cover, he is a
coward. When Mamie Saloam sought the underside of
the counterpane she was merely looking for future eth-
ics.

Mamie twisted the Bowery out of her hair, threw her
hips into the maelstrom of rightly moving things, and
raised an organism of potato and cod to the level of caviar
and champagne. When she turned about, she had taken
three steps in the direction of the proverbial gentleman
who follows after the world and the flesh.

The rich and the poor are divided only in the matter
of scorn, eye scorn, lip scorn, and the sudden rude laughter that runs the gamut of Broadway. All these leaped into
Mamie's saucy face as she looked at herself for the first
time in a mirror that gave her back, whole.

When she walked out, one heard only the sound of
slum slippers and the regular cadence of her knees as she
descended the steps. She was used to uneven footing.

After the mirror she swore that she had taken the last
cod bone from between her teeth and now she would
chew only after-dinner mints.

When a girl gives up gum and alleys, and has known
little else, she becomes something different, and the something different that Mamie became was a dancer, toe and
otherwise.

Into the little world of the painted came Mamie. Into

that place of press-agents and powder-puffs, of Lillian Russell and Raymond Hitchcock, of Irving and of Sarah, scented with lilac and Bel Bon, throbbing and pulsating with the sound of laughter; into that little stall called the dressing room, out of which none may come unchanged.

Mamie Saloam was a good medium on which to lay cosmetics. Everything merely accentuated those points that God and the Saloams had given her; in fact, the team-work between the two had been sublime. Mamie was beautiful.

She was loved by the men down front because she had mastered the technique of the tights.

Her world held rows and rows of dusty caned chairs, and over these, like migrating robins, the pink anatomy of the chorus—hips thrown out against the painted drop, listless eyes that saw only supper, a new step, and once in awhile, some other things. Mamie Saloam could go where she willed. She could stoop or look up because Mamie breathed true ambition and heroic drudgery.

When she passed the boundaries of decency it was a full run for your money; when she went up in smoke, those original little pasty pans of Egypt became chimney pots. If Helen of Troy could have been seen eating peppermints out of a paper bag, it is highly probable that her admirers would have been an entirely different class.

It is the thing you are found doing while the horde looks on that you shall be loved for—or ignored.

Billy had caught Mamie pinning "Thou shalt not sin" up high on the door of her room in the house of chameleon thoughts. He then knew—for even electricians can know things—that the way to approach Mamie was to sit close and abide in hope, for opportunity comes once to every man.

While he waited, Mamie made up her one philosophy. It was made, of course, for the benefit of women. It read: "A woman never knows what she sees; therefore, she tries to see what she knows."

"Listen," said the stage manager one night from out of the gloom where Mamie sat restringing the beads that passed for combinations, underskirt, shift, petticoat, bodice, skirt, and withal, propriety for Salome. "Listen, we are in a fix. The P.I.B. is on to us and you."

"In what way?" inquired Mamie Saloam.

"They have gotten on to the fact that early in the season we are to present you as *Salome*. They have prejudices—"

"Of course they have," said Mamie calmly; "they have seen Mme. Aguglia, Mary Garden, Gertrude Hoffman, and Trixie Friganza do the stunt; they have all seen what they wanted to see because the aforesaid showed them what they wanted to see; I'll admit that John hasn't been properly loved since the original gurgle ceased; I'll admit that as we have gotten further and further away from the real head, we have dealt with rather papier-mache passions.

"John was rather lethargic in his response even in the beginning, and we have made too much fuss over him. When a man is dead, a certain respect is due him; it is a proper and a joyous thing to dance about him, but I do think he has been rather overkissed. I will show the ladies of the P.I.B. the necessary moderation, even if the gentleman is helpless. Leave it to me."

"By the way," she added as the stage manager pondered, his hand in his hair, "what is the P.I.B.?"

"It is the Prevention of Impurities upon the Boards," he said, and smiled at her.

"And what do they want?"

"They either want the performance stopped or—they want to see a purely impartial rendering."

Billy looked at her from beneath his shaggy eyebrows. Then suddenly he let go of the thing that is called reserve and took her hand.

"Mamie," he said, "couldn't you respond to me; couldn't I ever be anything to you; couldn't I make up for all this"—he waved his arm broadcast—"this ambition stuff?"

"Billy," she said, and her voice was cold and practical, "I couldn't ever boil potatoes over the heat of your affection. Your love would never bridge a gap; it wouldn't even fill up the hole that the mice came through, and," she concluded, withdrawing her hand, "I couldn't ever consider anyone less than John."

Deep down in Billy's heart lay a terrible passion that itched to force this allegorical obstacle from between him and the woman. As he sat in his perch up in the wings and focused the blue light upon the platter and the white upturned plaster face, he knew what had put the word

"La mort" into the dictionary and into circulation, and he groaned within his soul.

The next day they took away the dusty rows of chairs, the heaps of discarded tights, shed by human butterflies that had grown into something more brilliant or had died emerging from the chrysalis prematurely. They did not notice that it was dusty until they saw two spots some three inches apart, which looked as if someone had been upon his knees.

They did not speculate any further, but Mamie saw.

The stage hands cleaned and fussed in preparation for the trial scene to be given for the benefit of the P.I.B. A pitcher, belonging to the dresser, very much cracked, and yet gaudy as the owner, was filled with lemonade, which first frosted the outside like a young woman's demeanor when holding the young man off, and finally broke out into great beads and slid over the hips of the pitcher to the table below like the tears that follow up the first grief.

It was quite dark backstage when they were through. The little bags of ballast that let down Florida or France from the ceiling hung swaying fifty feet above Billy as he tinkered with the lights. Out front sat the stage manager between the starched ladies of the P.I.B., drinking the lemonade gently yet firmly from tall, frail glasses. They looked at each other across the chain-encircled vest of the stage manager with the macaw look which is strictly limited to boards of prevention and committees for inspection.

They would like to think well of Mamie Saloam, but as Mamie said, they had seen Mme. Aguglia.

Then out across the dusky stage came Mamie, tall and dominating. Her bare shoulders supported vivid streams of her hair. For a minute she stood poised in the center of the stage, a voluptuous outline in the mist.

Then the spotlight fell, not upon Mamie, but upon the face of John, upturned and white, with half-closed lids, the hair and beard flowing over the edge of the plate. Dark loops broke the dead white of the forehead, a silent questioning of the painted lips awaiting the performance of Mamie Saloam, who had learned to kiss ten years before.

The ladies of the P.I.B, not to be fooled, leaned sternly over their glasses. They wanted to be sure that there was a simplicity in the way Mamie Saloam wallowed before her lord.

On she came, halting, and then suddenly broke into a semicircle of half-steps about the head of the dead Baptist, gurgling, throaty little noises escaping her lips. Slowly she lowered herself until, imperceptibly to the starched ladies, she lay upon the floor and sinuously wriggled toward the tin platter.

Sidewise, forward, approaching it with plastic hands, nearer and nearer and nearer till the platter was within the zone of her very breath. Over it she hovered, murmuring, while her eyes changed from blue to green and from green to deep opal. Then suddenly she dropped her chin among the strands of the flowing beard.

The starched ladies sighed and relaxed. Here was a woman at last who could do the thing with perfect impartiality. They turned approving eyes upon the manager.

"She has John under perfect control," they said, and passed out.

Then Mamie did a strange thing. She sat up, put her arms about her knees, and looked serenely at the face still motionless in the blue of the light from the unoccupied electrician's box. John the Baptist batted his right eye.

"Get up, Billy," she said. "It's all right. Let us thank the dark of a backstage night, and your ability to lie still. At last I have proved that a woman never knows what she is seeing."

Who Is This Tom Scarlett?

HE SNARLS.

It is a philosophy; one's lower teeth are always good.

On either side of him sit three men.

The room is long, narrow, and the heavy smoke creeps up and down, touching first one, then another, shuddering off. Seven bowls of soup stand at regular intervals upon the table. The imprint of foreign hostelries is upon the silver. On the walls, just behind the seven heads, are seven blue and white Dutch plates like halos, and above the seven plates the rising and placating star, a liquor license.

Tom Scarlett turns his face from side to side, brushing his shoulders as he does so with the ends of his long black sideburns. Like a bird whose wings have been plucked of their flight, this fall of hair seems to have been robbed of its support, clinging to the mouth, which is raised diagonally across fine yellow teeth. The head is magnificent and bald. Like a woman who is so beautiful that clothes instinctively fall from her, this head has risen above its hair in a moment of abandon known only to men who have drawn their feet out of their boots to walk awhile in the corridors of the mind.

His hands lie in front of him. They are long, white, convalescent hands, on which the dew of death is always apparent, the knuckles interrupting each pale space with a sudden symmetrical line of bone. These hands lie between the anchovies and the salt, and as he turns first to the right and then to the left, they move imperceptibly, as though reins were attached to them from the head. And as Tom Scarlett snarls, Tash laughs.

Spave torments a pickle that lies in front of him with a fork, squirting drops of green juice upon the bare boards. Some of the others talk of a person of bad repute. One calls loudly for a glass of rum, while the sixth breaks, one after another, the backs of toothpicks, littering them over the floor.

They have been jesting among themselves because Tom Scarlett has been lonely again. They tell him that he has too many interests, and he answers: "Should one pass you over with nose keen for the most fragrant portion of your souls, where the flowers of your persistency have left their perfume, that nose would stop between your first and second knuckle, for on your smoke you have concentrated, as I on my flame."

They look at one another, and move among themselves, and finally are swept away in a great gale of laughter, whereat Tom Scarlett snarls and lets his face fall back into its habitual calmness.

The clock in the street strikes three. In the tolling of the bell the six hear the voice of their trade. For Tom Scarlett alone does it strike off another morning in man's short life.

For Spave it means that his counter is waiting his cheating barter; for Glaub, that the little pigs in his rotisserie lie feet upward in anticipation of the spit that shall be a staff on which to climb to the eminence of man's stomach; while for Shrive the ink is drying in his bottles used so illy to amuse men; and for Tash that the lumber in his yard is growing gray in the rain. Freece seems to see his oils drying upon his canvas; while, last of all, it recalls to Umbas' mind the fact that there are three pretty little corpses waiting to be sent to heaven with becoming smiles upon their lips and a yard or two of lace bought at a great reduction from a dealer on Second Avenue, because slightly damaged, when his wife called him a fool and his hand shook.

To hurry matters, the six crane their necks in the direction of the kitchen, where Lizette is making sauce for the spaghetti. They cannot see, however, because Madame is sitting at her table drinking wine and snarling at her dog, and from time to time reaching down to rub forefinger and thumb in its hair, as though its fleas were her torment also. Tom Scarlett has often wondered how she kept her diners, so morose she is and so bitter. Her eyebrows twitch over her eyes like long black whips goading her eyeballs on to hate and menace.

Spave balances an almond on his polished fingernail and sends it up, up, spinning into the air, where it turns, striking Madame's glass, dashing a blot of red upon the tablecloth. Madame opens her mouth, the eyebrows raise themselves as if to strike.

Spave leans forward, extending a stick of celery. "For your little teeth," he says, and Madame's jaws snap to like a grate.

But Tom Scarlett is annoyed, and because he is annoyed he realizes that he is different. Madame's eyes have become gamin; they search the men, darting here and there. One would say that they concealed a tongue, hid a mouth, cloaked a fist. Madame is always one course ahead of her diners. She seems to derive a great deal of pleasure from the fact. She is especially pleased if she can have one dish that they will not get at all.

The dog, like his mistress, is bad tempered in a tricky way, standing with one paw upon a bone—one morsel ahead of the yellow cur sniffing by the lintel. Sometimes this dog smiles, the saliva running in a silver rim around his lips, dropping tearwise slowly.

Tom Scarlett and the dog have something in common; both reproduce the atmosphere under which they serve— the one his mistress and the other his time.

Who is this Tom Scarlett?

His friends have ceased to idolize him because they have caught him picking his teeth. Thus many deities take the toboggan. They no longer marvel at him because he has given them to eat of the fruit of his soul—and because it was tropical and strange and they could not eat it, they said it was not eatable. Tom Scarlett snarls and offers them cigars, which they are more than glad to get.

"You are like a steak," they tell him; "good only when digested."

Tash beats upon his vest and howls.

"How you will be appreciated when his stomach has appropriated you."

Tom Scarlett answers quietly: "Still, I shall be the dish."

"But we the approval. A great man should keep several stomachs as he keeps a wine chest."

Tears bulge out Tom Scarlett's eyelids, but he answers gently: "I stand alone among men."

"So the flower thinks."

"Well?"

"There are always dead flowers to nourish the living, as there are always dead minds to support the steps of greatness."

Tom Scarlett smiles, exposing his fine teeth.

"I have crawled around the rim of the world like a fly— I know what I know." He leaned forward, placing his finger on Tash. "If men," he said, ruminatively, "were forty feet taller, the screaming of those in death would sound like crickets chirruping in the grass in the evening. The greatest kiss would be but a little puckering, which, when interrupted, would give out a fleshy sigh." He tosses up his hands, laughing greatly down the hairs of his beard.

"You will die as others die."

He answers: "Yes, I shall die as others die—crying out. But here I shall differ. A great man gives birth to himself; for him the death rattle is the wail of birth."

Spave spits: "He will put his hand upon his stomach as one in mortal pain, but he will cry, 'My head! My head!' A last transaction in favor of the mind."

And so they grew merry tormenting him.

One day they came later than usual. Madame was not drinking; instead she kept passing her hand back and forth across her dog's spine. She scowled, it is true, giving the room more of its usual morose aspect, thereby maintaining its cheerful air—for only by maintaining established custom are we entirely content. Still she shook her head in a way that seemed to give her a good deal of sorrow.

And they shook themselves because it was raining outside, a peculiar dampness that suggests to mind the fact that all things must attach themselves to some ailment, even men, reminded them that the earth draws much back to herself in her rainstorms besides the growing river and the autumn leaves. So they shuddered, and Madame, eating her Parmesan, shuddered also and spoke to them.

"He is walking again today."

She pointed upward, for Tom Scarlett lodged on the parlor floor.

"Ah, he will be down presently."

"I do not think so."

"You will see. One's stomach is always the gendarme of one's mind."

"But listen."

Five of them try to, but Race, taking his coat off, knocks over a chair.

"Why in the name of the saints can't you be quiet?" they shouted, in the exasperated manner of men who, if thwarted in their silences, will at least not be thwarted in their uproars.

"It's well," said Madame, peeling an apple; "You could not hear him, anyway; one has to see him now."

"What is wrong?"

"He walks like a cat. Do you remember what a noise he used to make with his great feet, as though he wanted the furniture to know he approached." She clicked her tongue. "No more."

The six began at their soup. "He will come down, you will see." But when he failed to come at the appearance of the cheese and nuts they began to talk among themselves. They said, "What can this be?" And they said, "He has indeed altered: I no longer hear his great feet upon the boards. He had arrogant feet."

Old Tash chuckled.

"After all, in a monarchy or in a republic, it's us little men that count. We bear the children, then we sense that one among the lot is different. Is it not by our hand that its face is kept clean? Would it not be a dirty gamin running around the streets in tatters, holding up its hands to squint at the stars, but walking in prodigious puddles? Is it not our care that keeps the bib dry? Do we not hide our children's drool until they are old enough to hide it for themselves? And is it not by our hand that the child is fed, that he is brought up into manhood? Don't we print his books, don't we build his colleges, don't we sweep his streets, light his lamps, make his bed, and in the end is it not us who bury him, after building him that other house that he has peradventure to leave; and is it not we who write his biography? He may be the voice, but who are the ears? Eh? He may paint the pictures, but who are the eyes? He may be a rare flower, but who is the nose? He may have his head in the clouds, but who is the earth in which his feet are set?"

He gave vent to a loud, rich laugh, a laugh that wedged its way between much good eating to reach the ears of Madame. He leaned back, striking his vest, as a jockey strikes his horse, letting his breath escape him in that after-dinner sigh indulged in by the rotund. "After all is said and done, Madame, is it not we, I ask you, who are the great importance of the earth?"

Madame raised her eyebrows.

"He walks like a cat. I do not like it."

"So softly?"

"So softly, little dusty footfalls, like a cat, a small, profound cat. Men walk that way when they have changed their minds."

She did not explain what she meant by the word profound.

"A little, dusty cat, with a gray nose from prowling in among what people call great facts. Why, will you tell me, have all great things to be dusted? Cathedrals and books and windmills?"

They lit their cigars.

Madame snapped: "Eh, eh, and bric-a-brac and the inside of all empty bowls, the floors of reservoirs have known the feet of the sparrows."

"You talk in riddles, Madame."

"I talk one language; you hear another."

"The dog wants a bone," they suggested, and assumed a calm mien.

They asked Glaub about his rotisserie, and why he did not eat of his own little pigs for a change.

He answered: "Can one eat his own child? The aroma from my little pigs is like a sigh going up to heaven; it almost placates me. No, no," he added, "I cannot eat my little pigs; others must do that for me. We leave our children's seasoning to the public; they are the ones who make them tender and profitable. So with my little bits of pork with features at one end and a little exclamation point of a tail at the other. It is a waste of nature's talents that she gives features to her meats, but there it is."

"There are some who say that the odor of a butcher's shop is delicious—and fattening."

Glaub shuddered.

Like buzzards these six had flapped about the life of Tom Scarlett in that little basement room where Madame served her persistent table d'hote, and as such carrion swoop down and take away the eyes of the dead that have been its light, they swooped down upon the brilliancies of Tom Scarlett, thinking, animal-like, that they had its radiance between their teeth. But it was only the empty husk of a thought because they could not understand.

For long months they had tormented him so. For many long months they had been content to eat food that was at best a hollow mockery, as such food is liable to be. But to Tom Scarlett there was some dire truth in what they said—for he realized that around and around such men as he circled such a six and such another six interminably; and Tom Scarlett knew that because of him they gathered undue radiance.

So today when Madame failed to drink her red wine, while she rubbed the back of her dog and scowled and would say nothing to them that was either hard and biting, or soft and unctuous, they were uncomfortable. Was it not raining outside, and had not dampness settled down to a tete-a-tete with the smoke that hung like a yellow rag before the nose of each as they picked their teeth?

Shrive took another sip of wine. "If this country," he was saying in a garrulous tone to Glaub at his left, "does not give more chance to its public men—eh, I admit," he added hastily at the opening of Glaub's mouth, "that there should be places for the men of importance, of course, like the President and the deans of colleges and strike-breakers, but there should be one or two exalted chairs for its minor poets and its journalists. We can't all have a great man on ice."

*

The other four heard the last part of the speech and burst out laughing.

"Here," they cried, "may the ice soon melt."

They started to rise, and Tash got as far as the bending of his knees. Madame turned around with a hand in the hair of her dog. Presently she drank again, looking at the door.

It had swung open and the face of Tom Scarlett peered between the jamb and the outer edge. Tash sat down.

There was something in the eye of Tom Scarlett today

that they had not exactly expected to see. It was not the eye of an obscure celebrity like Tom.

He picked up an apple and bit into it.

"Ha!" he said, and once again, "Ha!" Then he burst into sudden laughter.

"Six great-little men," he shouted, abruptly, half shutting his eyes, and added sharply: "Carrion! The earth about the flower, the hand that holds the infant's mouth shut until it knows enough to be hypocritical about its saliva—" He jerked the apple away from his mouth. He bent forward until his long bathrobe touched the floor. Then his fine yellow teeth showed between his lips, held up a trifle crookedly, as a portiere upon a resplendent yet gloomy room.

"What are you now?" he demanded. "Sparrows—seaweed. No, no! Hold! Business men. Little, dirty, gravy-spilling bourgeoisie! Hereafter you will find it difficult to swallow your bird seed."

He laughed again, sitting down among them. "Yah!" he cried, more gently. "A great man among men, that helped you to be something, but what will happen to your stature if I become a little man among little men?"

"Now what have you done?"

"I am growing my own flowers. I, too, am eating bird seed with the sparrows."

He put a handful of apple pips upon the table.

"I think I shall open a little piggery also. I shall twitter." But tears bulged out his eyes.

The Jest of Jests

THE NAME of the heroine of the story is the Madeleonette. Why never seemed to matter any more than that the hero should have been called the Physician when he had never so much as seen a case of measles in his life.

The place of climax is Long Beach, but that you will not understand until you reach the very end, though I might as well warn you that it was there the Madeleonette and the Physician fell into each other's arms, much to the consternation of the "regulars" on the boardwalk.

However, there was a third party to this story, and his name was Josiah Illock, a small, good-for-nothing type of man, who looked as though he should have been laying drain pipes in a small suburban town rather than making love to the Madeleonette.

On the other hand, the Physician was tall and dark and even handsome. He wore a long, old-fashioned frock coat and gray tweed trousers, and had an habitual expression of forceful timidity. He kept his hands in his pockets much of the time, with that backward thrust that made him seem to be encouraging his receding backbone.

Now both of the gentlemen loved the Madeleonette, or they said so, and love and advertisements must be believed. For Josiah, she was the lily of existence; for the

Physician, she was the rock on which faith or a home is founded.

For herself the Madeleonette was only a fast aging woman, who had managed somehow to keep a certain amount of looks and some of youth's fine hair in spite of the ravages of time. She was a widow who had been left in rather comfortable circumstances. Her husband, who had been an antique collector, had supplied her with armchairs, sofas and cabinets enough to have started a small museum, but I would hesitate to say that this fact had anything to do with the affections of the two gentlemen just mentioned.

When upon occasion these men met in her green and white parlor, they glared, for they hated each other heartily. The Physician did not waste time intriguing to do away with Josiah, but when Josiah was alone with the Madeleonette, he could speak of little else until he defeated his own plans and sent the Madeleonette's heart over in the direction of the Physician.

Sometimes Josiah would say to her: "Some day you are going to wake up to the fact that the Physician is not as crazy about you as you think. All men begin by loving a woman for what she isn't and end by perceiving what she is. In the beginning they caress the skin with kisses, and in the end they puncture with the pistol."

"Great God!" the Madeleonette would cry. "Do you think so?"

And he would answer: "Always it's an instinct. Men shoot what they do not understand. That is, they track

the lion instead of the fox. They bring to the bitter dust
the highest flying hawk and to the pitfalls they at last drag
the antelope."

"There are no pitfalls for the woman over forty," the
Madeleonette would answer. "There's only one possibility for her, and that is she will end life on a sofa with hot
bottles at head and feet."

*

"Look here," he said, leaning forward. "You know what
I mean. Shooting is simple. A woman can get over that—
if—" There was a long pause. "If," he finished, "he keeps
right on loving her—but he won't. They never do."

"The Physician would die," she answered simply.

"Want to prove it?" Josiah questioned.

She looked at him a long time as a woman does who is
taking chances.

"All right," she said at last. "It's worth it."

He talked on, sketching his plan, but she did not pay
any attention until she heard him saying: "I'll see to it
that it's loaded with blanks, of course. All you have to do
is to fall over and pretend dead. Stop breathing for a few
seconds, but watch. If he really cares for you he will raise
hell. If he doesn't, he'll merely leave the room with you
and the revolver together to prove it suicide."

She laughed, "You're a fool, ain't you? As if any one,
especially the Physician, were going to risk his neck, even
if he does love me. What's he to shoot for?"

"A provocation."

"What provocation?"

"Jealousy," he answered, pretending to be absorbed in his cigar band.

"You're all crazy, you men," she said, dropping off into an acceptable silence.

In the meantime the Physician, who looked back upon a life of thirty-nine years of timid shudderings, catapulted out upon the veranda of his home and stood there breathing hard. He was more than a timid man. Like a carpenter's foot rule, he was long and powerful in sections, but too apt to double up and cease his calculations. He adored bravery because he had none of it. It was his reason for his affection for the Madeleonette. He knew her for a brave woman. He had a rock, while she had only a lover.

"Yet," he reflected sanely, "one should test the Madeleonette. A woman without courage would be my ruin. I lack that quality so myself."

He watched a long dust-gray line of children with a certain keen shrillness of breath that did more to eat up tobacco than forty mouths applied simultaneously.

Now while the Physician mused, the Madeleonette prepared for the death.

When a woman decides to lie down and play 'possum she always selects with fearful care her hosiery, her petticoats and her shoes.

The pumps that the Madeleonette picked out were chosen for the newness of soles, the petticoats for their lace and ribbons and the hosiery for its irreproachable unity.

In her daily life she had considered her hats, her gloves and her buckles. When she decided to lean back against destiny, she concentrated on her lingerie. She tied her laces tighter, powdered her neck lower, put her fingers into rings, her neck into the willing slavery of a halter of pearls, and upon her face she put that fixed smile which advertises a perception of the angels.

She knew that she was not going to die. Had not Josiah Illock assured her, and did not Josiah love her?

Once Juliet had done this thing.

"My God!" she said, and started toward the window. Sudden ideas always take us to the casement. The tears ran unmolested down her cheeks. "What if the Physician, swayed with remorse and with despair, should take the paper cutter or the curling irons and thrust them into his startled soul? What if he should lurch over to the window and fling himself to the pavement? What if he should tie a noose of handkerchiefs about his throat and spoil the gas fixture for the next tenant? What—"

The tears ceased. "What a fool I am," she thought as she smiled. "I should wake up directly."

She went back to her wardrobe to hunt for a becoming dress. She laid it out upon the bed and, taking the cologne bottle, doused a liberal quantity of its contents upon the chiffon exterior. Then she laid it to her nose to ascertain if it was scented within the bounds of delicacy.

Next she took her hair out of curl papers and combed

it into a ravishing coiffure. Presently, with her feet in bronze slippers and her electric coffee pot beside her, she gave herself up to pleasant expectancy, while she set the social crackers straight.

There was a sharp ring of the far distant bell. She ran out into the kitchen to press the button—waited at the door for the ascending steps to turn into a man.

Josiah Illock came in, removed his hat and shuffled over to a chair. He sat there gasping.

"You like it?" she said, indicating her gown.

"It is beautiful," he assented. "What is it?"

"Chiffon. It falls nicely," she confided with a slight blush. "It falls nicely."

He grinned. "It's going to be the jest of jests, ain't it," he remarked guardedly. But there was a nervous twitching of his mind that betrayed itself in the muscles of his neck.

"Yes," she answered. "I've been practicing the fall, Josiah. I'm black and blue, but I have made it not only a fall, but a disaster. It has become an art."

"Um," he answered. "You love him pretty much, don't you."

"Quite a bit," she assented. "But I love art more." She tried to look natural. "There must be some subtle, fine, masterful touch that will make him realize that not only has a candle been snuffed out, but that an arc light has given up its flame; not only that a soul has passed into the night, but that a professional has given her last performance on any stage; not only that a grave shall open for the Madeleonette, but that an abyss shall remain forever gaping."

Josiah Illock did not understand.

"What will you do?" he questioned.

"I shall die smoking a cigarette," she said and watched for the effect.

His eyes narrowed. "I don't see anything professional in that, though perhaps you are right," he assented and took to making nervous movements. Then abruptly he caught her hand.

"Can't you transfer that affection to me? Really it would be safer—please, I love you."

She drew her hand back. "You're messing things up a good bit, Josiah. I can love no one but the Physician. It is more than a conviction; it is something that has been bitten into my heart as a rose bug bites a rose."

Josiah winced. "You wouldn't have to go through this business then," he commented.

She turned upon him. "Not go through this business? Why, this is dress rehearsal. I wouldn't stop if I were married to him. You're a fool, Josiah. I have left the pistol in the hall on the stand. You'd better put those blanks in," she added as he arose.

When he returned, she failed to notice that perspiration stood out upon his upper lip. She set the teapot on. The doorbell rang. They both started. She opened the door.

The Physician entered, hat in hand, and bowed over his fingers. Then they both stood up.

"Give me your hat," she said.

Then Josiah came in with his behavior calculated to enrage to the point of madness. First he put his arm about the waist of the Madeleonette and, second, he kissed her. Third he opened his mouth to say some cutting things, but a look in the Physician's face stopped him with his tongue raised. The Physician was staring at the nodding pansies in their box at the window in a way that seemed to him little ease. Then with a long step he reached the door and, at the same instant, came the short contralto song of a revolver shot. The Madeleonette dropped over sideways, with her cigarette still in her fingers. As she hit the floor, an abrupt flare of smoke burst from between her lips and ascended slowly in a gravely widening ring.

There was silence which was in its turn broken by the shutting of a back door.

The Physician laughed. A short, sad and very disillusioned laugh, and tossed the weapon upon the couch. He did not lean over her to look into her face. He did not stoop to kiss her lips. He did not cross those still hands above her breast. Instead he reached for the handle of the door and was gone.

In an instant, like a cat the Madeleonette was on her feet. She whirled a chair against the jamb and, drawing her chin above the transom top, watched with blazing eyes the exit of the Physician.

She watched him pass down the carpeted stair and on the lower landing. She caught a tune from "Chin-Chin" as he went. She said sadly: "Now I shall have that little fool Josiah running around calling me beloved."

She dropped to the floor as a plumb to the sod.

"Josiah!" she called.

There was no answer. She groped her way into the kitchen.

It was empty.

She did not understand.

But one thing she did. It was growing in a widening pain. The Physician had been tested and found wanting.

He had not only tried to kill her and had, so far as he knew, but he had gone out as a man leaves a lavatory after washing his hands. She represented the suds after an experiment.

So that was the man he was. Just on outside appearances he had grown blindly jealous and flared up. Well, anyway, she knew him before it was too late. What was the matter with Josiah, though? Why had he bolted? She got up and went back into the parlor, where she wrote a note.

She even smiled now and finished the cigarette.

How frightened he would be when he found out that she was not dead after all. What would he not suffer in the way of humiliation and perception of his great inefficiency. How deliciously miserable he would be when he discovered he had lost her forever.

She went on to tell him of her trick to test him and added a bitter little jab such as women fashion. "I shall no longer darken the doors of this place, defiled as it is by its acquaintance with you. I am leaving—shall have left by the time this reaches you—for Long Beach. I shall need a little rest in which to recover from this wound."

She sent the note by messenger boy that it might reach its destination before the blood of self-accusation should recede from his cheeks.

Some five minutes later a small messenger boy appeared at the door. "No answer," he said, and departed with that casualness indulged in by Western Union children in the face of death and reunion.

The note was from the Physician.

"When you read this," it said, "I shall already be gone. I tested you and found you wanting. At the sound of a pistol shot you fainted. Oh, woman, that pistol was loaded with blanks! Ah, how shall I ever recover! You whom I loved—a coward! I shall always love you, but where I place that love there must I also have faith. Forever I leave this sad, disillusioned home. I go to Long Beach, there to recover a little of my former gaiety.

"P.S.—By the way, as I went out I found a loaded revolver on the table. What is the meaning of this?"

The Madeleonette sat down sharply. "I'm the antelope all right," she said.

Thus it comes about that the second paragraph of this story is the last.

Prize Ticket 177

CLOCHETTE BRIN felt pretty sure that no minister would throw the awakening gravel to her window, because Clochette had to admit that she was no longer young and alluring, that her voice had lost its color as a fading tulip loses its beauty, and her eyes were not so soft as they had once been, as the steel of strife had entered rather largely of late.

Therefore all that Clochette saw in her future was a good old age and a possible set of six rose-cluster, silver-plated after-dinner coffee spoons—if she could attain them.

Clochette Brin was a ticket seller. Into the hurry of five o'clock South Ferry workers and the breakfast-regretting uptowners she wedged her way in the morning and hoisted all of a passing fair form upon the high stool at the back of the wired opening of the ticket window. Perched there like a great god on a human scale, between the cracker box and the old roped-in chair, sagging and falling in like the knees of an ancient woman.

In the very beginning, when Clochette had been young, she knew that love and lottery went together, as do heaven and harp. Also she reckoned that no matter what number your lot was set on, premiums were not worth much anyhow.

Incidentally, Clochette was nearly right.

Now at the age of thirty she knew that life was altogether a lottery of a baser sort. Therefore, she passed out the change with a heroism that goes with a woman who has become a little overheavy. Whistling a popular air between bites of a ham sandwich and trips to the stove to stir coffee with a tarnished spoon, Clochette spent her life.

Her only family tie was a hard and uncompromising knot, a crippled mother, who hooped out the underside of a rose-strewn coverlet, a living trellis.

Some women, as they grow old, lose faith and avoirdupois and, sitting on hard lean cane, go down life's pages an exclamation point, to slip at last like a splinter into the River Styx. But not so Clochette, for, having lived in the shadow of many heavy dinners, she gloried in the fact that she would make some considerable splash when she went in over the side.

Clochette did not mind passing on with the fraternity of the Silent Cold, but she would continue to object until she had as many silver spoons to call her own as had a certain very small roomer on the floor below.

Du Berry was her name, this certain small roomer, and she was delicately pink and fresh, and had hair that curled above bewitching pale ears, and she smiled so that she maddened men. She painted porcelain or something, and spent most of her time hanging out of the window.

She knew nothing of the world that had made

Clochette's eyes hard. She had a gentle, generous heart, and she would have given Clochette anything she wanted if Clochette had asked. As it was, Du Berry knew Clochette only as an animated roll of "I" tickets that got unreamed by six of an evening, and then came home to be fed.

Du Berry was young and clean and wholesome, and pretty without powder, but having merely a back sink knowledge of Clochette, which lasted only through the washing of two potatoes, she never proffered her friendship.

There had come to the street a young man. He might have been twenty-five—a lean, dark, handsome, black-haired youth with a dilatory lilt.

He had no parents nor relations, little money and apparently no occupation, at least this is the set of conclusions that most of the street came to in regard to him. A man who has an occupation does not lie in bed until ten or eleven o'clock of a morning, and yet a man without one seldom comes in by seven at night to do Indian club and dumbbell practice.

This much Clochette and Du Berry knew of him; the shadows in his room knew more. They knew that he was making himself a personal proposition by adjusting a face strap under his chin just before getting into bed, and by pulling much bath towel across a perfect Grecian back while he waited for the water to boil. Also the shadows knew that the weight of such authors as George Sand,

Meredith, Moore and Dumas were the ones responsible for the knife-like crease in the young gentleman's trousers.

Doik was his name. Slender-handed as a pickpocket and warm-hearted as an Irishman, Doik crept into the street that now sheltered Du Berry and Clochette, the ticketseller.

Of course, Du Berry fell in love at first sight, as you all expected, and she would have asked nothing better than to have ironed out the white shirts that flapped from his window.

Clochette loved him also, but Clochette was different. She wanted to cook herring for his breakfast and take the lovers out of his cup of tea.

It was Clochette who got acquainted first.

It came through Doik's determination to have some sort of social life. He desired friendship. He also aspired to a better knowledge of The Avenue and of fragile teacups and the well-waxed mustache. He had heard that on The Avenue love and life were ripe for the picking, and he had seen the bus framed in the cut running south of Twenty-third Street.

In the meantime he talked to Clochette.

Clochette talked well because she had a great scorn for the rules of the seven-foot bookcase, and these things made her very human.

She knew that Doik was broke, that he was a gentleman, that he was extremely well built, that he might be called handsome, but beauty goes at naught in Baxter Street as a substitute for cash.

He was hoping silently to move uptown. It was while he hoped and waited that he heard from Clochette about the two yearly events in Baxter Street.

Event number one was the arrival of the man from the boggy parts of London, who did tricks on stilts. And event number two was the annual prize given by Loggie's moving picture house for unmarried women only.

"Ain't you never been there?" she asked, thrusting a hand back in the direction of Loggie's.

Doik shook his head.

"It's the darndest swell place," she went on. "They have regular prizes every Friday, and once a year, upon May 5, they have the lottery set aside for unmarried women only!"

She tossed her head a bit and smiled, liking to think that there was such preparation for the unattached women of the streets of the modern Babylon. It gave them a sort of dignity.

"The other prizes are about the same. Anyone can get in on them, but this isn't silver brushes and table scarfs, it's the regular thing."

"Um," assented Doik, "and what is it going to be this time?"

"You can't never tell," Clochette said, with averted eyes. "It's generally personal. Once they put up a joke on us. We women were all there, and we was all single, too, mind you, and all of us was in a flutter trying to make out of our numbers the winning one. The little painter girl, Du Berry, was there, too, when the award was given."

"And what was it?" Doik leaned closer.

"Wasn't nothing much," evaded Clochette.

"You ought to tell me, you know."

"Why?"

Doik reflected. Girls had been telling him things for a long while. He knew that he had a finely developed capacity for absorbing. Also he knew that nothing is withheld from Adonis, therefore he smiled and showed a fine row of even teeth. "Aw, come on, be a sport and tell Doik!"

She blushed and stirred up the grounds in the coffee pot.

"One of 'em was a teething ring, t'other was—"

"Yes?" he prompted.

"A smoking jacket."

She raised her eyes to get the full of his understanding and he laughed suddenly, without sound, his hands upon his knees; laughed and took his hat off and said he was confounded, and fully realized what it must have meant to the sisterhood of Baxter Street. "Who got the coat?"

"Mrs. Penell's daughter, Daisy."

"Who got the teething ring?"

"I did."

He said he was confounded again, and stood staring in the direction of Loggie's.

"What is it going to be this time?"

"I don't know," Clochette answered. "Nobody knows until the last film."

"Seems rather hard on the married women," he hazarded.

"They should worry," retorted Clochette, off guard. "Don't they get all there is in life without wanting all of the prizes? Why, it's almost an incentive to stay single, and the Lord knows," she added, "we do need an incentive."

"Yes," he said, "I suppose so—say!—" he halted, and suddenly darted off and down the stairs.

An hour later the boy was seen striding in the direction of Sam's lunch room, and three passengers in the street said they saw him bolting beef stew and a large wedge of apple pie, "and," they observed, "eating it as though he had almost forgotten how." Which he nearly had.

Clochette saw him again about two and asked him, from the tired depths of her, where he had been.

"You see," he said, "I had a dinner coming to me. So I went to it."

"I see," remarked Clochette, and added: "Say, when was you home last?"

"I haven't got any home."

"No home. Say, Doik—kid—you—ain't an orphan?"

He nodded.

"No relatives?"

"None. Last of my family, last of my name."

"No friends?"

"Only you."

"My Gawd, what are you going to do?"

"I'll stick it out," he said bravely.

"Look here," she said abruptly. "You can come up to

see me any evening you like, and me and my mother will try to make up for relations lost."

"You're awfully good," he said, and a film of tears passed across his eyes and sent into twisted lines the walls of the cage wherein sat his only friend.

"You can come up tonight," she added, and turned away.

The little painter girl, sitting with her feet up on the sofa and a drawing board in her lap, sang softly in the coming glow of evening. The odor of second-hand clothes and the labor of warm multitudes came to her. There had been such an evening as this once in Babylon. And now the wondrous incense was Pete's dray of onions and the wondrous flowing garments were Mrs. O'Shay's as she sipped lemonade upon the roof of her tenement. The soft sounds of an old world were just the ordinary high- pitched tones of Mrs. Skindisky calling her kids home.

The red lights gleamed down by Loggie's—the heart's blood to a never dead desire. The postbox had grown into the dim proportions of tomorrow's possibilities, and the gold and purple bottles in the apothecary's window took on a highlight as Danny, the druggist, turned the gas on.

Presently Du Berry put down the board and leaned out the window. The police station was waking into a flurry of lights, and a uniform or two stood upon the steps. The sharp shattered laughter of a girl reached Du Berry's ears, and she slowly turned her head and was sorry and somewhat sad. And then, returning to the lights of Loggie's, she smiled and passed indifferently on to the interminable ranges of tenement upon tenement stretching away into the unlimited reaches of the evening sun, and she started and drew in her head.

There was a step upon the stairs.

No one came up after Clochette, and she had closed her door a whole hour past. The step was a man's too, and it was light and almost hopeful, yet hesitant.

Du Berry's heart swung in great sweeps as she leaned weakly against the wall. Was it—could it be?

It paused, and then it went up and on, and she stood still and grasped the knob in her hand, and then as the step died out, she opened the door swiftly and leaned out. For one second she saw the blue of Doik's trousers, and the next, the blue had passed into Clochette's apartment.

But the thing that had stopped her heart was the look the owner of them had shot at her.

Remembering this same evening gave Clochette much to regret.

"No, thank you," said Doik, shaking the crumbs off his knees. "I don't think I will have any more."

"Can't I read to you, ma'am, or do something to have made this an evening for you as well as me?" He said it so simply, and in such good faith, and he held his hands so tight, and looked so kind and funny, that the woman beneath the counterpane suddenly found anguish in her dumbness, and regretted, with full eyes, the fact that her limbs had been taken into the ample palm of rheumatism.

"She can't understand you," Clochette said, but she turned around and stirred something in a pitcher.

The boy wandered aimlessly about, and said presently: "Can't she hear, don't you think?"

"Yes, she can hear," said Clochette.

Sitting beside her, he read to her, and Clochette, watching, wondered sometimes at the things that Baxter Street gets in its net.

She helped him on with his coat. "You're a good boy," she said, and something in her voice made him nod a little as he reached the door.

"You wouldn't be proud, or glad, to see me sell myself, would you?" he questioned, and not waiting for an answer, thanked her and told her he would come again, and shut the door.

Now Du Berry never stayed up this late, but she heard the door of Clochette's room open and she heard it shut, and swiftly coming out into the hall, because she wanted to see him, she found herself looking into his face without an excuse, so she took his hands, and they stood so for a minute. The life of the street died down, and the horses in the stable by Pete's sagged against their stalls and stamped at the length of a Baxter Street night. But this did not affect the lives of the boy who swung dumbbells and the girl who painted porcelain.

And then he blurted out: "Are you going, too?" and she answered "Yes," and he disappeared in the night, which held also the colored bottles in Danny's apothecary shop.

Was she going? Well, she certainly guessed she was. The very next day she proved it to the whole street by buying the ticket two hours before opening time. You see, Tommy Thrupp, who sold the tickets, knew the winning number (sometimes they do, you know), and he, being fond of a certain lady who painted china, slipped it to her and told her, in a whisper, that 54 was the rope around the neck of six rose cluster, silver-plated after-dinner coffee spoons. After supper, while she was rinsing out the tea-pot, Du Berry told Clochette about it, out by the back sink, and Clochette's eyes hardened. "Six silver after-dinner spoons?" she said, and pondered. She looked this little frail girl over, and in her heart of hearts she knew that Du Berry was capable of giving up her life for the asking. But Clochette hated the asking of favors. And yet six rose-cluster, silver-plated after-dinner coffee spoons just needed to make up the set.

"Say!" She turned so suddenly that Du Berry jumped. "Be a sport, will you? Take a chance. Let's swap tickets, mine is number 177. Let's see what will happen."

"But the spoons?" cried Du Berry, and opened her eyes, and then understood, and offered it immediately, and would have kissed Clochette besides. Therefore they swapped, and Du Berry went back into her room and closed the door, and said over and over: "Poor, poor old thing, poor dear, poor dear. I'm so glad I had it to give her. Oh! I hope Tommy was right."

The boy who played the piano at Loggie's grabbed the last handful of ragtime and sprinkled it over the audience in a closing crash of Spring sentiment, threw his knuckles into the back of the hardwood piano's trademark, threw his pompadour out of his eyes, and whirled around on his stool, accomplishing the death of the electric light over the sheets of music as he did so.

All of the sisterhood of the single waited in the dark along with Du Berry, who had come in late, and Clochette Brin, who had come in early.

One, two, three, of the sickly little lights blinked out of the dark at the side wings of the stage. Three, four, five, six, and Tommy stepped into view, whirling his great bag of numbers, and dashed to the middle of the stage, where (he hardly gave the numbers time) he proclaimed the winning number of the silver spoons to be 54, and waited.

There was a rustle as the whole of the maiden portion of Baxter Street focused their eyes upon their cards, the long disappointed sigh, as in full sight, Clochette Brin, the ticket seller, stood up, and with heroic Babylonian voice, told the residents of the unclaimed set of Baxter Street, that the rose cluster, silver-plated after-dinner spoons were hers.

Tommy's eyes roved a moment, and knowing Du Berry, smiled as he passed the prize over.

There was a stretching of necks as the sisterhood took in fully the person of the woman who had carried off their hopes.

And then all eyes went back to Tommy, who held up his hand. There was an awful silence. "The other winning number is 177," he said, and added, as Du Berry, breathless, half started from her chair: "Somebody is forfeiting her right to compete next year with this one. Allow me to present number 177."

Into the dim glow of the six lights upon the stage stepped—Doik. A little pale, his head thrust back, his chest unsteady. A splendid man in a moment when hard luck had brought him to this pass, and slowly his head came down level and he looked into the eyes of his fate.

"My Gawd!" breathed Clochette Brin, "I sold you, Doik, for a set of silver-plated spoons," and her voice broke, but Doik did not hear.

"Dear, the Lord has been merciful," said Doik, as he took the painter girl into his arms. "I got a hundred for this—and—you."

There was silence after that until one of them said: "I can't go again next year and compete for the prizes offered to"—a small catch in her voice—"unmarried ladies only—now," and something stopped the speech right there.

"No," said Clochette's voice out of the dark. "I ain't going to bother you, only I thought..." (her voice rambled off in a strained and pathetic way), "I thought this might come in handy next year, when—you can't compete," and she was gone.

They struck a match, and, standing close together in its blur, they saw a little red india rubber teething ring.

A Sprinkle of Comedy

HE WAS a tall man—with long, pale hands that swayed from the wrists like heavy flowers on slender stems.

His eyes were long, pointed and blue with a curious spray of blood-veins running through them as though the eyeballs themselves were small berries set in the center of a vine. He had a peculiar way of walking, half lounging, and though he never gave the impression of being in a hurry, he somehow managed to get about a little quicker than any one of his three friends. His hips flattened out abruptly from the base of the slender legs, and the bulging pockets of the tweed suit were always half full of paper clippings. A cigar usually hung in the corner of his mouth and sent an occasional wreath of smoke above the head which had already begun to lose its hair. The impression was the same as that obtained from a picture of a high mountain on which a cloud had descended. When he spoke it was in a short, sharp manner punctuated with an occasional drawled "and," "the," or "if."

He had done many things in his life, about which he told no one. He liked to think that he was yet able to astonish those few friends whom he had never even interested. Time and time again when he might have told his history with considerable profit he had failed to do so.

Why? Probably because it had, after all, been dreary, commonplace, uneventful.

This man's friends were of the type that in an instant descend from "friend" into a "gang."

It takes circumstances alone to make them either friend, lover, enemy, thief, brawler, what-not. It may be a hand on the shoulder, a word whispered in the ear, a certain combination of apparently unimportant incidents.

The man, Roger, knew this very well. In spite of his hesitant gait, in spite of his quietness, and in spite of his occasional quick speech, he had as yet not let them become aware of the fact that he was their master. He would sit among them, rubbing his chin, smoking his cigar, coughing, and say never a word. Sometimes he would drink with them, laugh when they were not laughing, remain immobile when they roared. It was only at such times as these that they would pause suddenly, and looking at him, break off with a half laugh or a counterfeit cough. He understood very well why. He never said anything.

This man had a wife and son. He never spoke of them, excepting once or twice when he mentioned his boy with a touch of ill-concealed pride.

His wife was the type of woman who, though large and sullen, always appears at parties and balls with a delicately fronded feather fan, or who is seen passing out of tea-rooms with a long rose between her teeth—a thing that has probably been done by every woman in the world.

She carried her passion for flowers into her own room and from there to the windowsills of every window in the apartment. Window boxes of green sheltered pansies and violets in season, which she watered so often that they died.

Her flowers were second only to her passion for her son. For her husband she had the kind of peculiar approval that a woman often displays in public by giving him too much sugar in his tea, and in leaving him entirely without it when dining alone. But for her, Roger would perhaps have been one of the great men of history.

The boy was frail and somewhat like his father—only shorter and more energetic. He had long, yellow hair, a straight nose, a manly chin, a great deal of plain honesty, and a marked talent for the piano. Yet at times, he would make short remarks warranted to anger his mother, who would raise her heavy eyebrows, and cause his father to move uneasily.

He was beginning to grow handsome and knew it. His attempt at a mustache had gone very well, and he twirled it so continuously that his finger-practice in the scales had markedly fallen off in the right hand.

He would say such things as: "It's no use, you needn't talk about the progress of civilization. We're nothing but expert monkeys."

"Ah, my dear."

"Yes, I know it doesn't sound nice—they haven't any manners. But that's the only difference, you see. Manners have franchised women to some extent—Shaw, for instance, has liberated them through the indefatigable politeness of his heroines' husbands. And no man was king until he had acquired the art of bowing without difficulty. The difference between the bow of the bourgeois and the aristocrat is, in the one, the face muscles are lazy and permit the cheeks and lips to fall forward, giving the face a sullen, ill-arranged look—while in the other, the face remains intact, even though you swing him feet first from a gibbet."

"My dear, you are what the English call horrid."

He twirled his light mustache. "You know I told you so," he said.

Then the mother would sigh, fold her handkerchief into a very small square, and say to Roger, "I'm sorry, but it seems to me that the lad is growing strange and of an odd material."

Roger answered always in a flat monotone: "If he were material he would be silk," and clicking his heels together, departed to drink with his three friends in abstract silence.

What was his great fear? It was simple.

He feared that his son would grow weary of the same round of existence—yet at the same time he knew that he was capable of nothing new unless fate pushed him into it. This is the fundamental reason for the silence on his past; even to his son he never betrayed a knowledge of having lived before the age of 29. He hoped that his silence on this interval in his existence would prove a source of romantic speculation on the part of his son, and thereby keep him a little closer to the family.

He desired an honorable career for his son. Why, we shall see.

He had suggested to him often the renown connected with chemistry. His son only laughed. He suggested a course in mathematics. His son answered instantly, "Two and two make five." He left that subject and went off into a eulogistic account of the life of an anthropologist. His son retorted, "Men have four legs, but they have learned to call two of them hands." His father sighed.

"Then why don't you go in for civil engineering?"

"To make a bridge," the son answered, "you burden a man with the things he loathes until, with his back bent to the ground, he once more calls his hands feet."

Roger turned from him suddenly and, pressing his hat over his eyes, went out into the street.

Well, what was he going to do about it? What did his son want to do? Idle?

"Eh, eh," he would mutter to himself "I'll teach him."

But when parents mutter that they will teach, it is about then that they are going to learn something.

Then one day his son came home without his mustache. Roger went into his own room and closed the door. There he paced back and forth for hours, his hands behind him, a strange look in his face, at once very sad and happy. In fact, he looked like a man who has just had a cup of cold water dashed into his face at the time that he has been presented with a material increase in salary.

Roger was perplexed on the one hand, and on the other, profoundly quiet. Something seemed to have broken in him, yet when he came out from that room later, a hard line had set about his mouth and shone coldly in his eyes.

As he went out, he fingered a little slip of paper earnestly and in complete absorption. He had placed it with the others in his bulging pockets.

He pushed open the door leading into the room so much frequented by himself and his three friends.

Finally, they were all silent.

They were even more than uneasy. Then they were startled. What they had been awaiting had come; what they had been expecting was about to happen. They felt themselves to be upon that brink which is called adventure, and which would change them for life from casual and uninteresting figures into something historic and terrible.

They ordered a round of beer and sandwiches. Of these Roger did not partake.

"No," he said as if in answer to something they had said in chorus. "No, boys, we don't need anything here but a little care and a great deal of alacrity."

One of them asked what was up.

"This," he said slowly, putting his hand upon his hip and softly reaching the fingers down by means of stretching them out to their entire length from the palm. "This is the matter—I need your combined help—do you understand?"

They assented.

"I also need secrecy—get that?"

They nodded.

"Can I depend upon you—all?"

They nodded a second time.

"You see, it can't be accomplished without your help, or I would do it alone. The boy is strong and I'm no longer young."

He placed the paper out smoothly in front of the three and looked up at them alternately as they read.

The note ran, in his son's hand: "It's all right. Charlie will make a great get-away tonight if it doesn't rain—if it does, we'll wait for a fair night. Don't exactly like starting an adventure that is likely to alter my life, in the rain."

And a straggling scrawl at the bottom of this: "Three cheers for the ever-increasing brotherhood of the ring!"

The men sat back.

"Well?"

They answered that they did not exactly get it.

Roger carefully explained: "It's my son, you see. He's always been threatening to run away. To become a circus rider at first was his idea. That was when he was 15. Then he wanted to be a policeman. And later, just lately, he didn't do a thing but read the sporting columns—that means that Jess Willard has got him by the soul. The rest of it is plain enough. He's going to run away with that boy friend of his, Charlie, a prizefighter himself in a small way. That is, if it doesn't rain—"

The three of them answered: "What have we got to do?"

Roger answered instantly: "Stop him, of course."

"How?"

He laughed, crumpling the note up in the first fist they had seen him make.

"Now, why do you ask me such a question as that? How should one prevent one's children from dropping from the tree unless one scares them?"

"Well, what are we to do? Details!"

Roger placed both arms on the table with his hands locked at their ends. "First you must all come to my house. Second you must have patience, much patience, because I'll have to put you in the cellar."

"Eh, that's cold," said one.

"It's necessary," Roger answered. "Then, when I give the signal, you all rush out and grab the kid. Give him the scare of his life and hand him over to me. Of course," he added "I could reason with him tonight. Tell him that I have found out. Show him the note—but—"

He paused, looking around: "But that would not deter him for long. That sort of thing only fires a boy's imagination."

They were a little disappointed: "That's nothing very dangerous nor very interesting."

Roger smote the table with his fist. "To me," he answered, "to me—that is sufficient. To me it is important. It means my lad's future."

He turned away. There were tears in his eyes.

"Have you told your wife?"

He shook his head. "No," he said. "I don't want to worry her—besides it will be sufficient for him that I know."

"Wouldn't it be better to catch him a little this side of the wood he has to pass at the end of the park?"

"No, no; the point is to prevent him from being successful enough to get three feet from the house—I want to—to—what is it they say—to nip this in the bud—I know to what it leads.

"Our children," he said, apparently unheedful for a moment where he was, "come to us and are content to stay with us only so long as the legs refuse to support them; only until they can hold the spoon, the glass and the fork themselves and then—they—fly." He added: "The child was right. We are monkeys, or something—we do not change. As soon as we can, we go; if it is a bird, it flies; if it is a calf, it walks; and if it is a fruit, it falls."

They whispered among themselves. His anger had altered them; his request for help pleased them, but his philosophy only puzzled them, made them laugh, which is often the same, because herein they realized lay the difference between the hand that does the deed and the brain that directs it.

They sat thus till toward dusk—then going arm in arm into the street they said that it looked like a stormy night, as there were no stars. They promised to come to Roger's house after dinner, and being cautioned to enter by the back way and to descend at once to the cellar, they parted.

The night had grown dark by 9:30, when Roger, excusing himself to his wife, descended to the cellar. His son had not put in an appearance for dinner—not unusual in itself, but tonight it made Roger unhappy and thoughtful.

Presently three knocks on the pane of glass at the windows warned him that his friends were without.

He whispered them to descend. In so doing their feet seemed already to have learned to murmur where they had always shuffled and made a great noise. They were armed with long sticks and presented such a terrifying aspect that even Roger was pleased.

"I don't think it will rain," he said, opening the little window an inch and thrusting his hand out to feel the temperature and moisture of the night.

They spoke softly, which was not necessary, but which seemed to them appropriate. When we are about to trip a man up, we usually do it in an undertone.

Said one:

"When do you think he will come out?"

Roger answered: "Any minute now."

Said a second: "Is there a door nearer the front?"

"Here," said Roger.

They waited in silence; a long time passed. Off and on Roger slipped his hand out of the window chink to make sure that it was not raining. Off and on, also, the three men arranged the contour of their faces that they might look frightful, indeed, when the attack began.

At eleven o'clock Roger was walking up and down impatiently.

"He's late," he said, "unless he's waiting until I come home." Here he laughed a little.

He went again to the window: "I thought I heard steps," he said. He thrust his hand out of the window again. A fine mistlike rain struck it softly, wetting his wrist. He drew it in suddenly with a grunt. His whole figure relaxed.

"It's raining," he said.

They looked at one another.

"Well!"

"Let us have a drink. I will present you to my wife." He laughed again. "And my son."

They tramped heavily upstairs. Roger pushed open the door of the sitting-room, let his friends in and called to his wife.

"Here!" she answered, and came in presently with a slow movement, her sullen eyes peering ahead of her.

Roger went to the window and closed it.

"Why do you leave it open?" he asked. "It's cold, my dear."

"I know," she answered, moving lazily across the room as he began introducing his friends. "How do you do? Yes, I left it open when I watered the pansies a minute ago. Sorry."

With a half cry, Roger sprang toward her. "When you what?" he demanded.

Very slowly he sat down. He put his hands to his face and began to laugh in a hard, catchy manner.

It was at this point that he changed from a silent man into a monologist.

Something had broken in him, and what had broken was his own repressed soul in the breaking away of his only son.

He made only one allusion to what had just passed before he launched out into a torrent of words about his youth.

"Gentlemen, you see by what a father and son are parted." He cleared his throat, and spreading both hands open in front of him, began:

"Well, in eighteen hundred and thirty-nine, I, having long desired to become a prizefighter, left my father's house one night by a back window …."

He was a gentle, childish man now. His friends sat and stared in rather a frightened way at three sticks of wood which lay on the carpet at their feet.

The Earth

UNA AND LENA were like two fine horses, horses one sees in the early dawn eating slowly, swaying from side to side, horses that plough, never in a hurry, but always accomplishing something. They were Polish women who worked a farm day in and day out, saying little, thinking little, feeling little, with eyes devoid of everything save a crafty sparkle which now and then was quite noticeable in Una, the elder. Lena dreamed more, if one can call the silences of an animal dreams. For hours she would look off into the skyline, her hairless lids fixed, a strange metallic quality in the irises themselves. She had such pale eyebrows that they were scarcely visible, and this, coupled with her wide-eyed silences, gave her a half-mad expression. Her heavy peasant face was fringed by a bang of red hair like a woolen table-spread, a color at once strange and attractive, an obstinate color, a color that seemed to make Lena feel something alien and bad-tempered had settled over her forehead; for, from time to time, she would wrinkle up her heavy white skin and shake her head.

Una never showed her hair. A figured handkerchief always covered it, though it was pretty enough, of that sullen blonde type that one sees on the heads of children who run in the sun.

Originally the farm had been their father's. When he died he left it to them in a strange manner. He feared separation or quarrel in the family, and therefore had bequeathed every other foot to Una, beginning with the first foot at the fence, and every other foot to Lena, beginning with the second. So the two girls ploughed and furrowed and transplanted and garnered a rich harvest each year, neither disputing her inheritance. They worked silently side by side, uncomplaining. Neither do orchards complain when their branches flower and fruit and become heavy. Neither does the earth complain when wounded with the plough, healing up to give birth to flowers and to vegetables.

After long months of saving, they had built a house, into which they moved their furniture and an uncle, Karl, who had gone mad while gathering the hay.

They did not evince surprise or show regret. Madness to us means reversion; to such people as Una and Lena it meant progression. Now their uncle had entered into a land beyond them, the land of fancy. For fifty years he had been as they were, silent, hard-working, unimaginative. Then all of a sudden, like a scholar passing his degree, he had gone up into another form, where he spoke of things that only people who have renounced the soil speak of—strange, fanciful, unimportant things, things to stand in awe of, because they discuss neither profits nor loss.

When Karl would strike suddenly into his moaning,

they would listen awhile in the field as dogs listen to a familiar cry, and presently Lena would move off to rub him down in the same hard-palmed way she would press the long bag that held the grapes in preserving time.

Una had gone to school just long enough to learn to spell her name with difficulty and to add. Lena had somehow escaped. She neither wrote her name nor figured, she was content that Una could do "the business." She did not see that with addition comes the knowledge that two and two make four and that four are better than two. That she would someday be the victim of knavery, treachery or deceit never entered her head. For her, it was quite settled that here they would live and here they would die. There was a family graveyard on the land where two generations had been buried. And here Lena supposed she, too, would rest when her wick no longer answered to the oil.

The land was hers and Una's. What they made of it was shared, what they lost was shared, and what they took to themselves out of it was shared also. When the pickle season went well and none of the horses died, she and her sister would drive into town to buy new boots and a ruffle for the Sabbath. And if everything shone upon them and all the crops brought good prices, they added a few bits of furniture to their small supply, or bought more silver to hide away in the chest that would go to the sister that married first.

Which of them would come in for this chest Lena never troubled about. She would sit for long hours after the field was cleared, saying nothing, looking away into the horizon, perhaps tossing a pebble down the hill, listening for its echo in the ravine.

She did not even speculate on the way Una looked upon matters. Una was her sister; that was sufficient. One's right arm is always accompanied by one's left. Lena had not learned that left arms sometimes steal while right arms are vibrating under the handshake of friendship.

Sometimes Uncle Karl would get away from Lena and, striding over bog and hedge, dash into a neighboring farm, and there make trouble for the owner. At such times, Lena would lead him home, in the same unperturbed manner in which she drove the cows. Once a man had brought him back.

This man was Swedish, pale-faced, with a certain keenness of glance that gave one a suspicion that he had an occasional thought that did not run on farming. He was broad of shoulder, standing some six feet three. He had come to see Una many times after this. Standing by the door of an evening, he would turn his head and shoulders from side to side, looking first at one sister and then at the other. He had those pale, well-shaped lips that give the impression that they must be comfortable to the wearer. From time to time, he wetted them with a quick plunge of his tongue.

He always wore brown overalls, baggy at the knee, and lighter in color where he leaned on his elbows. The sisters had learned the first day that he was "help" for the owner of the adjoining farm. They grunted their approval and asked him what wages he got. When he said a dollar and a half and board all through the Winter season, Una smiled upon him.

"Good pay," she said, and offered him a glass of mulled wine.

Lena said nothing. Hands on hips, she watched him, or looked up into the sky. Lena was still young and the night yet appealed to her. She liked the Swede too. He was compact and big and "well bred." By this she meant what is meant when she said the same thing of a horse. He had quality—which meant the same thing through her fingers. And he was "all right" in the same way soil is all right for securing profits. In other words, he was healthy and was making a living.

At first he had looked oftenest at Lena. Hers was the softer face of two faces as hard as stone. About her chin was a pointed excellence that might have meant that at times she could look kindly, might at times attain sweetness in her slow smile, a smile that drew lips reluctantly across very large fine teeth. It was a smile that in time might make one think more of these lips than of the teeth, instead of more of the teeth than the lips, as was as yet the case.

In Una's chin lurked a devil. It turned in under the lower lip secretively. Una's face was an unbroken block of calculation, saving where, upon her upper lip, a little down of hair fluttered.

Yet it gave one an uncanny feeling. It made one think of a tassel on a hammer.

Una had marked this Swede for her own. She went to all the trouble that was in her to give him the equivalent of the society girl's most fetching glances. Una let him sit where she stood, let him lounge when there was work to be done. Where she would have set anyone else to peeling potatoes, to him she offered wine or flat beer, black bread and sour cakes.

Lena did none of these things. She seemed to scorn him, she pretended to be indifferent to him, she looked past him. If she had been intelligent enough, she would have looked through him.

For him her indifference was scorn, for him her quietness was disapproval, for him her unconcern was insult. Finally he left her alone, devoting his time to Una, calling for her often of a Sunday to take a long walk. Where to and why, it did not matter. To a festival at the church, to a pig killing, if one was going on a Sunday. Lena did not seem to mind. This was her purpose; she was by no means generous, she was by no means self-sacrificing. It simply never occurred to her that she could marry before her sister, who was the elder. In reality it was an impatience to be married that made her avoid Una's lover. As soon as Una was off her hands, then she, too, could think of marrying.

Una could not make her out at all. Sometimes she would call her to her and, standing arms akimbo, would stare at her for a good many minutes, so long that Lena would forget her and look off into the sky.

One day Una called Lena to her and asked her to make her mark at the bottom of a sheet of paper covered with hard cramped writing, Una's own.

"What is it?" asked Lena, taking the pen.

"Just saying that every other foot of this land is yours."

"That you know already, eh?" Lena announced, putting the pen down. Una gave it back to her.

"I know it, but I want you to write it—that every other foot of land is mine, beginning with the second foot from the fence."

Lena shrugged her shoulders. "What for?"

"The lawyers want it."

Lena signed her mark and laid down the pen. Presently she began to shell peas. All of a sudden she shook her head.

"I thought," she said, "that second foot was mine—what?" She thrust the pan down toward her knees and sat staring at Una with wide, suspicious eyes.

"Yah," affirmed Una, who had just locked the paper up in a box.

Lena wrinkled her forehead, thereby bringing the red fringe a little nearer her eyes.

"But you made me sign it that it was you, hey?"

"Yah," Una assented, setting the water on to boil for tea.

"Why?" inquired Lena.

"To make more land," Una replied, and grinned.

"More land?" queried Lena, putting the pan of peas upon the table and standing up. "What do you mean?"

"More land for me," Una answered complacently.

Lena could not understand and began to rub her hands. She picked up a pod and snapped it in her teeth.

"But I was satisfied," she said, "with the land as it was. I don't want more."

"I do," answered Una.

"Does it make me more?" Lena asked suspiciously, leaning a little forward.

"It makes you," Una answered, "nothing. Now you stay by me as helper—"

Then Lena understood. She stood stock still for a second. Suddenly she picked up the breadknife and, lurching forward, cried out: "You take my land from me—"

Una dodged, grasped the hand with the knife, brought it down, took it away placidly, pushed Lena off and repeated: "Now you work just the same, but for me—why you so angry?"

No tears came to Lena's help. And had they done so, they would have hissed against the flaming steel of her eyeballs. In a level tone thick with a terrible and sudden hate, she said: "You know what you have done—eh? Yes, you have taken away the fruit trees from me, you have taken away the place where I worked for years, you have robbed me of my crops, you have stolen the harvest— that is well—but you have taken away from me the grave, too. The place where I live you have robbed me of and the place where I go when I die. I would have worked for you perhaps—but," she struck her breast, "when I die I die for myself." Then she turned and left the house.

She went directly to the barn. Taking the two stallions

117

out, she harnessed them to the carriage. With as little noise as possible she got them into the driveway. Then climbing in and securing the whip in one hand and the reins fast in the other, she cried aloud in a hoarse voice: "Ahya you little dog. Watch me ride!" Then as Una came running to the door, Lena shouted back, turning in the trap: "I take from you too." And flinging the whip across the horses, she disappeared in a whirl of dust.

Una stood there shading her eyes with her hand. She had never seen Lena angry, therefore she thought she had gone mad as her uncle before her. That she had played Lena a dirty trick, she fully realized, but that Lena should realize it also, she had not counted on.

She wondered when Lena would come back with the horses. She even prepared a meal for two.

Lena did not come back. Una waited up till dawn. She was more frightened about the horses than she was about her sister; the horses represented six hundred dollars, while Lena only represented a relative. In the morning, she scolded Karl for giving mad blood to the family. Then toward the second evening, she waited for the Swede.

The evening passed as the others. The Swedish working man did not come.

Una was distracted. She called in a neighbor and set the matter before him. He gave her some legal advice and left her bewildered.

Finally, at the end of that week, because neither horses nor Lena had appeared, and also because of the strange absence of the man who had been making love to her for some weeks, Una reported the matter to the local police. And ten days later they located the horses. The man driving them said that they had been sold to him by a young Polish woman who passed through his farm with a tall Swedish man late at night. She said that she had tried to sell them that day at a fair and had been unable to part with them, and finally let them go to him at a low price. He added that he had paid three hundred dollars for them. Una bought them back at the figure, from hard earned savings, both of her own and Lena's.

Then she waited. A sour hatred grew up within her and she moved about from acre to acre with her hired help like some great thing made of wood.

But she changed in her heart as the months passed. At times she almost regretted what she had done. After all, Lena had been quiet and hard working and her kin. It had been Lena, too, who had best quieted Karl. Without her he stormed and stamped about the house, and of late had begun to accuse her of having killed her sister.

Then one day Lena appeared carrying something in her arms, swaying it from side to side while the Swede hitched a fine mare to the barn door. Up the walk came Lena, singing, and behind her came her man.

Una stood still, impassible, quiet. As Lena reached her, she uncovered the bundle and held the baby up to her.

"Kiss it," she said. Without a word, Una bent at the waist and kissed it.

"Thank you," Lena said as she replaced the shawl.

"Now you have left your mark. Now you have signed." She smiled.

The Swedish fellow was a little browned from the sun. He took his cap off, and stood there grinning awkwardly.

Lena pushed in at the door and sat down.

Una followed her. Behind Una came the father.

Karl was heard singing and stamping overhead. "Give her some molasses water and little cakes," he shouted, putting his head down through the trap door, and burst out laughing.

Una brought three glasses of wine. Leaning forward, she poked her finger into the baby's cheek to make it smile. "Tell me about it," she said.

Lena began: "Well, then I got him," she pointed to the awkward father. "And I put him in behind me and I took him to town and I marry him. And I explain to him. I say: 'She took my land from me, the flowers and the fruit and the green things. And she took the grave from me where I should lie—'"

*

And in the end they looked like fine horses, but one of them was a bit spirited.

The Head of Babylon

IT HAD BEEN RAINING since Thursday. Furrows of muddy water ran across the stretches of road where the tufted grass had given out. The long ridge of moss and flowers that stretched itself like a snake through the town shook a little in the heavy gusts of rain. The cart with its flat-eared tandem labored slowly up and into the misty valley beyond, always avoiding the band of flowers which separated one ox from the other. The whiffletrees shook, jangling their iron hooks, and the cooing of the crated doves came down the wind.

Some laborers from the adjoining town plodded past, their picks and shovels across their shoulders. Their tan jumpers dripped a mixture of rain and sweat. Some of them smoked pipes upside-down. They slouched by the general store with its dripping awning, and away into the gloomy fields beyond.

Behind a grove of elms surrounded by a small court and row of fir trees, stood the house of Pontos—a heavily landed farmer of the city. Besides his cattle, amounting to several hundred head, he had some fifty fine horses, suitable both for ploughing and long team work. Pontos was a Pole, a tall, florid man, who always wore a black skull cap and long pale jacket. He had a small amount of knowledge connected with the problem presented to him each year by his land. His great ox eyes shone with a lazy good health. He stuck his thumbs beneath his girdle during the day while contemplating his crops, but of an evening he stuck them beneath his belt for pleasure as he looked over the heads gathered at his table.

His stomach and his house were both of the feudal type. A Roman would not have scoffed at the immense table running from one end of the room to the other. Nor would the epicure find it in his heart to sneer at his hung delightful hams with their sweet smoky taste and a tenderness that caused them to slip away beneath approving teeth.

Pontos had a great many children. He always alluded to them as one more finger than his hands. He would hold up his short fingers as he said this, counting along them, tapping them at the base of their hard topaz callouses, instead of on the tips—somehow he connected them in this way with his labor.

"There is Tina," he would say, going from the thumb to the first finger on, naming them until he reached the alternating thumb, and here he would finish, "And then there's Theeg."

His eleven children had grown up as healthily as his corn. They were all tall blond creatures with short upper lips and large ox-like eyes. Theeg alone resembled her mother. Her eyes were long and black and strange—lashes of silver covered them with a frosting of ice. Her nose was powerful where it flared into appreciative nostrils.

Her mouth was small and well shaped. The upper lip was heavy and lay upon the lower languidly. Her cheek bones were high but not so broad as her father's, and her chin deserted the family entirely. It was small and pointed and soft and usually sought her shoulder.

The mother of these children had grown old suddenly, but with that age which takes a long time to become old. She had been a thin woman, but was now stout and small and wrinkled, with a color about her like the color of the earth. Only her eyes had the same heavy silver lashes as her daughter's, and her mouth, too, had signs of having been at one time what Theeg's was now.

They were all good eaters and they were all fond of company. When Pontos kept open house it was for his family, his friends and his laborers. He saw no distinction in having risen to landowner. Somehow he connected it, in his mind, with his and his wife's and his children's hard, unending, untiring labor. He was much too dull of mind to be sharp of pride. He thanked God for his success and was glad when his friends and his "help" came to thank God with him. He needed help thanking God as he needed help in the harvest season. He figured that the more men there were, the heavier the harvest, and he let his landlust and crop law drift over into his belief in divinity. The more people giving praise, the more blessings.

On this particular night, his daughter was to be married to Slavin, a landowner in the neighboring village. Torches of wax had been set about the room. The youngest child crawled on its stomach, dabbling its fingers in the hot wax and smiling as it slowly hardened, covering its little hand with a white veil. At either end of the long room, two huge fireplaces were piled high with resin knots, while garlands of ground pine were stretched from rafter to rafter.

The table sagged in the middle like a loaded horse. Great white stalks of celery shot up from polished tumblers, and three yellow bowls of mush steamed on either side of a flank of venison. The musicians straggled in and took their places at the end of the room, tuning up their fiddles. One of them was an old Negro, who played through the summer season in the small towns in return for food and beer. Now he was clapping his hands and smiling and cracking jokes and thumping with his feet. While his friend, after the manner of white people, tuned up his instrument, this Negro tuned up his body, swaying this way and that, humming in the back of his throat and shaking his shoulders.

Pontos paid no heed to them, any more than he would have paid heed to the buzzing of flies over his pasties had he been a cook. Both stood for the same thing, appreciation of and participation in an excellent affair.

His wife sat in the old armchair at the foot of the table. For the occasion she had returned to the garments of her youth, a Polish dress of red and blue that had been worn in her seventeenth year. It had been altered now and made large around the waist. A handsome apron of yellow cloth with red and blue stitching lay across her knees, and for extra decoration she had removed her earrings.

The laborers who had been pushing their way through the rain in the twilight came in at the door now, shaking the mud from their heels and flinging their coats into a corner by the fire. One of them remarked that it looked like snow. Someone answered that it was likely; he had even known it to snow in June. Pontos did not desert his place by the lintel. Slavin had not shown up, and Pontos strained his ears trying to catch the sound of horses along the road that led away into the outlying village. The croaking of the frogs had ceased earlier in the evening, as if the rain had gotten into their throats. Across the stretch of cement yard, Pontos could see a bat hanging in a heavily branched tree, and beyond this the clouds seemed to be dispersing.

Pontos rested one hand high up on the door jamb and laid his head against it, his large booted foot thrust back. His wife had begun to talk to some of the laborers, and a decanter of wine had already been unstopped. Pontos looked upon his children much as he looked upon ungrown or unplanted stock. He hoped they would grow up well and marry well, as he trusted the seasons would treat his crops kindly. Theeg was his favorite; he could not quite make her out. She lay in bed all day like a child, yet he could not make up his mind to exact of his failing courage a caress that he would have been pleased to bestow upon her. He would have liked to stroke her beneath the chin. While still a child she had lost the entire use of her limbs, only moving her head and intelligent cold eyes; still, something in these eyes forbade that caress that always sprung to the tips of his fingers whenever he saw her turn her head in toward her shoulder.

Somehow he did not regret her unlikeness to her brothers and her sisters; if she had been corn he would have rooted her up, not being interested in natural phenomena and plant diseases; but with her it was only strange and different, and he did not resent her in the least. Somehow he liked and trusted her. That he trusted her, he never stopped to think about. Still, it was significant, as though he said, "I expect you to make the specimen one of the best."

A great dais was built for her at the head of the room between two long candles; a mat of flowers had been spread about this raised platform with its catafalque-like couch, and on the foot of the bed the little children of the neighborhood had littered small cakes and candles.

The priest had not yet arrived, though a great chair had been set for him near an open Bible. Pontos, leaning at the door, suddenly turned inward to survey the room, trying to see it as Slavin would see it, for he had heard the horses climbing the hill.

Slavin was a man who had started several local disputes in regard to agricultural improvements. He subscribed to several agricultural magazines, but seldom read them, feeling a sort of security in their mere presence. Sometimes he would take them to bed, but he never read more than three or four paragraphs before a feeling of great weariness would overcome him and he would fall asleep. Still, the other farmers considered him a dangerous unit, and found a great deal of satisfaction in the sight of his yearly crops, which were scarcely ever up to their own, owing to his many experiments.

He was a short dark-skinned man of about forty-five. He had fallen in love with Theeg at first sight; she seemed like something newer and stranger and more desirable because of her oddity. Tonight he was radiant but sad. He had stopped in at Leavitt's to get a drink before finishing the ascent of the hill, and Pontos caught the odor of it as Slavin's red lips moved beneath his bristling mustache.

He looked around eagerly for Theeg, and seeing the nest prepared for her, but without its bird, he went up to her mother, and dropping a heavy hand upon her shoulder, told her to cheer up.

She had been sitting in one of her contented and quiet moods, picking out the red threads of one of the embroidered flowers. She had such a profound expression of absolute and essential happiness that one would have found nothing astonishing in the fact had she mooed; but when Slavin told her to cheer up, two tears sprung instantly from her eyes and descended to her woolen waist, leaving brown spots as though she were of the earth.

The long table had already begun to fill before Slavin's arrival; now it was entirely surrounded by the friends and laborers not only of Pontos but of the bridegroom. Slavin would not sit down, but moved uneasily about the room. His stiff new shirt annoyed him, and he kept coughing a little. He had not dressed for the wedding excepting as such people dress. He had changed his boots and his collar and shirt, and had washed his face; and instead of speaking of the new mowing implements, so much in his mind lately, he spoke of the rain.

Finally they bore her in. Her four elder brothers were at the corners of a litter they had hastily constructed for the carrying. They placed her among the soft rugs of the couch upon the dais, where she looked like some splendid tranquil candied fruit with her heavy bands of dark hair and those strange silver lashes.

The great fires had been lit and the shavings caught, instantly shooting red and blue flames up the sides of the logs. Like gay colored lizards, they darted in and out, springing higher and higher at each renewed attempt.

Pontos was already experiencing that mingled feeling of loss and acquisition connected with the giving away in marriage of a favorite daughter. Theeg's mother, on the other hand, moved about hurriedly filling the tall glasses with fine old wine, and shouting, "You'll all drink now."

The priest had come in while the uproar was at its height and stood smacking his lips just behind Thalin, a younger brother who had his glass tilted over his nose.

Theeg had asked for a glass of wine, but in the excitement of drinking her health, she had been neglected. Now it was brought to her by one of her little brothers, who, reaching up to his full height and raising his arm above his head, could just touch it to her lips.

As she lay there, Theeg smiled. Her white feet showed

below the fringe of the rug—one slipper hung loose at the heel, slippers that never touched the floor excepting when they fell.

The little cakes the children had strewn over the couch lay unheeded, and one or two of the candy bells had rolled down between her ankles. Off and on, as they passed, the laborers took these cakes up and biting into them passed some remark to their neighbor.

The musicians were beginning to play snatches from songs, and the men were looking furtively at the steaming pasties that the cook had just brought in.

The priest began the ceremony, and it became mingled with the remarks of the mother asking her daughter if she was comfortable, and Theeg's answer to this question, "Yes," was taken for the answer to "Will you take this man?"

The night had grown dark outside, and as they feasted, the heavy rain could be heard dripping on the roof with a sound as though many fearful and light-footed animals were pacing up and down.

And as they ate and drank and grew loud under the wine, Pontos turned from time to time to look at his daughter where she lay upon her rugs. There was something in his heart that had not been there. Was it because Theeg was better than they? Because she was different merely? So from time to time the back of Pontos' neck gathered two long whitish creases where he turned his head; and from time to time he looked at Slavin wondering what Theeg would think of him later.

And once the merriment reached that point where drunkenness follows, Theeg's voice could be heard high above all, "The land is their land, and the house is their house, my father's and my father's people and their children. And the cows in the field are their cows, and the calves are their young and the things that grow in the Spring shall be theirs in the Fall. And all that's born for them in the Summer in long furrows shall be cut and die for them in the harvest. But this other is mine."

Some of them listened now; only her mother droned on as she picked at the embroidery, "The milk has been very poor this season; the cows don't get enough rain—"

Slavin got up; one of Theeg's slippers had fallen to the floor. He passed his hand over her foot gently before returning the little boot to its position.

"What was that?" Theeg inquired, raising her chin from her shoulder—"Thy hand, Slavin, or the earth?"

He laughed at the question and patted her.

Presently the torches guttered and went out one by one. The musicians had fallen asleep on their chairs. The priest dozed, his hands crossed over his stomach.

The trampling of horses in the court brought tears to the mother's eyes suddenly. Theeg was going now.

They dressed Theeg carefully in a long cloak of fur, and kissing her one after the other, the children filed by, standing in line, the first one looking back with a sensation of being a great distance from her sister.

Pontos got angry for a moment, and knocked Slavin

in passing; but he turned around instantly and smiled at him.

He went up to his daughter and kissed her on both cheeks. "A good, good child," he whispered, and made way for the mother. She was short and round, and could barely reach; her little stout arms on the side of the couch made her look as though she were leaning on a fence to gossip; but she was saying: "You will find it difficult. You will have to invent a way of living."

They bore Theeg out, and placed her in the center of the great wagon, and tucked the ends of the skin around her body. She began to laugh.

Slavin climbed in beside her, still shaking the hand of her brother. The driver, standing forward, took up the reins and the whip. Theeg spoke.

"Eh?" her father inquired.

"The glass of wine," she said, and, recalling, "and the little cakes."

She had the cakes put beside her, and Slavin took the glass.

She turned her head upon her shoulder: "Yea, the land and the moving things thereon, and all the young year that has begun, are theirs. All the grass that has found renewal, all the flowers that bloom, all the old hopes and the old manner—but this, this is mine. This new man and this new day are mine, and mine this task to make this lonely head a wild, grand thing upon its helpless pedestal." She began laughing again, the strange silver lashes shaking; and as the horses sprang forward under the driver's whip, the glass of wine spilled, staining the white fur.

The great peasant father looked after her. His gentle ox eyes had closed a little as though the tears standing beneath them hurt.

"She'll make a great thing of it," he said, and tramped in. But he stood at the door again listening to the wind in the trees and the faint sound of the rain, and to the horses galloping along the road and down into the valley beyond.

The little one had fallen asleep in the puddle of wax, and her mother struck her as she lifted her up.

No-Man's-Mare

PAUVLA AGRIPPA had died that afternoon at three; now she lay with quiet hands crossed a little below her fine breast with its transparent skin showing the veins as filmy as old lace, purple veins that were now only a system of charts indicating the pathways where her life once flowed.

Her small features were angular with that repose which she had often desired. She had not wanted to live, because she did not mind death. There were no candles about her where she lay, nor any flowers. She had said quite logically to her sisters: "Are there any candles and flowers at a birth?" They saw the point, but regretted the philosophy, for buying flowers would have connected them with Pauvla Agrippa, in this, her new adventure.

Pauvla Agrippa's hair lay against her cheeks like pats of plaited butter; the long golden ends tucked in and wound about her head and curved behind her neck. Pauvla Agrippa had once been complimented on her fine black eyes and this yellow hair of hers, and she had smiled and been quite pleased, but had drawn attention to the fact that she had also another quite remarkable set of differences—her small thin arms with their tiny hands and her rather long narrow feet.

She said that she was built to remain standing; now she could rest.

133

Her sister, Tasha, had been going about all day, praying to different objects in search of one that would give her comfort, though she was not so much grieved as she might have been, because Pauvla Agrippa had been so curious about all this.

True, Agrippa's husband seemed lost, and wandered about like a restless dog, trying to find a spot that would give him relief as he smoked.

One of Pauvla's brothers was playing on the floor with Pauvla's baby. This baby was small and fat and full of curves. His arms curved above his head, and his legs curved downward, including his picture book and rattle in their oval. He shouted from time to time at his uncle, biting the buttons on his uncle's jacket. This baby and this boy had one thing in common—a deep curiosity—a sense that somewhere that curiosity would be satisfied. They had all accomplished something. Pauvla Agrippa and her husband and her sister and the boy and Pauvla's baby, but still there was incompleteness about everything.

Nothing was ever done; there wasn't such a thing as rest, that was certain, for the sister still felt that her prayers were not definite, the husband knew he would smoke again after lunch, the boy knew he was only beginning something, as the baby also felt it, and Pauvla Agrippa herself, the seemingly most complete, had yet to be buried. Her body was confronted with the eternal necessity of change.

It was all very sad and puzzling, and rather nice too. After all, atoms were the only things that had imperishable existence, and therefore were the omnipotent quality and quantity—God should be recognized as something that was everywhere in millions, irrevocable and ineradicable—one single great thing has always been the prey of the million little things. The beasts of the jungle are laid low by the insects. Yes, she agreed that everything was multiple that counted. Pauvla was multiple now, and some day they would be also. This was the reason that she wandered from room to room touching things, vases, candlesticks, tumblers, knives, forks, the holy pictures and statues and praying to each of them, praying for a great thing, to many presences.

A neighbor from across the way came to see them while Pauvla's brother was still playing with the baby. This man was a farmer, once upon a time, and liked to remember it, as city-bred men in the country like to remember New York and its sophistication.

He spent his summers, however, in the little fishing village where the sisters, Pauvla and Tasha, had come to know him. He always spoke of "going toward the sea." He said that there was something more than wild about the ocean; it struck him as being a little unnatural, too.

He came in now grumbling and wiping his face with a coarse red handkerchief, remarking on the "catch" and upon the sorrow of the house of Agrippa, all in the one breath.

"There's a touch of damp in the air," he said, sniffing, his nose held back so that his small eyes gleamed directly behind it. "The fish have been bad catching and no-man's-mare is going up the headlands, her tail stretched straight out."

Tasha came forward with cakes and tea and paused, praying over them also, still looking for comfort. She was a small woman, with a round, wrinkled forehead and the dark eyes of her sister; today she felt inconvenienced because she could not understand her own feelings—once or twice she had looked upon the corpse with resentment because it had done something to Pauvla; however, she was glad to see the old man, and she prayed to him silently also, to see if it would help. Just what she prayed for she could not tell; the words she used were simple: "What is it, what is it?" over and over with her own childhood prayers to end with.

She had a great deal of the quietness of this village about her, the quietness that is in the roaring of the sea and the wind, and when she sighed it was like the sound made of great waters running back to sea between the narrow sides of little stones.

It was here that she, as well as her brothers and sisters, had been born. They fished in the fishing season and sold to the market at one-eighth of the market price, but when the markets went so low that selling would put the profits down for months, they turned the nets over and sent the fish back to sea.

Today Tasha was dressed in her ball-gown; she had been anticipating a local gathering that evening and then Pauvla Agrippa got her heart attack and died. This dress was low about the shoulders, with flounces of taffeta, and the sea-beaten face of Tasha rose out of its stiff elegance like a rock from heavy moss. Now that she had brought the cakes and tea, she sat listening to this neighbor as he spoke French to her younger brother.

When they spoke in this strange language she was always surprised to note that their voices became unfamiliar to her—she could not have told which was which, or if they were themselves at all. Closing her eyes, she tried to see if this would make any difference, and it didn't. Then she slowly raised her small plump hands and pressed them to her ears—this was better, because now she could not tell that it was French that they were speaking, it was sound only and might have been anything, and again she sighed, and was glad that they were less strange to her; she could not bear this strangeness today, and wished they would stop speaking in a foreign tongue.

"What are you saying?" she inquired, taking the teacup in one hand, keeping the other over her ear.

"Talking about the horse," he said, and went on.

Again Tasha became thoughtful. This horse that they were speaking about had been on the sands, it seemed to her, for as long as she could remember. It was a wild thing belonging to nobody. Sometimes in a coming storm, she had seen it standing with its head out toward the waters, its mane flying in the light air, and its thin sides fluttering with the beating of its heart.

It was old now, with sunken flanks and knuckled legs; it no longer stood straight—and the hair about its nose had begun to turn gray. It never interfered with the beach activities, and on the other hand it never permitted itself to be touched. Early in her memory of this animal, Tasha had tried to stroke it, but it had started, arched its neck and backed away from her with hurried jumping steps. Many of the ignorant fisherfolk had called it the sea horse and also "no-man's-mare." They began to fear it, and several of them thought it a bad omen.

Tasha knew better—sometimes it would be down upon the pebbly part of the shore, its head laid flat as though it were dead, but no one could approach within fifty feet without its instantly leaping up and standing with its neck thrust forward and its brown eyes watching from beneath the coarse lashes.

In the beginning people had tried to catch it and make it of use. Gradually every one in the village had made the attempt; not one of them had ever succeeded.

The large black nostrils were always wet, and they shook as though some one were blowing through them—great nostrils like black flowers.

This mare was old now and did not get up so often when approached. Tasha had been as near to it as ten paces, and Pauvla Agrippa had once approached so near that she could see that its eyes were failing, that a thin mist lay over its right eyeball, so that it seemed to be flirting with her, and this made her sad and she hurried away, and she thought, "The horse had its own defense; when it dies it will be so horrifying perhaps that not one of us will approach it." Though many had squabbled about which of them should have its long beautiful tail.

Pauvla Agrippa's husband had finished his cigar and came in now, bending his head to get through the low casement. He spoke to the neighbor a few moments and then sat down beside his sister-in-law.

He began to tell her that something would have to be done with Pauvla, and added that they would have to manage to get her over to the undertaker's at the end of the headland, but that they had no means of conveyance. Tasha thought of this horse because she had been thinking about it before he interrupted and she spoke of it timidly, but it was only an excuse to say something.

"You can't catch it," he said, shaking his head.

Here the neighbor broke in: "It's easy enough to catch it; this last week three children have stroked it—it's pretty low, I guess; but I doubt if it would be able to walk that far."

He looked over the rim of the teacup to see how this remark would be taken—he felt excited all of a sudden at the thought that something was going to be attempted that had not been attempted in many years, and a feeling of misfortune took hold of him that he had certainly not felt at Pauvla Agrippa's death. Everything about the place, and his life that had seemed to him quite normal and natural, now seemed strange.

The disrupting of one idea—that the horse could not be caught—put him into a mood that made all other accustomed things alien.

However, after this it seemed quite natural that they should make the effort and Tasha went into the room where Pauvla Agrippa lay.

DJUNA BARNES: COLLECTED STORIES

The boy had fallen asleep in the corner and Pauvla's baby was crawling over him, making for Pauvla, cooing softly and saying "mamma" with difficulty, because the little under lip kept reaching to the upper lip to prevent the saliva from interrupting the call.

Tasha put her foot in the baby's way and stood looking down at Pauvla Agrippa, where her small hands lay beneath her fine breast with its purple veins, and now Tasha did not feel quite the same resentment that she had felt earlier. It is true this body had done something irrevocable to Pauvla Agrippa, but she also realized that she, Tasha, must now do something to this body; it was the same with everything, nothing was left as it was, something was always altering something else. Perhaps it was an unrecognized law.

Pauvla Agrippa's husband had gone out to see what could be done with the mare, and now the neighbor came in, saying that it would not come in over the sand, but that he—the husband—thought that it would walk toward the headland, as it was wont.

"If you could only carry her out to it," he said.

Tasha called in two of her brothers and woke up the one on the floor. "Everything will be arranged for her comfort," she said, "when we get her up there." They lifted Pauvla Agrippa up and her baby began to laugh, asking to be lifted up also, and holding its little hands high that it might be lifted, but no one was paying any attention to him, because now they were moving his mother.

Pauvla Agrippa looked fine as they carried her, only

her small hands parted and deserted the cleft where they
had lain, dropping down upon the shoulders of her brothers. Several children stood hand in hand watching, and
one or two villagers appeared who had heard from the
neighbors what was going on.

The mare had been induced to stand and someone had
slipped a halter over its neck for the first time in many
years; there was a frightened look in the one eye and the
film that covered the other seemed to darken, but it made
no objection when they raised Pauvla Agrippa and placed
her on its back, tying her on with a fish net.

Then someone laughed, and the neighbor slapped his
leg saying, "Look what the old horse has come to—caught
and burdened at last." And he watched the mare with
small cruel eyes.

Pauvla Agrippa's husband took the strap of the halter
and began plodding through the sand, the two boys on
either side of the horse holding to all that was left of Pauvla
Agrippa. Tasha came behind, her hands folded, praying
now to this horse, still trying to find peace, but she noticed with a little apprehension that the horse's flanks had
begun to quiver, and that this quiver was extending to its
ribs and from its ribs to its forelegs.

Then she saw it turn a little, lifting its head. She called
out to Pauvla Agrippa's husband who, startled with the
movement and the cry, dropped the rope.

The mare had turned toward the sea; for an instant it
stood there, quivering, a great thin bony thing with
crooked legs; its blind eyes half covered with the black

coarse lashes. Pauvla Agrippa with her head thrown a bit back rested easily, it seemed, the plaits of her yellow hair lying about her neck, but away from her face, because she was not supported quite right; still she looked like some strange new sea animal beneath the net that held her from falling.

Then without warning, no-man's-mare jumped forward and plunged neck-deep into the water.

A great wave came up, covered it, receded, and it could be seen swimming, its head out of the water, while Pauvla Agrippa's loosened yellow hair floated behind. No one moved. Another wave rose high, descended, and again the horse was seen swimming with head up, and this time Pauvla's Agrippa's hands were parted and lay along the water as though she were swimming.

The most superstitious among them began crossing themselves, and one woman dropped on her knees, rocking from side to side; and still no one moved.

And this time the wave rose, broke and passed on, leaving the surface smooth.

That night Tasha picked up Pauvla Agrippa's sleepy boy and standing in the doorway prayed to the sea, and this time she found comfort.

Smoke

THERE WAS SWART with his bushy head and Fenken with the half shut eyes and the grayish beard, and there also was Zelka with her big earrings and her closely bound inky hair, who had often been told that "she was very beautiful in a black way."

Ah, what a fine strong creature she had been, and what a fine strong creature her father, Fenken, had been before her, and what a specimen was her husband, Swart, with his gentle melancholy mouth and his strange strong eyes and his brown neck.

Fenken in his youth had loaded the cattle boats, and in his twilight of age he would sit in the round-backed chair by the open fireplace, his two trembling hands folded, and would talk of what he had been.

"A bony man I was, Zelka—my two knees as hard as a pavement, so that I clapped them with great discomfort to my own hands. Sometimes," he would add, with a twinkle in his old eyes, "I'd put you between them and my hand. It hurt less."

Zelka would turn her eyes on him slowly—they moved around into sight from under her eyebrows like the barrel of a well-kept gun; they were hard like metal and strong, and she was always conscious of them, even in sleep.

When she would close her eyes before saying her prayers, she would remark to Swart, "I draw the hood over the artillery." And Swart would smile, nodding his large head.

In the town these three were called the "Bullets"— when they came down the street, little children sprang aside, not because they were afraid, but because they came so fast and brought with them something so healthy, something so potent, something unconquerable. Fenken could make his fingers snap against his palm like the crack of a cabby's whip just by shutting his hand abruptly, and he did this often, watching the gamin and smiling.

Swart, too, had his power, but there was a hint at something softer in him, something that made the lips kind when they were sternest, something that gave him a sad expression when he was thinking—something that had drawn Zelka to him in their first days of courting. "We Fenkens," she would say, "have iron in our veins—in yours I fear there's a little blood."

Zelka was cleanly. She washed her linen clean as though she were punishing the dirt. Had the linen been less durable there would have been holes in it from her knuckles in six months. Everything Zelka cooked was tender—she had bruised it with her preparations.

And then Zelka's baby had come. A healthy, fat, little crying thing, with eyes like its father's and with its father's mouth. In vain did Zelka look for something about it that would give it away as one of the Fenken blood—it had a maddeningly tender way of stroking her face; its hair was finer than blown gold; and it squinted up its pale blue eyes when it fell over its nose. Sometimes Zelka would turn the baby around in bed, placing its little feet against her side, waiting for it to kick. And when it finally did, it was gently and without great strength and with much good humor. "Swart," Zelka would say, "your child is entirely human. I'm afraid all his veins run blood." And she would add to her father, "Sonny will never load the cattle ships."

When it was old enough to crawl, Zelka would get down on hands and knees and chase it about the little ash-littered room. The baby would crawl ahead of her, giggling and driving Zelka mad with a desire to stop and hug him. But when she roared behind him like a lion to make him hurry, the baby would roll over slowly, struggle into a sitting posture, and, putting his hand up, would sit staring at her as though he would like to study out something that made this difference between them.

When it was seven, it would escape from the house and wander down to the shore, and stand for hours watching the boats coming in, being loaded and unloaded. Once one of the men put the cattle belt about him and lowered him into the boat. He went down sadly, his little golden head drooping and his feet hanging down. When they brought him back on shore again and dusted him off they were puzzled at him—he had neither cried nor laughed. They said, "Didn't you like that?" And he had only answered by looking at them fixedly.

And when he grew up he was very tender to his mother,

who had taken to shaking her head over him. Fenken had died the summer of his grandchild's thirtieth year, so that after the funeral Swart had taken the round-backed chair for his own. And now he sat there with folded hands, but he never said what a strong lad he had been. Sometimes he would say, "Do you remember how Fenken used to snap his fingers together like a whip?" And Zelka would answer, "I do."

And finally, when her son married, Zelka was seen at the feast dressed in a short blue skirt, leaning upon Swart's arm, both of them still strong and handsome and capable of lifting the buckets of cider.

Zelka's son had chosen a strange woman for a wife: a little thin thing, with a tiny waistline and a narrow chest and a small, very lovely throat. She was the daughter of a ship owner and had a good deal of money in her name. When she married Zelka's son, she brought him some ten thousand a year. And so he stopped the shipping of cattle and went in for exports and imports of Oriental silks and perfumes.

When his mother and father died, he moved a little inland away from the sea and hired clerks to do his bidding. Still, he never forgot what his mother had said to him: "There must always be a little iron in the blood, sonny."

He reflected on this when he looked at Lief, his wife. He was a silent, taciturn man as he grew older, and Lief had grown afraid of him, because of his very kindness and his melancholy.

There was only one person to whom he was a bit stern, and this was his daughter, "Little Lief." Toward her he showed a strange hostility, a touch even of that fierceness that had been his mother's. Once she had rushed shrieking from his room because he had suddenly roared behind her as his mother had done behind him. When she was gone, he sat for a long time by his table, his hands stretched out in front of him, thinking.

He had succeeded well. He had multiplied his wife's money now into the many thousands—they had a house in the country and servants. They were spoken of in the town as a couple who had an existence that might be termed as "pretty soft"; and when the carriage drove by of a Sunday with baby Lief up front on her mother's lap and Lief's husband beside her in his gray cloth coat, they stood aside not to be trampled on by the swift legged, slender ankled "pacer" that Lief had bought that day when she had visited the "old home"—the beach that had known her and her husband when they were children. This horse was the very one that she had asked for when she saw how beautiful it was as they fastened the belt to it preparatory to lowering it over the side. It was then that she remembered how, when her husband had been a little boy, they had lowered him over into the boat with this same belting.

During the winter that followed, which was a very hard one, Lief took cold and resorted to hot water bottles and thin tea. She became very fretful and annoyed at her husband's constant questionings as to her health. Even Little Lief was a nuisance because she was so noisy. She would steal into the room, and, crawling under her mother's bed, would begin to sing in a high, thin treble, pushing the ticking with her patent leather boots to see them crinkle. Then the mother would cry out, the nurse would run in and take her away, and Lief would spend a half hour in tears. Finally they would not allow Little Lief in the room, so she would steal by the door many times, walking noiselessly up and down the hall. But finally, her youth overcoming her, she would stretch her legs out into a straight goose step, and for this she was whipped because on the day that she had been caught, her mother had died.

And so the time passed and the years rolled on, taking their toll. It was now many summers since that day that Zelka had walked into town with Swart—now many years since Fenken had snapped his fingers like a cabby's whip. Little Lief had never even heard that her grandmother had been called a "beautiful woman in a black sort of way," and she had only vaguely heard of the nickname that had once been given the family, the "Bullets." She came to know that great strength had once been in the family to such an extent, indeed, that somehow a phrase was known to her, "Remember always to keep a little iron in the blood." And one night she had pricked her arm to see if there were iron in it, and she had cried because it hurt. And so she knew that there was none.

With her this phrase ended. She never repeated it because of that night when she had made that discovery.

Her father had taken to solitude and the study of sociology. Sometimes he would turn her about by the shoulder and look at her, breathing in a thick way he had with him of late. And once he told her she was a good girl but foolish, and left her alone.

They had begun to lose money, and some of Little Lief's tapestries, given her by her mother, were sold. Her heart broke, but she opened the windows oftener because she needed some kind of beauty. She made the mistake of loving tapestries best and nature second best. Somehow she had gotten the two things mixed—of course, it was due to her bringing up. "If you are poor, you live out-of-doors; but if you are rich, you live in a lovely house." So to her the greatest of calamities had befallen the house. It was beginning to go away by those imperceptible means that at first leave a house looking unfamiliar and then bare.

Finally she could stand it no longer and she married a thin, wiry man with a long, thin nose and a nasty trick of rubbing it with a finger equally long and thin—a man with a fair income and very refined sisters.

This man, Misha, wanted to be a lawyer. He studied half the night and never seemed happy unless his head was in his palm. His sisters were like this also, only for another reason: they enjoyed weeping. If they could find nothing to cry about, they cried for the annoyance of this dearth of destitution and worry. They held daily councils for future domestic trouble—one the gesture of emotional and one of mental desire.

Sometimes Little Lief's father would come to the big iron gate and ask to see her. He would never come in—why? He never explained. So Little Lief and he would talk over the gate top, and sometimes he was gentle and sometimes he was not. When he was harsh to her, Little Lief wept, and when she wept, he would look at her steadily from under his eyebrows and say nothing. Sometimes he asked her to take a walk with him. This would set Little Lief into a terrible flutter; the corners of her mouth would twitch and her nostrils tremble. But she always went.

Misha worried little about his wife. He was a very selfish man, with that greatest capacity of a selfish nature, the ability to labor untiringly for some one thing that he wanted and that nature had placed beyond his reach. Some people called this quality excellent, pointing out what a great scholar Misha was, holding him up as an example in their own households, looking after him when he went hurriedly down the street with that show of nervous expectancy that a man always betrays when he knows within himself that he is deficient—a sort of peering in the face of life to see if it has discovered the flaw.

Little Lief felt that her father was trying to be something that was not natural to him. What was it? As she grew older, she tried to puzzle it out. Now it happened more often that she would catch him looking at her in a strange way, and once she asked him half playfully if he wished she had been a boy. And he had answered abruptly, "Yes, I do."

Little Lief would stand for hours at the casement and, leaning her head against the glass, try to solve this thing about her father. And then she discovered it when he had said, "Yes, I do." He was trying to be strong—what was it that was in the family?—oh, yes—iron in the blood. He feared there was no longer any iron left. Well, perhaps there wasn't—was that the reason he looked at her like this? No, he was worried about himself. Why?—wasn't he satisfied with his own strength? He had been cruel enough very often. This shouldn't have worried him.

She asked him, and he answered, "Yes, but cruelty isn't strength." That was an admission. She was less afraid of him since that day when he had made that answer, but now she kept peering into his face as he had done into hers, and he seemed not to notice it. Well, he was getting to be a very old man.

Then one day her two sisters-in-law pounced upon her so that her golden head shook on its thin, delicate neck.

"Your father has come into the garden," cried one.

"Yes, yes," pursued the elder. "He's even sat himself upon the bench."

She hurried out to him. "What's the matter, father?" Her head was aching.

"Nothing." He did not look up.

She sat down beside him, stroking his hand, at first timidly, then with more courage.

"Have you looked at the garden?"

He nodded.

She burst into tears.

He took his hand away from her and began to laugh.

"What's the matter, child? A good dose of hog-killing would do you good."

"You have no right to speak to me in this way—take yourself off!" she cried sharply, holding her side. And her father rocked with laughter.

She stretched her long, thin arms out, clenching her thin fingers together. The lace on her short sleeves trembled, her knuckles grew white.

"A good pig-killing," he repeated, watching her. And she grew sullen.

"Eh?" He pinched her flesh a little and dropped it. She was passive; she made no murmur. He got up, walked to the gate, opened it and went out, closing it after him. He turned back a step and waved to her. She did not answer for a moment, then she waved back slowly with one of her thin, white hands.

She would have liked to refuse to see him again, but she lacked courage. She would say to herself, "If I am unkind to him now, perhaps later I shall regret it." In this way she tried to excuse herself. The very next time he had sent word that he wished speech with her, she had come.

"Little fool!" he said, in a terrible rage, and walked off. She was quite sure that he was slowly losing his mind—a second childhood, she called it, still trying to make things as pleasant as possible.

She had been ill a good deal that spring, and in the fall she had terrible headaches. In the winter months she took to her bed, and early in May the doctor was summoned.

Misha talked to the physician in the drawing-room before he sent him up to his wife.

"You must be gentle with her. She is nervous and frail." The doctor laughed outright. Misha's sisters were weeping, of course, and perfectly happy.

"It will be such a splendid thing for her," they said, meaning the beef, iron and wine that they expected the doctor to prescribe.

Toward evening Little Lief closed her eyes.

Her child was still-born.

The physician came downstairs and entered the parlor where Misha's sisters stood together, still shedding tears.

He rubbed his hands.

"Send Misha upstairs."

"He has gone."

"Isn't it dreadful? I never could bear corpses, especially little ones."

"A baby isn't a corpse," answered the physician, smiling at his own impending humor. "It's an interrupted plan."

He felt that the baby, not having drawn a breath in this world, could not feel hurt at such a remark, because it had gathered no feminine pride and, also, as it had passed out quicker than the time it took to make the observation, it really could be called nothing more than the background for medical jocularity.

Misha came into the room with red eyes.

"Out like a puff of smoke," he said.

One of the sisters remarked: "Well, the Fenkens lived themselves thin."

The next summer Misha married into a healthy Swedish family. His second wife had a broad face, with eyes set wide apart, and with broad, flat, healthy, yellow teeth. And she played the piano surprisingly well, though she looked a little heavy as she sat upon the piano stool.

The Coward

VARRA KOLVEED had led too long that life of unending sameness that has its end either in hysteria or melancholy. Twice a day the bodies of her little sisters were pushed and patted and shoved by her into and out of their shabby clothing. At six o'clock precisely the day found her laying the table for her sister's husband, her sister herself, and for those same smaller ones that had come into their care with the death of her mother. Every afternoon and every evening saw her shaking out the red tablespread also, and at nine o'clock exactly, Varra descended the first two steps leading into the street and waited for Karl.

Varra had been engaged to Karl going on three years now, and the three years were threatening to stretch into a fourth for lack of money. Romance had died there on that second step above the pavement and had given way to habit.

Varra had never been called pretty. She had even been termed rather plain. She had never admitted this judgment to be correct. She even thought, quite frankly, that she was a little more than passable. She had lived so long among dull things that anything with a bit of color in it seemed to her beautiful, and Varra had the red round spots high up on her cheeks that one sees occasionally in Breton peasants, and Varra had very splendid curling hair, which she had never allowed to grow long since it had been cropped the year of the fever—and this hair stood up on her head in a red flaming wedge which seemed to Varra very good.

One thing only had Varra that put her above those with whom she came in contact: she had what was called a reputation.

Just when this reputation began no one could remember; even Varra had forgotten. The incident that must have led to it was a thing of the past. Sometimes Varra tried to remember what it was that had given her this reputation for courage, as she plaited her hair before she went to bed. Was it that day that she had climbed across the roof and down into the gutter and saved the new spring robin when all the boys were timid? Or was it when she had used a knife to take out a splinter one evening as she sat on the steps? She remembered this knife, a long thin polished blade that seemed to demand bravery. And then the girl across the way had been watching, so Varra had cut herself quite a deep gash, dabbing the blood off with her handkerchief, but taking care to fold the scarlet spots out, so that they would be conspicuous all that evening when she rubbed her nose or wiped her forehead.

Anyway there the reputation was. It had become very precious to Varra because it was someone else's opinion and not her own. But gradually it became her own, and she could not always recollect whether people had said

she was beautiful or courageous until she stopped to consider which of these two qualities she had given herself
involuntarily.

As Varra grew up she became very proud of this reputation. She nursed it, and at the same time it kept her in a
great deal of anxiety. She had to keep thinking up little
things that would remind the neighbors that she was this
year what she had been last—the courage that had picked
her out for attention then was still one of her qualities. In
the end she thought herself a little braver than she really
was. Sincerely and honestly, she held to this opinion and
would have raged had she been denied this little grain of
personal elations.

For Varra there had been little youth, just a few hours
in the sun, just a moment snatched from romanticism with
some novel of the time, one short little moment of an appreciation that spring had come and spring would go, one
lilac bloom that had meant something to her, one moment when, lying face down in the June grass, she had
waited silently for her chance, had finally caught the one
bird that she could remember as having had freedom, one
acknowledgment that night was mysterious and frightful
and something to lie under as one would lie under a guillotine waiting for the moment when the knife should descend, the knife that must inevitably be there high up in
the dark against the ceiling, the something portentous that
gave her this feeling of impending doom, this tightening
of the feet, this thanksgiving for the heavy weave of the

sheet sensed against her nose and mouth and her closed lids.

And then Varra had gone past it, without memory when it stopped and without regrets for its ending because it had no definite boundary. And she only felt a sense that within her somewhere was an island surrounded by what she now was, that was, that had been her childhood.

Many times in the years that went to the making of Varra, she had silently regretted this name she bore for bravery. When a spider was seen about the place, it was she now who had to catch and kill it. The rest of the family had grown frankly timid as Varra had grown, to all appearances, more bold. When the frying pan handle was red hot, it was Varra who came up and took it off the stove in her bare hands, smiling. It was Varra also who had to part the pair of bull pups which had flown at one another's throats. It was she who put the ropes about their necks and she it was who finally parted them.

Once or twice in the beginning she had said timidly, "I am not so brave, you know," and they had all answered, "See, true courage. She is a brave child, yes, a modest one."

And then she had become engaged, and Karl flattered her and told her that he loved her for her bravery more than anything else. Karl's chum, Monk, had also flattered Varra. Indeed, toward the end of this third year of engagement, Varra had become so accustomed to this title that she no longer lay awake trying to remember where it had its beginning.

She read fairy tales where damsels with wands ruled over a world of the timid. She was always finding herself in love with the hero and the heroine of some novel. She came out of them into her own life with a little gasp of sorrow, and she went back into them again with a sigh of content.

Yet Varra had still a certain kind of acuteness. There were things that she liked and there were things that she did not like at all. The only trouble was that she failed to keep her sense of values separate. She had been called brave, so now she thought it was brave to like people that her instinct bade her to distrust. Monk was a man who instinctively bred dislike. His ill-shaped head gave her physical pain, and the wide low-set ears, set on at an angle seen commonly in monkeys, made her feel a repulsion for looking at him at all, and his jaunty, quick slang with its touch of false bravado made her unhappy because she sensed in this same bravado her own bravery; only in him there was something vulgar. The difference lay in this: he was trying to produce an illusion and Varra was trying not to disillusion.

And then had come that terrible hour when a little crowd collected about their door, overflowing into their parlor, talking all at once.

Karl and Monk had been arrested. Leaning with her forehead against the door, Varra tried to make out what they were saying. She put her hands to her throat and found it was not the spot that troubled her. Her hands slipped to her heart, and this was also lacking in appropriateness. She began untying her apron, and this was the gesture that seemed at last to be the right one. What was she doing? What were they saying? Robbery? Where? She pushed forward, still pulling at the knot in her apron.

"What is this?" she cried in a sharp voice.

"Karl and Monk have been arrested."

"What for?"

"They were under suspicion for some time—petty robberies, they said—jewelry—and then last night quite a haul from the Barnaby place."

She wasn't listening any more. Jewelry? Karl? She brought her two hands around with the apron in them, feeling for the little cheap ring on her third finger. Tears slowly rose to the borders of her pale eyes. Then she heard her sister saying, "You must be brave, dear."

Varra turned away and went upstairs.

She lay face up on the bed. This was another concession made to her reputation. She wanted to bury her eyes in the pillow, but she mustn't. What must she do? Get up, walk about? Yes, that was it—get up and walk about. Why? Where?

She went to the table and picked up a brooch Karl had given her. Stolen, too, eh? She rummaged through her bureau; a necklace of beads and a broad bracelet were all the things that she could remember as having come from Karl in their three years of courtship. She put these all together. She never stopped to question herself about her feeling in reaction to this change. She did not deny it to herself because in doing this she thought she would be a coward; and now she must show what she was really made of, if, indeed, she were a brave woman after all, or only a sham.

Toward eight o'clock, her sister knocked at her door.

"He is to be tried tomorrow," she whispered along the crack, and stole away again.

Suddenly Varra's courage gave out in one terrible storm of weeping, and she turned over on her bed heavily, pressing the bedding up around her as if she wanted to bury herself, to dig herself into oblivion. This reputation of hers had been built of the things the house was built of, the daily household sayings. It was in the atmosphere; it was a household quality, a something that had been given life by all these things that surrounded her, and she abruptly realized that it was with the household that she was trying to bury herself. She sat up, throwing the blankets away with a quick, frightened gesture. She felt dizzy and tried to weep again and could not. She stood up before her little cracked mirror. Was she really ugly? The color had left her cheeks, but it was in her lips.

She knew now what it was that had really brought on this great fit of weeping—it was because she knew what she had before her and what she must do for Karl. What was it they had said? Oh yes, of course, she was courageous; she must begin now. Tomorrow, her little sister had said. She would have to find out where the court was.

The mid-day session was in full swing. Petty lawyers

in frock coats promenaded the wide corridors like dogs on the track of game. Misery, despair, justice, injustice— all these things were their meal. They circled about this hall, their fat, small hands hidden in the tails of these sleek, shiny coats, and their bright, alert eyes darting here and there. One of these lawyers had been following a woman with his eyes for the last ten seconds as the woman stood in the shadow of the winding staircase, her hands clasped in front of her, holding a faded yellow box. She stood very still, and seemed to impart something like importance to the case. Only after he had finished his pleading and retired behind the railings did the case again drop into its poverty and ugly despair once more.

He approached Varra now, his oiled black hair shining as he stepped across the bar of light falling in at the wide entrance.

"Are you represented?" he spoke softly, pleasantly, and he dropped his hands to his side, his coat tails swinging. He was very proud of this coat; it had been nicknamed the "Case coat," or the "Coat of appeals."

Varra turned toward him slowly and looked at him a minute. Then she said, "What?" fearing that perhaps this man had something to do with the whole system of judicial ruling.

He repeated his question, adding that she really should have a lawyer. She shook her head and moved off. What she had to do must be done alone; therein lay the impetus. She did not need help to be courageous. She could save Karl alone. She could tell the lie that would set him free. She was strong enough to go straight up to the judge and pronounce the words that would throw suspicion on to herself. And besides, she had the necklace, the ring, the brooch and the bracelet, all together in this little yellow box. If they did not believe her, they would believe their eyes. How would she come by this plunder unless she herself had stolen it?

She moved toward the doors. She could see the benches filled with sleepy-looking people. She felt herself rudely pushed aside by a German woman who was speaking in a shrill voice to the court attendant who would not let her pass. Varra felt very lonely. After all, what was the use; no one was here to help her; no one was here to know what she was doing. She should have told them at home. No, Karl would be the only one to know.

A feeling of tenderness swept over her for Karl. After all, she loved him; and her own impending sacrifice made him seem newborn in all the splendor of the deed. She looked up into the face of the court attendant and smiled. "May I sit down and watch awhile?" she asked cunningly, hoping that he would be pleased with her and treat her as someone with a really superior nature, so it would give her confidence in herself.

He did like her frank smile, and the red-rimmed eyes looking up into his, coquettishly, made him stand aside for her, and made him watch her as she moved to a seat.

She leaned forward a little, looking straight ahead of her. There was the raised platform with the judicial desk.

There were the clerks, the court stenographer, the petty lawyers, the police—the relatives weeping, the dry-eyed curiosity seekers. The man in black sitting with slightly bowed head behind the desk must be the judge. She looked around, but could not see either Karl or Monk. Some dreary prisoners were sitting back to her on a bench within the railing, and a reporter stood beside the clerks' desk, pad in hand. Why were all these people sitting here? What did they want to see? What they themselves had escaped, what they themselves would have some day to go through, perhaps?

The dirty black curtains, with their heavy tassels at the windows, took her attention. They were like the smaller curtains at the windows of a hearse, only the tassels were too terrible and too heavy. They seemed like judges that had grown sulky beneath their wigs of dust, like something that would finally fall into the cup of life and lie there, black and horrible and menacing, spoiling it at the lips, as mother spoils the beauty of wine, the malignity of vinegar.

Varra looked at the judge. She wondered why people neglect to make friends with judges, as it would help so if they were on a calling basis. If this judge had said to her once, "Please pass the tea, Miss Kolveed," she would now be able to go right up to him and whisper into his ear to be kind to Karl, and all would be over. But she had neglected to do this, and so it was going to make a difference.

Some mean case of some sort had just come up. Two men, one an officer and the other a Pole, stood before this

bar of justice, holding up a strip of lace. She could not
hear a word that was said, and she was glad. It would not
spoil this great thing she had come to do. Yet she looked
at this length of lace, stretching away and coiling into a
senseless mass in a roll of silks in a box, as though it were
very strange. What had lace to do with prison? With good
and bad? Couldn't lace even escape this defiling exposi-
tion? Hereafter Varra knew that lace would be something
that she could no longer wear. She had thought dully that
inanimate objects could not be contaminated, could have
nothing in common with human beings; that was neither
here nor there. She closed her eyes.

She could hear a steady droning, the shuffling of feet,
a half-suppressed sob. She opened her eyes. The Pole
was being led away by an officer, and on this side near
her, a woman had arisen weeping. Something rose in
Varra's throat—it was her grief. Something dropped down
into her throat—it was her tears. She must not cry. If she
had wept, she would have been a coward. At that moment, she heard the names of Karl and Monk.

She half-started to her feet! Several heads turned toward her, and someone whispered: "A relative, probably."

Yes, that was Karl; that black, curly hair was Karl's,
but why did he hang his head? She did not even look
toward Monk. She was angry because they must be hurting Karl where they gripped his arms on either side. Yes,
she must get up now. She got up, holding the box in her
hand. She heard someone saying: "Is your name Karl
Handmann?" And she saw Karl move, but she could not

hear his answer. Then again the same voice: "And you, Monk Price?" And she heard Monk answering, loud and with his usual bravado: "That's me."

She was down by the railing now. Her heart was pounding terribly. God! was bravery as cruel as this? She held the yellow box out in front of her as though this were her first duty. Someone laid a hand on her. She heard her own voice, "I am coming, Karl." She saw him turn around. She saw the judge's astonished eyes. The clerks paused, the stenographer, without raising his head, waited for the next remark.

Now, now she must be brave. She was going to show Karl and all the world what she was made of—the stuff—what was it—iron—oh, yes, she was made of iron. Everything went black. She began again: "I—your Honor—I." She shook her head, laughed a little and turned abruptly, holding the box. "I can't," she said, and slid to her knees.

She heard the noise subsiding, the fluttering of paper cease. The footsteps no longer moved around her. She heard only the clock striking, but she could not move. Perhaps she was dying.

She came to. Several men were plying her with water. The court attendant was back at his place. She heard the people walking again. She got to her feet.

"How do you feel now?" someone asked her, and someone else said softly: "Poor girl, was he your sweetheart or a brother?"

Varra opened her mouth. "Did—did he get off?" They

seemed afraid to tell her something, and she demanded sharply in that voice she used to the children: "Come, come! Tell me."

"No. The little one with black, curly hair got—got several years."

"But," someone else chimed in, thinking it might comfort her, "the other one's case, Monk, has been suspended for a further hearing. He made a very good plea for himself—lively, rather impudent, but he made some laugh. That always helps."

Varra turned slowly to the steps and stood there staring out into the day. She was not thinking about Monk or about Karl. She was thinking about herself. After all, she was a coward. She could kill spiders and hold hot frying pans and save birds, but she was nothing more, a small town brave—a woman without real courage, something to despise, something to hate. God, how she hated herself—how she hated those people who had begun this defeat, those people who had started it all by praising her—oh, she was horrible. She was hungry and turned in at one of the dirty coffee stalls. She looked in the mirror—yes, she thought herself still beautiful, but now that was all.

She knew that Karl was innocent—she had seen it in his eyes. And she knew that Monk was all that was low and base and mean. She felt that he had drawn Karl into this to save his own skin. What an ugly beast he was, how red the tips of his ears had been that moment in court when she had looked at him.

She began to justify herself. Could she have confessed to something she had not done to save Karl, who wasn't guilty? No, a thousand times no. Why? Because it would have placed her below him. It would have made her something vicious and criminal. She would have allied herself to save him (it's true) with all the dirt and filth that was in that corrupt body of Monk. How could she have done this? Would he still have loved her? Perhaps the sacrifice would have been too splendid, and besides he would have known that she wasn't really guilty. Perhaps too, he would have denied her, refused her sacrifice. Then, what a beautiful thing it would have been. Perhaps he would have gotten off altogether and she also. How wonderful that would have been! And then he would have said to her again, "I love you because you are brave more than for anything else."

And now he had got several years, and Monk was as yet unsentenced.

When she reached home, she trembled, as though the street must already know her for what she was. She crept to her room, fearing that she would wake the family, and opened the door carefully, hardly daring to breathe. She undressed slowly, standing in the middle of the room. She got into bed as she had never gotten into it since she was a child, furtively, with a crouching movement, and drew the sheets over her throat.

She lay there, staring into the darkness—yes, that was it, that was the reason she had failed, because she could not make herself seem so low, so mean, so petty before Karl, who was really good and clean and strong.

But what hurt most was her lost pride in herself; this was terrible. All through the night she kept saying to herself, "What must I do now?"

She got up again, lighting a candle. Was she still beautiful? People had called her ugly—she grinned at herself in the mirror. No, she was really ugly. She blew the light out, then lit it again. "How can I tell if I am ugly or handsome if I make faces?" She looked. She saw her face, a rigid, set, white thing shining out of the glass at her. No, she was not so bad.

She went back to the cot and sat on it, her bare feet touching the floor. Was there anything that she could do yet? She decided that she was not really good looking at all, and now she was not even brave.

She could not cry. She said these things to herself, half aloud; still, they did not make her wince—neither beautiful nor brave—ugly, a coward. Yet she loved Karl—she hated Monk. She was more like Monk after all—quite a lot like Monk.

She fell asleep.

The next afternoon when Monk's case came up, a woman holding a yellow box walked briskly into the court and down the aisle. The attendant went after her. This time he did not like something in her step.

She spoke in a loud, resolute, almost coarse voice, directly at the judge, paying no attention whatsoever to Monk.

And this time she went through with it.

When, with extreme reluctance, Monk was released, she did not even look at him. Instead, she smiled and asked for a mirror. People moved aside to let the slimy, ugly body of Monk pass, but Varra was paying no attention to them. She put down the pocket glass and said hurriedly, softly, "No, I am really quite ugly."

She had forgotten Karl, she had forgotten Monk. She looked at the black curtains with their heavy tassels.

Monsieur Ampee

STEP UPON A WORM and the worm becomes a butterfly
—Ampee, the unknown, suddenly and with a supreme
gesture, took what had been a tradesman's nose out of
his wine cup to discover that it was looked upon as a feature not only of rare excellence, but of superior distinction.

Ampee had the worm's nature. Had he done what
worms are supposed to do—in other words, had he
"turned"—those watching the convulsion would not have
been very pleased with the hitherto unseen surface thus
exposed. Ampee was not the insinuating, crawling, slimy
type; he was, rather, the coldest of persons, theoretical,
persistent, quiet—one of those men who live out their
forty years or so as one wears one's only coat, carefully,
with seeming indifference, but sending it to be cleaned
and pressed once in a while, and ever as it wears out having it patched and turned and mended—with the same
finish in view—a coat that had once been of one piece
and had come to an end of many pieces; a life that had
once been just a life and had ended as a crowd—for Ampee
could not have laid his hand on anything in himself that
he did not eventually know for someone else's.

Ampee had lived in a sort of obscure comfort. His wife,

171

Lyda, had long ago submerged herself. She had been an almost aristocratic lady when Ampee had married her, a woman who had always taken care to dress simply, like the queen, to act as artificially as her frank nature would permit, and to live all the necessary lies that keep a household from becoming an item in the paper and the occupants from the public eye.

He looked upon his wife as upon the public. She was what all the world was—instead of buying a morning paper, he had taken Lyda to church with him and married her—thus he had subscribed to the events of the day with a wedding certificate; instead of propping up the paper of a morning, he looked at his wife. It was a saving, too. She lived as the mass lived, on air existing plain, and she complained not in a dangerous but a human way.

She had borne him three children as the world bore children. He was amused at her docility and her helplessness. She subscribed to things that the world in general subscribed to; and she renounced the usual things that are deemed injurious to the world as a rising generation. She looked to evolution and the future with an ant-like perseverance. She hurried her children into the best of health as an ant stores away food for a day to come, or as a fowl is placed on a block of ice. And she shed over them only those numbered tears that the world has discovered to be absolutely necessary for the preservation of a sufficient quantity of regret to insure tact and feeling among people who rely on the existence of those they move among.

Yet Lyda was honest, was faithful, was as happy as the people in general are happy. She, on her side, looked upon her husband as a great phenomenon, the question beyond answer, the problem without a possibility of a final footing up—he represented inexorable and unending time, and in acknowledging this she acknowledged that time would never rise above what was petty, self-seeking and indifferent. Ampee lived among his fellow beings as though he were the only pardonable mistake among a million errors.

Ampee had been successful in a certain way—his business had grown and prospered quietly, he had achieved a fair income, and no place on men's tongues was set aside for his name. This he had taken good care of. A man with ambitions in a mercantile line could not afford to be personally renowned as the revolutionists were renowned, or as artists and bohemians in general were renowned.

He drank excellent wines and contented himself with being ugly and common; indeed he would have regretted extremely any exceptional trait or feature. He was glad that his physique was of an appropriate and unnoticeable quality. He wanted to attract as little attention to himself as a soldier wants to be conspicuous; he had as usual the obscure exterior that is required of those who go out to conquer.

Ampee had only one enemy. This was Fago, whom he called "the Nihilist," because Fago spoke occasionally of "the people" in a tone of voice that had no quality of business about it. He distrusted Fago because Fago was one of those men who could talk for half an hour about civilization without once making any allusion to their pockets, who could hold a cool argument about any subject without once bringing in profit or loss.

And then, to make it worse, Fago was owner of a rival store. Ampee had gone in for a side branch, the selling of wines, to outdo this same Fago, who had his chief trade on his excellence in his bottled produce. Still Fago had kept his customers, and Ampee had racked his mind for a solution. This was in 1842. In the summer of 1846 Ampee bought a vineyard, set a caretaker on the place, ate a good dinner, and approached his wife.

"Lyda," he said, looking at her with the judicial eye that one turns upon a crowd, "what do you think of what I have done today?"

Lyda had long ago, probably with the birth of the second child, forgotten how the queen dressed, and no longer relied on her looks. She had only a smattering of her best quality left, her honesty—and this was subject to her fatigue and her nervousness.

"I have bought up a little vineyard," he continued. "Something like ten or twelve hundred bottles of wine should be the result. Only I have yet to install new machinery and labor, and to pay off the mortgage. To do that, I need money."

He never smoked, because it tainted his breads and cheeses. He never walked around to ease his tension, because Lyda had a habit of saying: "Sh-h, Ampee, the cakes are in the oven and you will certainly make them fall." On the other hand, he did not like a man who rubbed his hands together or bit his nails, because this was commonly called the habit of a shifty nature, and he wanted no such speculations going abroad in connection with his daily habits. Instead, Ampee would see how long he could hold his eyes very wide open without flickering the lashes; a prolonged, steady gaze was well received, and was the work of an honest, well-meaning man.

In this way he stared at his wife, and she, in turn, looked down, as she always did on such occasions. His eyes gave her a sad, expectant feeling of failure; she was always fearing that Ampee would at some inopportune moment fail, and these lids would fall with a suddenness and a finality that would leave no further doubt in the world's eyes of the subterfuge of their owner.

"What are your plans?"

"Start a corporation, consisting of our two selves; call it something with a sound of reliability about it, and sell shares."

"At how much per head?" She had a practical streak in her as well as others, and at times, if she was occupied in darning, she let her sense of fair play fall a little in the background, because the very fact that she had still to mend and patch reminded her that they were not quite as well off as they should be, if only for the good of their children.

"Oh, that can be settled later."

"And when would the stockholders receive their first dividend?"

"Plenty of time, plenty of time. Don't you think I will act squarely?" he added, fixing her finger with his wideset eyes. He laughed, too, without much facial exertion, pleasantly, hopefully.

Whenever Ampee set out to cheat the people, he always gave his wife some little present; he was kinder, too. He went so far as to kiss her. On the day following, she found a gold piece beneath her plate, and somehow she forgot to thank him.

During the two years that followed, Fago was slowly pressed out of the lead. He fell back; people began to turn toward Ampee's cellars. They talked of the flavor of the most excellent wine and waited hopefully for the day when their shares would show cash returns.

Ampee began to cultivate Fago's friendship: he feared him. This was an unexpected feeling for Ampee. He almost regretted having put himself in a position where he feared.

Fago had begun to doubt Ampee. He could see that there was some sort of swindle beneath the whole thing, and he felt a little contemptuous when now he saw Ampee standing in his doorway, or when he heard a customer make remarks upon the superior quality of Ampee's wine.

And then, Fago had been changing, too, as Ampee changed. As Ampee grew gross and expectant, Fago began to doubt. He grew restless and he turned over in his honest head many an old idea. Sometimes this had a most astonishing effect. In altering his former views he came to like people he had disliked and vice versa. He began to

be dissatisfied with himself, although having to acknowl-
edge that, for his former turn of mind, he had been all
that could be expected. It seemed strange that he could
find in himself two fairly decent men; he had always
thought that there was only one kind of good and one
kind of bad.

Then, too, Fago had allied himself with a semi-radical
crowd, who came to drink in his back room. At first he
had stood aloof, but finally, out of his friendliness, he had
been drawn in, and now he did not care to contradict
Ampee when Ampee called him "Nihilist," though
Ampee's evident ignorance of just what constituted a nihilist made him smile.

Then one day the people, who had grown restive and
angry at the nonexistence of their hopes in the vineyard,
began to demand of Ampee. He saw that it was about
time to draw out with his little haul and to change his
quarters or play bankrupt. Lyda had been very silent for
the past few weeks, and was uncommunicative; as a ther-
mometer she was beginning to fail him and Ampee resented her.

Sitting on the edge of his bed that night, he told her
something.

"Lyda, we have come off very nicely—very nicely, indeed. What do you say if we retire into the country for a
while, or take a trip abroad?"

"You are going to close the shop! You are going to
swindle the people! You have never done this before,

excepting in short measure. I do not like it. It does not stand in with my principle. It is a mean man's trick. It will leave you worse off in the end than you are. Let us put it entirely on a practical footing. What are you going to do when next you want to show your face?"

"Show it," he answered, looking at her fixedly.

"And what will happen to you?"

"Nothing," he answered, crossing his long legs. "Nothing ever does. This is the way all big men have started—that is, all my kind of big men."

"What do you call your kind?"

"The obscure. I am satisfied with gain in a financial way. I have no personal pride. I do not long to become one of the peerage or to hold a place in politics. Therefore, it was quite correct."

"You must take me into account. I have certain qualities. You must not overlook them."

"Such as?" There was a hint of a sneer in Ampee's face.

"I come of a good family."

"Yes, you do."

"I have my reputation for honesty."

"That too, yes."

"Well, what are you going to do with them?"

"My dear woman, you speak as though they were a stock—as though they were packages."

"Well, yes, that's so."

"I will let you keep them."

"Good of you," she answered with a touch of her old refinement. Then she broke out into stormy abuse.

"You are a pitiable thing, Monsieur Ampee, and we are not going to stand for you, I tell you. I shall tell your children what you are."

"They have guessed."

She said with a flash of sudden illumination, "Are you there?" And he sprung up, startled and puzzled and shocked. He half turned and looked at himself from the shoulder down.

"What is it?" he cried excitedly. "What is it—"

She burst into tears.

So he looked at her as she lay face to the wall. That must have been a whim of hers, calling that out, treating him as something so small that he might get lost. He stretched himself beside her and looked up at the ceiling.

He had always been able to treat his wife as one treats algebra or a simple sum; go so far, do thus and thus and it would have this and that effect. Whenever he wanted to see how far his calculations had gone, all he had to do was to add up, and this simply by the means of his wife's face, actions or phraseology. Presently, without emotion, only curious of the sum he had now to contend with, he reached his hand over and dropped his fingers into the hollows of his wife's closed eyes. He lifted them up and looked at them, spreading the fingers and closing them. They were wet with her tears. That meant that the experiment had gone up to its unanswerable quantity, i.e., that Lyda would reach reaction and come down the balance side and with a probable mistake in calculation.

But this time it did not have quite the result that he expected. She did not turn around. She continued to weep silently but firmly, as a person weeps who has a fair foundation based on a condition of long standing.

This annoyed Ampee, and to his annoyance he probably owed his life. He got up, put his dressing gown on and went downstairs to extinguish the kitchen lamp and the light in the front of the store, as was his usual custom, but which he had neglected to see to on this particular night.

Then came the explosion—a slight sound of tearing wood, a curtain caught fire from a gust from the window—and bewildered, frightened and almost paralyzed, Ampee picked himself up with the flaming curtain in his hand. He looked at it, then dashed it into a vat of wine and turned toward the stairs. He ran up them lightly, quickly, and, still running, entered his wife's room.

The floor sagged where a great hole had been torn in it near the window. The bedstead on which Lyda was lying was intact, but Lyda herself remained motionless.

He approached her half-choking on a terrible thought. He said, "Ayah," and put his hand upon her face.

So the experiment could go farther, the figures could be made to add up to an answer he had not expected.

He turned his wife's face toward him. Death from shock, probably. He hadn't expected this. He didn't like it. How in God's name had all this happened? Then it flashed through his mind. The revolutionists. Fago!

His eyelids dropped. He began to cry.

He wept as a man weeps who is terribly frightened.

Two months later, a well-known figure, a bereaved man, a broken tradesman as far as outside appearances went, but with plenty of money for drinks and such entertainment, Ampee again comes upon the scene.

He has gotten nicely out of his obligations along with the wreck of his home—the safe, everything, money, bonds, deeds, capital, all went with the rest of the things.

It does not matter who believed or who did not believe—he cast out dark hints that it was due to the "Nihilists" and those scurvy fellows the revolutionists, bohemians and writers. It does not matter to him that it was proved to be carelessness on his own or on someone else's part, due to the explosion among some cans of powder and other things kept in the cellar. No, undoubtedly it was chiefly due to the fact that as a business his had outstripped a certain man on the opposite side of the street. At this Fago did not so much as laugh, it seemed so utterly ridiculous. "You know," he said, "we don't do such dirty little tricks as cleaning rats out or stepping on worms." And strangely enough, Ampee laughed and took no offense.

Of an evening, people would nudge one another as he sat in the cafes. He had become what he had never expected to be—personally renowned through police investigation and local comment and newspaper mention. When the case finally blew over—he was willing enough—he had become quite a "Dandy" and was considered quite charming.

But one night he sat himself down among the very circle he had abused.

They held him in contempt, but liked to play with him, turning him this way and that.

They would say, "Well, how is life now, Tradesman Ampee?"

And he would slap his knee and pound his free foot, and he would light a cigarette and, waving his arms, say excellent things humorously, finally ending up on the middle of the table in a drunken dance. And one night, as he swung his arms as if they had been wings, he leaned down and whispered to Fago:

"There are some things that will not bear stirring up, my little revolutionists, and one of them is clear water." Here he shouted with laughter and then, drawing his brows together, he solemnly got down from the table amid the taunts of the group, who had overheard him.

"No," they said, "not when the water is a puddle and it stirs up mud; not when it is likely to drain off all the innocent looking surface and leave behind the dirt." He knew that by drawing off the pure water they referred to Lyda.

He shouted: "I tell you, you will see there are some things that you can't blow up. There are some things you can't thrust your fingers into without making them worse. Listen, I'm telling you something—listen to me while I am in emotion. Go ahead, be mad, try to right things, but you see, you see—I fly. You say draw off the water, and I say beware of what is beneath the water. It is not always so pleasant to look upon. It is not always so nice—and people like to see nice things, don't they? Well, step on the worm—so." He ground his heels into an imaginary insect.

He turned away amid the shouts from the company grouped around Fago, and as they derided him on his wings, one of them asked him where he was going, and he turned his head over his shoulder and answered with fixed eyelids, "To wash my hands."

The Terrorists

IN EARLY YOUTH Pilaat had been very melancholy, though vigorous. This was due to his healthy body and to his imaginative mind.

Those people who are in the habit of assuming that a melancholy stomach must accompany a sad mind, were rather disconcerted with Pilaat's indomitable digestion, about his excesses that never gave him punishment in their passing, and about his unalterable decision to become a necessity in the community.

Then his hair had been long and his dress decidedly on the "artistic" plan. His straight nose had below it a very full and perhaps weak mouth, and above it, eyes of a strange, large and mournful turn.

Time shortened the hair a little and the mouth was covered by a graying mustache. The eyes watered easily, and sometimes, during an evening, blood veins would stretch across them.

Pilaat was no longer vigorous, though for a man of fifty odd, he was robust enough. On the other hand, his melancholy had, so people seemed to think, disappeared altogether. Those who knew him longest made the mistake of calling him "more like a human being"; and those who knew him the shortest made the correct judgment, that he was "drinking too much."

His early love of the people had sent him toward them eagerly. Being close to them and in with them, he learned how pitifully weak they all were, and his strong digestion made him despise them for those qualities that, somehow, he blamed on environment and not heredity, excepting as one can inherit the filth of the gutter and the starvation of the ash pile. And along with his interest, his study and his acknowledgment of its inevitability, came this robust hate.

From speaking of the people as the "Unfortunate," he spoke of them as the "Miserable." And in the way he said this word there was no sound of pity for their sad, shabby hearts; there was only a knowledge that their garments were also shabby and mournful. Had Pilaat come from a less cleanly family, he would have loved them very strongly and gently to the end. But he had been comforted and maimed in his conceptions and his fellow love by too many clean shirts in youth. He still longed to correct things, but he wanted to correct them as one cleans up a floor, not as one binds up a wound.

He shouted because his heart was heavy. He began to awe those of his own group. Soon enough, they called him the "Terrorist," and, in the end, when he made a gesture of pity, people raised their arms to protect themselves.

He had a very young wife, a weak-chinned, small thing about 27 years old. She had been nicknamed Joan d'Arc, because of a certain pale loveliness about the frail oblong of her face. She had lost two or three teeth, and she smoked innumerable cigarettes, drank beer on half- holidays, and flirted with anyone whom she despised.

She believed in the vanity of all things and the pessimism in all things, and she wanted to annihilate any slovenly ease of mind in herself, so she deliberately set about annihilating her own soul and her own delicate, sensitive, and keen insight.

She wore heavy boots that seemed to be drawing her down; thus her five feet looked like three.

Her hair was cut short after the manner of intellectuals among the women of her set, and she wore loose and dirty blouses, smeared with paint and oil.

She was in the cafes all the afternoon from three till six, when she "cleared out" for "the pigs," the smug and respectable who brought their wives and children to dine. Again at nine she was back talking about the revolutionists.

Pilaat had written some poems and had them published obscurely; these she always carried around with her, reading them aloud or studying them nonchalantly. She had long grown tired of them, but she wanted to puzzle the strangers who filtered in, and she wanted to add, when asked about them, "By Pilaat Korb—you know, the Terrorist," never referring to the fact that he was her husband; this she left for others to whisper. She liked to be the center of whispers, for then she could be impersonal and forget herself without any danger of falling into obscurity.

Among her friends she would permit herself the pleasure of pretending to feel human suffering very deeply. She would swing her arms about, imitating Pilaat. She would lean far back in her chair as he did when he had finished a sentence, as "I know, you call me crazy—but that is not all. I have a retort to make, an accusation. You, the people—what do you know?—are you not being swindled on every side, and yet you submit? Ah, fools! Fools!" he would shout. "You are always horribly conscious of your bones, and you begin to think that it is as it should be. You say this is life—bah!" He would then end up leaning far back as his wife did when she copied him, thinking that she was expressing herself. And sometimes her friends said, "Certainly, there you are," while they drank beer or devoured large, ill-shaped sandwiches.

She would say, "You wander, my poor friends, about the world like shadows. We must find you your bodies once again." She said "we" with that intonation used by agitators.

These two lived in a dismal little garret high above the rest of the sad houses of the shabby side street. The building had once been some kind of church or house of devotion, but had long ago been turned into rooms, and was now frequented by a vocalist, a violin and piano teacher, and a few out-at-knee artists.

There was never any lock on the outer door, approached by three rickety steps. Two or three iron mailboxes clung to the walls, and in the winter, when the wind howled hardest and the snow made park benches impossible, tramps and derelicts of all kinds would creep in here and sleep along the walls near the dry wood of the steps.

Their garret had been at one time very dignified and almost elegant, as its tall lines and its heavy wood proclaimed. Its windows and the architecture of the roof spoke of a past that had been no mean thing. Now it was like a woman who had fallen from wealth and distinction and esteem, who had lost all her admirers, but not quite all her looks, who passes her remaining days in that odd mixture of clothes that look so strange together—a silk and beribboned petticoat hidden by a calico dressing gown, a torn stocking thrust into small and delightfully fashioned slippers, a well-appointed mouth closing on crumbs. Such was the room to which of an evening Pilaat and his little wife climbed.

Sometimes the sleeping men in the hall would be awakened by their late arrival and would turn over muttering abuse, or some of them accepted Pilaat's invitation to have a drink with him.

Thus he would collect a party that often made merry until the small hours of the morning. Or Pilaat would bring some of his friends with him—they led the life of actors—sleeping into the late afternoon and staying up half or all of the night.

Toward the end of his career, Pilaat began to tear his mustache out. When remonstrated with, he would say, "I am preparing to show my teeth." He had become very nervous and excitable and unhappy. He felt that the world was not going in the direction that he had wished. It neither turned toward his solution early enough, nor did it, on the other hand, succumb to its final end, as he had predicted, soon enough for him. He was tired of living out his life and watching others live out theirs on the prescribed gradual plan. He was annoyed with the passage of time; it infuriated him that twenty-four hours were still a day and that there were seven days a week, as there had been when he was born.

He no longer wrote poetry or plays, nor did he keep up his connection with a paper which he had started, and which spoke harshly of all things. He had taken more and more to his bottle, and because he was very nervous he drank too much, and because he drank too much, he became more and more excitable.

Instead of writing his poetry, now he laid it in among the strands of his wife's hair in his occasional tender strokings, when he would call her Little One and, sometimes, Sniffle Snuffle, when he would burst out laughing heartily at her disconcerted countenance. She knew well enough that Pilaat saw through her would-be ferocity and her assumed interest in the world. After all, she was only a little girl who, because she was interested, thought that she must assume fury, and because she was too lazy to dress her hair after the fashion, cut it off.

Yet there was something strange about Pilaat's wife. She did not like the society of silly and vain women, and she did turn most naturally to such men as her husband moved among. Perhaps it started in a torn shoe and a consciousness that only in such society are shoes valued more for the pass they have come to than for what they had been originally.

She had never much sympathy for "society," and a marriage of money disgusted her, though her family had, in the beginning, some such vain ideas about her. They were respectable people who owned a little estate somewhere near the sea, and who had been dropped in successive generations into the midst of old and tarnished jewelry comprising the family splendor. Most of this they had given to their daughter when they had their first ambitions in the way of a well-to-do doctor in the village, and which their daughter had promptly pawned. Sometimes, it is true, this jewelry would come back, piece by piece, and appear on her wrist or about her neck or from her ears, and at such times she drew a little aside from her husband and his friends, and would sit dreaming in a corner, her red wrists about her little crooked knees.

On one such night as this Pilaat had acted very strangely indeed. He had passed several morose hours by himself, and finally at a cafe located his wife, wearing this mysterious and migratory jewelry.

The sight of these gems and silvers always put him into a passion either of avarice or contempt—he would get hold of them and realize money on the spot, or he would very bitterly place them on the table before him and solemnly demand that they be cleared away with the rest of the "rubbish."

His wife would become silent, smiling a little, her head thrown back. Or, if the waiter did make a motion to sweep the trinkets away, she would say in a loud voice, "Yes, that's right: take them away. Feed them to the chickens or make a meal off them. I'm tired of supporting them." Then Pilaat cried in a terrible fury, catching the dazed waiter by the wrist and swearing at the top of his voice in Rumanian, Italian and French, saying that he was being treated like a man "who has not come honestly by his decorations."

From this, he went off into a melancholy reverie. He answered nothing in the way of a question, and ordered innumerable bottles of wine.

When, accompanied by three or four friends, they finally reached their house, Pilaat threatened to kill the vocalist who was teaching someone to sing in the room below them, it being half-past twelve.

"What is all that racket about?" he demanded, flying down the steps and pounding on the door of the vocalist's room. A thin, yellow-faced woman, the vocalist in question, opened the door sharply, thrust her head out, and said: "Be off with you, you lazy vagabond. In my country such people as you would be locked up."

Pilaat struck his chest with his fist. "Locked up, is it?" he demanded, smiling fiercely. "Locked up, is it? That is what I have against this country. They do not let you go home unless you commit something that makes you a little ashamed to say 'How do you do?' to the mother of all things, the cell."

She slammed the door on the implication. "You're crazy!" Pilaat flew back upstairs, shouting: "Crazy! and did I not warn you that I was crazy, you poor, senseless thing? Did I not give myself full credit for it in the very beginning? But does that make it necessary for me to be tortured with the horrible sounds issuing from such lovely throats as Maria's [the pupil who took the vocal lessons]? And must I forever regret the inferiority of the things Maria is forced to swallow, and of the noise Maria tosses from out her little throat?"

He was in the middle of the room by this time, and much amused his friends. His wife leaned back in the corner and twisted the bracelets around and around, blinking her eyelids and shuffling with her feet.

"What is it you would do with the little Maria if you had her and could dispose of her case as you would, eh?" inquired one man, with a bristling beard and an odor about him of tar.

"What would I do?" demanded Pilaat, seating himself with his back to the fire. "I would have her singing in Paradise by dawn. After all, I am a man of force. Some day I shall march upon the town and shall show you. It's about time for an uprising when little girls think they can sing and young men think they can govern."

"Ah, well, it's a dull season; the autumn is nearly here."

"Autumn, " retorted Pilaat, flourishing his arm, "is the season for destruction—but we are weak, miserable creatures, and we leave to nature all the tearing down of the scenery, and to her we leave all the building up of the same scenery next year and the year after for interminable and tireless and wearisome years."

"Well?"

"I would tear down the scenery better than all of them," he said irrelevantly. "Than all of them I would rip the whole existing plan of nature to pieces. How she would shiver, how she would implore. But I should have no mercy. No, not even when she got upon her knees and wept at my feet and covered them with her insufferable tears. I would invite her to suicide. I would mock at the stains upon her cheeks. I would glory at the dirt on the imploring knees. I would laugh aloud, and shake her by those horrible, ample shoulders of hers, and would cry out to her, 'Now die, die; we do not care! Tear the little leaves out of your heart. We are in need of them for a bed. Weep; we need a drink. Destroy yourself, for we need a harp on which to sing the song of freedom.'" He had become half drunk with his frenzy, and he stood up.

"I tell you, I would say to her: 'We are tired of you. I, Pilaat, am tired of you, and she, my little girl, is tired of you, and Maria is tired of you. We are tired of your spontaneity and your persistency and your punctuality. We want to see you dead and smoldering. What will we do? We will thrust our feet into your heart because they are cold, and our hands we will warm at your palms. And we will shake them at your death, saying: "At last you have accomplished more than seasons and beauty; you have created destruction." We can no longer rise in the morn-

DJUNA BARNES: COLLECTED STORIES

ing and say, "Behold, the sun has arisen." We shall no
longer send our children to school to learn mathematics.
We shall never be connected with you any longer as the
outcome of your whims. We are set free—thus.'" He
snapped his fingers and executed a pirouette on his heel,
and sat down, discussing the feasibility of destruction on
a large scale.

His wife still blinked her eyes in the corner, and continued to roll her bracelets. The whole room had such a
menacing aspect, such a sad and gloomy atmosphere, and
contained so many odors and voices that she was annoyed
and wanted to sleep. Sleep had overcome one of the men
who leaned against a table; his head had fallen forward
and he snored a little.

In the other corner of the room, the conversation had
taken a decidedly revolutionary turn. They were beginning to talk of besieging the town. Names were mentioned
as persons to destroy. They began to collect things that
would do as missiles.

The room began to bristle. Dark beards stood out as
though their wearers had been scratched. Lips protruded,
ears trembled, the very beards began to shake. Fists
doubled up, eyes sparkled, and the tongue knew no forbidden thing. There was something at once terrible and
beautiful about these men, who, rising, suddenly turned
for a moment toward the old boards of that room such a
searching and melancholy gaze that tatters and misery
might have seemed for one instant something splendid.

"Eh, it will be magnificent. In the dawn we shall do it. In the dawn we shall creep forth to make the world better for men. They will see us coming, creeping on all fours, and they will say, 'Here are the rats.' They shall learn what rats can do." Some of the men stretched a little among the empty bottles. Pilaat began to drowse, a heavy paperweight in his hand. John, his bosom friend, leaned near with the broken leg of a chair firmly clutched in his hand, and he whispered a little to make it more menacing.

The fire had died down and barely a light flickered. Pilaat's head fell forward on his chest. The bristling beards one by one relaxed and rested once more down in smooth, silky lines. Deep breathing took the place of cries, oaths, imprecations. Pilaat's wife stirred uneasily in her corner, dreaming, her hand over her bracelets.

She woke up—it was midday. She looked out into the street. A postman was standing on the steps of the door opposite, and a woman with a baby in pink ribbons moved slowly out toward the park.

She stumbled over Pilaat and two or three of the men huddled together for warmth. All of them, in their sleep, had moved away from those things that they had collected as weapons. They had rolled onto them, and they found that they hurt and were uncomfortable. The chair leg lay beside the paperweight. She stretched, opened her mouth, and yawned. She looked about for a cigarette stub, and found it, lighting it slowly. She prepared the little oil stove for the reception of the old and stained coffeepot.

She looked out of the window again; it was a splendid day. She thought of her favorite cafe, and she smiled as she contemplated one or two new phrases she would use in relation to life. She put Pilaat's book in her pocket. The coffee began to boil.

The Rabbit

THE ROAD had been covered with leaves on the day that the little tailor had left his own land. He said good day and good-bye in the one breath, with his broad teeth apart as if he had been hauled out of deep water. He did not leave Armenia because he wanted to, he left because he had to. There wasn't a thing about Armenia that he did not want to stay with for ever; it was necessity, he was being pushed out. In short, he had been left a property in New York City.

Leave-taking did not tear him to pieces, he wept no tears, the falling leaves sent no pang through him, he treated the whole business as a simple and resigned man should. He let Armenia slip through his fingers.

His life had been a sturdy, steady, slow, pleasant sort of thing. He ploughed and tended his crops. Hands folded over the haft of his scythe, he watched his cow grazing. He groomed the feathers and beaks of his ducks to see that the feathers lay straight, the bills unbroken and shining. He liked to pass his hands over the creatures of his small land, they were exactly as pleasing as plants; in fact he could not see much difference, when you came right down to it.

Now it was otherwise. His people advised him (as he

DJUNA BARNES: COLLECTED STORIES

was a single man) to accept his inheritance, a small tailoring business his uncle had left him. With a helper, they said, it might be the very best thing for him. It might "educate" him, make him into an "executive," a "boss," a man of the world.

He protested, but not with any great force; he was a timid man, a gentle man. He cleaned the spade, sharpened the saws, shook the shavings out of the plane, oiled his auger and bit, rubbed fat into the harness, and pulling his last calf from the drenched and murmuring cow, wondered what to do.

The day he was to leave he went first into the forest where he had brought boughs down, tying them, to make a hut against the sun. His jug of molasses and cinnamon water was still there by his sitting log. The woods spilled over into the road; the shadows, torn through with bright holes of sunlight, danced in patches of bloom. Mosquitoes from the swamp sang about his head. They got into the long hairs of his beard below his chin, and clung, whining in the mesh, wheeled against his cheek, flying up above his clashing hands, and as he slapped his face he thought of himself sitting in quiet misfortune, sewing, up on a table, as though he had died and had to work it out.

So one day, to the lower part of Manhattan (to the street of the shop of Amietiev the tailor) came a stranger, the latest Amietiev, with a broom. The passers-by saw him swinging it over the boards of his inheritance, a room not much more than twelve by twenty-four, the back third curtained off, to hide the small bed and the commode beside it. He tested the air, as he had tested the air of his country, he sneezed; he held the room up in his eye by the scruff of its neck, as you might say, and shook it in the face of his lost acres.

He had learned the tailors' trade when he was a young boy, when this now dead uncle had been his guardian, but his fingers were clumsy and he broke the needle. He worked slowly and painfully, holding his breath too long, puffing it out in loud sighs. He toiled far into the night, the goose between his knees. People on the way home peered in at him as he sat on his table-top, half hidden by the signs in his windows, the fly-specked fashion book open at the swaggering gentlemen in topcoats; out-of-date announcements of religious meetings, and bills for the local burlesque. Loiterers, noting how pale he was, remarked to each other, "That one will die of the consumption, see if he doesn't!"

Across the way, laid out on a butcher's slab (vying with Armietiev's remnants of silk linings, shepherd checks and woollen stuffs), were bright quarters of beef, calves' heads and knuckle bones; remnants of animals, pink and yellow layers of fat. There were muscle meats and kidneys, with their webbings of suet; great carcasses, slashed down the center showing the keyboard of the spine, and hanging on hooks, ducks dripping, head down, into basins.

When the little tailor looked up, it made him horribly sad; the colors were a very harvest of death. He remembered too easily the swinging meadows of his own country, with the cows in the lanes and the fruits overhead, and he turned away and went on stitching.

Behind the curtain was a small gas-ring on which he warmed his breakfast; sometimes a sausage, always coffee, bread, cheese. In the summer it was too hot, in the winter the shop was deadly with heavy air; he could not risk opening the door. He was flooded with chill whenever a customer came in (no one ever seemed to think he might feel the wind); so he sat in the foul air, made infinitely worse by the gas stove, and day by day his eyes grew farther back in his head, the dark brows more and more prominent. The children of the neighborhood called him "coal eye."

In the second summer business picked up, he worked more quickly, did excellent patchwork, charged very little and never gave himself any time for his own life at all; he stitched, turned, pressed, altered, as though the world were a huge barricade of old clothes. At about this time he had become attached to a small, ill, slender Italian girl, who had first appeared carrying her father's coat. She smelled tart, as of lemons.

Her straight black hair, parted in the middle, was as black as her eyes; under a dipping nose blazed her mouth, firm, shut. Almost anything bright caught at him. He thought of all the calendars with all the Madonnas that he had seen, and he made the mistake of shuffling this girl in with them. The sharp, avaricious cruelty of her face pleased him; he confused the quick darting head with brightness. He himself was not a good-looking man; this did not trouble him, he was as good-looking as anyone in his family and that was that. He was quite unconscious that for the size of his head, his body was rather small; the fact that he had coarse hair made matters worse.

This girl, Addie, mentioned all these things. It hurt him because he was beginning to like her. He noticed that when he showed it, by the trembling of his needle, she laughed and looked starved. He was puzzled. "Why," he asked, "when you say such things about me, do you look so pretty?"

This being the very worst thing he could say, it encouraged her, it flattered her. She throve on whetting, and he was always putting an edge on her: after all, she was neither as nice as he thought, nor as young. Finally, after much debate with himself, with slow tortuous convulsions of mind, he asked her if she had thought of love and marriage. Of course she had; here was a business right there before her for the taking, it was promising and seemed to be going to "flourish" as you might put it, and wasn't she already used to him? In a quiet, canny, measured way (that he was much too much of an idiot to notice) she had made her plans. She was pleased to admit the attachment, but what she said was, "You are a poor sort of man!" She said it roughly (as if blaming him for something). She said it bridling, pulling her pleated skirt between two fingers in a straight line. He felt that she was very stout; himself, very nothing.

"What do you want that I shall do?"

She shrugged, flipped her hair back, opened her entire mouth, exposing the full length of the crouching tongue.

"I mean, if I must do something, what is it? If as you say, I am only—"

"You'll never *be* anything," she said, then she added, "You'll never be anything *else*."

"True, not something else, but perhaps more?"

"Now there's a likely." She had a way of clipping her meanings short, it was her form of scorn.

"What do you mean by 'a *likely*'?"

"You are not the sort, for instance…"

"For?" He turned his body, looking at her closely.

"You are hardly a *hero*!" She laughed in a series of short snapping sounds, like a dog.

"Are heroes the style?" he asked, with such utter guile and with such a troubled face that she tittered.

"Not in your family, I take it."

He nodded. "That is true, yes, that is quite true. We were quiet people. You do not like quiet people?"

"Foo!" she said, "they are women!"

He pondered this a long time. Slowly he got off his table; he took her by both shoulders, shaking her softly from side to side.

"That is not true and you know it; they are something else."

She began shouting, "*So*, now I'm a liar. This is what it has come to! I'm abominable, unnatural, unnatural!" She had managed to get herself into the highest sort of pretended indignation, pulling her hair, swinging it like a whip from side to side. In so laying hold on herself, in disarranging her usually composed, almost casual ease, the sly baggage had him in as great a state of distress, as if he had had to witness the shaking of an holy image.

"No, no!" he cried, clapping his hands together. "Don't do it, leave yourself alone! I'll do something, I'll make everything as it should be." He came to her, drawing her hair out of her fist. "For you I will do *anything*. Yes, surely, I will do it, I will, I will!"

"You will do *what*, Amietiev?" she asked, with such sudden calm that his anxiety almost stumbled over her. "What is it that you will do?"

"I shall be less like a woman. You called me a woman; a terrible thing to say to a man, especially if he is small, and I am small."

She came forward, her elbows tight to her sides, her palms out, walking sideways: "You'll do anything for me? What? Something daring, something really *big*, something grand, just for me?"

"Just for you." He looked at her in sorrow. The cruel passing twist of the mouth—(everything about her was fleeting)—the perishing thin arms, the small cage of the ribs, the too long hair, the hands turning on the wrists, the sliding narrow feet, and the faint mournful sharp odor of lemons that puffed from her swinging skirt, moved him away from her; grief in all his being, snuffed him out. She came up behind him, caught both his hands, pulling them backward, and leaning against him, kissed him on the neck. He tried to turn around, but she held him; so they stood for a moment, then she broke away and ran out into the street.

He set to work again, sitting cross-legged on the table. He wondered what he was supposed to do. Nothing like this had happened before; in fact he had always told her how he longed for a country life, with her beside him in the fields, or sitting among the plants and vegetables. Now here he was faced with himself as a hero...what was a hero? What was the difference between himself and that sort of man? He tried to think if he had ever known one. He remembered tales told him by the gypsies, a great time ago, when he was in his own land; they had certainly told him of a lad who was a tremendous fighter, who wrestled with his adversary like a demon, but at the end, not being able to kill anything, had thrown himself off a mountain. But for himself, a tailor, such a thing would be impossible...he would only die and that would not get him anywhere. He thought of all the great people he had read of, or heard of, or might have brushed against. There was Jean the blacksmith, who had lost an eye saving his child from a horse; but if he, Amietiev, lost an eye, Addie would not like him at all. How about Napoleon? There was a well-known man; he had done everything, all by himself, more or less, so much so that he even crowned himself Emperor without any help at all, and people so admired him they hung his picture all over the world, because of course he had been such a master at killing. He thought about this a long time, and finally came to the inevitable conclusion: all heroes were men who killed or got killed.

Well, that was impossible; if he were killed he might

as well have stayed in the country and never laid eyes on Addie—therefore he must kill—but what?

He might of course save someone or something, but there would have to be danger of one kind or another, and there might not be any for days and days, and he was tired and afraid of waiting.

He laid his work aside, slid off the table, lowered the light, and lying face down on his cot, tried to think the whole thing out.

He sat up, rubbing both hands on the sides of his face; it was damp under the beard, he could feel it. He tried to make a picture for his mind, a picture of what killing was like. He sat on the edge of the cot, staring at the small piece of carpet with its Persian design, his mind twisted in it.

He thought of trees, the brook where he went fishing, the green fields, the cows who breathed a long band of hot air from their nostrils when he came close; he thought of the geese, he thought of thin ice on the ponds with bushes bristling out of it…he thought of Addie, and Addie was entwined with the idea of killing. He tried to think of himself as of someone destroying someone. He clapped his palms together, lacing the fingers in a lock. No, no, no! That wouldn't press out the life of a thrush. He held his hands apart, looking at the thumbs. He rubbed them down the sides of his legs. What a terrible thing murder was! He stood up, shaking his body from side to side, as if it hurt him. He went out into the shop, pulling up the shade as high as it would go.

Exactly opposite, two bright lights burned in the butcher's window. He could see sides of beef hanging from their hooks, the chilled lakes of blood in the platters, the closed eyes of the calves' heads in ranks on their slabs, looking like peeled women, and swaying in the wind of the open door, game, with legs knocked down.

He came out of his shop carefully, stepping into the street on the tips of his toes, as though someone might see or hear him. He crossed, and butting his forehead against the butcher's plate-glass front, stared at all the hooded eyes of the squabs, the withered collapsed webs of the ducks' feet, the choked scrap barrel, spilling out its lungs and guts. His stomach gave way, he was sick. He put his hand on the pit of his belly and pressed. He pulled at his beard, rolling the russet hairs that came away between his fingers.

He knew the butcher well; he also knew when he stepped out for a short beer at the saloon. He knew his habit of keeping the back door on the latch, he knew exactly what was stored in the back room. He expected no hindrance and got none. He pushed the back door in easily enough. For a moment the dimness left him blind, the next instant he emerged carrying a box. Now furtive, hurried, stumbling, he crossed back to his own door, opened it with his foot, and all but fell in.

The reflection of the ruby glass of the butcher's lamps ran red over his fashion-plates and strutting cardboard gentlemen. The little tailor put the box down in the farthest corner. His heart was beating high up in his neck.

He groped about in his mind for something to stop at, some place to steady himself. He must make himself resolute. He clenched his chattering teeth, but it only made him cry. To stop that, he clasped both hands behind his neck, bending his neck down, and at the same time he sank to his knees beside the box and lowered his hands and forehead to the floor. He must do it! He must do it! He must do it *now*! His mind began its wandering again. He thought himself into his own country, in another season. Sunlight on the forest floor. He remembered the mosquitoes. He leaned back upon his heels, his arms hanging. The bright and sudden summer! Ploughing, seeding, the harvesting—what a pity it was. He paused, what was a pity? He only noticed it now!

Something moved in the box, breathing and kicking away from him; he uttered a cry, more grunt than cry, and the something in the box struck back with hard drumming fright.

The tailor bent forward, hands out, then he shoved them in between the slats of the box opening, shutting them tight! tight! tighter! The terrible, the really terrible thing, the creature does not squeal, wail, cry: it puffs, as if the wind were blunt; it thrashes its life, the frightful scuffling of the overwhelmed, in the last trifling enormity.

The tailor got to his feet, backing away from what he had done; he backed into the water pail, and turning, plunged his hands in. He beat the water, casting the waves up into his face with the heels of his hands. Then he went straight for the door and opened it. Addie fell face in, she had been standing straight up against the panel, her hands behind her back.

She righted herself without excuse or apology; she could tell by his face that he had done something enormous for the first time in his life, and without any doubt, for her. She came close to him, as she had to the door, her arms behind her. "What have you done?" she said.

"I—I have killed—I think I have killed—"

"Where? What?" She moved away from him, looking into the corner at the box. "*That!*" She began to laugh, harsh, back-bending laughter.

"Take it or leave it!" he shouted, and she stopped, her mouth open. She stooped and lifted up a small grey rabbit. She placed it on the table; then she came to Amietiev and wound her arms around him. "Come," she said. "Comb your hair."

She was afraid of him, there was something strange about his mouth swinging slightly sidewise. She was afraid of his walk, loud and flat. She pushed him toward the door. He placed one foot after the other, with a precision that brought the heel down first, the toe following....

"Where are you going?"

He did not seem to know where he was, he had forgotten her. He was shaking, his head straight up, his heart wringing wet.

She said tartly, "At least shine your boots!"

Indian Summer

AT THE AGE of fifty-three Madame Boliver was young again. She was suddenly swept away in a mad current of reckless and beautiful youth. What she had done with those years that had counted up into such a perfect conclusion, she could not tell—it was a strange, vague dream. She had been plain, almost ugly, shy, an old maid. She was tall and awkward—she sat down as if she were going to break when she was in those new years that girls call early bloom.

When she was thirty she had been frankly and astonishingly Yankee; she came toward one with an erect and angular stride. She was severe, silent and curious. It was probably due to this that she was called Madame. She dressed in black outlined with white collar and cuffs, her hair was drawn straight back and showed large-lobed and pale ears. The tight-drawn hair exposed her features to that utter and unlovely nakedness that some clean rooms are exposed to by the catching back of heavy and melancholy curtains—she looked out upon life with that same unaccustomed and expectant expression that best rooms wear when thrown open for the one yearly festivity that proclaims their owners well to do.

She had no friends and could not keep acquaintances—her speech was sharp, quick and truthful. She spoke seldom, but with such fierce strictness and accuracy that those who came into contact with her once, took precautions not to be thus exposed a second time.

She grew older steadily and without regret—long before the age of thirty she had given up all expectations of a usual life or any hopes of that called "unusual"; she walked in a straight path between the two, and she was content and speculated little upon this thing in her that had made her unloved and unlovely.

Her sisters had married and fallen away about her as blossoms are carried off, leaving the stalk—their children came like bits of pollen and she enjoyed them and was mildly happy. Once she, too, had dreamed of love, but that was before she had attained to the age of seventeen—by that time she knew that no one could or would ask for her hand—she was plain and unattractive and she was satisfied.

She had become at once the drudge and the adviser—all things were laid upon her both to solve and to produce. She labored for others easily and willingly and they let her labor.

At fifty-three she blazed into a riotous Indian Summer of loveliness. She was tall and magnificent. She carried with her a flavor of some exotic flower; she exhaled something that savored of those excellences of odor and tone akin to pain and to pleasure; she lent a plastic embodiment to all hitherto unembodied things. She was like some rare wood, carved into a melting form—she breathed abruptly as one who has been dead for half a century.

Her face, it is true, was not that plump, downy and senseless countenance of the early young—it was thin and dark and marked with a few very sensitive wrinkles; about the mouth there were signs of a humor she had never possessed, of a love she had never known, of a joy she had never experienced and of a wisdom impossible for her to have acquired. Her still, curious eyes with their blue-white borders and the splendid irises were half veiled by strange dusty lids. The hair, that had once been drawn back, was still drawn back, but no appallingly severe features were laid bare. Instead the hair seemed to confer a favor on all those who might look upon its restrained luxury, for it uncovered a face at once valuable and unusual.

Her smile was rich in color—the scarlet of her gums, the strange whiteness of her teeth, the moisture of the sensitive mouth, all seemed as if Madame Boliver were something dyed through with perfect and rare life.

Now when she entered a room every one paused, looking up and speaking together. She was quite conscious of this and it pleased her—not because she was too unutterably vain, but because it was so new and so unexpected.

For a while her very youth satisfied her—she lived with herself as though she were a second person who had been permitted access to the presence of some lovely and some longed-for dream.

She did not know what to do. If she could have found

religion newly with her new youth she would have wor-
shipped and have been profoundly glad of the kneeling
down and the rising up attendant with faith, but this was
a part of her old childhood and it did not serve.

She had prayed then because she was ugly; she could
not pray now because she was beautiful—she wanted
something new to stand before, to speak to.

One by one the old and awkward things went, leaving
in their wake Venetian glass and bowls of onyx, silks, cushions and perfume. Her books became magazines with
quaint, unsurpassable and daring illustrations.

Presently she had a salon. She was the rage. Gentlemen in political whiskers, pomaded and curled, left their
coats in the embrace of pompous and refined footmen.

Young students with boutonnières and ambitions
came; an emissary or two dropped in, proffered their
hearts and departed. Poets and musicians, littérateurs and
artists experimenting in the modern, grouped themselves
about her mantels like butterflies over bonbons and
poured sentiment upon sentiment into her ears.

Several gentlemen of leisure and millions courted her
furiously with small tears in the corners of their alert eyes.
Middle-aged professors and one deacon were among the
crowd that filled her handsome apartment on those days
when she entertained.

There was something about Madame Boliver that
could not quite succumb to herself. She was still afraid;
she would start, draw her hand away and pale abruptly in
the middle of some ardent proposal—she would hurry to

the mirror at such times, though she never turned her head to look in.

Was it possible that she was beautiful now? And if so, would it remain? And her heart said, "Yes, it will remain," until at last she believed it.

She put the past behind her and tried to forget it. It hurt her to remember it, as if it were something that she had done in a moment of absent-mindedness and of which she had to be ashamed. She remembered it as one remembers some small wrong deed hidden for years. She thought about her past unattractiveness as another would have thought of some cruelty. Her eyes watered when she remembered her way of looking at herself in her twenties. Her mouth trembled when she thought back to its severity and its sharp retorts.

Her very body reproached her for all that had been forced upon it in her other youth, and a strange passion came upon her, turning her memory of her sisters into something at times like that hatred felt by the oppressed who remember the oppression when it has given way to plenty.

But now she was free. She expanded, she sang, she dreamed for long hours, her elbows upon the casement, looking out into the garden. She smiled, remembering the old custom of serenading, and wondered when she, too, would know it.

That she was fifty-three never troubled her. It never even occurred to her. She had been fifty-three long ago at twenty, and now she was twenty at fifty-three, that was all—this was compensation, and if she had been through her middle age in youth she could go through her youth in middle age.

At times she thought how much more beautiful nature is in its treacheries than its remedies.

Those who hovered about her offered, time on time, to marry her, to carry her away into Italy or to Spain, to lavish money and devotion on her, and in the beginning she had been almost too ready to accept them in their assurances, because the very assurances were so new and so delightful.

But in spite of it she was, somewhere beneath her youth, old enough to know that she did not love as she would love, and she waited with a patience made pleasant by the constant attentions of the multitude.

And then Petkoff, "the Russian," had come, accompanied by one of the younger students.

A heavy fur cap came down to the borders of his squinting and piercing eyes. He wore a mixture of clothing that proclaimed him at once foreign and poor. His small mustache barely covered sensitive and well shaped lips, and the little line of hair that reached down on each side of his close-set ears gave him an early period expression as if he, too, in spite of his few years, might have lived in the time when she was a girl.

He could not have been much over thirty, perhaps just thirty—he said little but never took his eyes off the object of his interest.

He spoke well enough, with an occasional lapse into

Russian, which was very piquant. He swept aside all other
aspirants with his steady and centered gaze. He ignored
the rest of the company so completely as to rob him of
rudeness. If one is ignorant of the very presence of his
fellow beings, at most he can only be called "strange."

Petkoff was both an ambitious and a self-centered
man—all his qualities were decisive and not hesitatingly
crooked, providing he needed crookedness to win his
point. He was attractive to Madame Boliver because he
was as strange as she was herself, her youth was foreign,
and so was Petkoff.

He had come to this country to start a venture that
promised to be successful; in the meantime, he had to be
careful both in person and in heart.

What he felt for Madame Boliver was at first astonishment that such a woman was still unmarried; he knew
nothing of her past, and guessed at her age much below
the real figure. After awhile this astonishment gave way
to pleasure and then to real and very sincere love.

He began to pay court to her, neglecting his business a
little and worrying over that end of it, but persisting, nevertheless.

He could see that she, on her side, was becoming
deeply attached to him. He would walk about in the park
for hours arguing this affair out to himself. Both the
shoulds and should nots.

It got him nowhere except into a state of impatience.
He liked clear-cut acts and he could not decide to go or
stay. As it was, nothing could be worse for his business

than this same feverish indecision. He made up his mind.

Madame Boliver was radiantly happy. She began to draw away from a life of entertainment and, instead, turned most of her energies into the adoration of her first real love. She accepted him promptly, and with a touch of her old firm and sharp decisiveness, and a hint of her utter frankness. He told her that she took him as she would have taken a piece of cake at a tea party, and they both laughed.

That was in the winter. Madame Boliver was fifty-five —he never asked her how old she was and she never thought to tell him. They set the day for their wedding early in the following June.

They were profoundly happy. One by one the younger, more ardent admirers fell off, but very slowly; they turned their heads a little as they went, being both too vain and too skeptical to believe that this would last.

She still held receptions and still her rooms were flooded, but when Petkoff entered, a little better dressed but still a bit heedless of the throng, they hushed their highest hilarities and spoke of the new novels and the newest trend in art.

Petkoff had taken notice of them to that degree necessary to a man who knows what he has won, and from whom and how many. He looked upon them casually, but with a hint of well-being.

Madame Boliver grew more beautiful, more radiant, more easeful. Her movements began to resemble flowing water; she was almost too happy, too supple, too conscious of her well-being. She became arrogant, but still splendid; she became vain, but still gracious; she became accustomed to herself, but still reflective. She could be said to have bloomed at too auspicious an age; she was old enough to appreciate it, and this is a very dangerous thing.

She spent hours at the hairdresser's and the dress-maker's. Her dressing table resembled a battlefield. It supported all the armament for keeping age at a distance. She rode in the avenue in an open carriage, and smiled when the society notices mentioned her name and ran her picture.

She finally gave one the impression of being beautiful, but too conscious of it; talented, but too vain; easy of carriage, but too reliant on it; of being strange and rare and wonderful, but a little too strange, a little too rare, a little too wonderful. She became magnificently complex to outward appearances, yet in her soul Madame Boliver still kept her honesty, her frankness and her simplicity.

And then one day Madame Boliver took to her bed. It began with a headache and ended with severe chills. She hoped to get up on the following day, and she remained there a week; she put her party off, expecting to be able to be about, but instead she gave it sitting in a chair supported by cushions.

Petkoff was worried and morose. He had given a good deal of time to Madame Boliver, and he cared for her in a selfish and all-engrossing way. When she stood up no longer he broke a Venetian tumbler by throwing it into the fireplace. When she laughed at this he suddenly burst out into very heavy weeping. She tried to comfort him, but he would not be comforted. She promised him that she would walk soon, as a mother promises a child some longed-for object. When she said, "I will be well, dear, soon; after all I'm a young woman," he stopped and looked at her through a film of painful tears.

"But are you?" he said, voicing for the first time his inner fear.

And it was then that the horror of the situation dawned upon her. In youth, when youth comes rightly, there is old age in which to lose it complacently, but when it comes in old age there is no time to watch it go.

She sat up and stared at him.

"Why, yes," she said in a flat and firm voice, "that's so. I am no longer of few years."

She could not say "no longer young," because she was young.

"It will make no difference."

"Ah," she said, "it will make no difference to you, but it will make a difference to us."

She lay back and sighed, and presently she asked him to leave her a little while.

When he had gone she summoned the doctor.

She said: "My friend—am I dying—so soon?"

He shook his head emphatically. "Of course not," he assured her; "we will have you up in a week or so."

"What is it, then, that keeps me here now?"

"You have tired yourself out, that is all. You see, such

extensive entertaining, my dear madame, will tax the youngest of us." He shook his head at this and twisted his mustache. She sent him away also.

The next few days were happy ones. She felt better. She sat up without fatigue. She was joyful in Petkoff's renewed affections. He had been frightened, and he lavished more extravagant praise and endearing terms on her than ever before. He was like a man who, seeing his fortune go, found how dear it was to him after all and how necessary when it returned to him. By almost losing her he appreciated what he should have felt if he had lost her indeed.

It got to be a joke between them that they had held any fears at all. At the club he beat his friends on the back and cried:

"Gentlemen, a beautiful and young woman." And they used to beat his back, exclaiming: "Lucky, by God!"

She ordered a large stock of wine and cakes for the wedding party, bought some new Venetian glasses and indulged in a few rare old carpets for the floor. She had quite a fancy, too, for a new gown offered at a remarkably low sum, but she began to curb herself, for she had been very extravagant as it was.

And then one day she died.

Petkoff came in a wild, strange mood. Four candles were burning at head and feet, and Madame Boliver was more lovely than ever. Stamping, so that he sent up little spirals of dust from the newly acquired carpet, Petkoff strode up and down beside the bier. He leaned over and lit a cigarette by one of the flickering flames of the candles. Madame Boliver's elderly sister, who was kneeling, coughed and looked reproachfully upward at the figure of Petkoff, who had once again forgotten every one and everything. "Damn it!" he said, putting his fingers into his vest.

A Night in the Woods

FOR TRENCHARD the town jail represented freedom
he had always wanted so passionately, communal freedom that those enjoying it call social boredom. To him
who must ever serve in his little cellar where he baked
bread, this square and rickety edifice seemed something
holy, until the day he and his wife got locked up in it only
to discover that they were the only transgressors in a community of five thousand inhabitants—and this rather
spoiled matters.

Jennie and he had been married something like those
proverbial happy thirty years or so. They were both stout,
small, and good natured. They were both gentle with
downy complexions and easy smiles. They were both so
exactly suited to each other that it seemed as though they
must have been born somewhere in a nest together.

Both of them came originally from the south of France;
neither of them remembered much about it, though they
would cry excitedly, "Ah, what a world that was, my dear.
Full of sunlight and leaves, upturned earth and flowers."

Both of them throughout their married existence had
spoken almost reverently about freedom—meaning such
freedom as these youthful memories cast back—the freedom of the out-of-doors.

Jennie could have adapted herself to things as they were if it had not been for her loyalty to Trenchard. True, she often looked out into the streets to breathe in the beauties of the newly budded trees that flanked the library on either side, but it was a passive sort of longing that would have gone with her to the grave but for the corresponding longing in her husband's breast.

They had no children to free them with the delightful bondage of new youth; they had no relatives and no very close friends saving their dog Pontz. They lived in a world of exactly one—for Jennie Trenchard, for Trenchard Jennie, with their love for their dog entering in as part of them.

In youth Jennie had been round, rosy, kind, of quick action and of slow mind. She had been born to a world of chickens and ducks, of cows and horses and casual springs and casual autumns. She had been pig-tailed then, had worn blue pinafores and had been the quietest girl in school. When the boys teased her she would frown a little; when they would pull her braids she would turn her head slowly and say nothing very marked in contempt, but very hesitant in coming. She would never cry, never whine, never complain. Finally, they let her alone, this sort of young person being the bane of a naughty boy's existence.

In youth Trenchard had been small also, plump, exceedingly good natured, but quick tempered. He was slow with his lessons, dreamy in his method and much petted by his parents.

He had large and thick-lidded eyes and the whitest of

skins. His mouth and nose were like something against a hard and determined wall. The nose pugged abruptly.

She was still blonde, though turning to something paler. He still possessed black hair, though of late years it had begun to curl a little, the only sign that he had grown up, he would say, and she: "You are going to be still younger than when you were born, my dear."

Of course, their tempers were not always mild. They had some few fallings out as is not only necessary, but customary in good families. He could not smoke, therefore he chewed. She had forgiven him long ago for this "filthy trick, never indulged in by my father." She could not sew, but he had forgiven her, though "all the women in my family had been par excellence at needlework."

At times Trenchard would fall into a morose silence; then Jennie smiled and served the customers herself. At night, when the oven door shone out like the bleeding mouth of some demon, Trenchard, stripped to the waist, pulled out little biscuits for the morning trade. His wife would say, quite resolutely: "My dear, you are working too hard. There is plenty of time and money now for both our old age and a little vacation."

He would shake his head.

"Yes, you need a little rest," and he would always add: "Bah, I need freedom."

She would sit down resting her hands on the check of her apron, saying, "Well then, your freedom; let us buy a little land."

"Where from? We have not enough capital."

"Let us venture," she would say.

"One may speculate before the age of twenty, but not after," he would answer. And so the days would pass with the little longings of both stilled by the respective kindnesses and forethought of each of them.

And then the crash comes. A man and his wife somewhere on the border of town die suddenly, and the cause has been traced back to poison found in a loaf of bread. As Jennie and Trenchard are the only bakers in the town, they are immediately pounced upon by the marshal, and both of them landed securely in that very jail that Trenchard had been longing to inhabit.

Like little birds they begin to pick at each other, questioning, talking, laughing, weeping. Trenchard always weeps easily; now his face is composed of laughter, tears, astonishment and fear, pleasure and disappointment.

"Is this the place," he seems to say as he turns around and around in what is like an ordinary room with a few rusty bars up at the windows.

Impossible, he begins to laugh. "My dear Jennie," he says with great excitement, "here is the freedom and the holiday we have been talking about."

"Do not laugh," she answers severely, "there is real danger here. We have been accused of a frightful thing—do you understand?" Here she catches him by the sleeve and pulls at it. "We are in for murder—poisoning. Of course," she adds logically, "we did not do it, so that's off our minds. But perhaps they will think we did all the same, and then we die—yes, assuredly we die, little Trenchard, and I do not like to think of that so soon."

"Eh, that's so." He sits down and begins to cry again heartily in great sobs. Jennie, dry-eyed and calm, folds her hands over her apron as she has so often done in the little shop.

"What shall we do?"

"There is nothing to do."

As if this had struck a terrible pang to his ear, Trenchard begins to weep afresh, while Jennie pats him on the shoulder. "There, there," she says comfortingly, "you must remember, little one, that all things come to all men, or so they say. And here we are."

"But, Jennie, we may be hung."

"Very true."

"But it is terrible. We must do something. Are there no ways in the world of showing these people that we did not poison the bread?"

"Oh yes, there are a lot of ways, if they will let us show them."

"Then let us do it immediately." He stands up at this and starts for the door.

"The door is locked, Trenchard. At last you know what it is like to be in jail."

"You need not remind me."

"I do not want you to forget."

"Is it you, Jennie, who have held me back always?"

"What do you mean?"

"It is because of you that I have never had my freedom, my little beloved freedom, the love of my heart."

"Trenchard, you are a wretch."

"Jennie, you are a willful and bad woman."

Whereat they both fall to weeping and kissing each other and patting each other as if they were trying to mend a broken image, something they have reared up in their thirty years of married life.

The night has begun to fall in great shadows, as though it, too, were in prison. The air has begun to chill, for it is late summer, and the two cling closer together, waiting for the tread of the watchman.

Trenchard begins to dream—not far away are the woods, the great, clean, sheltering woods, with the moss and the leaves that he has so often longed to explore, but which he has never had time to so much as visit. Jennie begins to worry about the biscuits that had been left to rise.

From the window, he can see the great pines, and beyond this, the dying sun. A little puff of fresh air blows against his cheek and he sighs, feeling for his tobacco. He bites off a little piece and begins to chew slowly.

"Life is not freedom after all, eh, Jennie?" She shakes her head, still worrying about the biscuits.

Leaning close to the bars of the window, he looks away into the great dark and the greater silence of the woods. A few wild birds, startled by nightfall, circle far overhead, calling out in a lonely and barren way, as they descend into the shelter of the forest.

Suddenly Trenchard says: "Jennie," stealthily, "we are going to escape."

There is more in this one word "escape" than just the meaning that he would seem to give it! There is in it all the longing of their lives, for that remembered freedom of their youth, the play-time they were both too young to appreciate but also too young to forget.

"Is there a way?"

He says grandly: "I shall make a way."

And he does. Standing on tip-toes, he goes about the worm eaten and rickety room, feeling along the floor, looking up at the ceiling, testing it with his eyes.

"Try the window."

He is in an ecstasy of anticipation of a romance that at last he shall know the taste and the smell of as he tries the window bars, which shake in their sockets, but do not bend.

Alas, it is fruitless; but not so the door. Jennie, going boldly up to it, as small children go up to what sometimes they fear to bully it, shakes it, only to have the door open slowly with a creaking noise that had only a few moments before been the sound of bondage.

They peer out into the darkness. Someone snores gently. They begin to run, clumsily at first and then swifter. Toward the shadows of the woods, toward the great out-of-doors and that great freedom. Jennie had not forgotten the biscuits however, and pants out: "Hadn't we better go back to the shop, Trenchard, and see to the dough?" But he does not hear her; his soul is filled with the new freedom, his first breath of night air and the trees in thirty years.

He shivers a little. "Isn't it glorious?" And she says, "Yes, it is lovely." And they run on.

But they cannot run very far, because, after all, they are very old for such things, and it is, for Trenchard, chew or flight; and you must remember that tobacco is a thirty years' habit, and longing for freedom only a thirty years' desire, and the one is always stronger than the other.

*

They fall beside a clump of bushes.

The smell of fresh sod and moss comes to their nostrils, the odor of a crushed flower, of a few bleeding berries. The sound in the air of leaves and wind seems good. The birds that Trenchard had watched have now disappeared altogether, and everything is still save something moving under earth and the restless noises of a forest that grows always, leaving the earth for the air.

Presently they move on again, striking deeper into the forest where pursuit is almost impossible. They go down on hands and knees and creep; they fall on their faces once or twice, and Jennie whispers, "That time I kissed the earth."

It is chilly, even colder than they expected, and they have no shelter save the bushes under which they lie and the coat of Trenchard.

"Do you think," she begins, "that they will ever find us here?"

He says grandly: "I doubt it."

"But what about our shop?"

"How could we return to that—we are fugitives, don't you understand, Jennie?"

"Yes," she says, "I understand." But she doesn't, and she looks at Trenchard with sorrowful eyes, thinking how much, indeed, he must have longed for his freedom.

"But what would they do to us?"

"Do you know the import of the offense charged against us?"

"Yes, I know."

"Then you know what they will do with us."

"We will die."

"Yes, we will die—provided they catch us."

"Will they catch us, Trenchard?"

"I do not know—why do you worry? We are at present free, Jennie. Lie down and look at the stars."

"I can't lie down!" she cries, suddenly, catching hold of Trenchard. "What if you should get caught and killed, and I also?"

"No, no, it is all right; we shan't be."

"But perhaps?"

Presently they both start up.

"What was that?"

"It sounded like a dog barking."

"And that?"

"We are being pursued already," he says drearily, getting once more to his knees. "Let us move on."

They hear the dog barking again, nearer now and plainly gaining on them.

"Hark!" Jennie exclaims. "It sounds like our Pontz."

"I left him in the cellar. He will betray us—our child will surely betray us."

They hear him so near now that they think he must be beside them, but it was not so. In a moment more, however, Pontz flings his heavy white body upon them, yelping in little short, mad cries of delight—leaping up about them, licking their hands and faces.

Then they hear men's voices.

"Ah, mon Dieu!" they both exclaim. "The little one has betrayed us already."

Trenchard, on his knees, tries to hold the mouth of Pontz close. "Not yet," he whispers.

Pontz begins to whine, to twist—escaping again he barks louder, more joyfully.

"It must be," Trenchard says, and catches the dog by the throat. He sets his hands about him, presses slowly, and as he presses tears come into his eyes. Jennie sits forward, her hands in her lap. She begins to count the squares in her apron. Presently they begin to dig.

Will they have time to bury him—their little one—so glad to see them, so happy, so faithful?

No. They are too exhausted. Finally they lie down beside the body of the dead Pontz.

"Will they find us?"

"Probably."

"Isn't that a lantern light?"

"Yes, I think it is."

"It has cost us dear, Trenchard."

"But it is freedom—for a little while."

"Wouldn't it be better to die now—than later—when—"

"No. Just lie here. This is beautiful."

"It is terrible."

He sits up suddenly and savagely.

"Let them think we are happy, contented."

"I can hear what they are saying, Trenchard; they are almost upon us."

"Now let us lie still—this is freedom."

Finale

IN THE CENTER of the room lay the corpse.

The proper number of candles burned at head and feet.

The body had been duly attended to. The undertaker had pared the nails, put the tongue back in the mouth, shut the eyes, and with a cloth dusted with bismuth had touched the edges of the nostrils.

It had been washed and dressed and made to assume the conventional death pose—the hands crossed palm over knuckles. Everything else in the room seemed willing to go on changing—being. He alone remained cold and unwilling, like a stoppage in the atmosphere.

His wife, his mother, and his children knelt about him. His wife cried heavily, resting the middle of her breasts on the hard side of the coffin boards. His mother wept also, but with that comfort of one who has seen both the beginning and the end; with that touch of restfulness that comes to those who like the round, the complete, the final.

His children knelt and did not weep. The little girl's closed palms were damp, and she wanted to look at them but dared not. The boy had that very morning discovered the pleasure of rubbing his head under the nurse's arm when she said "Come, put your shirt on," and he wanted to smile about this, but his eyes refused to grow damp, he could not permit himself the satisfaction.

On the floor, in a corner, lay what had been the dead man's dearest possession—a bright blue scarf embroidered with spots of gold. It had been given to him when passing through Italy, by a long legged Sicilian whom he had loved as one loves who must catch a train.

It was a lovely thing, but much treasuring had lined it; and the marks of his thumbs as they passed over it in pleasant satisfaction had left their tarnish on the little spots of gold.

The shadows grew and darkness fell. The room was silent save for that melancholy murmur of lips that taste tears.

A large rat put his head out of a hole, long dusty, and peered into the room.

The children were going to rise and go to bed soon. The bodies of the mourners had that half-sorrowful, half-bored look of people who do something that hurts too long.

Presently the rat took hold of the scarf and trotted away with it into the darkness of the beyond.

One thing only had the undertaker forgotten to do; he had failed to remove the cotton from the ears of the dead man, who had suffered from earache.

Renunciation

SKIRL PAVET leaned forward, resting his head against the back of the pew; he wanted to look up but he dared not.

His prayer had been said long ago before he had slid to his knees; now he kept his head bowed not to be in the way of other people's prayers.

He fumbled in the dark for his hymn book and could not find it. He contented himself by feeling of the sole of his boot where a hole was coming.

The dim church and the odor of incense seemed to him to be quite wonderful, a sort of darkened sachet for pain. Here one shook out the garments of sin and if they could not be cleansed at least they could be perfumed. He'd heard that chorus girls did something like this— used cologne water when they hadn't time for the next curtain.

The high ceiling looked like an inverted mold to Skirl, a place where formless, terrible and ugly things were made beautiful. He crossed himself thinking about this and his trouble, looking around a little furtively with his yellow eyes set in pale firm wrinkles, like new flowers.

He could see the altar far away at the end of his supplication, its two incense burners sending up slow thin threads of scented smoke on either side of the scarlet figure of the priest.

Skirl Pavet looked into this distance, thinking how much this altar resembled a dressing table—a dressing table for the soul—and that scarlet priest like a lovely red autumn leaf blow up against that polished thing of wood, with its great open Bible. He moved like a leaf too, here, there, as if he were trying to play a song and couldn't find the tune.

He raised his face toward the picture of the Virgin. He liked her look of dawning innocence. There was the figure on the cross, that too was beautiful, like a splendid pathetic fruit—some super-effort of nature—yet somehow too sorrowful to pluck.

The sun beating upon the stained glass of the windows threw colored lights face down upon the floor, and this was like sunlight in a forest. Everything seemed like a forest to Skirl, a great dense wood; a place where everything was in bloom—sorrow was in bloom, and repentance and hope and virtue and sin.

He thought how sweet a thing sin was. It was so fine and strong and universal. All the bowed heads with their moving mouths were impelled by sin. Sin rushed by his neck in two fine acrid streams. It was like the odor of a tanning factory where leather is made. He moved his lips also now, but only because he was troubled into nervousness about the gap left by a tooth that had loosened that morning.

He saw figures moving about; people were leaving,

some of them came out of their pews on one leg, bent on it and went away quickly. He smiled a little and got up also. Two men and a woman were dipping their hands in the holy water and, waiting until they were within the shadow of the pillar, they crossed themselves.

He dipped his own thick hand and touched himself four times, looking about slowly at the frightened people; he splashed himself comfortably, as a bird bathes in a public puddle, throwing up myriad drops of water.

He was not ashamed, and he dried his short fingers as he descended the steps.

He remembered, now that he was in the sunlight, that he had been praying for strength, for a terrible kind of enduring strength, a fulfillment of a possible power that might have been his had he wished it, long ago.

His acknowledgment that sin was beautiful and strong was only another way of saying farewell intelligently and gratefully to what he had been, toward what he had done, giving way to what he must now do, must now be, with a sort of superb charm, a subtle and philosophic bow.

Skirl Pavet was returning after twenty-five years of absence to his wife and to his home. He pictured to himself the old house, the familiar street, the former acquaintances. Most of those people who had known him would have forgotten his name by now, even his nickname, even his pet name. They would fumble in obscure and forgotten corners for it, searching his face for a clue to the peculiarity that had given him names of any kind. He was returning with a sharp desire and a sharp dread. He knew how many windows there were to the kitchen, but he could not remember just how his wife's hands felt.

He looked away into the tall intricacies of New York's roofs. He thought back to a day when the first robin called him from the city and the quick hard life of competition. He dreamed slowly as he turned downtown.

Strange, that he, a Pole, should be here. He looked at the sky through sudden tears. Strange too that he should be setting his face toward home and those things that had broken him, driving him like a leaf in a forest, shaken loose from its branch, stumbling in among the trunks of alien trees, beating its way toward the open, finding the fields at last, only to creep among strong growing green things, to flutter helplessly over full round stretches of earth, slowly dying, become brittle, growing brown and melancholy and still more agile, till finally—

Strange the he, Skirl Pavet, whose lips had touched every holy image in Poland, had spread themselves on many an ikon's glass, had settled about many a cross, should come to this at last. To this dry renouncing of all his youth's sap and its sweetness, of all his wander-love, of his freedom. How wonderful it had been. What throats the Finnish girls had, what hands the English!

He stumbled over an unevenness in the pavement, and turned looking into the face of the crowd. Dark faces and pale, some stupid, some gay. An officer passed swinging his cane, jangling the little spur-chains that passed under his boots.

Skirl dropped his hands at his sides swinging them

slowly; he always did this when he was perplexed, it gave him a feeling of such hopelessness that something would have to happen to him, something would have to come to relieve him of this awful stupidity, this idle dreaming weariness.

He thought of Polly, his wife, a middle-sized woman, with stout knees and full lips too colorless and amiable. He remembered that her nose set in well at the corners, and he reflected that this type always grow stout. She had always been a good natured woman, but mundane, jocose.

She was the daughter of a western hotel keeper. He went back over his first meeting with her. She was a favorite in the family and would have been quite spoiled, had she been quick, apprehensive or sharp. As it was she smiled at those who petted her, flourishing under kindness like a kitten, and like a kitten missed it not at all when it ceased. He had gone out there because he had heard of the opportunities the West afforded; he had come back empty-handed with this buxom fresh-faced Polly—daughter of a hotel keeper. She soon fell into the old business, opened a restaurant in the early Thirties, near Seventh Avenue, and from that time he began to grow restless.

That was long ago. He thought of it now, moving his nose in quick successive shivers of savory memories, closing his eyes, trying to recall the pattern in the carpet one had to cross before one came to the table. Two crouching dragons, a square and two crouching dragons reversed—was that it, or had he made a mistake about the whole design. He puzzled his mind about the way she used her English; she had strange tricks with little words, a manner with her lips; he could not recall what words, what manner.

She used to sit at a long table with their oldest patrons, stout, middle-aged, stupid men. Some were dry goods merchants, some were tailors, one was a banker, another a broker.

Later when the lunch crowd had gone, the cooks and the waiters would sit at another long table in the rear, in white caps and aprons, talking slowly, softly about the making of butter sauce, of tripe *sauté*.

He smiled suddenly recalling the name of the chef, Bradley, that was a strange name. He had no teeth and his ample jowl swung in great satisfied rhythms, while a small moustache rose and fell on the sunken upper lip.

And there was Sammie, who always peered into the syrup and milk jugs, sighing and shaking his head at the manner in which they both emptied, hurrying with his food, moving his body, his arms never still, in a passion to be at the remainder of the meal before it should be lost in the stomachs that surrounded him.

Skirl had called this sordid, dirty. He had always loved the country, the open fields, the smell of spring, like the breath of a dear one after months of dreary death. The sense of buds breaking and the early rains that took liberty with the newly-sown flower beds, chasing small particles of loam into hurrying rivulets, making an effort to drag something back with them into the bowels of the earth. The sound of animals running through bramble and swamp, the crackling of little hoofs in the twigs, and the odor of new calves with moist hair. And this had been the argument he had used against her, excusing himself for going away, to have his fill of life, love, the earth.

He had a child of his own, but he had forgotten that too, laid it aside, put it back in his memory to bring out when it should please him, with the tranquillity of one who takes what he desires, never quite relinquishing what he does not, holding it to make it serve in time of need. Polly had brought it up to its fourth year with comfortable and hearty slaps on its plump, glowing cheeks, with many an apprehensive face as she picked it up, fondling it, pinching it on either side of its little wet mouth, squealing at it, becoming intoxicated with the excitement and energy of mothers who like their own; kissing its tiny white teeth, and finally, standing hands on hips, would watch it as it crawled away saying: "Isn't he a beggar?" making those animal noises that save the child from too early terror of civilization.

He had pretended to be jealous of the fat comfortable men with whom Polly sat, cracking nuts, laughing, though he knew well enough that it was part of the business of a restaurant keeper to be amiable with the guests. But somehow he didn't like the way she got their histories out of them. This he really resented. He felt that he was the only person that Polly should know all about, that where other men bought their clothes, met their brides or took their sorrows, were things about which Polly should not be curious. He resented the way these well-fed gentlemen would move back from the table, puffing out their cheeks, snapping bands from cigars, sprawling as if to say "This is an excellent place to dine, but a better place to rest."

He resented their comfortable sighs, their after-dinner circular movement of the closed mouth, their persistent heavy smoking. He hated their laughter, he hated their satisfaction with the city, the dirty streets, their tiring, dull trades. This wasn't life. He felt then that they had been swamping him, drawing in on him, killing him with gross layers of flesh, moving over and around him like a boat full of restlessly dying fish.

And because of these things, he had prayed for strength, strength to keep away from all he loved, strength to go back to all that hurt and smothered him, to renounce all, that he might end his days at last with this woman who had always been kindly, stupid, amused. To leave those others who were young and bright and who understood.

There was Ollie, tall splendid Ollie with her strange large eyes and her way of saying, "You'll not forget me, my little man."

She had been the one real passion of his life, he thought, but he had not stayed long with her. There were others, sweet women, warm, gentle creatures—all but one who had slapped his face one night in Java.

He didn't mind now, he was glad that his face would tingle with any memory, such things were seasoning to the great seasonless mass that is a man before he has loved.

He knew that he had not always been happy, perhaps he would admit that to Polly when he returned, she might be glad to know that there were times when he had missed her, had even compared her with others. He liked admitting things to Polly, she always looked cheerful and nodded, seeming to say, "That's right, keep alive."

That was the strange thing about Polly, she never resented, never rebuked, did not even seem to think what he did strange; a sort of philosophy that had its culminating belief in just that "Keep alive,"—sensing that any way people kept alive was a sort of excuse in itself.

This was a lower way of looking at it, perhaps, but it had often comforted him. Even in those days when lying awake in the four-posted bed of yellow wood, in the garret whose roofs nearly touched his head, he had decided that he wanted no other shelter than the sky.

How he felt again the soft blankets of that bed against his unshaven chin, the cool edge of the sharp sheets that he could never bear against his throat, a feeling as if he were going to be strangled, beheaded!

He had written to Polly after these twenty-five years of absence and she had written him to come. Would she really be glad to see him? It must be that, for she had no real curiosity, no comparative valuation, no desire to put one and one together to make up the whole of the fabric of life, portions, edges were enough for her. She had no other reason than just that, to let him return when he wanted to.

And suddenly there came over him a hot flush because he knew how good she was, had always been.

And the boy he would be far along in the twenties, grown up. Yet he could not visualize him. He held his hand up in the air on a level with his shoulder. People stopped, turned around, smiled. He colored and lowered it. There was where his boy would stand. Of course the people could not know what he was thinking. It was just a gesture that he had to make to feel in some way the passage of time.

He must be good to him now, must devote the rest of his life to him and to her. No more turning aside, no more running after nature, no more appreciation of lovely throats, hands, faces.

He knew how weak he was, what his passions were, great overwhelming passions, and Ollie lived here, very near his own house—and he had cared—

Well, that was the reason why he had prayed—prayed for strength to keep him straight for wisdom—to shut his eyes on everything but the inner self, on everything but those things of home that were his.

He was a Pole and he loved his God, and he recalled again the picture of the Virgin and the image of Christ taking that downward course of all things that sorrow— tears, flesh—and he thought of all the holy images of other countries that had become stained with the mark of his great caressing mouth.

He was very tired, he did not know that he could be so tired. He had walked these few blocks so many times in the past, and they had not tired him, and he remembered that he had been tired when he knelt to pray.

And then he was in their street, at their door, turning

the knob, walking in, and he seemed to have been away only yesterday, and the geranium flowering in the pots were those he had planted there a sun before, and the table full of stout gentlemen were those he had hated but a dawn away. And there was Polly, rising, scattering crumbs, smiling, a little stouter, gay, mundane, jocose.

And the table at the far end was surrounded by a pack of white-capped, white-aproned cooks and waiters. Only Bradley was not there, someone with a small and narrow chin had the place of honor, and no one jumped up to look into the syrup and milk pitchers.

He asked questions hurriedly to keep from losing all of his past at once, for what he had been but yesterday seemed suddenly to be less than a dream. And less than a mist were the splendid days he had spent with Ollie in Huntington, a little town through whose streets gray-faced clerks hurried, gathering at lunch time about the low ivy-covered stone wall that skirted the cemetery. Birds were in the grass then and there the lovers dodged the eyes of acquaintances behind the decaying symbol on some old stone that had expressed a person's love for a person long gone.

And she, Ollie had thrown back her naked arms into the grass behind her head talking of a new gingham gown, of the colored post cards that were being sold to the countryside, little pictures of the mill, of the church, of the library—well—

He asked about old acquaintances too and Polly answered him smiling whimsically, telling of her life; how the son of one of their customers had taken a commission and was already at sea, and how Tessie had taken ill and passed away in the fall.

*

Finally he sat on the edge of his bed. Coming back had been so easy, he remembered now how her hand felt. The way she twisted her mouth, he had always known somehow, was toward the left, and her western accent was quite a thing of his life.

And the boy?

The boy was married.

He hadn't thought of that.

He fumbled in his pocket for his pipe, found it and looking around at the old rafters and the four-posted bed, sighed. Polly was stouter, much, and yet only by a double chin was she strange to him.

He closed his eyes. He had prayed for strength—Polly was getting his slippers, and an inertia seemed to leave him powerless to get them for himself. Then he reached for them hurriedly.

"And Ollie?"

"Her granddaughter was christened last June."

He looked away into the street from the dirty little oblong pane.

"Let me put them on, you can't bend so easily as once, Skirl."

"I prayed today—down on my knees—" still he reached out a stockinged foot. He was almost nodding, he laughed a little, contentedly.

But later, turning his face to the wall, crossing himself with one finger, his eyes shed tears. He could hear Polly talking downstairs to the help, clattering with the pans, but he was tired and he dozed.

A Night Among the Horses

TOWARD DUSK, in the summer of the year, a man in evening dress, carrying a top hat and a cane, crept on hands and knees through the underbrush bordering the pastures of the Buckler estate. His wrists hurt him from holding his weight and he sat down. Sticky ground-vines fanned out all about him; they climbed the trees, the posts of the fence, they were everywhere. He peered through the thickly tangled branches and saw, standing against the darkness, a grove of white birch shimmering like teeth in a skull.

He could hear the gate grating on its hinge as the wind clapped. His heart moved with the movement of the earth. A frog puffed forth its croaking immemoried cry; the man struggled for breath, the air was heavy and hot; he was nested in astonishment.

He wanted to drowse off; instead he placed his hat and cane beside him, straightening his coat tails, lying out on his back, waiting. Something quick was moving the ground. It began to shake with sudden warning and he wondered if it was his heart.

A lamp in the far away window winked as the boughs swung against the wind; the odor of crushed grasses mingling with the faint reassuring smell of dung, fanned up and drawled off to the north; he opened his mouth, drawing in the ends of his moustache.

The tremor lengthened, it ran beneath his body and tumbled away into the earth.

He sat upright. Putting on his hat, he braced his cane against the ground between his out-thrust legs. Now he not only felt the trembling of the earth but caught the muffled horny sound of hooves smacking the turf, as a friend strikes the back of a friend, hard, but without malice. They were on the near side now as they took the curve of the Willow road. He pressed his forehead against the bars of the fence.

The soft menacing sound deepened as heat deepens; the horses, head-on, roared by him, their legs rising and falling like savage needles taking purposeless stitches.

He saw their bellies pitching from side to side, racking the bars of the fence as they swung past. On his side of the barrier he rose up running, following, gasping. His foot caught in the trailing pine and he pitched forward, striking his head on a stump as he went down. Blood trickled from his scalp. Like a red mane it ran into his eyes and he stroked it back with the knuckles of his hand, as he put on his hat. In this position the pounding hoofs shook him like a child on a knee.

Presently he searched for his cane; he found it snared in the fern. A wax Patrick-pipe brushed against his cheek, he ran his tongue over it, snapping it in two. Move as he would, the grass was always under him, crackling with twigs and cones. An acorn fell out of the soft dropping powders of the wood. He took it up, and as he held it between finger and thumb, his mind raced over the scene back there with the mistress of the house, for what else could one call Freda Buckler but "the mistress of the house," that small fiery woman, with a battery for a heart and the body of a toy, who ran everything, who purred, saturated with impudence, with a mechanical buzz that ticked away her humanity.

He blew down his moustache. Freda, with that aggravating floating yellow veil! He told her it was "aggravating," he told her that it was "shameless," and stood for nothing but temptation. He puffed out his cheeks, blowing at her as she passed. She laughed, stroking his arm, throwing her head back, her nostrils scarlet to the pit. They had ended by riding out together, a boot's length apart, she no bigger than a bee on a bonnet. In complete misery he had dug down on his spurs, and she: "Gently, John, gently!" showing the edges of her teeth in the wide distilling mouth. "You can't be ostler *all* your life. Horses!" she snorted. "I like horses, but—" He had lowered his crop. "There are other things. You simply can't go on being a groom forever, not with a waist like that, and you know it. I'll make a gentleman out of you. I'll step you up from being a 'thing'. You will see, you will enjoy it."

He had leaned over and lashed at her boot with his whip. It caught her at the knee, the foot flew up in its stirrup, as though she were dancing.

And the little beast was delighted! They trotted on a way, and they trotted back. He helped her to dismount, and she sailed off, trailing the yellow veil, crying back:

"You'll love it!"

Before they had gone on like this for more than a month (bowling each other over in the spirit, wringing each other this way and that, hunter and hunted) it had become a game without any pleasure; debased lady, debased ostler, on the wings of vertigo.

What was she getting him into? He shouted, bawled, cracked whip—what did she figure she wanted? The kind of woman who can't tell the truth; truth ran out and away from her as though her veins wore pipettes, stuck in by the devil; and drinking, he swelled, and pride had him, it floated him off. He saw her standing behind him in every mirror, she followed him from show-piece to show-piece, she fell in beside him, walked him, hand under elbow.

"You will rise to governor-general—well, to inspector—"

"Inspector!"

"As you like, say master of the regiment—say cavalry officer. Horses, too, leather, whips—"

"O my God."

She almost whinnied as she circled on her heels:

"With a broad, flat, noble chest," she said, "you'll become a pavement of honors...Mass yourself. You will leave affliction—"

"Stop it!" he shouted. "I *like* being common."

"With a quick waist like that, the horns will miss you."

"What horns?"

"The dilemma."

"I *could* stop you, all over, if I wanted to."

She was amused. "Man in a corner?" she said.

She tormented him, she knew it. She tormented him with her objects of "culture." One knee on an ottoman, she would hold up and out, the most delicate miniature, ivories cupped in her palm, tilting them from the sun, saying: "But look, look!"

He put his hands behind his back. She aborted that. She asked him to hold ancient missals, volumes of fairy tales, all with handsome tooling, all bound in corded russet. She spread maps, and with a long hatpin dragging across mountains and ditches, pointed to "just where she had been." Like a dry snail the point wandered the coast, when abruptly, sticking the steel in, she cried "*Borgia!*" and stood there, jangling a circle of ancient keys.

His anxiety increased with curiosity. *If* he married her—after he *had* married her, what then? Where would he be after he had satisfied her crazy whim? What would she make of him in the end; in short, what would she leave of him? Nothing, absolutely nothing, not even his horses. Here'd be a damned fool for you. He wouldn't fit in anywhere after Freda, he'd be neither what he was nor what he had been; he'd be a *thing*, half standing, half crouching, like those figures under the roofs of historic buildings, the halt position of the damned.

He had looked at her often without seeing her; after a while he began to look at her with great attention. Well, well! Really a small mousy woman, with fair pretty hair that fell like an insect's feelers into the nape of her neck, moving when the wind moved. She darted and bobbled about too much, and always with the mindless intensity of a mechanical toy kicking and raking about the floor.

And she was always a step or two ahead of him, or stroking his arm at arm's length, or she came at him in a gust, leaning her sharp little chin on his shoulder, floating away slowly—only to be stumbled over when he turned. On this particular day he had caught her by the wrist, slewing her around. This once, he thought to himself, this once I'll ask her straight out for truth; a direct shot might dislodge her.

"Miss Freda, just a moment. You know I haven't a friend in the world. You know positively that I haven't a person to whom I can go and get an answer to any question of any sort. So then, just what *do* you want me for?"

She blushed to the roots of her hair. "Girlish! are you going to be girlish?" She looked as if she were going to scream, her whole frame buzzed, but she controlled herself and drawled with lavish calm:

"Don't be nervous. Be patient. You will get used to everything. You'll even like it. There's nothing so enjoyable as climbing."

"And then?"

"Then everything will slide away, stable and all." She

caught the wings of her nose in the pinching folds of a lace handkerchief. "Isn't that a destination?"

The worst of all had been the last night, the evening of the masked ball. She had insisted on his presence. "Come" she said, "just as you are, and be our whipper-in." That was the final blow, the unpardonable insult. He had obeyed, except that he did not come "just as he was." He made an elaborate toilet; he dressed for evening, like any ordinary gentleman; he was the only person present therefore who was not "in dress," that is, in the accepted sense.

On arrival he found most of the guests tipsy. Before long he himself was more than a little drunk and horrified to find that he was dancing a minuet, stately, slow, with a great soft puff-paste of a woman, showered with sequins, grunting in cascades of plaited tulle. Out of this embrace he extricated himself, slipping on the bare spots of the rosin-powdered floor, to find Freda coming at him with a tiny glass of cordial which she poured into his open mouth; at that point he was aware that he had been gasping for air.

He came to a sudden stop. He took in the whole room with his frantic glance. There in the corner sat Freda's mother with her cats. She always sat in corners and she always sat with cats. And there was the rest of the cast—cousins, nephews, uncles, aunts. The next moment, the *galliard*. Freda, arms up, hands, palm out, elbows buckled in at the breast, a praying mantis, was all but tooth to

253

tooth with him. Wait! He stepped free, and with the knob end of his cane, he drew a circle in the rosin clear around her, then backward went through the French windows.

He knew nothing after that until he found himself in the shrubbery, sighing, his face close to the fence, peering in. He was with his horses again; he was where he belonged again. He could hear them tearing up the sod, galloping about as though in their own ballroom, and oddest of all, at this dark time of the night.

He began drawing himself under the lowest bar, throwing his hat and cane in before him, panting as he crawled. The black stallion was now in the lead. The horses were taking the curve in the Willow road that ran into the farther pasture, and through the dust they looked faint and enormous.

On the top of the hill, four had drawn apart and were standing, testing the weather. He would catch one, mount one, he would escape! He was no longer afraid. He stood up, waving his hat and cane and shouting.

They did not seem to know him and they swerved past him and away. He stared after them, almost crying. He did not think of his dress, the white shirt front, the top hat, the waving stick, his abrupt rising out of the dark, their excitement. Surely they must know him—in a moment.

Wheeling, manes up, nostrils flaring, blasting out steam as they came on, they passed him in a whinnying flood, and he damned them in horror, but what he shouted was "Bitch!," and found himself swallowing fire from his heart, lying on his face, sobbing, "I *can* do it, damn everything, I can get on with it; I can make my mark!"

The upraised hooves of the first horse missed him, the second did not.

Presently the horses drew apart, nibbling and swishing their tails, avoiding a patch of tall grass.

The Valet

T HE FIELD S about Louis-Georges' house grew green
in very early spring, leaving the surrounding countryside
to its melancholy gray, for Louis-Georges was the only
farmer who sowed his fields to rye.

Louis-Georges was a small man with a dark oval face
that burned like a Goya and supported a long raking nose
in which an hoar-frost of hair bristled. His arms swung
their stroke ahead of his legs; his whole person knew who
he was—that sort.

He had fierce pride in everything he did, even when
not too well executed, not too well comprehended; he
himself was so involved in it.

Sometimes standing in the yard, breathing the rich air,
nose up, he enjoyed his lands utterly, rubbing the fingers
of one hand with the fingers of the other, or waving the
hands above the horns of his cattle where, in buzzing
loops, flies hung, or slapping the haunches of his racers,
saying to the trainer: "There's more breeding in the rump
of one of these, than any butt in the stalls of Westminster!"
—pretending that he understood all points from muzzle
to hoof—in short, a man who all but had a "hand in being."

Sometimes he and Vera Sovna would play hide-and-seek about the grain bins and through the mounds of hay, she in her long flounces and high heels, screaming and leaping among the rakes and flails.

Once Louis-Georges caught a rat, bare hand, and with such skill that it could not use its teeth. He disguised his elation, showing her how it was done, pretending it a cunning he had learned in order to protect the winter grain.

Vera Sovna was a tall creature with thin shoulders which she shrugged as if the blades were too heavy. She usually dressed in black, and she laughed a good part of the time in a rather high key.

She had been the great friend of Louis-Georges' mother, but since the mother's death she had, by her continued intimacy, fallen into disrepute. It was whispered that she was "something" to Louis-Georges. When the landholders saw her enter his house, they could not contain themselves until they saw her leave it; if she came out holding her skirts carefully above her ankles, they found the roofs of their mouths with disapproving tongues; if she walked slowly, dragging her dress, they would say: "What a dust she brings up in the driveway!"

If she knew anything of their feelings she did not show it. Driving through the town, turning neither to right nor left, she passed right through the market square, looking at nobody, but obviously delighted with the rosy bunches of flowers, the bright tumble of yellow squash and green cucumbers, the fruits piled in orderly heaps on the stands. But on the rare occasions when Louis-Georges accompanied her, she would cross her legs at the knee, or lean forward, or shake a finger at him, or turn her head from side to side, or lean back laughing.

Sometimes she visited the maids' quarters to play with Leah's child, a little creature with bandy legs and frail neck, who thrust out his stomach for her to pat.

The maids, Berthe and Leah, were well-built complacent women with serene blue eyes, fine teeth and round firm busts that flourished like pippins. They went about their duties chewing stalks of rye and salad leaves, reefing with their tongues.

In her youth Leah had evidently done something for which she now prayed at intervals, usually before a wooden Christ, hanging from a beam in the barn, who was so familiar that she did not notice Him until, sitting down to milk, she raised her eyes; then, putting her forehead against the cow's belly, she prayed, the milk splashing over her big knuckles and wasting into the ground, until Berthe came to help her carry the pails, when she would remark, "We are going to have rain."

Vera Sovna spent hours in the garden, the child crawling after her, leaving the marks of his small hands, wet with saliva, on the dusty leaves; digging up young vegetable roots with such sudden ease that he would fall on his back, blinking up at the sun.

The two maids, the valet Vanka, and Louis-Georges were the household, except when augmented by the occasional visits of Louis-Georges' aunts, Myra and Ella.

Vanka was Russian. He bit his nails. He wore his

clothes badly, as though he had no time for more than the master's neatness. His rich yellow hair was dishevelled though pomaded, his eyebrows shaggy and white. His eyes, when he raised their heavy lids, were gentle and intelligent. He was absolutely devoted.

Louis-Georges would say to him, "Now, Vanka, tell me again what it was they did to you when you were a boy."

"They shot my brother," Vanka would answer, pulling at his forelock. "They shot him for a 'red.' They threw him into prison with my father. Then one day my sister, who took them their food in two pails, heard a noise; it sounded like a shot and that day father returned only one pail, and they say he returned it like a person looking over his shoulder." Vanka told that story often, sometimes adding with a sigh, "My sister, who had been a handsome woman (the students used to visit her just to hear her talk)—became bald—overnight."

After such confidences, Louis-Georges would shut himself up in his study where, in a large scrawling hand, he wrote to his aunts. Sometimes he would put in a phrase or two about Vanka.

Sometimes Vera Sovna would come in to watch, lifting her ruffles, raising her brows. If Vanka was present they would stare each other down, she with her back to the fireplace, her heels apart, saying:

"Come, come, that is enough!" adding, "Vanka, take his pen away."

Louis-Georges went on, smiling and grunting, but

never lifting his hand from his written page. As for Vanka, he simply stood catching the pages as they were finished.

Finally with a loud scrape and a great shove, Louis-Georges would push back his chair and standing up would say, "Now, let us have tea."

In the end he fell into a slow illness. It attacked his limbs; he was forced to walk with a cane. He complained of his heart, but he persisted in going out to look at the horses, and to amuse Vera Sovna he would slash at the flies with his stick, enjoying the odor of milk and dung.

He had plans for the haying, for getting in the crops, but he had to give over to the farm hands who, left to themselves, wandered off at any odd hour, to their own acres, to their own broken fences.

Six months later Louis-Georges took to his bed.

The aunts came, testing the rate of decay with their leathery noses, as they portioned out paregoric, like women in charge of a baby, remarking to each other with surprise, "He never used to be like this," easing the velvet straps that bit into their shoulder flesh, peering at each other, from either side of his bed.

They were afraid of meeting Vera Sovna. Their position was difficult. Having been on friendly terms with her while Louis-Georges' mother was alive, they felt that once the old lady was dead, they had to increase in dignity and reserve. Then, too, the townsfolk seemed to have turned against Vera. Still, the aunts did not wish to be too harsh, so they left Louis-Georges' bedside for an hour every evening that Vera Sovna might come to see him, and Vera

Sovna came, creeping softly and saying, "Oh, my *dear!*"
She would tell him stories, told before, all about her own
life, as if that life, not yet spent, might be of help. She told
him of her week in London, of a visit to The Hague; of
adventures with hotel keepers in impossible inns, and
sometimes, leaning close to him, he thought he heard her
weeping.

But in spite of this—the illness and the tension in the
air—Vera Sovna seemed strangely gay.

During the foundering of Louis-Georges, Leah and
Berthe served as nurses, changing his sheets, turning him
over to rub him with oil and alcohol, crossing themselves
and giving him the spoon.

The valet stood at the foot of the bed trying not to
cough or sigh or annoy his master in any way. But sometimes he would fall asleep holding to the bedpost, and
wake to dreams of the "revolution," a dream which faded
as he caught himself.

Vera Sovna had taken to dining with the girls in the
kitchen, a long bare room that pleased her. From the window one could see the orchard and the pump and the
long easy slope of the meadow. From the beams braided
onions and smoked meats dangled over the long table,
strewn with a thin snow of flour, and hot loaves of new
bread.

The girls accepted Vera Sovna's company cheerfully.
When she went away, they cleared the board, talking of
other things, sharpening knives, forgetting.

The matters of the estate went on as usual. Nothing

suffered because of the master's infirmity. Crops ripened, the haying season passed; the orchard sounded with the thud of falling fruit. Louis-Georges ripened into death, detached, as if he had never been. About Vera Sovna there was a quiet brilliance. She tended the medicine bottles as though they were musical intervals; she arranged him bouquets as though they were tributes. And Vanka?

There was the one who took on utter anguish, he bent under the shortening shadow of his master as one at last permitted the use of grief for himself.

Myra and Ella in shock, shook crumbs from their laps, sending each other in to visit Louis-Georges, and pretending, each to the other, he was much improved. It was not that they were afraid he might die, they were afraid they were not prepared.

When the doctor arrived they shifted their uncertainty. They rushed about getting subscriptions filled, spoons polished; they closed their eyes, sitting on either side of his bed, picturing him already shriven and translated, in order to find pleasure in opening their eyes to find him just as usual.

When they knew that he was dying indeed, the aunts could not keep from touching him. They tried to cover him up in those parts that too plainly exposed the rate of his departure; the thin arms, the damp pulsing spot in the neck, the fallen pit of his stomach. They fondled his knuckles and generally drove the doctor and the new nurse frantic. At last, in desperation, Myra, eluding everyone, knelt by Louis-Georges and stroked his face.

Death did not seem to be anywhere; that is, it did not seem to stay in one place, but with her caresses, seemed to move from quarter to quarter. At this point, she was locked out with her sister. They wandered up and down the hall, afraid to speak, unable to cry, passing each other, bracing their palms against the walls.

Then when Louis-Georges did die, there was the problem of Vera Sovna. However, they soon forgot her, trying to follow the instructions left by the dead man. Louis-Georges had seen to it that everything should go on as usual; he would not interrupt the seasons, he had "planned" next year.

The hens praised their eggs as usual, as usual the stables resounded with good spirits. The fields shed their very life upon the earth, and Vanka folded and put away the dead man's clothes.

When the undertaker arrived, Vanka would not let him touch the body. He washed and dressed it himself. It was he who laid Louis-Georges in the shining coffin that smelled like violin rosin; it was he who banked the flowers, and he who finally left the scene, on the whole flat of his suddenly clumsy feet. He went to his room and shut the door.

He paced. It seemed to him that he had left something undone. He loved service and order; he loved Louis-Georges who had made service necessary and order desirable. This made him rub his palms together, holding them close to his sighing mouth, as if the sound might teach him some secret of silence. Of course Leah had made a scene, hardly to be wondered at, considering. She had brought her baby in, dropping him beside the body, giving her first order: "You can play together, now, for a minute.

Vanka had not interfered. The child had been too frightened to disturb the arranged excellence of Louis-Georges' leavetaking, and both the child and mother soon left the room in stolid calm. Vanka could hear them descend to the lower parts of the house, the deliberate thump of Leah, the quick clatter of the child.

Walking to his room, Vanka could hear the trees beating the wind; an owl called from the barn, a mare whinnied, stomped and dropped her head back into her bin. Vanka opened the window. He thought he caught the sound of feet on the pebbled border that rounded the hydrangea bushes; a faint perfume, such as arose from the dancing flounces of Vera Sovna's dress seemed to hang in the air. Irritated, he turned away; then he heard her calling.

"Vanka," she said, "come, my foot is caught in the vine."

Her face, with its open mouth came up above the sill, and the next moment she jumped into the room. And there they stood, looking at each other. They had never been alone before. He did not know what to do.

She was a little dishevelled; twigs clung to the flounces of her skirts. She raised both shoulders and sighed; she reached out her hand and said his name.

"Vanka."

He moved away from her, staring.

"Vanka," she repeated, and came close to him, leaning on his arm. With great simplicity she said, "You must tell me everything."

"I'll tell you," he answered automatically.

"Look, your hands!" Suddenly she dropped her head into his palms. He shivered; he drew his hands away.

"Oh, look, you fortunate man!" she cried. "Most fortunate man, most elected Vanka! He let you touch him, close, close, near the skin, near the heart. You knew how he looked, how he stood, how the ankle went into the foot!"—he had ceased to hear her, he was so astonished—"his shoulders, how they set. You dressed and undressed him. You knew him, all of him for years. Tell me—tell me, what was he like?"

He turned. "I will tell you," he said, "if you are still, if you will sit down, if you are quiet."

She sat down: she watched him with great joy.

"His arms were too long," he said, "but you know that, you could see that, but beautiful; and his back, his spine, tapering slender, full of breeding—"

Spillway

BEHIND TWO SPANKING HORSES, in the heat of noon, rode Julie Anspacher. The air was full of the sound of windlasses and well water, and full too of the perfumed spindrift of flowers, and Julie stared as the road turned into the remembered distance.

The driver, an old Scandinavian and a friend of the family, who knew exactly two folk tales, one having to do with a partridge, the other with a woman, sat stiffly on his box, holding the reins slack over the sleek-rumped mares; he was whistling the score of the story about the partridge, rocking slowly on his sturdy base, and drifting back with the tune came the strong herb-like odor of hide, smarting under straining leather.

The horses began ascending the hill, moving their ears, racking down their necks. Reaching the ridge, they bounded forward in a whirl of sparks and dust. The driver, still rigid, still whistling, taking in rein in a last flourish, raised the whipstock high in the air, setting it smartly into its socket. In a deep-pitched voice he said, "It's some time since we have seen you, Mrs. Anspacher."

Julie raised her long face from her collar and nodded.

"Yes," she said shortly, and frowned.

"Your husband has gathered in the corn already, and the orchards are hanging heavy."

266

"Are they?" She tried to recall how many trees were of apple and pear.

The driver changed hands on the reins, turned around: "It's good to see you again, Mrs. Anspacher." He said it so simply, with such hearty pleasure, that Julie laughed outright.

"Is it," she answered, then checked herself, fixing her angry eyes straight ahead.

The child sitting at her side, loose limbed from excessive youth, lifted her face up, on which a small aquiline nose perched with comic boldness. She half held, half dropped an old-fashioned ermine muff, the tails of which stuck out in all directions. She looked excited.

"You remember Mrs. Berling?" the driver went on. "She married again."

"Did she?"

"Yes, ma'am, she did."

He began to tell her of a vacancy in the office for outgoing mails, taken by her husband's nephew.

"Corruption!" she snorted.

The child started, then looked quickly away as children do when they expect something and do not understand what. The driver brought the whip down on the horses, left and right; a line of froth appeared along the edges of the trappings.

"You were saying, Mrs. Anspacher?"

"I was saying nothing. I said, all is lost from the beginning, if we only knew it—always."

The child looked up at her, then down into her muff.

"Ann," said Julie Anspacher suddenly, lifting the muff

away from the child. "Did you ever see such big horses before?"

The child turned her head with brightness and bending down tried to see between the driver's arms.

"Are they yours?" she whispered.

"You don't have to whisper," Julie said. She took a deep breath, stretching the silk of her shirtwaist across her breasts. "And no, they are not mine, but we have two—bigger—blacker—"

"Can I see them?"

"Of course you will see them—don't be ridiculous!"

The child shrank into herself, clutching nervously at her muff. Julie Anspacher returned to her reflections.

It was almost five years since Mrs. Anspacher had been home. Five years before, in just such an autumn, the doctors had given her six months to live…one lung gone, the other going. They sometimes call it the "white death," sometimes the "love disease." She coughed a little, remembering, and the child at her side coughed too, as if in echo. The driver, puckering his forehead, reflected that Mrs. Anspacher was not cured.

She was thirty-nine; she should have died at thirty-four. In those five years of grace her husband Paytor had seen her five times, coming in over fourteen hours of rail, at Christmastide. He cursed the doctors, called them fools, and each time asked her when she was coming home.

The house appeared, dull white against locust trees.

Smoke, the lazy smoke that rises in the autumn in a straight column, rose up into an empty sky as the driver pulled the horses in, their foaming jaws gagging at the bit. Julie Anspacher jumped the side of the carriage at a bound, the short modish tails of her jacket dancing above her hips. She turned around, thrusting her black gloved hands under the child, lifting her to the path. A dog barked somewhere as they turned in at the gate.

A maid in a dust-cap put her head out of a window, clucked, drew it in and slammed the sash. Paytor, with slow, deliberate steps, moved across the gravel toward his wife and the child.

He was a man of middle height with a close cropped beard that ended in a grey wedge on his chin. He was sturdy, pompous, and walked with his knees out, giving him a rocking, dependable gait; he had grave eyes and a firm mouth. He was slightly surprised. He raised the apricot-colored veil that hid Julie's face, and leaning, kissed her on both cheeks.

"And where does the child come from?" he inquired, touching the little girl's chin.

"Come along, don't be ridiculous," Julie said impatiently, and swept on toward the house.

He hurried after her. "I am so glad to see you," he said, trying to keep up with her long swinging stride, that all but lifted the child off her feet in a trotting stumble.

"Tell me what the doctors said—cured?"

There was happiness in his voice as he went on: "Not that I really care *what* they think—I always predicted a ripe old age for you, didn't I? What were the doctors' methods in regard to Marie Bashkirtseff, I ask you? They locked her up in a dark room with all the windows shut—and so of course she died—that was the method then; now it's Koch's tuberculin—and that's all nonsense too. It's good fresh air does the trick."

"It has worked for some people," she said, going ahead of him into the living room. "There was one boy there—well, of that—later. Will you have someone put Ann to bed—the trip was hard for her—see how sleepy she is. Run along, Ann," she added, pushing her slightly but gently toward the maid. When they disappeared she stood looking about her, taking off her hat.

"I'm glad you took down the crystals—I always hated crystals—" She moved to the window.

"I didn't, the roof fell in—just after my last visit to you in December. You're looking splendid, Julie." He colored. "I'm so pleased, glad you know, awfully glad. I was beginning to think—well, not that doctors *know* anything—but it has been so long—" He tried to laugh, thought better of it, and stammered into, "It's a drop here of about fifteen hundred feet—but your heart—that is good—it always was."

"What do you know about my heart?" Julie said angrily. "You don't know what you are talking about. Now the child—"

"Yes, well?"

"Her name is Ann," she finished sulkily.

"A sweet name—it was your mother's. Whose is she?"

"Oh, good heavens!" Julie cried, moving around the room on the far side of the furniture. "Mine, mine, mine, of course! Whose would she be if not mine?"

He looked at her. "Yours? Why, Julie, how absurd!" All the color had drained from his face.

"I know—we've got to talk it over—it's all got to be arranged, it's terrible; but she is nice, a bright child, a good child."

"What in the world is all this about?" he demanded, stopping in front of her. "What are you in this mood for— what have I done?"

"Good heavens, what have *you* done! What a ridiculous man you are. Nothing, of course, absolutely nothing!" She waved her arm. "That's not it; why do you bring yourself in? I'm not blaming you, I'm not asking to be forgiven. I've been on my knees, I've beaten my head against the ground, I've abased myself, but—" she added in a terrible voice, "it's not low enough, the ground is not low enough; to bend down is not enough, to beg forgiveness is not enough; to receive?—it would not be enough. There just isn't the right kind of misery in the world for me to suffer, nor the right kind of pity for you to feel; there isn't a word in the world to heal me; penance cannot undo me—it is a thing beyond the end of everything—it's suffering without a consummation, it's like insufficient sleep; it's like anything that is without proportion. I am not asking for anything at all, because there is nothing that can be given or got—how primitive to be able to receive—"

"But, Julie—"

"No, no, it's not that," she said roughly, tears swimming in her eyes, "of course I love you. But think of this: me, a danger to everyone—excepting those like myself—in the same sickness, and expecting to die: fearful, completely involved in a problem affecting a handful of humanity—filled with fever and lust—not a self-willed lust at all, a matter of heat. And frightened, frightened! And nothing coming after, no matter what you do, nothing at all, nothing at all but death—and one goes on—it goes on—then the child—and life, hers, probably, for a time—"

"So."

"So I couldn't tell you. I thought, I'll die next month, no one will ever see anything of any of us in no time now. Still, all in all, and say what I like, I didn't want to go—and I *did*—well, you know what I mean. Then her father died—they say her lungs are weak—death perpetuating itself—queer, isn't it—and the doctors—" She swung around: "You're right, they lied to me, and I lived through—all the way."

He had turned away from her.

"The real, the proper idea is," she said in a pained voice, "—is design, a thing should make a design; torment should have some meaning. I did not want to go beyond you, or to have anything beyond you—that was not the idea, not the idea at all. I thought there was to be no more me. I wanted to leave nothing behind but you, only you. You must believe this or I can't bear it…and still," she continued, walking around the room impatiently, "there was a sort of hysterical joy in it too. I thought, if Paytor has perception, that strange other 'something,' that must be at the center of everything (or there wouldn't be such a passionate desire for it), that something secret that is so near that it is all but obscene—well, I thought, if Paytor has this knowledge, (and mind you, I knew all the time that you didn't have it), this 'grace,' I thought, well, then he will understand. Then at such times I would say to myself, after you had been gone a long time, '*now* he has the answer, at this very moment, at precisely ten-thirty of the clock, if I could be with him *now*, he would say to me, "I see."' But as soon as I had the timetable in my hand, to look up the train you would be on; I knew there was no such feeling in your heart— nothing at all."

"Don't you feel horror?" he asked in a loud voice.

"No, I don't feel horror—horror must include conflict, and I have none; I am alien to life, I am lost in still water."

"Have you a religion, Julie?" he asked her, in the same loud voice, as if he were addressing someone a long way off.

"I don't know, I think so, but I am not sure. I've tried to believe in something external and enveloping, to carry me away, beyond—that's what we demand of our faiths, isn't it? It won't do, I lose it; I come back again to the idea that there is something more fitting than release."

He put his head in his hands. "You know," he said "I've always thought that a woman, because she *can* have children, ought to know everything. The very fact that a woman can do so preposterous a thing as have a child, ought to give her prophecy."

She coughed, her handkerchief before her face. "One learns to be careful about death, but never, never about...." She didn't finish, but stared straight before her.

"Why did you bring the child here, why did you return at all then, after so long a time?—it's so dreadfully mixed up."

"I don't know. Perhaps because there is a right and a wrong, a good and an evil, and I had to find out. If there is such a thing as 'everlasting mercy,' I wanted to find out about that. There's such an unfamiliar taste to Christian mercy, an alien sort of intimacy...." She had a way of lifting the side of her face, closing her eyes. "I thought, Paytor may know—"

"Know what?"

"Division. I thought, he will be able to divide me against myself. Personally I don't feel divided; I seem to be a sane and balanced whole, but hopelessly estranged. So I said to myself, Paytor will see where the design divides and departs, though all the time I was making no bargain, I wasn't thinking of any system—well, in other words, I wanted to be set *wrong*. Do you understand?"

"No," he said in the same loud voice, "and what's more, you yourself must know what you have done to me. You have turned everything upside down. Oh, I won't say you betrayed me—it's much less than that, and more, it's what most of us do, we betray circumstances, we don't hold on. Well," he said sharply, "I can't do anything for you, I can't do anything at all; I'm sorry, I'm very sorry, but there it is." He was grimacing and twitching his shoulders.

"The child has it too," Julie Anspacher said, looking up at him. "I shall die soon. It's ridiculous," she added, the tears streaming down her face. "You are strong, you always were, and so was your family before you—not one of them in their graves before ninety—it's all wrong—it's quite ridiculous!"

"I don't know, perhaps it's not ridiculous; one must be careful not to come too hastily to a conclusion." He began searching for his pipe. "Only you must know yourself, Julie, how I torment myself, if it's a big enough thing, for days, years. Why? Because I come to conclusions instantly and then have to fight to destroy them!" He seemed a little pompous now. "You see," he added, "I'm human, but frugal. Perhaps I'll be able to tell you something later—give you a beginning at least. Later." He turned, holding his pipe in the cup of his hand, and left the room, closing the door behind him. She heard him climbing the stairs, the hard oak steps that went up into the shooting loft, where he practised aim at the concentric circles of his targets.

Darkness was closing in, it was eating away the bushes and the barn, and it rolled in the odors of the orchard. Julie leaned on her hand by the casement edge and listened. She could hear far off the faint sound of dogs, the brook running down the mountain, and she thought, "Water in the hand has no voice, but it really roars coming over the falls. It sings over small stones in brooks, but it only tastes of water when it's caught, struggling and running away in the hands." Tears came into her eyes, but they did not fall. Sentimental memories of childhood, she said to herself, which had sometimes been fearful, and had strong connections with fishing and skating, and the day they had made her kiss the cheek of their dead priest—*Qui habitare facit sterilem—matrem filiorum laetantem*—then *Gloria Patri*—that had made her cry with a strange backward grief that was swallowed, because in touching his cheek, she kissed aggressive passivity, entire and cold.

She wondered and wandered in her mind. She could hear Paytor walking on the thin boards above, she could smell the smoke of his tobacco, she could hear him slashing the cocks of his guns.

Mechanically she went over to the chest in the corner; it was decorated with snow scenes. She lifted the lid. She turned over the upper layer of old laces and shawls until she came to a shirtwaist of striped silk...the one she had worn years ago, it had been her mother's. She stopped. The child? Paytor didn't seem to like the child. "Ridiculous!" she said out loud. "She is quiet, good, gentle. What more does he want? But no, that wasn't enough now." She removed her gloves (why hadn't she done that at once?) Perhaps she had made a mistake in coming back. Paytor was strong, all his family had been strong like that before him, and she was ill and coughing. And Ann? She had made a mistake in coming back. She went towards the stairs to call Paytor and tell him about it, pinning up her veil as she went. Time drew out. But no, that wasn't the answer, that wasn't the right idea.

The pendulum of the wooden clock, on the mantel above the fireplace, pulled time back and forth with heavy ease, and Julie, now at the window, nodded without sleep—long grotesque dreams came up to her, held themselves against her, dispersed and rolled in again. Somewhere Ann coughed in her sleep (she must be in the guest room); Julie Anspacher coughed also, holding her handkerchief to her face. She could hear feet walking back and forth, back and forth, and the smell of tobacco growing less faint.

What could she do, for God's sake, what was there that she could do? If only she had not this habit of fighting death. She shook her head. Death was past knowing and one must be certain of something else first. "If only I had the power to feel what I should feel, but I've stood so much so long, there is not too long, that's the tragedy... the interminable discipline of learning to stand everything." She thought, "If only Paytor will give me time, I'll get around to it." Then it seemed that something must happen. "If only I could think of the right word before it happens," she said to herself. She said it over. "Because I am cold I can't think. I'll think soon. I'll take my jacket off, put on my coat...."

She got up, running her hand along the wall. Where was it? Had she left it on the chair? "I can't think of the word," she said, to keep her mind on something.

She turned around. All his family...long lives..."and me too, me too," she murmured. She became dizzy. "It's because I must get on my knees. But it isn't low enough," she contradicted herself, "but if I put my head down, way down—down, down, down, down…."

She heard a shot. "He has quick warm blood—"

Her forehead had not quite touched the boards, now it touched them, but she got up immediately, stumbling over her dress.

Oscar

BEFORE THE HOUSE rose two stately pine trees, and all about small firs and hemlocks. The garden path struggled up to the porch between wild flowers and weeds, and looming against its ancient bulk the shadows of out-houses and barns.

It stood among the hills, and just below around a curve in the road, lay the placid gray reservoir.

Sometimes parties would cross the fields, walking slowly toward the mountains. And sometimes children could be heard murmuring in the underbrush of things they scarcely knew.

Strange things had happened in this country town. Murder, theft, and little girls found weeping, and silent morose boys scowling along in the ragweed, with half-shut sunburned eyelids.

The place was wild, deserted and impossible in winter. In summer it was overrun with artists and town folk with wives and babies. Every Saturday there were fairs on the green, where second-hand articles were sold for a song, and flirting was formidable and passing. There were picnics, mountain climbings, speeches in the town hall, on the mark of the beast, on sin, and democracy, and once in a while a lecture on something that "everyone should know," attended by mothers, their offspring left with servants who knew what everyone shouldn't.

Then there were movies, bare legs, deacons, misses in cascades of curls and on Sunday one could listen to Mr. Widdie, the clergyman, who suffered from consumption, speak on love of one's neighbor.

In this house and in this town had lived, for some fifteen years or so, Emma Gonsberg.

She was a little creature, lively, smiling, extremely good-natured. She had been married twice, divorced once, and was now a widow still in her thirties.

Of her two husbands she seldom said anything. Once she made the remark: "Only fancy, they never did catch on to me at all."

She tried to be fashionable, did her hair in the Venetian style, wore gowns after the manner of Lady de Bath entering her carriage; and tried to cultivate only those who could tell her "where she stood."

Her son Oscar was fourteen or thereabouts. He wore distinctly over-decorative English clothes, and remembered two words of some obscure Indian dialect that seemed to mean "fleas," for whenever he flung these words defiantly at visitors they would go off into peals of laughter, headed by his mother. At such times he would lower his eyes and show a row of too heavy teeth.

Emma Gonsberg loved flowers, but could not grow them. She admired cats because there was "nothing servile about them," but they would not stay with her; and though she loved horses and longed to be one of those daring women who could handle them "without being crushed in the stalls," they nevertheless ignored her with calm indifference. Of her loves, passions and efforts, she had managed to raise a few ill-smelling pheasants, and had to let it go at that.

In the winter she led a lonely and discriminating life. In the summer her house filled with mixed characters, as one might say. A hot melancholy Jew, an officer who was always upon the point of depreciating his medals in a conceited voice, and one other who swore inoffensively.

Finally she had given this sort of thing up, partly because she had managed, soon after, to get herself entangled with a man called Ulric Straussmann. A tall rough fellow, who said he came from the Tyrol; a fellow without sensibilities but with a certain bitter sensuality. A good-natured creature as far as he went, with vivid streaks of German lust, which had at once something sentimental and something careless about it; the type who can turn the country, with a single gesture, into a brothel, and makes of children strong enemies. He showed no little audacity in putting things into people's minds that he would not do himself.

He smelled very strongly of horses, and was proud of it. He pretended a fondness for all that goes under hide or hair, but a collie bitch, known for her gentleness, snapped at him and bit him. He invariably carried a leather thong, braided at the base for a handle, and would stand for hours talking, with his legs apart, whirling this contrived whip, and, looking out of the corner of his eyes would pull his mustache, waiting to see which of the ladies would draw her feet in.

He talked in a rather even, slightly nasal tone, wetting his lips with a long out-thrust of tongue, like an animal. His teeth were splendid and his tongue unusually red, and he prided himself on these and on the calves of his legs. They were large, muscular and rather handsome.

He liked to boast that there was nothing that he could not do and be forgiven, because, as he expressed it, "I have always left people satisfied." If it were hate or if it were love, he seemed to have come off with unusual success. "Most people are puny," he would add, "while I am large, strong, healthy. Solid flesh through and through," whereat he would pound his chest and smile.

He was new to the town and sufficiently insolent to attract attention. There was also something childishly naive in him, as there is in all tall and robust men who talk about themselves. This probably saved him, because when he was drinking he often became gross and insulting, but he soon put the women of the party in a good humor by giving one of them a hearty and good-natured slap on the rear that she was not likely to forget.

Besides this man, Emma had a few old friends of the less interesting, though better-read, type. Among them, however, was an exception, Oliver Kahn, a married man with several children one heard of and never saw. A strange, quiet man who was always talking. He had splendid eyes and a poor mouth—very full lips. In the beginning one surmised that he had been quite an adventurer.

He had an odor about him of the rather recent cult of the "terribly good." He seemed to have been unkind to his family in some way, and was spending the rest of his life in a passion of regret and remorse. He had become one of those guests who are only missed when absent. He finally stayed for good, sleeping in an ante-room with his boots on—his one royal habit.

In the beginning Emma had liked him tremendously. He was at once gentle and furious, but of late, just prior to the Straussmann affair, he had begun to irritate her. She thought to herself, "He is going mad, that's all." She was angry at herself for saying "that's all," as if she had expected something different, more momentous.

He had enormous appetites, he ate like a Porthos and drank like a Pantagruel, and talked hour after hour about the same thing, "Love of one's neighbor," and spent his spare time in standing with his hands behind him, in front of the pheasants' cage. He had been a snipe hunter in his time, and once went on a big game hunt, but now he said he saw something more significant here.

He had, like all good sportsmen, even shot himself through the hand, but of late he pretended that he did not remember what the scar came from.

He seemed to suffer a good deal. Evil went deep and good went deep and he suffered the tortures of the damned. He wept and laughed and ate and drank and slept, and year by year his eyes grew sweeter, tenderer, and his mouth fuller, more gross.

The child Oscar did not like Kahn, yet sometimes he

would become extraordinarily excited, talk very fast, almost banteringly, a little malignly, and once when Kahn had taken his hand he drew it away angrily. "Don't," he said.

"Why not?"

"Because it is dirty," he retorted maliciously.

"As if you really knew of what I was thinking," Kahn said, and put his own hands behind him.

Emma liked Kahn, was attached to him. He mentioned her faults without regret or reproval, and this in itself was a divine sort of love.

He would remark: "We cannot be just because we are bewildered; we ought to be proud enough to welcome our enemies as judges, but we hate, and to hate is the act of the incurious. I love with an everlasting but a changing love, because I know I am the wrong sort of man to be good—and because I revere the shadow on the threshold."

"What shadow, Kahn?"

"In one man we called it Christ—it is energy; for most of us it is dead, a phantom. If you have it you are Christ, and if you have only a little of it you are but the promise of the Messiah."

These seemed great words, and she looked at him with a little admiring smile.

"You make me uneasy for fear that I have not said 'I love you with an everlasting love,' often enough to make it an act of fanaticism."

As for Oscar, he did what he liked, which gave him character, but made him difficult to live with.

He was not one of those "weedy" youths, long of leg, and stringy like "jerked beef, thank God!" as his mother said to visitors. He was rather too full-grown, thick of calf and hip and rather heavy of feature. His hands and feet were not out of proportion as is usually the case with children of his age, but they were too old looking.

He did not smoke surreptitiously. On the contrary he had taken out a pipe one day in front of his mother, and filling it, smoked in silence, not even with a frightened air, and for that matter not even with a particularly bold air;—he did it quite simply, as something he had finally decided to do, and Emma Gonsberg had gone off to Kahn with it, in a rather helpless manner.

Most children swing in circles about a room, clumsily. Oscar on the contrary walked into the four corners placidly and officially, looked at the back of the books here and a picture there, and even grunted approvingly at one or two in quite a mature manner.

He had a sweetheart, and about her and his treatment of her there were only a few of the usual signs—he was shy, and passionately immersed in her, there was little of the casual smartness of first calf love about it, though he did in truth wave her off with a grin if he was questioned.

He took himself with seriousness amounting to a lack of humor—and though he himself knew that he was a youth, and had the earmarks of adolescence about him—and know it he certainly did—once he said, "Well, what of it—is that any reason why I should not be serious about everything?" This remark had so astonished his mother that she had immediately sent for Kahn to know if he thought the child was precocious—and Kahn had answered, "If he were, I should be better pleased."

"But what is one to expect?"

"Children," he answered, "are never what they are supposed to be, and they never have been. He may be old for his age, but what child hasn't been?"

In the meantime, she tried to bring Straussmann and Kahn together—"My house is all at odds," she thought, but these two never hit it off. Straussmann always appeared dreadfully superficial and cynical, and Kahn dull and good about nothing.

"They have both got abnormal appetites," she thought wearily. She listened to them trying to talk together of an evening on the piazza steps. Kahn was saying:

"You must, however, warn yourself, in fact I might say arm yourself, against any sensation of pleasure in doing good; this is very difficult, I know, but it can be attained. You can give and forgive and tolerate gently and, as one might say, casually, until it's a second nature."

"There you have it, tolerate—who wants tolerance, or a second nature? Well, let us drop it. I feel like a child—it's difficult not to feel like a child."

"Like Oscar—he has transports—even at his age," Emma added hesitatingly. "Perhaps that's not quite as it should be?"

"The memory of growing up is worse than the fear of death," Kahn remarked, and Emma sighed.

"I don't know; the country was made for children, they

say—I could tell you a story about that," Straussmann broke off, whistling to Oscar. "Shall I tell Oscar about the country—and what it is really like?" he asked Emma, turning his head.

"Let the boy alone."

"Why, over there in that small village," Straussmann went on, taking Oscar by the arm. "It is a pretty tale I could tell you—perhaps I will when you are older—but don't let your mother persuade you that the country is a nice, healthful, clean place, because, my child, it's corrupt."

"Will you let the boy alone!" Emma cried, turning very red.

"Ah, eh—I'll let him alone right enough—but it won't make much difference you'll see," he went on. "There is a great deal told to children that they should not hear, I'll admit, but there wasn't a thing I didn't know when I was ten. It happened one day in a hotel in Southampton—a dark place, gloomy, smelling frightfully of mildew, the walls were damp and stained. A strange place, eh, to learn the delights of love, but then our parents seldom dwell on the delights,—they are too taken up with the sordid details, the mere sordid details. My father had a great beard, and I remember thinking that it would have been better if he hadn't said such things. I wasn't much good afterwards for five or six years, but my sister was different. She enjoyed it immensely and forgot all about it almost immediately, excepting when I reminded her."

"Go to bed, Oscar," Emma said abruptly.

He went, and on going up the steps he did not let his fingers trail along the spindles of the banisters with his usual "Eeny meeny miny mo," etc.

Emma was a little troubled and watched him going up silently, hardly moving his arms.

"Children should be treated very carefully, they should know as much as possible, but in a less superficial form than they must know later."

"I think a child is born corrupt and attains to decency," Straussmann said grinning.

"If you please," Emma cried gaily, "we will talk about things we understand."

Kahn smiled. "It's beautiful, really beautiful," he said, meaning her gaiety. He always said complimentary things about her lightness of spirit, and always in an angry voice.

"Come, come, you are going mad. What's the good of that?" she said, abruptly, thinking, "He is a man who discovered himself once too often."

"You are wrong, Emma, I am not worthy of madness."

"Don't be on your guard, Kahn," she retorted.

Oscar appeared before her suddenly, barefoot.

She stared at him. "What is it?" she at last managed to ask in a faint almost suffocated voice.

"I want to kiss you," he whispered.

She moved toward him slowly, when, half way, he hurried toward her, seized her hand, kissed it, and went back into the house.

"My God," she cried out. "He is beginning to think for himself," and ran in after him.

She remembered how she had talked to him the night before, only the night before. "You must love with an everlasting but a changing love," and he became restless. "With an everlasting but a changing love."

"What do you mean by 'changing'?" His palms were moist, and his feet twitched.

"A love that takes in every detail, every element—that can understand without hating, without distinction, I think."

"Why do you say, 'I think'?"

"I mean, I know," she answered, confused.

"Get that Kahn out, he's a rascal," he said, abruptly, grinning.

"What are you saying, Oscar?" she demanded, turning cold. "I'll never come to your bed again, take your hands and say 'Our Father.'"

"It will be all right if you send that man packing," he said, stressing the word "packing."

She was very angry, and half started toward the door. Then she turned back. "Why do you say that, Oscar?"

"Because he makes you nervous—well, then—because he crouches"; he saw by his mother's face that she was annoyed, puzzled, and he turned red to his ears. "I don't mean that, I mean he isn't good; he's just watching for something good to happen, to take place—" His voice trailed off, and he raised his eyes solemn and full of tears to her face. She leaned down and kissed him, tucking him in like a "little boy."

"But I'm not a little boy," he called out to her.

And tonight she did not come down until she thought Kahn and Straussmann had gone.

Kahn had disappeared, but Straussmann had taken a turn or two about the place and was standing in the shadow of the stoop when she came out.

"Come," he said. "What is it that you want?"

"I think it's religion," she answered abruptly. "But it's probably love."

"Let us take a walk," he suggested.

They turned in toward the shadows of the great still mountains and the denser, more arrogant shadows of the outhouses and barns. She looked away into the silence, and the night, and a warm sensation as of pleasure or of something expected but intangible came over her, and she wanted to laugh, to cry, and thinking of it she knew that it was neither.

She was almost unconscious of him for a little, thinking of her son. She raised her long silk skirts about her ankles and tramped off into the dampness. A whippoorwill was whistling off to the right. It sounded as if he were on the fence, and Emma stopped and tried to make it out. She took Ulric's arm presently, and feeling his muscles swell began to think of the Bible. "Those who take by the sword shall die by the sword. And those who live by the flesh shall die by the flesh."

She wished that she had some one she could believe in. She saw a door before her mental eye, and herself opening it and saying, "Now tell me this, and what it means,— only to-day I was thinking 'those who live by the flesh'"—

and as suddenly the door was slammed in her face. She started back.

"You are nervous," he said in a pleased whisper.

Heavy stagnant shadows sprawled in the path. "So many million leaves and twigs to make one dark shadow," she said, and was sorry because it sounded childishly romantic, quite different from what she had intended, what she had meant.

They turned the corner of the carriage-house.

Something moved, a toad, gray and ugly, bounced across her feet and into the darkness of the hedges. Coming to the entrance of the barn they paused. They could distinguish sleeping hens, the white films moving on their eyes—and through a window at the back, steam rising from the dung heap.

"There don't seem to be any real farmers left," she said aloud, thinking of some book she had read about the troubles of the peasants and landholders.

"You're thinking of my country," he said smiling.

"No, I wasn't," she said. "I was wondering what it is about the country that makes it seem so terrible?"

"It's your being a Puritan—a tight-laced delightful little Puritan."

She winced at the words, and decided to remain silent.

It was true, Straussmann was in a fever of excitement—he was always this way with women, especially with Emma. He tried to conceal it for the time being, thinking, rightly, that a display of it would not please her just at the moment—"but it would be only a matter of minutes when she would welcome it," he promised himself, and waited.

He reflected that she would laugh at him. "But she would enjoy it just the same. The way with all women who have had anything to do with more than one man and are not yet forty," he reflected. "They like what they get, but they laugh at you, and know you are lying—"

"Oh, my God!" Emma said suddenly, drawing her arm away and wiping her face with her handkerchief.

"What's the matter?"

"Nothing, it's the heat."

"It is warm," he said dismally.

"I despise everything, I really despise everything, but you won't believe—I mean everything when I say everything—you'll think I mean some one thing—won't you?" she went on hurriedly. She felt that she was becoming hysterical.

"It doesn't matter," he rejoined, walking on beside her, his heart beating violently. "Down, you dog," he said aloud.

"What is that?" She raised her eyes and he looked into them, and they both smiled.

"That's better. I wish I were God."

"A desire for a vocation."

"Not true, and horrid, as usual," she answered, and she was hot and angry all at once.

He pulled at his mustache and sniffed. "I can smell the hedges—ah, the country is a gay deceiver—it smells pleasant enough, but it's treacherous. The country, my dear Emma, has done more to corrupt man, to drag him down, to turn him loose upon his lower instincts, than morphine, alcohol and women. That's why I like it, that's why it's the perfect place for women. They are devils and should be driven out, and as there's more room in the country and consequently less likelihood of driving them out in too much of a hurry, there is more time for amusement." He watched her out of the corner of his eye as he said these things to note if they were ill advised. They seemed to leave her cold, but tense.

A little later they passed the barns again.

"What was that?" Emma asked suddenly.

"I heard nothing."

But she had heard something, and her heart beat fearfully. She recognized Oscar's voice. She reached up, signing Straussmann to be quiet. She did not want him to hear; she wished that the ground would yawn, would swallow him up.

"See that yellow flower down there," she said, pointing toward the end of the path they had just come. "I want it, I must have it, please." He did as he was bid, amiably enough.

She listened—she heard the voice of Oscar's little sweetheart: "It seems as if we were one already."...It was high, resolute, unflagging, without emotion, a childish parroting of some novel. Oscar's voice came back, half smothered:

"Do you really care—more than you like Berkeley?"

"Yes, I do," she answered in the same false treble, "lots more."

"Come here," he said softly—the hay rustled.

"I don't want to—the rye gets into my hair and spoils it."

"Dolly, do you like the country?"

"Yes, I do,"—without conviction.

"We will go to the city," he answered.

"Oh, Oscar, you're so strong," she giggled, and it sent a cold shudder through Emma's being.

Then presently, "What's the matter, Oscar—why, you're crying."

"I'm not—well, then yes, I am—what of it?—you'll understand, too, some day."

She was evidently frightened, because she said in a somewhat loosened key, "No one would ever believe that we were as much in love as we are, would they, Oscar?"

"No, why do you ask that?"

"It's a great pity," she said again with the false sound, and sighed.

"Do you care? Why do you care?"

Straussmann was coming back with the yellow flower between thumb and forefinger. Emma ran a little way to meet him.

"Come, let us go home the other way."

"Rather, let us not go home," he said, boldly, and took her wrist, hurting her.

"Ah," she said. "Vous m'avez blessée d'amour"—ironically.

"Yes, speak French, it helps women like you at such moments," he said, brutally, and kissed her.

But kissing him back, she thought, "The fool, why does Oscar take her so seriously when they are both children, and she is torturing him?"

"My love, my sweet, my little love," he was babbling.

She tried to quench this, trembling a little. "But tell me, my friend—no, not so hasty—what do you think of immortality?" He had pushed her so far back that there was no regaining her composure. "My God, in other words, what of the will to retribution!"

But she could not go on. "I've tried to," she thought.

Later, when the dawn was almost upon them, he said: "How sad to be drunk, only to die. For the end of all man is Fate, in other words, the end of all man is vulgar."

She felt the need of something that had not been.

"I'm not God, you see, after all."

"So I see, madam," he said. "But you're a damned clever little woman."

When she came in, she found Kahn lying flat on his back, his eyes wide open.

"Couldn't you sleep?"

"No, I could not sleep."

She was angry. "I'm sorry—you suffer."

"Yes, a little."

"Kahn," she cried in anguish, flinging herself on her knees beside him. "What should I have done, what shall I do?"

He put his hand on her cheek. "My dear, my dear," he said, and sighed. "I perhaps was wrong."

She listened.

"Very wrong, I see it all now; I am an evil man, an old and an evil being."

"No, no!"

"Yes, yes," he said gently, softly, contradicting her. "Yes, evil, and pitiful, and weak"; he seemed to be trying to remember something. "What is it that I have overlooked?" He asked the question in such a confused voice that she was startled.

"Is it hate?" she asked.

"I guess so, yes, I guess that's it."

"Kahn, try to think—there must be something else."

"Madness."

She began to shiver.

"Are you cold?"

"No, it's not cold."

"No, it's not cold," he repeated after her. "You are not cold, Emma, you are a child."

Tears began to roll down her cheeks.

"Yes," he continued sadly. "You too will hear: remorse is the medium through which the evil spirit takes possession."

And again he cried out in anguish. "But I'm *not* superficial—I may have been wanton, but I've not been superficial. I wanted to give up everything, to abandon myself to whatever IT demanded, to do whatever IT directed and willed. But the terrible thing is I don't know what abandon is. I don't know when it's abandon and when it's just a case of minor calculation.

"The real abandon is not to know whether one throws oneself off a cliff or not, and not to care. But I can't do it, because I must know, because I'm afraid if I did cast myself off, I should find that I had thrown myself off the lesser thing after all, and that," he said in a horrified voice, "I could never outlive, I could never have faith again. And so it is that I shall never know, Emma; only children and the naive know, and I am too sophisticated to accomplish the divine descent."

"But you must tell me," she said, hurriedly. "What am I to do, what am I to think? My whole future depends on that, on your answer—on knowing whether I do an injustice not to hate, not to strike, not to kill—well, you must tell me—I swear it is my life—my entire life."

"Don't ask me, I can't know, I can't tell. I who could not lead one small sheep, what could I do with a soul, and what still more could I do with you? No," he continued, "I'm so incapable. I am so mystified. Death would be a release, but it wouldn't settle anything. It never settles anything, it simply wipes the slate, it's merely a way of putting the sum out of mind, yet I wish I might die. How do I know now but that everything I have thought, and said, and done, has not been false, a little abyss from which I shall crawl laughing at the evil of my own limitation."

"But the child—what have I been telling Oscar—to love with an everlasting love—"

"That's true," he said.

"Kahn, listen. What have I done to him, what have I done to myself? What are we all doing here—are we all mad—or are we merely excited—overwrought, hysterical? I must know, I must know." She took his hand and he felt her tears upon it.

"Kahn, is it an everlasting but a changing love—what kind of love is that?"

"Perhaps that's it," he cried, jumping up, and with a gesture tore his shirt open at the throat. "Look, I want you to see, I run upon the world with a bared breast—but never find the blade—ah, the civility of our own damnation—that's the horror. A few years ago, surely this could not have happened. Do you know," he said, turning his eyes all hot and burning upon her, "the most terrible thing in the world is to bare the breast and never to feel the blade enter!" He buried his face in his hands.

"But, Kahn, you must think, you must give me an answer. All this indecision is all very well for us, for all of us who are too old to change, for all of us who can reach God through some plaything we have used as a symbol, but there's my son, what is he to think, to feel, he has no jester's stick to shake, nor stool to stand on. Am I responsible for him? Why," she cried frantically, "must I be responsible for him? I tell you I won't be, I can't. I won't take it upon myself. But I have, I have. Is there something that can make me immune to my own blood? Tell me—I must wipe the slate—the fingers are driving me mad—can't he stand alone now? Oh, Kahn, Kahn!" she cried, kissing his hands. "See, I kiss your hands, I am doing so much. You must be the prophet—you can't do less for the sign I give you—I must know, I must receive an answer, I will receive it."

He shook her off suddenly, a look of fear came into his eyes.

"Are you trying to frighten me?" he whispered. She went into the hall, into the dark, and did not know why, or understand anything. Her mind was on fire, and it was consuming things that were strange and merciful and precious.

Finally she went into her son's room and stood before his bed. He lay with one feverish cheek against a dirty hand, his knees drawn up; his mouth had a peculiar look of surprise about it.

She bent down, called to him, not knowing what she was doing. "Wrong, wrong," she whispered, and she shook him by the shoulders. "Listen, Oscar, get up. Listen to me!"

He awoke and cried out as one of her tears, forgotten, cold, struck against his cheek. An ague shook his limbs. She brought her face close to his.

"Son, hate too, that is inevitable—irrevocable—"

He put out his two hands and pushed them against her breast and in a subdued voice said, "Go away, go away," and he looked as if he were about to cry, but he did not cry.

She turned and fled into the hall.

However, in the morning, at breakfast, there was nothing unusual about her, but a tired softness and yielding of spirit; and at dinner, which was always late, she felt only a weary indifference when she saw Straussmann coming up the walk. He had a red and white handkerchief about his throat, and she thought, "How comic he looks."

"Good evening," he said.

"Good evening," she answered, and a touch of her old gaiety came into her voice. Kahn was already seated, and now she motioned Straussmann to follow. She began slicing the cold potted beef and asked them about sugar in their tea, adding, "Oscar will be here soon." To Kahn she showed only a very little trace of coldness, of indecision.

"No," Straussmann said, still standing, legs apart: "If you'll excuse me, I'd like a word or two with Kahn." They stepped off the porch together.

"Kahn," he said, going directly to the point, "listen." He took hold of Kahn's coat by the lapel. "You have known Emma longer than I have, you've got to break it to her." He flourished a large key under Kahn's nose, as he spoke.

"I've got him locked up in the outhouse safe enough for the present, but we must do something immediately."

"What's the matter?" A strange, pleasant but cold sweat broke out upon Kahn's forehead.

"I found Oscar sitting beside the body of his sweetheart, what's-her-name; he had cut her throat with a kitchen knife, yes, with a kitchen knife—he seemed calm, but he would say nothing. What shall we do?"

"They'll say he was a degenerate from the start—"

"Those who live by the flesh—eh?"

"No," Kahn said, in a confused voice, "that's not it."

They stood and stared at each other so long that presently Emma grew nervous and came down the garden path to hear what it was all about.

Mother

A FEEBLE LIGHT flickered in the pawn shop at Twenty-nine. Usually, in the back of this shop, reading by this light—a rickety lamp with a common green cover—sat Lydia Passova, the mistress.

Her long heavy head was divided by straight bound hair. Her high firm bust was made still higher and still firmer by German corsets. She was excessively tall, due to extraordinarily long legs. Her eyes were small, and not well focused. The left was slightly distended from the long use of a magnifying glass.

She was middle-aged, and very slow in movement, though well balanced. She wore coral in her ears, a coral necklace, and many coral finger rings.

There was about her jewelry some of the tragedy of all articles that find themselves in pawn, and she moved among the trays like the guardians of cemetery grounds, who carry about with them some of the lugubrious still-ness of the earth on which they have been standing.

She dealt, in most part, in cameos, garnets, and a great many inlaid bracelets and cuff-links. There were a few watches, however, and silver vessels and fishing tackle and faded slippers—and when, at night, she lit the lamp, these and the trays of precious and semi-precious stones, and the little ivory crucifixes, one on either side of the window, seemed to be leading a swift furtive life of their own, conscious of the slow pacing woman who was known to the street as Lydia Passova.

No one knew her, not even her lover—a little nervous fellow, an Englishman quick in speech with a marked accent, a round-faced youth with a deep soft cleft in his chin, on which grew two separate tufts of yellow hair. His eyes were wide and pale, and his eye-teeth prominent.

He dressed in tweeds, walked with the toes in, seemed sorrowful when not talking, laughed a great deal and was nearly always to be found in the café about four of an afternoon.

When he spoke it was quick and jerky. He had spent a great deal of his time in Europe, especially the watering places—and had managed to get himself in trouble in St. Moritz, it was said, with a well-connected family.

He liked to seem a little eccentric and managed it simply enough while in America. He wore no hat, and liked to be found reading the *London Times,* under a park lamp at three in the morning.

Lydia Passova was never seen with him. She seldom left her shop; however, she was always pleased when he wanted to go anywhere: "Go," she would say, kissing his hand, "and when you are tired come back."

Sometimes she would make him cry. Turning around she would look at him a little surprised, with lowered lids, and a light tightening of the mouth.

"Yes," he would say, "I know I'm trivial—well, then, here I go, I will leave you, not disturb you any longer!" and darting for the door he would somehow end by weeping with his head buried in her lap.

She would say, "There, there why are you so nervous?"

And he would laugh again: "My father was a nervous man, and my mother was high-strung, and as for me—" He would not finish.

Sometimes he would talk to her for long hours, she seldom answering, occupied with her magnifying glass and her rings, but in the end she was sure to send him out with: "That's all very true, I have no doubt; now go out by yourself and think it over"—and he would go, with something like relief, embracing her large hips with his small strong arms.

They had known each other a very short time, three or four months. He had gone in to pawn his little gold ring, he was always in financial straits, though his mother sent him five pounds a week; and examining the ring, Lydia Passova had been so quiet, inevitable, necessary, that it seemed as if he must have known her forever—"at some time," as he said.

Yet they had never grown together. They remained detached, and on her part, quiet, preoccupied.

He never knew how much she liked him. She never told him; if he asked she would look at him in that surprised manner, drawing her mouth together.

In the beginning he had asked her a great many times,

clinging to her, and she moved about arranging her trays with a slight smile, and in the end lowered her hand and stroked him gently.

He immediately became excited. "Let us dance," he cried, "I have a great capacity for happiness."

"Yes, you are very happy," she said.

"You understand, don't you?" he asked abruptly.

"What?"

"That my tears are nothing, have no significance, they are just a protective fluid—when I see anything happening that is about to affect my happiness I cry, that's all."

"Yes," Lydia Passova said, "I understand." She turned around, reaching up to some shelves, and over her shoulder she asked, "Does it hurt?"

"No, it only frightens me. You never cry, do you?"

"No, I never cry."

That was all. He never knew where she had come from, what her life had been, if she had or had not been married, if she had or had not known lovers; all that she would say was, "Well, you are with me, does that tell you nothing?" and he had to answer, "No, it tells me nothing."

When he was sitting in the café he often thought to himself, "There's a great woman"—and he was a little puzzled why he thought this because his need of her was so entirely different from any need he seemed to remember having possessed before.

There was no swagger in him about her, the swagger he had always felt for his conquests with women. Yet there was not a trace of shame—he was neither proud nor shy about Lydia Passova, he was something entirely different. He could not have said himself what his feeling was—but it was in no way disturbing.

People had, it is true, begun to tease him:

"You're a devil with the ladies."

Where this had made him proud, now it made him uneasy.

"Now, there's a certain Lydia Passova, for instance, who would ever have thought—"

Furious he would rise.

"So, you do feel—"

He would walk away, stumbling a little among the chairs, putting his hand on the back of every one on the way to the door.

Yet he could see that, in her time, Lydia Passova had been a "perverse" woman—there was, about everything she did, an economy that must once have been a very sensitive and a very sensuous impatience, and because of this every one who saw her felt a personal loss.

Sometimes, tormented, he would come running to her, stopping abruptly, putting it to her this way:

"Somebody has said something to me."

"When—where?"

"Now, in the café."

"What?"

"I don't know, a reproach—"

She would say:

"We are all, unfortunately, only what we are." She had a large and beautiful angora cat, it used to sit in the tray of amethysts and opals and stare at her from very bright cold eyes. One day it died, and calling her lover to her she said:

"Take her out and bury her." And when he had buried her he came back, his lips twitching.

"You loved that cat—this will be a great loss."

"Have I a memory?" she inquired.

"Yes," he answered.

"Well," she said quietly, fixing her magnifying glass firmly in her eye. "We have looked at each other, that is enough."

And then one day she died.

The caretaker of the furnace came to him, where he was sipping his liqueur as he talked to his cousin, a pretty little blonde girl, who had a boring and comfortably provincial life, and who was beginning to chafe.

He got up, trembling, pale, and hurried out.

The police were there, and said they thought it had been heart failure.

She lay on the couch in the inner room. She was fully dressed, even to her coral ornaments; her shoes were neatly tied—large bows of a ribbed silk.

He looked down. Her small eyes were slightly open, the left, that had used the magnifying glass, was slightly wider than the other. For a minute she seemed quite natural. She had the look of one who is about to say: "Sit beside me."

Then he felt the change. It was in the peculiar heaviness of the head—sensed through despair and not touch.

The high breasts looked very still, the hands were half closed, a little helpless, as in life—hands that were too proud to "hold." The drawn-up limb exposed a black petticoat and a yellow stocking. It seemed that she had become hard—set, as in a mold—that she rejected everything now, but in rejecting had bruised him with a last terrible pressure. He moved and knelt down. He shivered. He put his closed hands to his eyes. He could not weep.

She was an old woman, he could see that. The ceasing of that one thing that she could still have for any one made it simple and direct.

Something oppressed him, weighed him down, bent his shoulders, closed his throat. He felt as one feels who has become conscious of passion for the first time, in the presence of a relative.

He flung himself on his face, like a child.

That night, however, he wept, lying in bed, his knees drawn up.

The Robin's House

IN A STATELY DECAYING MANSION, on the lower end of the Avenue, lived a woman by the name of Nelly Grissard.

Two heavy cocks stood on either side of the brownstone steps, looking out toward the park; and in the back garden a fountain, having poured out its soul for many a year, still poured, murmuring over the stomachs of the three cherubim supporting its massive basin.

Nelly Grissard was fat and lively to the point of excess. She never let a waxed floor pass under her without proving herself light of foot. Every ounce of Nelly Grissard was on the jump. Her fingers tapped, her feet fluttered, her bosom heaved; her entire diaphragm swelled with little creakings of whale-bone, lace and taffeta.

She wore feathery things about the throat, had a liking for deep burgundy silks, and wore six petticoats for the "joy of discovering that I'm not so fat as they say." She stained her good square teeth with tobacco, and cut her hair in a bang.

Nelly Grissard was fond of saying: "I'm more French than human." Her late husband had been French; had dragged his nationality about with him with the melancholy of a man who had half-dropped his cloak and that cloak his life, and in the end, having wrapped it tightly about him, had departed as a Frenchman should.

There had been many "periods" in Nelly Grissard's life: a Russian, a Greek, and, those privileged to look through her key-hole said, even a Chinese.

She believed in "intuition," but it was always first-hand intuition; she learned geography by a strict system of love affairs—never two men from the same part of the country.

She also liked receiving "spirit messages"—they kept her in touch with international emotion—she kept many irons in the fire and not the least of them was the "spiritual" iron.

Then she had what she called a "healing touch"—she could take away headaches, and she could tell by one pass of her hand if the bump on that particular head was a bump of genius or of avarice—or if (and she used to shudder, closing her eyes and withdrawing her hand with a slow, poised and expectant manner) it was the bump of the senses.

Nelly was, in other words, dangerously careful of her sentimentalism. No one but a sentimental woman would have called her great roomy mansion "The Robin's House"; no one but a sentimentalist could possibly have lived through so many days and nights of saying "yes" breathlessly, or could have risen so often from her bed with such a magnificent and knowing air.

No one looking through the gratings of the basement window would have guessed at the fermenting mind of Nelly Grissard. Here well-starched domestics rustled about, laying cool fingers on cool fowls and frosted bottles. The cook, it is true, was a little untidy; he would come and stand in the entry, when spring was approaching, and look over the head of Nelly Grissard's old nurse, who sat in a wheel-chair all day, her feeble hands crossed over a discarded rug of the favorite burgundy color, staring away with half-melted eyes into the everlasting fountain, while below the cook's steaming face, on a hairy chest, rose and fell a faded holy amulet.

Sometimes the world paused to see Nelly Grissard pounce down the steps, one after another, and with a final swift and high gesture take her magnificent legs out for a drive, the coachman cracking his whip, the braided ribbons dancing at the horses' ears. And that was about all— no, if one cared to notice, a man, in the early forties, who passed every afternoon just at four, swinging a heavy black cane.

This man was Nicholas Golwein—half Tartar, half Jew.

There was something dark, evil and obscure about Nicholas Golwein, and something bending, kindly, compassionate. Yet he was a very Jew by nature. He rode little, danced less, but smoked great self-reassuring cigars, and could out-ponder the average fidgety American by hours.

He had traveled, he had lived as the "Romans lived," and had sent many a hot-eyed girl back across the fields with something to forget or remember, according to her nature.

This man had been Nelly Grissard's lover at the most depraved period of Nelly's life. At that moment when she was coloring her drinking water green, and living on ox liver and "testina en broda," Nicholas Golwein had turned her collar back, and kissed her on that intimate portion of the throat where it has just left daylight, yet has barely passed into the shadow of the breast.

To be sure, Nelly Grissard had been depraved at an exceedingly early age, if depravity is understood to be the ability to enjoy what others shudder at, and to shudder at what others enjoy. Nelly Grissard dreamed "absolutely honestly"—stress on the absolutely—when it was all the fashion to dream obscurely,—she could sustain the conversation just long enough not to be annoyingly brilliant, she loved to talk of ancient crimes, drawing her stomach in, and bending her fingers slightly, just slightly, but also just enough to make the guests shiver a little and think how she really should have been born in the time of the Cenci. And during the craze for Gauguin she was careful to mention that she had passed over the same South Sea roads, but where Gauguin had walked, she had been carried by two astonished donkeys.

She had been "kind" to Nicholas Golwein just long enough to make the racial melancholy blossom into a rank tall weed. He loved beautiful things, and she possessed them. He had become used to her, had "forgiven" her much (for those who had to forgive at all had to forgive Nelly in a large way), and the fact that she was too fluid to need one person's forgiveness long, drove him into slow bitterness and despair.

The fact that "her days were on her," and that she did

not feel the usual woman's fear of age and dissolution, nay, that she even saw new measures to take, possessing a fertility that can only come of a decaying mind, drove him almost into insanity.

When the autumn came, and the leaves were falling from the trees, as nature grew hot and the last flames of the season licked high among the branches, Nicholas Golwein's cheeks burned with a dull red, and he turned his eyes down.

Life did not exist for Nicholas Golwein as a matter of day and after day—it was flung at him from time to time as a cloak is flung a flunkey, and this made him proud, morose, silent.

Was it not somehow indecent that, after his forgiveness and understanding, there should be the understanding and forgiveness of another?

There was undoubtedly something cruel about Nelly Grissard's love; she took at random, and Nicholas Golwein had been the most random, perhaps, of all. The others, before him, had all been of her own class—the first had even married her, and when she finally drove him to the knife's edge, had left her a fair fortune. Nicholas Golwein had always earned his own living, he was an artist and lived as artists live. Then Nelly came and went— and after him she had again taken one of her own kind, a wealthy Norwegian—Nord, a friend of Nicholas'.

Sometimes now Nicholas Golwein would go off into the country, trying to forget, trying to curb the tastes that Nelly's love had nourished. He nosed out small towns, but he always came hurriedly back, smelling of sassafras, the dull penetrating odor of grass, contact with trees, half-tamed animals.

The country made him think of Schubert's Unfinished Symphony—he would start running—running seemed a way to complete all that was sketchy and incomplete about nature, music, love.

"Would I recognize God if I saw him?" The joy of thinking such thoughts was not every man's, and this cheered him.

Sometimes he would go to see Nord; he was not above visiting Nelly's lover—in fact there was that between them.

He had fancied death lately. There was a tremendously sterile quality about Nicholas Golwein's fancies; they were the fancies of a race, and not of a man.

He discussed death with Nord—before the end there is something pleasant in a talk of a means to an end, and Nord had the coldness that makes death strong.

"I can hate," he would say, watching Nord out of the corner of his eye; "Nelly can't, she's too provincial—"

"Yes, there's truth in that. Nelly's good to herself—what more is there?"

"There's understanding." He meant compassion, and his eyes filled. "Does she ever speak of me?"

It was beginning to rain. Large drops struck softly against the café window and thinning out ran down upon the sill.

"Oh, yes."

"And she says?"

"Why are you never satisfied with what you have, Nicholas?"

Nicholas Golwein turned red. "One dish of cream and the cat should lick his paws into eternity. I suppose one would learn how she felt, if she feels at all, if one died."

"Why, yes, I suppose so."

They looked at each other, Nicholas Golwein in a furtive manner, moving his lips around his cigar—Nord absently, smiling a little. "Yes, that would amuse her."

"What?" Nicholas Golwein paused in his smoking and let his hot eyes rest on Nord.

"Well, if you can manage it—"

Nicholas Golwein made a gesture, shaking his cuff-links like a harness—"I can manage it," he said, wondering what Nord was thinking.

"Of course it's rather disgusting," Nord said.

"I know, I know I should go out like a gentleman, but there's more in me than the gentleman, there's something that understands meanness; a Jew can only love and be intimate with the thing that's a little abnormal, and so I love what's low and treacherous and cunning, because there's nobility and uneasiness in it for me—well," he flung out his arms—"if you were to say to Nell, 'He hung himself in the small hours, with a sheet'—what then? Everything she had ever said to me, been to me, will change for her—she won't be able to read those French journals in the same way, she won't be able to swallow water as she has always swallowed it. I know, you'll say there's nature and do you know what I'll answer: that I have a contempt for animals—just because they do not have to include Nelly Grissard's whims in their means to a living conduct—well, listen, I've made up my mind to something"— he became calm all of a sudden and looked Nord directly in the face.

"Well?"

"I shall follow you up the stairs, stand behind the door, and you shall say just these words, 'Nicholas has hung himself.' "

"And then what?"

"That's all, that's quite sufficient—then I shall know everything."

Nord stood up, letting Nicholas open the café door for him.

"You don't object?" Nicholas Golwein murmured.

Nord laughed a cold, insulting laugh. "It will amuse her—"

Nicholas nodded, "Yes, we've held the coarse essentials between our teeth like good dogs—" he said, trying to be insulting in turn, but it only sounded pathetic, sentimental.

Without a word passing between them, on the following day, they went up the stairs of Nelly Grissard's house, together. The door into the inner room was ajar, and Nicholas crept in behind this, seating himself on a little table.

He heard Nord greet Nelly, and Nelly's voice answering—"Ah, dear"—he listened no further for a moment, his mind went back, and he seemed to himself to be peaceful and happy all at once. "A binding up of old sores," he thought, a oneness with what was good and simple—with everything that evil had not contorted.

"Religion," he thought to himself, resting his chin on his hands—thinking what religion had meant to all men at all times, but to no man in his most need. "Religion is a design for pain—that's it." Then he thought, that, like all art, must be fundamentally against God—God had made his own plans—well, of that later—

Nelly had just said something—there had been a death-like silence, then her cry, but he had forgotten to listen to what it was that had passed. He changed hands on his cane. "There is some one in heaven," he found his mind saying. The rising of this feeling was pleasant—it seemed to come from the very center of his being. "There's some one in heaven—who?" he asked himself, "who?" But there was no possible answer that was not blasphemy.

"Jews do not kill themselves—"

Nelly's voice. He smiled—there was some one in heaven, but no one here. "I'm coming," he murmured to himself—and felt a sensuous going away in the promise.

His eyes filled. What was good in death had been used up long ago—now it was only dull repetition—death had gone beyond the need of death.

Funnily enough he thought of Nelly as she was that evening when she had something to forgive. He had pulled her toward him by one end of a burgundy ribbon,

"Forgive, forgive," and she had been kind enough not to raise him, not to kiss him, saying, "I forgive"—she just stood there showing her tobacco-stained teeth in a strong laugh, "Judas eliminated." He put his hand to his mouth, "I have been *There*," and *There* seemed like a place where no one had ever been. How cruel, how monstrous!

Some one was running around the room, heavy, ponderous. "She always prided herself on her lightness of foot," and here she was running like a trapped animal, making little cries, "By the neck!"—strange words, horrifying, unreal—

"To be a little meaner than the others, a little more crafty"—well, he had accomplished that, too.

Some one must be leaning on the couch, it groaned. That took him back to Boulogne; he had loved a girl once in Boulogne, and once in the dark they had fallen—it was like falling through the sky, through the stars, finding that the stars were not only one layer thick, but that there were many layers, millions of layers, a thickness to them, and a depth—then the floor—that was like a final promise of something sordid, but lasting—firm.

Sounds rose from the streets; automobiles going up town, horses' hoofs, a cycle siren,—that must be a child,— long drawn out, and piercing—yes, only a child would hold on to a sound like that.

"Life is life," Nelly had just said, firmly, decisively. After all he had done this well—he had never been able to think of death long, but now he had thought of it, made it pretty real—he remembered sparrows, for some unknown reason, and this worried him. "The line of the hips, simply Renoir over again—"

They were on the familiar subject of art.

The sounds in the room twittered about him like wings in a close garden, where there is neither night nor day. "There is a power in death, even the thought of death, that is very terrible and very beautiful—" His cane slipped, and struck the floor.

"What was that?" the voice of Nelly Grissard was high, excited, startled—

"A joke."

Nicholas Golwein suddenly walked into the room.

"A joke," he said and looked at them both, smiling.

Nelly Grissard, who was on her knees, and who was holding Nord's shoe in one hand, stared at him. It seemed that she must have been about to kiss Nord's foot.

Nicholas Golwein bowed, a magnificent bow, and was about to go.

"You ought to be ashamed of yourself," Nelly Grissard cried, angrily, and got to her feet.

He began to stammer: "I—I am leaving town—I wanted to pay my respects—"

"Well, go along with you—"

Nicholas Golwein went out, shutting the door carefully behind him.

The Doctors

"WE HAVE FASHIONED ourselves against the Day of Judgement." This remark was made by Dr. Katrina Silverstaff at the oddest moments, seeming without relevance to anything at all, as one might sigh, "Be still." Often she said it to herself. She thought it when on her way home, walking along the east wall of the river, dangling from her finger the loop of string about the box of seed cakes she always brought home for tea; but she always stopped to lean over the wall to watch the river barges, heavy with bright brick, moving off to the Islands.

Dr. Katrina, and her husband Dr. Otto, had been students in the same *gymnasium* at Freiburg-in-Breisgau. Both had started out for a doctorate in gynecology. Otto Silverstaff made it, as they say, but Katrina lost her way somewhere in vivisection, behaving as though she were aware of an impudence. Otto waited to see what she would do. She dropped out of class and was seen sitting in the park, bent forward, holding Otto's cane before her, its golden knob in both hands, her elbows braced on her legs, slowly poking the fallen leaves. She never recovered her gaiety. She married Otto but did not seem to know *when*; she knew why—she loved him—but he evaded her, by being in the stream of time; by being absolutely *daily*.

They came to America in the early twenties and were instantly enjoyed by the citizens of Second Avenue. The people liked them, they were trustworthy, they were durable; Doctor Katrina was useful to animal and birds, and Doctor Otto was, in his whole dedicated round little body, a man of fervor, who moved about any emergency with no dangling parts, aside from the rubber reins of his stethoscope. When he rapped his knuckles on a proffered back, he came around the shoulder with bulging eyes and puffing tense mouth, pronouncing verdict in heavy gusts of hope, licorice and carbolic acid.

The doctors' name plates stood side by side in the small tiled entry, and side by side (like people in a Dutch painting) the doctors sat at their table facing the window. The first day was the day she first remarked: "We have fashioned ourselves against the Day of Judgement." A globe of the world was between them, and at his side, a weighing machine. He had been idly pushing the balancing arm on its rusting teeth when she began speaking, and when she finished abruptly, he stopped, regarding her with a mild expression. He was inordinately pleased with her; she was "sea water" and "impersonal fortitude," neither asking for, nor needing attention. She was compact of dedicated merit, engaged in a mapped territory of abstraction, an excellently arranged encounter with estrangement; in short she was to Otto incomprehensible, like a decision in chess, she could move to anything but whatever move, it appeared to the doctor, would be by the rules of that ancient game. The doctors had been in office no more than a year when their first child was born, a girl, and in the year following, a boy; then no more children.

Now as Doctor Otto had always considered himself a liberal in the earlier saner sense of the word (as he would explain later, sitting with his neighbors in the Hungarian grill, his wife beside him), he found nothing strange in his wife's abstraction, her withdrawal, her silence, particularly if there was a xylophone and a girl, dancing on her boot's pivot, in the pungent air of the turning spit. Katrina had always been careful of music, note for note she can be said to have "attended." She collected books on comparative religions, too, and began learning Hebrew. He said to everybody, "So? are we not citizens of *anything*?"

Thus their life went into its tenth year. The girl had taken up dancing lessons, and the boy (wearing spectacles) was engrossed in insects. Then something happened that was quite extraordinary.

One day Doctor Katrina had opened the door to the ring of a travelling pedlar of books. As a rule she had no patience with such fellows, and with a sharp "No, thank you !" would dismiss them. But this time she paused, the door knob in her hand, and looked at a man who gave his name as Rodkin. He said that he was going all through that part of the city. He said that he had just missed it last year when he was selling Carlyle's *French Revolution*; this time however he was selling the Bible. Standing aside, Doctor Katrina let him pass. Evidently surprised, he did pass and stood in the hall.

"We will go into the waiting room," she said. "My husband is in consultation and must not be disturbed." He said, "Yes, of course, I see." Though he did not see anything.

The waiting room was empty, dark and damp, like an acre risen from the sea. Doctor Katrina reached up and turned on a solitary light, which poured down its swinging arc upon the faded carpet.

The pedlar, a slight pale man with an uncurling flaxen beard, more like the beard of an animal than of a man, and with a shock of the same, almost white hair, hanging straight down from his crown, was—light eyes and all—hardly menacing; he was so colorless as to seem ghostly.

Doctor Katrina said, "We must talk about religion."

He was startled and asked why.

"Because," she said, "no one remembers it."

He did not answer until she told him to sit down, and he sat down, crossing his knees; then he said, "So?"

She sat opposite, her head slightly turned, apparently deliberating. Then she said, "I must have religion become out of the reach of the *few*; I mean out of reach *for* a few; something impossible again; to find again."

"*Become*?" he repeated, "that's a queer word."

"It is the only possible word," she said with irritation, "because, at the moment, religion is claimed by too many."

He ran a small hand through his beard. "Well, yes," he answered, "I see."

"No, you don't!" she rapped out sharply. "Let us come to the point. For me everything is too arranged. I'm not saying this because I need your help. I shall never need your help." She stared straight at him. "Understand that from the beginning."

"Beginning," he repeated in a loud voice.

"From the beginning, right from the start. Not help, *hindrance*."

"Accomplish what, Madame?" He took his hand away from his beard and lowered his left arm, dropping his books.

"That is my affair," she said, "it has nothing to do with you, you are only the means."

"So, so," he said. "The means."

A tremor ran off into her cheek, like a grimace of pain. "You can do nothing, not as a person." She stood up. "I must do it all. No!" she said, raising both hands, catching the ends of her shoulder scarf in a gesture of anger and pride, though he had not moved, "I shall be your mistress." She let her hands fall into the scarf's folds. "But," she added, "do not intrude. Tomorrow you will come to see me, that is enough; that is all." And with this "all," the little pedlar felt fear quite foreign to him.

However he came the next day, fumbling, bowing, stumbling. She would not see him. She sent word by the maid that she did not need him, and he went away abashed. He came again the day following, only to be told that Doctor Katrina Silverstaff was not in. The following Sunday she was.

She was quiet, almost gentle, as if she were preparing him for a disappointment, and he listened. "I have deliberately removed remorse from the forbidden; I hope you understand."

He said "Yes" and understood nothing.

She continued inexorably: "There will be no thorns for you. You will miss the thorns but do not presume to show it in my presence." Seeing his terror, she added: "And I do not permit you to suffer while I am in the room." Slowly and precisely she began unfastening her brooch. "I dislike all spiritual decay."

"Oh, oh !" he said under his breath.

"It is the will," she said, "that must attain complete estrangement."

Without expecting to, he barked out, "I expect so."

She was silent, thinking, and he could not help himself, he heard his voice saying, "I want to suffer!"

She whirled around. "Not in my house."

"I will follow you through the world."

"I shall not miss you."

He said, "What will you do?"

"Does one destroy oneself when one is utterly disinterested?"

"I don't know."

Presently she said: "I love my husband. I want you to know that. It has nothing to do with this, still I want you to know it. I am *pleased* with him, and very proud."

"Yes, yes," Rodkin said, and began shaking again; his hand on the bedpost set the brasses ringing.

"There is something in me that is mournful because it is being."

He did not answer; he was crying.

"There's another thing," she said with harshness, "that I insist on—that you will not insult me by your attention while you are in the room."

He tried to stop his tears, and he tried to comprehend what was happening.

"You see," she continued, "some people drink poison, some take the knife, others drown. I take you."

In the dawn, sitting up, she asked him if he would smoke, and lit him a cigarette. After that she withdrew into herself, sitting on the edge of the mahogany board, her hands in her lap.

Unfortunately there was new ease in Rodkin. He turned in bed, drawing his feet under his haunches, crossed, smoking slowly, carefully.

"Does one regret?"

Doctor Katrina did not answer, she did not move, she did not seem to have heard him.

"You frightened me last night," he said, pushing his heels out and lying on his back. "Last night I almost became somebody."

There was silence.

He began quoting from his Bible: "Shall the beasts of the field, the birds of the air forsake thee?" He added, "Shall any man forsake thee?"

Katrina Silverstaff remained as she was, but something under her cheek quivered.

The dawn broke, the street lamps went out, a milk-cart rattled across the cobbles and into the dark of a side street.

"One. One out of many...*the* one."

Still she said nothing and he put his cigarette out. He was beginning to shiver; he rolled over and up, drawing on his clothes.

"When shall I see you again?" A cold sweat broke out over him, his hands shook. "Tomorrow?" He tried to come toward her, but he found himself at the door. "I'm nothing, nobody,"—he turned toward her, bent slightly, as though he wished to kiss her, but no move helped him. "You are taking everything away. I can't feel—I don't suffer, nothing you know—I can't—" He tried to look at her. After a long time he succeeded.

He saw that she did not know he was in the room.

Then something like terror entered him, and with soft and cunning grasp, he turned the handle of the door and was gone.

A few days later, at dusk, his heart the heart of a dog, he came into the street of the doctors and looked at the house.

A single length of crêpe, bowed, hung at the door.

From that day he began to drink heavily. He became quite a nuisance in the cafes of the quarter; and once, when he saw Doctor Otto Silverstaff sitting alone in a corner with his two children, he laughed a loud laugh and burst into tears.

The Diary of a Dangerous Child

September first:

Today I am fourteen; time flies; women must grow old.

Today I have done my hair in a different way and asked myself a question: "What shall be my destiny?"

Because today I have placed my childhood behind me, and have faced the realities.

My uncle from Glasgow, with the square whiskers and the dull voice, is bringing pheasants for my mother. I shall sit in silence during the meal and think. Perhaps someone, sensitive to growth, will ask in a tense voices, "What makes you look thoughtful, Olga?"

If this should be the case, I shall tell.

Yes, I shall break the silence.

For sooner or later they must know that I am become furtive.

By this I mean that I am debating with myself whether I shall place myself in some good man's hands and become a mother, or if I shall become wanton and go out in the world and make a place for myself.

Somehow I think I shall became a wanton.

It is more to my taste. At least I think it is.

I have tried to curb this inner knowledge by fighting down that bright look in my eyes as I stand before the mirror, but not ten minutes later I have been cutting into lemons for my freckles.

"Ah woman, thy name, etc."—

September third:

I could not write in my diary yesterday, my hands trembled and I started at every little thing. I think this shows that I am going to be anemic just as soon as I'm old enough to afford it.

This is a good thing; I shall get what I want. Yes, I am glad that I tremble early. Perhaps I am getting introspective. One must not look inward too much, while the inside is yet tender. I do not wish to frighten myself until I can stand it.

I shall think more about this tonight when mother puts the light out and I can eat a cream slowly. Some of my best thoughts have come to me this way.

Ah! What ideas have I not had eating creams slowly, luxuriously.

September tenth:

Many days have passed; I have written nothing. Can it be that I have changed? I will hold this thought solitary for a day.

September eleventh:

Yes, I have changed. I found that I owed it to the family.

I will explain myself. Father is a lawyer; mother is in society.

Imagine how it might look to the outer world if I should go around looking as if I held a secret.

If the human eye were to fall upon this page I might be so easily misunderstood.

What shame I might bring down upon my father's head—on my mother's too, if you want to take the whole matter in a large sweeping way—just by my tendency to precocity.

I should be an idiot for their sakes.

I will be!

October fourth:

I have succeeded. No one guesses that my mind teems. No one suspects that I have come into my own, as they say.

But I have. I came into it this afternoon when the diplomat from Brazil called.

My childhood is but a memory.

His name is Don Pasos Dilemma. He has great intelligence in one eye; the other is preoccupied with a monocle. He has comfortable spaces between his front teeth, and he talks in a soft drawl that makes one want to wear satin dresses.

He is courting my sister.

My sister is an extremely ordinary girl, older than I, it is true, but her spirit has no access to those things that I almost stumble over. She is not bad looking, but it is a vulgar beauty compared to mine.

There is something timeless about me, whereas my sister is utterly ephemeral.

I was sitting behind the victrola when he came in. I was reading *Three Lives*. Of course, he did not see me.

Alas for him, poor fellow!

My sister was there too; she kept walking up and down in the smallest sort of space, twisting her fan. He must have kissed her because she said, "Oh," and then he must have kissed her more intensely, because she said, "Oh," again, and drew her breath in, and in a moment she said softly, "You are a dangerous man!"

With that I sprang up and said in a loud and firm voice: "Hurrah, I love danger!"

But nobody understood me.

I am to be put to bed on bread and milk.

Never mind, my room in which I sleep overlooks the garden.

October seventh:

I have been too excited to make any entry in my diary for a few days. Everything has been going splendidly.

I have succeeded in becoming subterranean. I have done something delightfully underhand. I bribed the butler to give a note to Don Pasos Dilemma, and I've frightened the groom into placing at my disposal a saddled horse. And I have a silver handled whip under my bed.

God help all men!

This is what I intend to do. I am going to meet Don Pasos Dilemma at midnight at the end of the arbor, and give him a whipping. For two reasons: one, because he deserves it, second, because it is Russian. After this I shall wash my hands of him, but the psychology of the family will have been raised one whole tone.

I'm sure of this.

Yes, at the full of the moon, Don Pasos Dilemma will be expecting me. His evil mind has already pictured me falling into his arms, a melting bit of tender and green youth.

Instead he will have a virago on his hands! How that word makes me shiver. There's only one other word that affects me as strongly—Vixen! These are my words!

Oh to be a virago at fourteen! What other woman has accomplished it?

No woman.

October eighth:

Last night arrived. But let me tell it as it happened.

The moon rose at a very early hour and hung, a great cycle in the heavens. Its light fell upon the laburnum bushes and lemon trees and gave me a sense of ice up and down my spine. I thought thoughts of Duse and how she had suffered on balconies a good deal; at least I gathered that she did from most of her pictures.

I too stood on the balcony and suffered side-face. The silver light glided over the smooth balustrade and swam in the pool of gold fishes.

In one hand I held the silver mounted whip. On my head was a modish, glazed riding hat with a single loose feather, falling sideways.

I could hear the tiny enamel clock on my ivory mantle

ticking away the minutes. I began striking the welt of my riding boot softly. A high-strung woman must remember her duties to the malicious. I bit my under lip and thought of what I had yet to do. I leaned over the balcony and looked into the garden. There stood the stable boy in his red flannel shirt and beside him the fiery mare.

I tried to become agitated, my bosom refused to heave. Perhaps I am too young.

I shall leap from the balcony onto the horse's back. I whistled to the boy, he looked up, nodding. In a moment the mare was beneath my window. I looked at my wrist watch, it lacked two minutes to twelve. I jumped.

I must have miscalculated the shortness of the distance, or the horse must have moved. I landed in the stable boy's arms.

Oh well, from stable boy to prince, such has been the route of all fascinating women.

I struck my heels into the horse's side and was gone like the wind.

I can feel it yet—the night air on my cheeks, the straining of the great beast's muscles, the smell of autumn, the gloom, the silence. My own transcendent nature—I was coming to the man I hated—hated with a household hate. He who had kissed my sister, he who had never given me a second thought until this evening, and yet who was now all eagerness,—yes counting the minutes with thick, wicked, middle-aged poundings of a Southern heart.

When one is standing between life and death (any moment might have been my last), they say one reviews one's whole childhood. One's mind is said to go back over every little detail.

Anyway mine went back. The distance being so short it went back and forth.

I thought of the many happy hours I had spent with my youngest sister putting spiders down her back, pulling her hair, and making her eat my crusts. I thought of the hours I had lain in the dust beneath the sofa reading Petronius and Rousseau and Glyn. I thought of my father, a great, grim fellow standing six feet two in his socks, but mostly sitting in the Morris chair. Then I remembered the day I was fourteen, only a little over a month ago.

How old one becomes, and how suddenly!

I grew old on horseback, between twelve and twelve one.

For at twelve one precisely, I saw the form of Don Pasos Dilemma in the shadow of the trees, and my heart stopped beating, and I could feel all the childish uncertainties I had suffered become hard and firm, and I knew that I should never again be a child.

I could scarcely see how the betrayer was dressed, but I sensed that he had tricked himself out for the occasion. Had I been challenged, I should have wagered that he had perfumed himself behind the ears and under the chin. That's the kind of trick those foreign men are always up to.

I read that somewhere in a book.

Such men plan downfalls; they are so to speak connoisseurs of treachery; they are the virtuosi of viciousness.

I drew rein on the full four strokes of my horse's hoofs; I raised my silver mounted whip. I threw back my head. A laugh rang out in the stillness of midnight.

It was my laugh, high, drenched with the scorn of life and love and men.

It was a good laugh.

I brought the whip down—

October twenty-seventh:

I have changed my mind.

Yes, I have quite changed my mind. I am neither going to give myself into the hands of some good man, and become a mother, nor am I going to go out into the world and become a wanton. I am going to run away and become a boy.

For this Spaniard, this Brazilian, this Don Pasos Dilemma scorned my challenge, the fine haughty challenge of a girl of youth and vigor, he scorned it, and cringing behind my mother, as it were, left me to face disillusion and chagrin at a late hour at night, when no nice girl should be out, much less facing anything.

For as you may have guessed, it was not Don Pasos who rode to meet me, it was my mother, wearing his long Spanish cloak.

November third:

In another year I shall be fifteen, a woman must grow young again. I have cut off my hair and I am asking myself nothing.

Absolutely nothing.

The Diary of a Small Boy

August seventh:

I am fourteen years old. I wear long trousers and stiff collars and I no longer turn around in the road to see if I am being watched. Nevertheless, I am told that I am not old enough to make any important observations.

I may not be old enough to put what I feel politely, but I feel what I feel, even if it is unpopular.

One of my most unpopular feelings, for instance, is Cousin Elda. She is a tall, obnoxious woman in her twenties, with great coarse, blonde braids. She comes from a far country—England or one of the Rhine towns, I forget which; and there she leaned out of a window a long time, watching the swift-running water on its way to sea, or she said she did. I guess it's true, because she has a water-watching look, and she smiles all funny and interwoven and quiet.

She is not the only unnecessary woman around our place. There are my mother's two sisters, Clovine and Cresseda. They are insufficient as friends and practically evaporated as relatives.

They are little and whispering, and they are always making you nervous by the number of things they put their hands on. I wouldn't mind if they really wanted the

336

things, or if they would only keep hold of them when then have got them. But they never do. They are always dropping them, and they are awfully sure about criminal law and how much punishment men should get.

They sit for hours talking of ways to make bad men sorry. Sometimes I see them from afar off, dropping their knitting and working themselves up.

Sometime I'm going to think up a brand-new crime and see what they suggest.

I think my mother is not very partial to them. She always goes by them without stopping, even when she is talking to them, and if she has much to say, she goes by three or four times.

I have a little sister, but she is beside the point—she is only old enough to see people's good sides. I'm a little cool to her because she is eternally falling down and grinning about it in a way that proves her immature.

I'm going to leave her out of this diary because she is too young to resent it.

But wait until I get thru with the rest of them!

August tenth:

I have not taken my pen in hand for many days because I have been harassed.

There have been lots of people at our house, with many different ways, and it has taken me a long time to make up an idea of each of them.

But I'm settled about it now.

Yesterday there was a hunting party, and all the dogs

and horses assembled on the green, down the driveway, and my mother came out of the house wearing a smart little riding-habit, and swinging a small whip in tiny, dangerous circles.

My father was there holding a gun at his side, and he kept patting it and looking it over, and locking it into second, or half-cock as it is called, and he looked very grand and handsome and superior to accident.

He has always been a very important man, but yesterday he claimed it.

My father is very great. He has dominating whiskers cut square for strength, and thinned out for delicacy. He wears quite a lot of rings because he is vain of his hands.

Usually one of his hands is between the leaves of some important book. Yesterday it was *War and Peace* and this morning it was *The Life of a Volupté,* whatever kind of life that is. But I like his hands best when he is cleaning his guns, or mending a saddle, or stroking the dogs.

He is broad-minded. He takes in all human aspects.

I wonder when I'm going to be a human aspect?

Anyway, they all went off, my cousin Elda looking every inch a woman in a riding-habit of gray and black.

She rode beside my father, and my mother went on in front without turning her head.

August twelfth:
I've been silent these past two days because I could not think up a name that was both beautiful enough, and strong enough to describe my mother.

If I say she is perilous, you get the feeling of trumpets and wars, and men riding down to doom. (Why is doom always down, and never up?) And if I say she is rare, you'll get an idea that she hardly ever comes down for breakfast and that she is inarticulate, and that won't do at all. If I say she is stupendous, you'll think that she must be over six feet tall, that she speaks in a loud voice, demands Shaw at the theaters, and expects strength from men and implacable democracy from women. All these impressions would be wrong.

She is small and dark and there is a hard softness about the place you put your head when you lean on her. She says "Dear" in a tone that makes you want to keep it away from everyone else.

She wears more rings than father, and her hands are kind, but they hurt if she wants them to. She wears loose clinging dresses, she walks in the garden with a hidden anger, and she cuts flowers for the house as if she were displeased, but all the time there is a smile in her face that makes you wait for something grand and terrible to occur.

August sixteenth:

I talked to the stable boy this morning. It seems to me that he is not so easy with me as he used to be. I must be growing up. Something is taking place in me.

I no longer feel dislike for my cousin Elda.

August eighteenth:

Today I walked about the outhouses and went down to examine the pump. I saw Elda coming around from the lilac bushes, smiling out of her large ox-eyes, the two braids falling down, one in front and one in back, and she was singing and walking slow.

She stopped a step or two away from me and said nothing for a minute, and then she asked me if I would like to go to the woods with her to gather wild flowers, and I said no, and she answered, "No?" in the same way I said it, only it sounded more hopeful.

She put her arm around me and said "No?" again, and I felt all disintegrated then she said, "Wouldn't you like to be a brave boy and go with me to protect me from the water snakes?"

Then that made me think of my father, and how safe it was for a long away all around him, when he held his gun that way in his hands, and patted it or cocked it, or just swung it down beside his leg with a careless air, and I said suddenly that I would go if I had a gun, but that I would not go otherwise.

She laughed and said, "Very well, I know where there is a beauty, and if you'll go with me I'll get it for you, but you must not tell, because you are your mother's darling and hope, and," she added suddenly, leaning down and looking into my face, "you are the link that binds them together, forever and ever." And I said I guessed so, and I felt all hot and excited and fearless.

She went away then to the house, and I stood by the

trough dipping my hand in, so anyone seeing me would think me careless and occupied and would not question me.

The stable boy went by. "Growing up, kid?" he said, but I did not answer him. Presently she came out of the house carrying a basket on her arm. She came up to me and I looked in it and there lay one of father's South American pistols—one he had used when he was in charge of one of the more important of the canals; the pistol with the dull, dangerous, smoldering look of passion. And then we walked toward the woods saying nothing. Presently she gave me the pistol. "Now remember, be careful, and shoot only if there is danger."

She went on ahead of me, singing under her breath, the two braids thrown back where I could see them, going down, down beyond the place for braids.

Presently she began turning the moss over with a stick and picking up things, green and damp and pretty, but nameless. The swamp water was black and thick. She went nearer and nearer, holding her blue dress up about her ankles, stepping over the black, wet stones—her feet kept sinking in, and she moved them softly and quickly. The skunk-cabbages were standing up out of the swamp angrily, all colored a boastful green.

"Do you love your mother?" she asked soon, and I answered:

"Yes. My father is a great man—"

She said: "Do you want to grow up some day like your father, and marry a beautiful woman and have a son to tie you together forever and forever, so no other beautiful woman can tear you apart?"

I said: "No beautiful woman could make me lose my head."

She laughed right out loud and stood up, looking at me, and said: "You are a baby—younger than I had imagined—"

"I'm old when I'm alone."

Then somehow, all of a sudden, everything got tangled up. She turned her head toward the swamp, screamed and slipped, and I saw a little water snake leaning over a rock, turning his tail around in a curl, and I saw the two yellow braids bent and funny and not straight as they always were and she fell against me, the gun went off, and the snake disappeared and I heard people shouting and running and my mother's voice high above everything: "Now she is trying those tricks on your son!" And her face was over me, looking as if the something terrible and tremendous that I had been waiting for, had happened—then I forgot—

October second:

We are not going to have hunting parties anymore. My father has put away all the guns and he sits on the porch for hours staring at the sun. My mother walks in the garden cutting flowers for the house.

Cousin Elda is gone. I guess she is leaning out of her window again, watching the water on its way to the sea.

I am not going to write any more in my diary, it is a girl's pastime—besides it hurts the wound in my side.

P.S. My mother's sisters talk more than ever about punishment for men— and it seems to be some man near the house here.

A Boy Asks a Question

THE DAYS had been very warm and close. It was fall now and everything was drawing in for winter. It had been a bad but somehow pleasant year. It seemed that a great number of people had been disillusioned about one thing or another, or perhaps it was the drought; whatever it was, fewer people were seen hurrying from one place to another; winter with frost and snow would be welcome.

Carmen la Tosca (with a name like that, what could she be but an actress?) was in the habit of riding at a swift gallop down the lane and into the copse beyond. She leaned in the saddle as she went under the boughs, the plume of her hat bending smartly back as she rounded the curve.

Her horse was a bolt of white, with shining fetlock, hard tense descending plane of frontal bone, blowing nostrils; but when Carmen la Tosca broke the line of the horse's back with her own, the spine flowed deftly under her like quick water, quivering into massive haunches, socketing a foaming flair of tail.

She rode well. She dropped her pelvis lightly upon the saddle, she kept her grip purposely slack.

She had been in stock for some time. Earlier on she

had been in opera; she had been the queen in *Aida* (among other parts) and she had played boys in vaudeville.

She was not the kind of woman who makes a habit of visiting the country, at least not the sort of country that people refer to as "a jolly place, snuggling among the foothills"...not at all, but this particular summer did find her trying out its simple pleasures.

To country folk she was absolutely stupendous. The boys who lolled about the general store said she was "staggering;" smaller children backed away from her when she walked in the road, calling, "Red mouth! Red mouth!"—but no one knew her.

She had appeared in the spring of the year with a man-servant and a maid. She had taken the "chalet," as the long empty house was called. It had two verandahs running clear around, and it had dozens of windows. All three of the new tenants were seen, all at one time, hanging new curtains. When they were in place, no one saw anyone for days, that is, no one saw *her* for days. Then she brought out the white horse and rode it. Before the season was over, she had hired five or six others, but she herself always singled out the white for her own mount. For a while she rode alone, then parties of four or five were seen with her, and now and again a gentleman (a birthmark twisting his face into unwilling scorn) rode beside her. There was a goat-path in the underbrush, here two boys sometimes came, and lying on their stomachs whispered together, waiting for her, walking or riding.

The boys were Brandt and Baily Wilson, farmer's sons. Sometimes, having waited in vain, they took the mountain road, berry-buckets in hand, because the mountain road went right past her house, where they could hear her people laughing behind the casement.

Sometimes she walked out, descending the hill, carefully, avoiding the crab-grass and the melon patches, talking brightly to the scarred gentleman, but paying little attention to the effect of her words, not through discourtesy but because she let things drift away.

Of course there was no end to the gossip, she did not court attention, she got attention. People said she was not exactly handsome, but neither was she ugly; her face held a perfect balance of the two—and then she was outrageously "*chic.*"

One of the women of the village, who had once, years ago, been to London "to see the Queen," said la Tosca's back was "just like;" this was without doubt sheer nonsense, but it did no harm; indeed it pleased everyone.

Carmen la Tosca breakfasted in bed, and late. Having caught herself out of sleep in a net of bobbin-lace, she broke fast with both food and scent, lazily dusting her neck and arms with perfumed talc, lolling on the bed (which stood between two ovals of pear-wood, framing versions of Leda and the swan), ripping through the wrappers of Puerto Rican journals and French gazettes with the blade of a murderous paper-cutter, and finally, in the total vacancy of complete indulgence, her hand sprawling across a screaming headline, would stare out into the harsh economy of russet boughs, pranked out in fruit.

The room and its occupant were a total discord. The beams, in that part of the country usually stained with walnut juice, were here jackass grey and plainly pegged, the walls ashen, and the doors, opening into the orchard, let pass a line of ragged grass. Carmen la Tosca liked that; but as the mornings were growing chill, she drew a quilted throw about her, and at night, when it rained, the shutters were thrown open that she might watch it falling down.

The particular morning the boy chose for his daring visit was waist-deep in fog, rain dripped from every branch and leaf, but by eleven the sun had managed to get out. He waited outside the doors until she turned her face to the wall, then he stepped in.

It was Brandt Wilson, fourteen. He was short, his hands, feet and head were large. He was splashed with mud, and rumpled. His tie stuck out ridiculously over the top of his tight little vest. He stood before her on the rug, hat in hand.

With a single movement she turned in bed.

"*Well*, who are you?"

"I'm Brandt Wilson, I live out there."

She said without smiling: "What is it?"

The boy hesitated, "I have a brother—"

Carmen la Tosca pushed the papers away, regarding him with amusement.

347

"Have you?"

"He's older than I am—and you know everything…."

"I do, do I. Who said so?"

"Everybody. The postman says you are a 'woman of the world—'"

"Gracious!"

"My brother Baily"—his breaking voice came up in a quivering treble—"well, my sister says, 'I don't like Baily any more—he has lost his plain look'. And I said, 'he's just the same, when you give him a present, and he is bending down untying it.'"

"What is this all about?"

"Out there, on the hill, we were lying in the sun—" he stared at her blankly, "He said he cried when it was over."

"When *what* was over?"

"I don't know; he said 'I am a man now,' and he grabbed me, and he was crying, and we rolled down the hill. Will I be like that?"

She rose on her elbow and looked at him with suffused eyes.

"How many of you are there?"

"Four."

"And how old is the oldest?"

"Twenty-three. He cried too, about his girl, she died. When they told him, he beat the open door on both sides, and shouted: 'I could have stopped her.' He wouldn't tell us how, but he told mother. 'I would have said I love you'. Is that a power?"

"Yes, it is innocence. We are all waiting for someone

who will learn our innocence—all over again." She lay back on her pillow.

"Am *I* going to cry?"

"I don't know, why not? Everyone suffers—all of us. In spite of all the things people say and explain, it is the same thing for everyone; men cry too—men *can* hurt."

He moved his hand on the footboard of the bed.

"I'm sorry," she said, "it's my indolence that does it."

"Does what?"

"Embarrasses you."

"It's all right."

"It is not," she answered. "Do you observe animals?"

He did not answer.

"*Do* you?"

"Yes."

She clapped her hands. "What would all your troubles mean to an animal?"

"I don't know."

"You don't?"

He looked down. "What does it mean?" As he spoke, he forgot what he had come for. "What is going to happen?—"

"Let the evil of the day—"

He said breathlessly. "That's what I want to know—"

"Listen. Do you know what makes the difference between the wise man and the fool? Never do evil to good people, they always forgive, and that's too much for anybody. In the end," she said, "when it is all over, you'll listen to nothing at all; only the simple story, told by everything."

"But I want to know now."

"Now," she said, "now is the time when you leave everything alone."

"But *why* did he cry?"

"Dignity—and despair—and innocence."

"Is that all?"

She had taken up her paper. "That is everything. In the end it will be the death of you."

He did not move.

"Come here," she said, and he came quickly. She drew his head toward her until their foreheads met.

"Start all over again," she said. He went away then.

And that very afternoon, Carmen la Tosca rode off, with her entire *entourage*.

The Nigger

JOHN HARDAWAY was dying. That wasn't what he minded. His small, well-shaped hands twitched at the soft coverlet which rose and fell slowly with his breathing, and he breathed hard with mouth open, showing all his teeth.

Rabb, the nigger, crouched in the corner. The air about her was heavy with her odor. She kept blinking her eyes. She was awed at the presence of her master, but ashamed too, ashamed that he was dying—ashamed as she would have been had he been caught at his toilet.

Rabb was a good nigger; she had served John Hardaway's mother, she had seen her die—old Mrs. Hardaway fluttered against her lace like a bird caught in deep foliage—Rabb had been able to do something about Mrs. Hardaway's death because Mrs. Hardaway had loved her, in her way.

Mrs. Hardaway had died understandably—she had breathed hard too, opening her mouth, but it was gentle and eager, like a child at the breast.

Rabb had tried to be near her, had put her hands on her. But the thing she was trying to touch lay in some hidden corner of Mrs. Hardaway, as a cat hides away under a bed, and Rabb had done nothing after all.

But it was different with John Hardaway. She watched

life playing coquettishly with him. It played with him as a dog plays with an old coat. It shook him suddenly in great gusts of merriment. It played with his eyelids; it twisted his mouth, it went in and out of his body, like a flame running through a funnel—throwing him utterly aside in the end, leaving him cold, lonely, and forbidding.

John Hardaway hated negroes with that hate a master calls love. He was a Southerner and never forgot it. Rabb had nursed him when he was an infant, she had seen him grow up into a big boy, and then she had been there when he broke his mistress's back by some flaw in his otherwise flawless passion.

From time to time John Hardaway called for water. And when Rabb tried to lift his head, he cursed her for a "black bitch"—but in the end he had to let her hold it.

John Hardaway was fifty-nine, he had lived well, scornfully, and this always makes the end easier; he had been a gentleman in the only way a Southerner has of being one—he never forgot that he was a Hardaway—

He called out to her now:

"When I die—leave the room."

"Yes, sah," she whispered sadly.

"Bring me the broth."

She brought it trembling. She was very tired and very hungry, and she wanted to whistle but she only whispered:

"Ain't there nothing I kin do for you?"

"Open the window."

"It's night air, sah—"

"Open it, fool—"

She went to the window and opened it. She was handsome when she reached up, and her nose was almost as excellent as certain Jewish noses; her throat was smooth, and it throbbed.

Toward ten o'clock that night John Hardaway began to sing to himself. He was fond of French, but what he learned in French he sang in English.

"Ah, my little one—I have held you on my knee—
"I have kissed your ears and throat—
"Now I set you down—
"You may do as you will."

He tried to turn over—but failed, and so he lay there staring into the fire.

At this point in the death of John Hardaway, Rabb, the nigger, came out of her corner, and ceased trembling. She was hungry and began heating some soup in a saucepan.

"What are you doing?" John Hardaway inquired abruptly.

"I's hungry, sah."

"Then get out of here—get into the kitchen."

"Yes, sah," but she did not move.

John Hardaway breathed heavily, a mist went over his eyes—presently, after interminable years, he lifted his lids. Rabb was now slowly sipping the steaming soup.

"You damned nigger!"

She got up from her haunches hurriedly—placing her hand in front of her, backing toward the door.

"Little one, I have taken you on my knee—"

Rabb crept back—she came up to the bed.

"Massah, don't you think—?"

"What?"

"A priest—maybe?"

"Fool!"

"Yes, sah, I only wanted to make safe."

He tried to laugh. He pressed his knees together. He had forgotten her.

Finally toward dawn he began to wander.

Rabb moistened the roll of red flesh inside her lip and set her teeth. She began to grin at nothing at all, stroking her hips.

He called to her.

"I want to tell you something."

She came forward—rolling her eyes.

"Come closer."

She came.

"Lean down!" She leaned down, but already the saliva began to fill her mouth.

"Are you frightened?"

"No, sah," she lied.

He raised his hand but it fell back, feebly.

"Keep your place," he whispered, and instantly went to sleep.

He began to rattle in his throat, while Rabb crouched in the corner, holding her breasts in her folded arms and rocking softly on the balls of her feet.

The rattling kept on. Rabb began creeping toward him on hands and knees.

"Massah!"

He did not move.

"John!"

He felt a strange sensation—he lifted his eyelids with their fringe of white lashes and almost inaudibly said:

"Now go!"

He had closed his eyes a long time, when he was troubled with the thought that some one was trying to get into his body as he left it. He opened his eyes and there stood Rabb the nigger very close, looking down at him.

A gush of blood sprang from his nose.

"No, sah!"

He began to gasp. Rabb the nigger stood up to her full height and looked down at him. She began to fan him, quickly. He breathed more hurriedly, his chest falling together like a house of cards. He tried to speak, he could not.

Suddenly Rabb bent down and leaning her mouth to his, breathed into him, one great and powerful breath. His chest rose, he opened his eyes, said "Ah!" and died.

Rabb ran her tongue along her lips, and raising her eyes, stared at a spot on the wall a little higher than she was wont to. After awhile she remembered her unfinished soup.

Madame Grows Older:
A Journal at the Dangerous Age

September seventh.

I must face the fact that I am no longer a young woman. I am a widow, mother of two thoroughly dressed, handsomely educated, spiteful daughters. Nevertheless I am starved. I am starved for youth. There must be, I tell myself, new worlds to conquer; there simply must be. It's only right.

When I was a child, and had curls down my back, I realized that it was horrible to be a child. Now that I am a matron, I realize that its horrible to be a matron. But I must not admit it, even to myself, I'm *so* volatile. In this year alone I've read *Frühlings Erwachen*, *A Night in the Luxembourg* and *Salomé* in Greek. Successively I've burned, buried and mutilated them, but their message flames in my soul, only I can't read the message until the fire burns down. I must have patience.

September eighth.

I am about to confess in a big way. This is my confession. I have an unsatisfied, insubordinate gland somewhere about me, the same identical gland, I'm convinced, that produced the *Blue Bird* and gave that determined look of cheerfulness to the Hapsburgs. I think it is called the infantile gland; any way, there it is. It must have its day.

September ninth.

I have been all around the border of my lake. Leaning down I drew ever so many water lilies to me, crushing them against my heart—but my better nature bid me let them go. Then I gathered a handful of gravel and started tossing it at the goldfish, until it dawned upon me that I was satisfying an impulse to cruelty in a small way. Now I am resting under the sun-dial trying to calm my riotous nerves. As I sit I toy with a fallen maple leaf. Life and the seasons are so implacable, aren't they? They are here to-day and gone tomorrow, it's so splendid and heartless!

My God, as I sit here I realize that I am perishable! O if that brute of an Einstein had only taken a fancy to my relativity! Time and space are my enemies. If it were not for time, I should not be dangerous, and if it were not for space, I should not feel so limited! How cruel is reason! How sharper than a serpent's tooth is meditation! How subtle is the lack of reason!

September tenth.

I said that I had made what was possibly my greatest confession. I lied! This is it: I am a girl, a mere child, amid my years. I have a sweet, forgiving nature, and I long to exert it, the trouble is that I've forgiven everything and everybody three or four times. I want to exert my womanly impulses, but there are so many womenly women exerting theirs, what chance have I who am no longer what I was?

On the other hand, of course, I have my feline qualities. I long to stretch out, at full length, on a couch, and hear men moaning about the corridors because I am indisposed. Ah how charming! I yearn to take up art. I feel, with my natural untrained instinct, I could mean a great deal to some new movement if I could only get it before it had moved much.

Then I want to be a psychic. I think there are ever so many messages just lost in space, waiting for a friend. For instance, I get a number of undefined feelings in a single day. Only yesterday I was mute with a sense of impending doom. The sense, or the doom, I don't know which, ran right through me. It was colossal! Might it not have heralded something of import? Perhaps it meant that red shoes were giving way to green; perhaps it presaged new dimensions; perhaps it meant there will be no more war. How can one tell? And I *must* know. I'm that way.

September eleventh.

Today I went driving. I got down at the park and went among those strangely innocent children one always sees in parks, pulling the swans about by their tails, sticking pins into the fish, and sitting on dogs. My arms were full of Little Elsie books, and a few copies of the *Story of Mankind* for those who are interested in retaliation. But no one seemed to want them.

I had half a dozen of those little rubber balls on elastic that come back at you, no matter what you do. These were for children at the breast. I sat a long time by the duck pond watching my reflection in the water, thinking on the inhumanity of man.

I was about to reenter my carriage, still thinking it, when my attention was attracted by a very young man. He could not have been over twenty-five. He had that peculiar dazed expression seen on the faces of immigrants who have been stunned in a foreign country. He might have been a Russian, a Swede, a Pole, an Italian, a Frenchman, he might have been anything. I did not know. I got hurriedly into my carriage and, directing the coachman to the Shelborne for tea, kept my eyes firmly fixed on the middle of his back.

September twelfth.

Today I returned to the park. I came empty handed, to be free, untroubled. "Alice," I said, "be vibrant, you are still young, you love life. A woman is as young as she looks, a man as young as he feels." "Alice," I said, "be a man, pull yourself together. You still pulse with the eternal scheme of things. You know you do." But my pulse tires me!

September thirteenth.

I cannot leave the park alone. I have become passionately attached to it. I sit by the pond and my thoughts revert to the young man of a day or two back. He was so manly. The perfect gentleman, so experienced without having learned anything, so tender and yet so racial. I think he would make my daughter Mariann, a fate second to none. I must meet him socially.

September fourteenth.

The welfare of my daughter is close to me—he is sitting on the bench just opposite. He is reading something. Is it Lettish, Finnish, Swedish? How beautiful is uncertainty!

September fifteenth. All is well. My brother Alex happened to know the young man. He had no sooner set eyes on him than he exclaimed: "As I live, Prendaville Jones!" Imagine my delight. Prendaville Jones! The name is alive with possibilities!

September seventeenth.

The whole family has met him. Mariann has lost her appetite, she avoids me. Can it be that her heart has learned that secret gesture called love?

September eighteenth.

I have made a perfectly ghastly discovery! Oh, I can't write it! It has sent me to bed where I now lie writing it. The ink has dried on my pen for the hundredth time. I cannot put pen to paper. I am wrapped up in arnica and my head is done up in towels. Near at hand are the smelling salts, the Social Register and a guide to Monte Carlo. I am not myself.

I light cigarette after cigarette, and cast them all into that space outside my window that I used to call nature. Now I will not recognize nature. I have turned the lights off and on twenty times trying to calm myself. In vain! I am a moral and physical menace to human nature. This is it: I am in love with Prendaville Jones! I, a woman of forty, know once again the anguish of spring, the torture of love! I sleep badly, I scorn food. The fires of jealousy leap through me. I thirst for my daughter's life! My own daughter! And now I know what I must do. I don't want youth. I don't want passion. I want those dear, dead days that I used to spend thinking of my lost youth, imagining I wanted it back. I want those long, pleasant, unproductive moments with my Elsie books and my water lilies. I want those hours spent in mild, unfertile thoughts of danger. I want those basking, middle-years among my beautifully worn out acquaintances. I long for rest and the noneventful forties. I tell you, I want to be untroubled once more.

This is what I am going to do. At midnight, on the hour, I shall dress myself in my lace dressing gown, and, taking the paper weight with the picture of St. George driving out the dragons on the reverse side, I shall go down though the tall grasses, as a matron should, who is encased in her implacable years, and there, at the pond's edge, cast myself in. No one shall know that I blossomed again at the age of discretion.

For I cannot bear the return of youth. It's too much, I am too tired. I shall kill myself!

September nineteenth.
I have killed myself!

Aller et Retour

THE TRAIN travelling from Marseilles to Nice had on board a woman of great strength.

She was well past forty and a little top-heavy. Her bosom was tightly cross-laced, the busk bending with every breath, and as she breathed and moved she sounded with many chains in coarse gold links, the ring of large heavily set jewels marking off her lighter gestures. From time to time she raised a long-handled *lorgnette* to her often winking brown eyes, surveying the countryside blurred in smoke from the train.

At Toulon, she pushed down the window, leaning out, calling for beer, the buff of her hip-fitting skirt rising in a peak above tan boots laced high on shapely legs, and above that the pink of woollen stockings. She settled back, drinking her beer with pleasure, controlling the jarring of her body with the firm pressure of her small plump feet against the rubber matting.

She was a Russian, a widow. Her name was Erling von Bartmann. She lived in Paris.

In leaving Marseilles she had purchased a copy of *Madame Bovary*, and now she held it in her hands, elbows slightly raised and out.

She read a few sentences with difficulty, then laid the book on her lap, looking at the passing hills.

Once in Marseilles, she traversed the dirty streets slowly, holding the buff skirt well above her boots, in a manner at once careful and absent. The thin skin of her nose quivered as she drew in the foul odors of the smaller passages, but she looked neither pleased nor displeased.

She went up the steep narrow littered streets abutting on the port, staring right and left, noting every object.

A gross woman, with wide set legs, sprawled in the doorway to a single room, gorged with a high-posted rusting iron bed. The woman was holding a robin loosely in one huge plucking hand. The air was full of floating feathers, falling and rising about girls with bare shoulders, blinking under coarse dark bangs. Madame von Bartmann picked her way carefully.

At a ship-chandler's she stopped, smelling the tang of tarred rope. She took down several colored postcards showing women in the act of bathing; of happy mariners leaning above full-busted sirens with sly cogged eyes. Madame von Bartmann touched the satins of vulgar, highly colored bedspreads laid out for sale in a side alley. A window, fly-specked, dusty and cracked, displayed, terrace upon terrace, white and magenta funeral wreaths, wired in beads, flanked by images of the Bleeding Heart, embossed in tin, with edgings of beaten flame, the whole beached on a surf of metal lace.

She returned to her hotel room and stood, unpinning

DJUNA BARNES: COLLECTED STORIES

her hat and veil before the mirror in the tall closet door. She sat, to unlace her boots, in one of eight chairs, arranged in perfect precision along the two walls. The thick boxed velvet curtains blocked out the court where pigeons were sold. Madame von Bartmann washed her hands with a large oval of coarse red soap, drying them, trying to think.

In the morning, seated on the stout linen sheets of the bed, she planned the rest of her journey. She was two or three hours too early for her train. She dressed and went out. Finding a church, she entered and drew her gloves off slowly. It was dark and cold and she was alone. Two small oil lamps burned on either side of the figures of St. Anthony and St. Francis. She put her leather bag on a form and went into a corner, kneeling down. She turned the stones of her rings out and put her hands together, the light shining between the little fingers; raising them she prayed, with all her vigorous understanding, to God, for a common redemption.

She got up, peering about her, angry that there were no candles burning to the *Magnifique*—feeling the stuff of the altar-cloth.

At Nice she took an omnibus, riding second class, reaching the outskirts about four. She opened the high rusty gates to a private park, with a large iron key, and closed it behind her.

The lane of flowering trees with their perfumed cups, the moss that leaded the broken paving stones, the hot musky air, the incessant rustling wings of unseen birds—

all ran together in a tangle of singing textures, light and dark.

The avenue was long and without turning until it curved between two massive jars, spiked with spirals of cacti, and just behind these, the house of plaster and stone.

There were no shutters open on the avenue because of insects, and Madame von Bartmann went slowly, still holding her skirts, around to the side of the house, where a long-haired cat lay softly in the sun. Madame von Bartmann looked up at the windows, half shuttered, paused, thought better of it and struck off into the wood beyond.

The deep pervading drone of ground insects ceased about her chosen steps and she turned her head, looking up into the occasional touches of sky.

She still held the key to the gate in her gloved hand, and the seventeen-year-old girl who came up from a bush took hold of it, walking beside her.

The child was still in short dresses, and the pink of her knees was dulled by the dust of the underbrush. Her squirrel-colored hair rose in two ridges of light along her head, descending to the lobes of her long ears, where it was caught into a faded green ribbon.

"Richter!" Madame von Bartmann said (her husband had wanted a boy).

The child put her hands behind her back before answering.

"I've been out there, in the field."

Madame von Bartmann, walking on, made no answer.

"Did you stop in Marseilles, Mother?"

She nodded.

"Long?"

"Two days and a half."

"Why a half?"

"The trains."

"Is it a big city?"

"Not very, but dirty."

"Is there anything nice there?"

Madame von Bartmann smiled: "The Bleeding Heart—sailors—"

Presently they came out into the open field, and Madame von Bartmann, turning her skirt back, sat down on a knoll, warm with tempered grass.

The child, with slight springiness of limb, due to youth, sat beside her.

"Shall you stay home now?"

"For quite a while."

"Was Paris nice?"

"Paris was Paris."

The child was checked. She began pulling at the grass. Madame von Bartmann drew off one of her tan gloves, split at the turn of the thumb, and stopped for a moment before she said: "Well, now that your father is dead—"

The child's eyes filled with tears; she lowered her head.

"I come flying back," Madame von Bartmann continued good-naturedly, "to look at my own. Let me see you," she continued, turning the child's chin up in the palm of her hand. "Ten, when I last saw you, and now you are a woman." With this she dropped the child's chin and put on her glove.

"Come," she said, rising, "I haven't seen the house in years." As they went down the dark avenue, she talked.

"Is the black marble Venus still in the hall?"

"Yes."

"Are the chairs with the carved legs still in existence?"

"Only two. Last year Erna broke one, and the year before—"

"Well?"

"I broke one."

"Growing up," Madame von Bartmann commented. "Well, well. Is the great picture still there, over the bed?"

The child, beneath her breath, said: "That's my room."

Madame von Bartmann, unfastening her *lorgnette* from its hook on her bosom, put it to her eyes and regarded the child.

"You are very thin."

"I'm growing."

"I grew, but like a pigeon. Well, one generation can't be exactly like another. You have your father's red hair. That," she said abruptly, "was a queer, mad fellow, that Herr von Bartmann. I never could see what we were doing with each other. As for you," she added, shutting her glasses, "I'll have to see what he has made of you."

In the evening, in the heavy house with its heavy furniture, Richter watched her mother, still in hat and spotted veil, playing on the sprawling lanky grand, high up behind the terrace window. It was a waltz. Madame von Bartmann played fast, with effervescence, the sparkles of her jewelled fingers bubbled over the keys.

In the dark of the garden, Richter listened to Schubert streaming down the light from the open casement. The child was cold now, and she shivered in the fur coat that touched the chill of her knees.

Still swiftly, with a *finale* somewhat in the Grand Opera manner, Madame von Bartmann closed the piano, stood a moment on the balcony inhaling the air, fingering the coarse links of her chain, the insects darting vertically across her vision.

Presently she came out and sat down on a stone bench, quietly, waiting.

Richter stood a few steps away and did not approach or speak. Madame von Bartmann began, though she could not see the child without turning:

"You have been here always, Richter?"

"Yes," the child answered.

"In this park, in this house, with Herr von Bartmann, the tutors and the dogs?"

"Yes."

"Do you speak German?"

"A little."

"Let me hear."

"Müde bin Ich, geh' zu Ruh."

"French?"

"O nuit désastreuse! O nuit effroyable!"

368

"Russian?"

The child did not answer.

"Ach!" said Madame von Bartmann. Then: "Have you been to Nice?"

"Oh, yes, often."

"What did you see there?"

"Everything."

Madame von Bartmann laughed. She leaned forward, her elbow on her knee, her face in her palm. The earrings in her ears stood still, the drone of the insects was clear and soft; pain lay fallow.

"Once," she said, "I was a child like you. Fatter, better health—nevertheless like you. I loved nice things. But," she added, "a different kind, I imagine. Things that were positive. I liked to go out in the evening, not because it was sweet and voluptuous—but to frighten myself, because I'd known it such a little while, and after me it would exist so long. But that—" she interrupted herself, "is beside the point. Tell me how you feel."

The child moved in the shadow. "I can't."

Madame von Bartmann laughed again, but stopped abruptly.

"Life," she said, "is filthy; it is also frightful. There is everything in it: murder, pain, beauty, disease—death. Do you know this?"

The child answered, "Yes."

"How do you know?"

The child answered again, "I don't know."

"You see!" Madame von Bartmann went on, "you

know nothing. You must know *everything*, and *then* begin. You must have a great understanding, or accomplish a fall. Horses hurry you away from danger; trains bring you back. Paintings give the heart a mortal pang—they hung over a man you loved and perhaps murdered in his bed. Flowers hearse up the heart because a child was buried in them. Music incites to the terror of repetition. The crossroads are where lovers vow, and taverns are for thieves. Contemplation leads to prejudice; and beds are fields where babies fight a losing battle. Do you know all this?"

There was no answer from the dark.

"Man is rotten from the start," Madame von Bartmann continued. "Rotten with virtue and with vice. He is strangled by the two and made nothing; and God is the light the mortal insect kindled, to turn to, and to die by. That is very wise, but it must not be misunderstood. I do not want you to turn your nose up at any whore in any street; pray and wallow and cease, but without prejudice. A murderer may have less prejudice than a saint; sometimes it is better to be a saint. Do not be vain about your indifference, should you be possessed of indifference; and don't," she said, "misconceive the value of your passions; it is only seasoning to the whole horror. I wish…" She did not finish, but quietly took her pocket handkerchief and silently dried her eyes.

"What?" the child asked from the darkness.

Madame von Bartmann shivered. "Are you thinking?" she said.

"No," the child answered.

"Then *think*," Madame von Bartmann said loudly, turning to the child. "Think everything, good, bad, indifferent; everything, and *do* everything, *everything*! Try to know what you are before you die. And," she said, putting her head back and swallowing with shut eyes, "come back to me a good woman."

She got up then and went away, down the long aisle of trees.

That night, at bedtime, Madame von Bartmann, rolled up in a bed with a canopy of linen roses, frilled and smelling of lavender, called through the curtains:

"Richter, do you play?"

"Yes," answered Richter.

"Play me something."

Richter heard her mother turn heavily, breathing comfort.

Touchingly, with frail legs pointed to the pedals, Richter, with a thin technique and a light touch, played something from Beethoven.

"*Brava!*" her mother called, and she played again, and this time there was silence from the canopied bed. The child closed the piano, pulling the velvet over the mahogany, put the light out and went, still shivering in her short coat, out on to the balcony.

A few days later, having avoided her mother, looking shy, frightened and offended, Richter came into her mother's room. She spoke directly and sparingly:

"Mother, with your consent, I should like to announce my engagement to Gerald Teal." Her manner was stilted.

"Father approved of him. He knew him for years: if you permit—"

"Good heavens!" exclaimed Madame von Bartmann, and swung clear around on her chair. "Who is he? What is he like?"

"He is a clerk in government employ; he is young—"

"Has he money?"

"I don't know: father saw to that."

There was a look of pain and relief on Madame von Bartmann's face.

"Very well," she said, "I shall have dinner for you two at eight-thirty sharp."

At eight-thirty sharp they were dining. Madame von Bartmann, seated at the head of the table, listened to Mr. Teal speaking.

"I shall do my best to make your daughter happy. I am a man of staid habits, no longer too young," he smiled. "I have a house on the outskirts of Nice. My income is assured—a little left me by my mother. My sister is my housekeeper, she is a maiden lady, but very cheerful and very good." He paused, holding a glass of wine to the light. "We hope to have children—Richter will be occupied. As she is delicate we shall travel, to Vichy, once a year. I have two very fine horses and a carriage with sound springs. She will drive in the afternoons, when she is indisposed—though I hope she will find her greatest happiness at home."

Richter, sitting at her mother's right hand, did not look up.

Within two months Madame von Bartmann was once again in her travelling clothes, hatted and veiled, strapping her umbrella as she stood on the platform, waiting for the train to Paris. She shook hands with her son-in-law, kissed the cheek of her daughter, and climbed into a second class smoker.

Once the train was in motion, Madame Erling von Bartmann slowly drew her gloves through her hand, from fingers to cuff, stretching them firmly across her knee.

"Ah, how unnecessary."

The Passion

EVERY AFTERNOON at four-thirty, excepting Thursday, a smart carriage moved with measured excellence through the Bois, drawn by two bays in shining patent leather blinkers, embellished with silver R's, the docked tails rising proudly above well-stitched immaculate cruppers.

In this carriage, with its half closed curtains, sat the Princess Frederica Rholinghausen, erect, in the dead center of a medallioned cushion.

Behind the tight-drawn veiling that webbed the flaring brim of a Leghorn hat burdened with ribbons and roses, the imperturbable face was no longer rouged to heighten contour, but to limn noble emaciation. The tall figure, with its shoulders like delicate flying buttresses, was encased in grey moiré, the knees dropping the stiff excess in two sharp points, like the corners of a candy box. No pearl in the dog-collar shook between the dipping blue of the veins, nor did the radiance on the fingernails shift by any personal movement; the whole glitter of the jewelled bones and the piercing eye, turned with the turning of the coach, as it passed the lake with creaking water-fowl, and rolled free from the trapping shadow of branchless boles.

The coachman, sitting up on the box with his son, was

breaking the young man in for a life of driving, in which
the old man would have no part. On every Thursday,
when the princess was at home, the empty carriage was
driven at a smart rocking pace, and every Thursday the
Allée de Longchamp rang with the old man's shouts of
"*Eh, doucement, doucement!*"

The family retainers, now only five, worked with as
little effort as was compatible with a slowing routine. Every morning the books in the library, with their white kid
bindings and faded coat of arms, were dusted, and every
afternoon, when the sun wasn't too blazing, the curtains
in the conservatoire were drawn back, but as the princess
moved from room to room less every year, one chamber
was closed for good every twelvemonth.

In the kitchen, regular as the clock, the cook whipped
up the whites of three eggs, with rum and sugar, for the
evening *soufflé*; and just as regularly, the gardener watered
the plants at nightfall, as though promoted, for in the still
splendor of the chateau gardens, one drank the dark cum-
bersome majesty as of Versailles.

The lapdog, long since too old to lift from her basket
of ruffled chintz, slept heavily, a mass of white fur, un-
marked of limb, or feature, save for the line of dark hair
that placed the eyelids, and the moist down-drooping
point below the chin.

On her Thursdays the princess arose at three, dressing herself before a long oak stand, blazing with faceted
bottles. She had been nearly six feet tall; now she had
waned but little under it. There were cut flowers where

she went, but she did not tend them. The scenes of the chase, hanging on the wall between the tall oak chairs, were feathered with dust and out of mind. She had painted them when she was young. The spinet in the corner, covered with a yellow satin throw, embroidered by her own hand, was crumbling along the bevel of the lid, signifying silence of half a century. The scores, lying one above the other, were for soprano. One was open at *Liebes-lied*. The only objects to have seen recent service were the candelabrum, the candles, half burnt upon their spikes, for the princess read into the night.

There were only two portraits, they were in the dining hall; one, her father, in uniform, standing beside a table, his plumed hat in his hand, his hand on the hilt of a sword, his spurred heels lost in the deep pile of a rug. The other, her mother, seated on a garden bench, dressed in hunter green, a little mannish hat tilted to one side. In one fist she held a cascade of ruffles above high riding- boots. A baroque case held miniatures of brothers and cousins; rosy-cheeked, moon-haired, sexless children smiling among the bric-à-brac; fans, coins, seals, porcelain platters (fired with eagles), and, incongruously, a statuette of a lady looking down through the film of her nightshift at her colorless breasts.

Sometimes it rained, splashing drops on the long French windows, the reflection stormed in the mirrors. Sometimes the sun struck a crystal, which in turn flung a cold wing of fire upon the ceiling.

In short, the princess was very old. Now it is said that

the old cannot approach the grave without fearful apprehension or religious rite. The princess did. She was in the hand of a high decay: she was *sèche*, but living on the last suppuration of her will.

Sometimes, not often, but sometimes she laughed, with the heartiness of something remembered inappropriately, and laughter in an ancient is troubling, because inclement and isolated. At times, raising her eyeglasses at the uncompromising moment, she had surprisingly, the air of a *galant*, a *bon-vivant*—but there was a wash of blue in her flesh that spoke of the acceptance of mortality. She never spoke of the spirit.

Now and again two rusty female aunts called, accompanied by tottering companions, equally palsied and broken, who nevertheless managed to retrieve fallen objects, mislaid spectacles, and crumbled cake—patiently bending and unbending, their breast watches swinging from silver hooks.

Sometimes an only nephew, a "scamp," not too childish in his accomplishments, impudent and self-absolved, strolled in—after stabling his horse—walking with legs well apart, slapping his puttees with the loop of his crop, swaggering the length of the room, promising "deathless devotion," holding out, at arm's length, a sturdy zinnia. Then collapsing into a chair (with the ease of inherited impudence, in courtly femur and fibula, in unhampered bone and unearned increment) he sipped at the frail teacup and, biting wide crescents in the thin buttered bread, stared out into the fields with a cold and calculating eye;

377

and when the princess left the room, he really didn't care.

Kurt Anders, a Polish officer, of some vaguely remembered regiment, who almost never appeared in uniform, was the chiefest among her callers. Once a month, on the second Thursday, for some thirty years, he had presented himself, drinking delicately from the same china as though he were not a giant, well trussed and top heavy. Two long folds spread away from the long dipping hooked nose under which his mouth, too small and flat for the wide teeth, pursued the cup. He spoke with a marked accent.

He was a widower. He collected plate and early editions, firearms and stamps. He was devoted to the seventeenth century. He wore puce gloves which, when he rolled them down in one true stroke, sent a faint odor of violet into the room. He had the bearing of one who had abetted licence, he looked as though he had eaten everything: but though elegant in his person, there was something about him not far from the stool.

Sometimes calling a little early, he would go off to the stables where the two bays, now the only horses, stamped and were curried, and where a pleasing brawl of bitches, weighed down with the season's puppies, fawned and snapped. Anders would stoop to stroke their muzzles, pulling at their leather collars, pausing long enough to balance their tails.

This man, whose history was said to have been both *éblouissant* and dark, and who, the gossips said, had most certainly disappointed his family in youth, was, without doubt, a figure of *scandale*. He had been much too fond

of the *demi-monde*. He enjoyed any great man's "favorite." He had a taste for all who would have to be "forgiven." He had been much in the company of a "darling"
of the academy, scion of the house of Valois, the one they
called "L'Infidèle"—or so he said—who, though passionately "modern" could not keep away from museum or
waxwork (particularly the roped-off sections housing
royal equipages, or the presently historically safe beds of
lost kings) and who, on one or more occasion, had been
seen to wipe the corner of his eye with a fine pocket handkerchief.

The truth? Anders enjoyed the maneuvre, the per-
fected "leap," the trick pulled off. Imposing, high
stomached, spatted, gloved, he strolled the Luxembourg,
watching the leaves falling on the statues of dead queens,
the toy boats on the pond, the bows bobbing on the back-
sides of little girls, the people sitting and saying nothing.
If one is some day to enjoy paradise? Then the one ir-
reparable loss is any park in Paris that one can no longer
visit.

Later, coming into the music-room, stripping off his
gloves, he would speak of the dogs, of the races, of the
autumn, of the air in relation to the autumn and the air of
other countries; he would speak in praise of this or that
cathedral, this or that drama. Sometimes he set up before
the princess a rare etching that he hoped she would like,
or he would walk up and down before her until she noticed the pockets of his coat, into which he had stuck small
flowers. Sometimes he forgot horses and dogs, etchings

and autumns, and would concentrate on the use and the decline of the rapier, and of the merit of the high boot for the actor. The princess would quote Schiller. Then Anders would plunge into the uses of the fool in Shakespeare, turning and turning a thin gold band on his little finger (winking with a ruby as tender as water), weighing a point the princess had made, regarding the impracticability of maintaining tradition, now that every man was his own fool. They might get off on to literature in general, and she would ask if he were well versed in the poetry of Britain. He would answer that Chaucer caught him, and was a devil of a fellow to shake off. She would inquire gravely "Why shake?" and then drift on to a discussion of painting, and how it had left the home *genre* when the Dutch gave way to the English. They would argue for and against indoor and outdoor subjects for oils; and now and then the whole dispute would turn off to a suggested trip, to view a fine piece of Spanish furniture. Sometimes he left the etching.

Of course everyone assumed the princess the one true passion of his life. It was taken for granted that, but for a rupture suffered in the Franco-Prussian War, he would have claimed her for bride. Others were just as certain the princess was far too niggardly to share the half of her bed. The rest insisted that they had been lovers in youth and were now as good as husband and wife.

All of this was nonsense.

They were pages in an old volume, brought together by the closing of the book.

On the last call but one, there had been something of a strain. He had mentioned Gesualdo and the sorrows of the assassin; and from the assassin to the passion of Monteverdi "at the tomb of the beloved."

"The 'walking straight up to dreadfulness'," he said, "that is love."

He stopped directly in front of her as he spoke, leaning toward her to see how she did, and she, bent back and peering, said: "The last attendant on an old woman is always an 'incurable'." She set her teacup down with a slight trembling of the hand, then drawing her eyeglasses up, she added with mordant acerbity, "But—if a little light man with a beard had said 'I love you,' I should have believed in God."

He called only once after that, and only once was the princess seen riding in the Bois, a mist behind a tightdrawn veil. Shortly after, she did not live.

Cassation

"Do you know Germany, Madame, Germany in the spring? It is charming then, do you not think so? Wide and clean, the Spree winding thin and dark—and the roses! the yellow roses in the windows; and the bright talkative Americans passing through groups of German men staring over their steins, at the light and laughing women.

"It was such a spring, three years ago, that I came into Berlin from Russia. I was just sixteen, and my heart was a dancer's heart. It is that way sometimes; one's heart is all one thing for months, then—altogether another thing, *nicht wahr*? I used to sit in the café at the end of the Zelten, eating eggs and drinking coffee, watching the sudden rain of sparrows. Their feet struck the table all together, and all together they cleared the crumbs, and all together they flew into the sky, so that the café was as suddenly without birds as it had been suddenly full of birds.

"Sometimes a woman came here, at about the same hour as myself, around four in the afternoon; once she came with a little man, quite dreamy and uncertain. But I must explain how she looked: *temperamentvoll* and tall, *kraftvoll* and thin. She must have been forty then, dressed richly and carelessly. It seemed as though she could hardly keep her clothes on; her shoulders were always coming out, her skirt would be hanging on a hook, her pocket book would be mislaid, but all the time she was savage with jewels, and something purposeful and dramatic came in with her, as if she were the center of a whirlpool, and her clothes a temporary debris.

"Sometimes she clucked the sparrows, and sometimes she talked to the *Weinschenk*, clasping her fingers together until the rings stood out and you could see through them, she was so vital and so wasted. As for her dainty little man, she would talk to him in English, so that I did not know where they came from.

"Then one week I stayed away from the café because I was trying out for the *Schauspielhaus*, I heard they wanted a ballet dancer, and I was very anxious to get the part, so of course I thought of nothing else. I would wander, all by myself, through the *Tiergarten*, or I would stroll down the *Sieges-Allee* where all the great German emperors' statues are, looking like widows. Then suddenly I thought of the Zelten, and of the birds, and of that tall odd woman and so I went back there, and there she was, sitting in the garden sipping beer and chuck-chucking the sparrows.

"When I came in, she got up at once and came over to me and said: 'Why, how do you do, I have missed you. Why did you not tell me that you were going away? I should have seen what I could do about it.'"

"She talked like that; a voice that touched the heart because it was so unbroken and clear. 'I have a house', she said, 'just on the Spree. You could have stayed with me. It is a big, large house, and you could have the room just off my room. It is difficult to live in, but it is lovely—Italian you know, like the interiors you see in Venetian paintings, where young girls lie dreaming of the Virgin. You could find that you could sleep there, because you have dedication.'

"Somehow it did not seem at all out of the way that she should come to me and speak to me. I said I would meet her again some day in the garden, and we could go 'home' together, and she seemed pleased, but did not show surprise.

"Then one evening we came into the garden at the same moment. It was late and the fiddles were already playing. We sat together without speaking, just listening to the music, and admiring the playing of the only woman member of the orchestra. She was very intent on the movement of her fingers, and seemed to be leaning over her chin to watch. Then suddenly the lady got up, leaving a small rain of coin, and I followed her until we came to a big house and she let herself in with a brass key. She turned to the left and went into a dark room and switched on the lights and sat down and said: 'This is where we sleep; this is how it is.'

"Everything was disorderly, and expensive and melancholy. Everything was massive and tall, or broad and wide. A chest of drawers rose above my head. The china stove was enormous and white, enameled in blue flowers. The bed was so high that you could only think of it as something that might be overcome. The walls were all bookshelves, and all the books were bound in red morocco, on the back of each, in gold, was stamped a coat of arms, intricate and oppressive. She rang for tea and began taking off her hat.

"A great painting hung over the bed; the painting and the bed ran together in encounter, the huge rumps of the stallions reined into the pillows. The generals, with foreign helmets and dripping swords, raging through rolling smoke and the bleeding ranks of the dying, seemed to be charging the bed, so large, so rumpled, so devastated. The sheets were trailing, the counterpane hung torn, and the feathers shivered along the floor, trembling in the slight wind from the open window. The lady was smiling in a sad grave way, but she said nothing, and it was not until some moments later that I saw a child, not more than three years old, a small child, lying in the center of the pillows, making a thin noise, like the buzzing of a fly, and I thought it was a fly.

"She did not talk to the child, indeed she paid no attention to it, as if it were in her bed and she did not know it. When the tea was brought in she poured it, but she took none, instead she drank small glasses of Rhine wine.

"'You have seen Ludwig,' she said in her faint and grieving voice, 'we were married a long time ago, he was just a boy then. I? Me? I am an Italian, but I studied English and German because I was with a travelling company. You,' she said abruptly, 'you must give up the ballet—the theater—acting.' Somehow I did not think it odd that she should know of my ambition, though I had not mentioned it. 'And,' she went on, 'you are not for the stage; you are for something quieter, more withdrawn. See here, I like Germany very much, I have lived here a good many years. You will stay and you will see. You have seen Ludwig, you have noticed that he is not strong; he is always declining, you must have noticed it yourself; he must not be distressed, he can't bear anything. He has his room to himself.' She seemed suddenly tired, and she got up and threw herself across the bed, at the foot, and fell asleep, almost instantly, her hair all about her. I went away then, but I came back that night and tapped at the window. She came to the window and signed to me, and presently appeared at another window to the right of the bedroom, and beckoned with her hand, and I came up and climbed in, and did not mind that she had not opened the door for me. The room was dark except for the moon, and two thin candles burning before the Virgin.

"It was a beautiful room, Madame, '*traurig*' as she said. Everything was important and old and gloomy. The curtains about the bed were red velvet, Italian you know, and fringed in gold bullion. The bed cover was a deep red velvet with the same gold fringe: on the floor, beside the bed, a stand on which was a tasselled red cushion, on the cushion a Bible in Italian, lying open.

"She gave me a long nightgown, it came below my feet and came back up again almost to my knees. She loosened my hair, it was long then, and yellow. She plaited it in two plaits; she put me down at her side and said a prayer in German, then in Italian, and ended, 'God bless you,' and I got into bed. I loved her very much because there was nothing between us but this strange preparation for sleep. She went away then. In the night I heard the child crying, but I was tired.

"I stayed a year. The thought of the stage had gone out of my heart. I had become a *religieuse*; a gentle religion that began with the prayer I had said after her the first night, and the way I had gone to sleep, though we never repeated the ceremony. It grew with the furniture and the air of the whole room, and with the Bible lying open at a page that I could not read; a religion, Madame, that was empty of need, therefore it was not holy perhaps, and not as it should have been in its manner. It was that I was happy, and I lived there for one year. I almost never saw Ludwig, and almost never Valentine, for that was her child's name, a little girl.

"But at the end of that year I knew there was trouble in other parts of the house. I heard her walking in the night, sometimes Ludwig would be with her, I could hear him crying and talking, but I could not hear what was said. It sounded like a sort of lesson, a lesson for a child to repeat, but if so, there would have been no answer, for the child never uttered a sound, except that buzzing cry.

"Sometimes it is wonderful in Germany, Madame, *nicht wahr?* There is nothing like a German winter. She and I used to walk about the Imperial Palace, and she stroked the cannon, and said they were splendid. We talked about philosophy, for she was troubled with too much thinking, but she always came to the same conclusion, that one must be, or try to be, like everyone else. She explained that to be like everyone, all at once, in your own person, was to be holy. She said that people did not understand what was meant by 'Love thy neighbor as thyself.' It meant, she said, that one should be like all people and oneself, then, she said, one was both ruined and powerful.

"Sometimes it seemed that she was managing it, that she was all Germany, at least in her Italian heart. She seemed so irreparably collected and yet distressed, that I was afraid of her, and not afraid.

"That is the way it was, Madame, she seemed to wish it to be that way, though at night she was most scattered and distraught, I could hear her pacing in her room.

"Then she came in one night and woke me and said that I must come into her room. It was in a most terrible disorder. There was a small cot bed that had not been there before. She pointed to it and said that it was for me.

"The child was lying in the great bed against a large lace pillow. Now it was four years old and yet it did not walk, and I never heard it say a thing, or make a sound, except that buzzing cry. It was beautiful in the corrupt way of idiot children; a sacred beast without a taker, tainted with innocence and waste time; honey-haired and failing, like those dwarf angels on holy prints and valentines, if you understand me, Madame, something saved for a special day that would not arrive, not for life at all: and my lady was talking quietly, but I did not recognize any of her former state.

"'You must sleep here now,' she said, 'I brought you here for this if I should need you, and I need you. You must stay, you must stay forever.' Then she said, 'Will you?' And I said no, I could not do that.

"She took up the candle and put it on the floor beside me, and knelt beside it, and put her arms about my knees. 'Are you a traitor?' she said, 'have you come into my house, Ludwig's house, the house of my child, to betray us?' And I said, no, I had not come to betray. 'Then,' she said, 'you will do as I tell you. I will teach you slowly, slowly; it will not be too much for you, but you must begin to forget, you must forget everything. You must forget all the things people have told you. You must forget arguments and philosophy. I was wrong in talking of such things; I thought it would teach you how to lag with her mind, to undo time for her as it passes, to climb into her bereavement and her dispossession. I brought you up badly; I was vain. You will do better. Forgive me.' She put the palms of her hands on the floor, her face to my face. 'You must never see any other room than this room. It was a great vanity that I took you out walking. Now you will stay here safely, and you will see. You will like it, you will learn to like it the very best of all. I will bring you breakfast, and luncheon, and supper. I will bring it to you both, myself. I will hold you on my lap, I will feed you like the birds. I will rock you to sleep. You must not argue with me—above all we must have no arguments, no talk about man and his destiny—man has no destiny—that is my secret—I have been keeping it from you until today, this very hour. Why not before? Perhaps I was jealous of the knowledge, yes, that must be it, but now I give it to you, I share it with you. I am an old woman,' she said, still holding me by the knees. 'When Valentine was born, Ludwig was only a boy.' She got up and stood behind me. 'He is not strong, he does not understand that the weak are the strongest things in the world, because he is one of them. He cannot help her, they are adamant together. I need you, it must be you.' Suddenly she began talking to me as she talked with the child, and I did not know which of us she was talking to. 'Do not repeat anything after me. Why should children repeat what people say? The whole world is nothing but a noise, as hot as the inside of a tiger's mouth. They call it civilization— that is a lie! But some day you may have to go out, someone will try to take you out, and you will not understand them or what they are saying, unless you understand nothing, absolutely nothing, then you will manage.' She moved around so that she faced us, her back against the wall. 'Look,' she said, 'it is all over, it has gone away, you do not need to be afraid; there is only you. The stars are out, and the snow is falling down and covering the world, the hedges, the houses and the lamps. No, no!' she said to herself, 'wait. I will put you on your feet, and tie you up in ribbons, and we will go out together, out into the garden where the swans are, and the flowers and the bees and small beasts. And the students will come, because it will be summer, and they will read in their books….' She broke off, then took her wild speech up again, this time as though she were really speaking to the child, 'Katya will go with you. She will instruct you, she will tell you there are no swans, no flowers, no beasts, no boys—nothing, nothing at all, just as you like it. No mind, no thought, nothing whatsoever else. No bells will ring, no people will talk, no birds will fly, no boys will move, there'll be no birth and no death; no sorrow, no laughing, no kissing, no crying, no terror, no joy; no eating, no drinking, no games, no dancing; no father, no mother, no sisters, no brothers—only you, only you!'

"I stopped her and I said, 'Gaya, why is it that you suffer so, and what am I to do?' I tried to put my arms around her, but she struck them down crying, 'Silence!' Then she said, bringing her face close to my face, 'She has no claws to hang by; she has no hunting foot; she has no mouth for the meat—vacancy!'

"Then, Madame, I got up. It was very cold in the room. I went to the window and pulled the curtain, it was a bright and starry night, and I stood leaning my head against the frame, saying nothing. When I turned around, she was regarding me, her hands held apart, and I knew that I had to go away and leave her. So I came up to her and said, 'Good-bye, my Lady.' And I went and put on my street clothes, and when I came back she was leaning against the battle picture, her hands hanging. I said to her, without approaching her, 'Good-bye, my love,' and went away.

"Sometimes it is beautiful in Berlin, Madame, *nicht wahr*? There was something new in my heart, a passion to see Paris, so it was natural that I said *lebe wohl* to Berlin.

"I went for the last time to the café in the Zelten, ate my eggs, drank my coffee and watched the birds coming and going just as they used to come and go—altogether here then altogether gone. I was happy in my spirit, for that is the way it is with my spirit, Madame, when I am going away.

"But I went back to her house just once. I went in quite easily by the door, for all the doors and windows were open—perhaps they were sweeping that day. I came to the bedroom door and knocked, but there was no answer. I pushed, and there she was, sitting up in the bed with the child, and she and the child were making that buzzing cry, and no human sound between them, and as usual, everything was in disorder. I came up to her, but she did not seem to know me. I said, 'I am going away; I am going to Paris. There is a longing in me to be in Paris. So I have come to say farewell.'

"She got down off the bed and came to the door with me. She said, 'Forgive me—I trusted you—I was mistaken. I did not know that I could do it myself, but you see, I can do it myself.' Then she got back on to the bed and said, 'Go away,' and I went.

"Things are like that, when one travels, *nicht wahr*, Madame?"

The Grande Malade

"AND THERE WE WERE, my sister Moydia and I, Madame. Moydia was fifteen and I was seventeen and we were young all over. Moydia has a thin thin skin, so that I sit and look at her and wonder how she has opinions. She is all white except the cheekbones, then rosy red; her teeth are milk-teeth and she has a small figure, very pretty and droll. She wanted to become '*tragique*' and '*triste*' and 'tremendous' all at once, like the great period Frenchwomen, only fiercer and perhaps less pure, and yet to die and give up the heart like a virgin. It was a noble, an impossible ambition, *n'est-ce pas*, Madame? But that was the way it was with Moydia. We used to sit in the sun when we were in Norway and read Goethe and did not agree with him at all. 'The man is *pompeux* and too *assuré*,' she would say, shutting her teeth, 'and very much too *facile*.' But then, people say we do not know.

"We are Russian, Moydia and I, and but for an accident, the most terrifying of our life up to then, we would not have known that our grandmother was a Jew—why? because she was *allowed* to drink champagne on her deathbed, and Jews are forbidden champagne you know. So, being 'damned' as it were (both in her dying *and* the 'permission,') she forced mother to drink champagne too,

393

that she might be damned in living as the dying in extremity. So we are Jew and not Jew. We are where we are. We are Polish when we are in Poland, and when in Holland we are Dutch, and now in France we are French, and one day we will go to America and be American; you will see, Madame.

"Now I have forgotten all the Polish I knew and all the Russian I knew and all the Dutch, except, that is, a poem. Ah, that poem, that small piece of a poem! a very touching thing, heavy, sweet—a fragment of language. It makes you feel pity in your whole body, because it is complete but mutilated, like a Greek statue, yet whole, like a life, Madame.

"Now I have come to Paris and I respect Paris. First I respected it in a great hat. I am short and a great hat would not, you see, become me, but I wore it for respect. It was all a jumble of flowers and one limber feather; it stood out so that my face was in the middle of a garden. Now I do not wear it any more. I have had to go back in my knowledge, right back to the remembrance, which is the place where I regard my father, and how he looked when in from the new snow. I did not really see him then. Now I see he was truly beautiful all the time that I was thinking nothing about him at all—his astrakhan cap, his frogged coat, with all those silver buttons, and the tall shining boots that caught him just under the knee. Then I think of the window I looked down from and saw the crown of that hat—a wonderful, a mysterious red felt. So now, out of respect for that man, I wear my hats small. Some day, when I have money, my shoes will be higher and come under my knee. This is my way, Madame, but it is not the way it is with Moydia. She has a *great memory in the present*, and it all turns about a cape, therefore now she wears a cape, until something yet more austere drives the cape away. But I must explain.

"First, we are very young as I said, so because of that one becomes *tragique* very quickly, if one is brave, is it not so? So Moydia, though she is two years younger than I, became exhausted almost at once.

"You know how it is in Paris in the autumn, when the summer is just giving up the leaf. I had been here with Moydia two autumns; the first was sad and light on the heart, the way it is when all one's lovers live in spite of the cold. We walked in the Tuileries, I in my small cap and Moydia in a woolly coat, for that was the kind of coat she wore then, and we bought pink and blue candies outside the Punch and Judy show and laughed when the puppets beat each other, Moydia's face tight beneath her skin with the lemon flavor, and tears coming down from her eyes as we thought how perfect everything was; the dolls at their fight and the trees bare, the ground all shuffled in with their foliage—then the pond. We stopped at the pond. The water was full to the edge with water-lily pads and Moydia said it was a shame that women threw themselves in the Seine, only to become a part of its sorrow, instead of casting themselves into a just-right pond like this, where the water would become a part of them. We felt a great despair that people do not live or die beautifully, nor plan anything at all; and then and there we said we would do better.

"After that I noticed, almost at once, that Moydia had become a little too florid. She sprinkled her sugar in her tea from too great a height, and she talked very fast. That was how it was with my sister Moydia in that autumn.

"And of course sophistication came upon us suddenly. We hung long curtains over our beds and we talked of lovers and we smoked. And me? I went about in satin trousers for respect to China, which is a very great country and has *majesté* because you cannot know it. It is like a big book which you can read but not understand. So I talked of China to Moydia; and we kept three birds that did not sing, as a symbol of the Chinese heart; and Moydia lay on her bed and became more and more restless, like a story that has no beginning and no end, only a passion like flash lightning.

"She was always kicking her feet in the air and tearing handkerchiefs and crying in her pillow, but when I asked her why she was doing all this, she sat straight up, wailing, 'Because I want *everything,* and to be consumed in my youth!'

"So one day she knew everything. Though I am two years older than Moydia, it is different with me. I live more slowly, only women listen to me, but men adore Moydia. To her they do not listen, they look. They look at her when she sits down and when she walks. All at once she began to walk and to sit down quite differently. All her movements were a sort of *malheureuse* tempest. She had her lover and she laughed and cried, lying face down, and whimpering, 'Isn't it *wonderful!*' And perhaps it was indeed wonderful, Madame. From all her admirers she had chosen the most famous, none other than Monsieur x. His great notoriety had thinned him. He dressed very *soigneusement*; white gloves, you know, and spats and a cape, a very handsome affair with a military collar; and he was *grave* and *rare* and stared at you with one eye not at all, but the other looked out from a monocle, like the lidless eye of a fish that keeps deep water. He was the *protégé* of a Baron. The Baron liked him very much and called him his '*Poupon prodigieux*,' and they played farces together for the amusement of the Faubourg. That was the way it was with Monsieur x, at least in his season when he was, shall we say, the *belle-d'un-jour* and was occupied in writing fables on mice and men, but he always ended the stories with paragraphs *très acre* against women.

"Moydia began to cultivate a throaty voice. She became an *habitué* of the opera; fierce and fluttering, she danced about Monsieur x during the *entr'acte*, pulling her flowers to pieces and scattering them as she went, humming, '*Je suis éternellement!*' The audience looked on with displeasure, but the Baron was enchanted.

"Because I and my sister have always been much together, we were much together now. Sometimes I visited the Baron with her and had many hours of dignity just watching them. When the Baron was entertaining, he was very gay and had great control of a sort of aged immaturity, and Moydia would play the kitten or the great lady, as the occasion demanded. If he seemed to forget her for an instant, she became a *gamine*, sticking her tongue out at his turned back, hissing, '*Ah, tu es belle!*' at which he would turn about and laugh, she falling into his lap, all in one piece, stiff and *enragé*. And he would have a long time stroking her and asking her, in his light worn feminine voice, what was the matter. And once she would not open her eyes, but screamed and made him hold her heart, saying, 'Does not the creature beat dreadfully?' and he entreated her, 'Because? Because?'

"Then clapping her hands she would burst into tears and cry: 'I give you too many destinies with my body. I am Marie on the way to the *guillotine*. I am Bloody Mary but I have not seen blood. I am Desdemona, but Othello—where is he? I am Hecuba and Helen. I am Graetal and Brunhilda, I am Nana and Camille. But I'm not as bored as they are! When shall I become *properly* bored?'

"He was bored, and he put her off his knee. She flew at him then and pulled his clothes about and ripped his gloves, and said with absolute quiet: 'It amazes me how I do not love you.'

"But when we got home, I had to put her to bed. She was shivering and laughing and she seemed to be running a fever.

"'Did you see his face? He is a monster! A product of *malaise*. He *wants* me to be his sacristan. He'd like me to bury him. I am positive of it, Katya; are you not positive of it? He is an old soul. He has come to his mortal end.

He is beastly with *finis*. But Death has given him leave. Oh!' she cried, 'I adore him! I adore him! I adore him! Oh, I do adore him !' And she refused to see him until he went quite out of his head and called for himself. She went running before him all down the hall. I could hear the sharp report of her heels, and her lisping voice quoting: '*Le héron au long bec emmanché d'un long cou*,' in a sing-song as she jumped the last step into the day, exclaiming, '*C'est la Fontaine, la Fontaine magnifique!*' And you could hear his cane tapping after her.

"Then this last autumn, before this last winter set in (you were not here then, Madame), Moydia had gone to Germany to visit papa, and all the night before we had sat up together, the three of us, Moydia, her lover and I. We drank a great deal too much, I sang my Dutch song and talked a long time, rambling on about father and his cap and boots, and that splendid coat of his. It pleased Moydia and it pleased me, but to Monsieur x, probably we seemed like beggars recalling remembered gold. So I danced a Tartar dance and raged that my boots did not reach to my knees, and all the time Moydia was lying on her lover's shoulder, both welded as if they were an emblem. But when I stopped whirling, he called me over, and he whispered that I should have a pair of great boots some day, which gave me great joy. But Moydia sprang up. 'I do not love this man, Cookoo, do I?' She always called him Cookoo when she was most fond, as though she were talking about someone else. 'I only love Cookoo when I am drunk. So now I do not love him at all, because I am not drunk at all. Oh, we Russian women drink a great deal but it is to become sober—this is something the other peoples do not take into account! Is it not so, Katya? It's because we are so extravagant that we do not reach justice…we reach poetry. You adore me, you see,' she said to him, 'and I *let* you, but that is the way it is with Polish women.'

"'Russian,' he corrected, and sat staring through the boss of his monocle straight at the wall.

"Well then, Moydia went away to Germany to visit papa, who is a travelling man now and buys and sells diamonds. He will not send us money unless he sees us at least once a year. He's that way. He says he will not have his girls grow up into something he does not like paying for. Sometimes he sends money from Russia, sometimes from Poland, sometimes from Belgium, sometimes from England. He has said that some day he will come to Paris, but he does not come. It is very confusing to get so many kinds of moneys, we never know what we will have to spend, we have to be very careful; perhaps that is the whole idea. But at this point Moydia had lost all caution. She bought herself a new dress to please Monsieur x, and to go away in, and not to alarm father—all at the same time. So it was a cunning dress, very deft and touching. It was all dotted suisse, with a very tight bodice, and into this bodice, just between the breasts, was embroidered, in very fine twist, a slain lamb. It might, you see, mean everything and it might mean nothing, and it might bring pleasure to both father and lover.

"After she had gone, I sat in the café every afternoon and waited for her return. She was not to be gone longer than two weeks. That was the autumn that I felt great sadness, Madame, I read a great deal and I walked about all by myself; I was in need of solitude. I walked in the Tuileries and visited the pond again, and went under the trees where the air was cool and there were numbers of people who did not seem to be gay. The autumn had come differently this year; it was already oppressive in September—it was as though there were a catafalque coming into Paris from a long way and everyone knew it; men buttoned their coats tight and the women tipped their sunshades down, as if for rain.

"So ten days passed, and the season hung heavy in a mist that blotted almost everything out. You could scarcely see the Seine when you went walking on the bridges, the statues in the parks were altogether withdrawn, the sentries looked like dolls in boxes, the ground was always damp, the café *brasiers* were going full heat. Then I knew, suddenly I knew—Moydia's lover was dying! And indeed that night he died. He had caught a chill the evening that Moydia left, and it had grown worse and worse. It was reported the Baron was always with him, and when the Baron saw that Monsieur x was truly going to die, he made him drink. They drank together all night and into the morning. The Baron wanted it that way: 'For that,' he said, 'he might die as he was born, without knowing.'

"So I went straight to the Baron's house, and right up

to the door, and rapped—but he would not let me in. He said through the door that Moydia's lover had been buried that very morning, and I said, 'Give me something for Moydia,' and he said, 'What shall I give you?' and he added, 'He left nothing but a deathless name!' And I said, 'Give me his cape.' And he gave me his cape, through the leeway of the chain on the door, but he did not look out at me, and I went away.

"That night Moydia arrived back from Germany. She had a terrible fever and she talked very fast, like a child. She wanted to go directly to Monsieur's house; I had great difficulty in keeping her in. I put her to bed and made her tea, but I could not keep still, so I brought her the cape and I said, 'Cookoo is dead and this is his cape and it is for you.' She said, 'How did he die?' and 'Why?'

"I said, 'He was taken ill the night you left, and it became a fever that would not leave him, so the Baron sat with him and they drank all night that he might die as he was born, without knowing.'

"Moydia began beating on the bed then with both hands and saying, 'Let us drink, and pray God I shall die the same death!' We sat up all night drinking and talking together without much sense. Toward morning she said, 'Now I have a great life!' and she wept and went to sleep, and by noon she was quite well.

"Now, Madame, she wears it always. The cape. Men admire her in it, indeed she looks very well in it, do you not think so? She has grown faster than I; you would take her for the elder, would you not? She is gay, spoiled, *tragique.* She sugars her tea from far too great a height. And that's all. There's nothing else to tell, except—in the débâcle my boots were quite forgotten. The next day all the papers carried pages and pages about Monsieur x, and in all of them he was wearing a cape. We, Moydia and I, read them together. They may even have printed something about him in America? Truly, we speak a little French; now we must be moving on."

Dusie

IT IS ABOUT DUSIE, madame, she was very young, perhaps only a year older than I, and tall, very big and beautiful, absent and so pale. She wore big shoes, and her ankles and wrists were large, and her legs beyond belief long. She used to sit in the corner of the café, day after day, drinking, and she had a bitter careless sort of ferocity with women. Not in anything she said, for she spoke seldom, but she handled them roughly, yet gladly. She was *dégagé*, but you could not know her well.

Sometimes, walking down the Rue D—, I saw her standing out on the balcony of her room, in a white dressing gown, like a man's, and sometimes she called to me, if she was not singing, and sometimes she did not. So it is with people in Paris, *n'est-ce-pas?*

After a while I did not see her in the café much, but often in the house of Madame K—. It was a splendid house, with footmen standing behind the great iron doors, in white gloves. They looked always as if they expected you, yet did not care.

The house was very French. All gold and blue, and, in the boudoirs, pink. There were three, but the part of the house I saw most often was blue and white, with much lace and gold. The walls were blue satin, and hanging from tasseled cords were many golden framed women hung. They were all reclining, and they looked at you sideways, smiling from beneath hives of honey-colored hair, and they had little with them but birds and flowers, and all were anaemic and charming, as if they had been handled too much. Sometimes a bar of music was near to them, but you would not think of humming it, it so belonged to them, just as it was.

There were many chrysanthemums, and a long white harp in the embrasure of the window, and in the dust lying upon it many women had written "Dusie." And above all, in an enamelled cage, two canaries, the one who sang, and the one who listened.

But in the boudoirs there was much pink, and everything was brittle and glazed and intricate. Ribbons dangled from everything and bon-bons were everywhere, and statuettes of little boys in satin breeches, offering tiny ladies in bouffant skirts, fans and finches and flowers, and all about in the grass were stuck shiny slinking foxes.

A thin powder was over everything upon the dressing table, mauve and sweet smelling, and a great litter of *La Vie Parisienne* and *Le Rire*, and when you picked up the most solemn looking volume, engravings of Watteau fell out and Greuze, and in the hall a tall clock tinkled and rang.

Madame K— was large, very full and blond. She went with the furniture as only a childless Frenchwoman can. She had been a surgeon, a physician, but nothing remained of it, only the tone of her voice when she was angry; then she removed the argument within the exact bounds of its sickness.

When there was talk of spiritual matters, and there is always such talk, madame, when women, many women, are closed up together in a room, she listened, but she let you know definitely that she was mortal.

There were always a large number of women in her house. It was like a Northern *gare,* and no trains running. There especially was Clarissa.

With Clarissa it was like this: it was as if everyone was her torment, as if she lived only because so many people had seen and spoken to her and of her. If she had been forgotten for a month, entirely, by everyone, I am sure she would have died. Everyone was her wound, and this made her sly, and sweet, and attractive too. For alone of them all, Madame K— had the great indifference for her, and was about her in no way occupied at all.

But for Dusie, Madame K— had love. You knew, because when Dusie was with her, Madame K— looked like a precaution all at once.

For that is the way it was with Dusie always. All people gave her their attention, stroking her, and calling her pet or beast, according to their feelings. They touched her as if she were an idol, and she stood tall, or sat to drink, unheeding, absent. You felt that you must talk to Dusie, tell her everything, because all her beauty was there, but uninhabited, like a church, *n'est-ce-pas,* madame? Only she was not holy, she was very mortal, and sometimes vulgar, a ferocious and oblivious vulgarity. She cursed

406

when corks would not come out of bottles; when women moved their knees if she were lying on them; when some-one said men were wise.

She had long, heavy hair, yet it looked like a splendid shame, and I could not tell why. Then one time, in Mi Carême, she cut it away; she said she had done it to be just. No one knew quite what she meant.

It is simple to understand why it was good to be near her. She had a strong bodily odor, like sleep and a tree growing, and yet she was not strong. Her movements were like vines growing over a ruin. When she was ill it was sorrowful to see her, she suffered such shallow pain, as if her body were in the toils of a feeble and remorseless agony. Then she would lie over, her knees up, her head down, laughing and crying and saying, "Do you love me?" to every woman, and every woman answered that they loved her. But it did not change her, and suddenly she would shout: "Get out, get out of my room!" Something in her grew and died for her alone.

When they were gone, thrown out, she would sit up in bed and amuse herself with the dolls they had brought her, wooden animals and tin soldiers, and again she would cast them from her with cunning energy. I know, she let me stay with her, yet when I asked her what she was think-ing, she would say "Nothing." Always she said that when anyone asked her what she was thinking, and in the end, madame, it produced upon them all a sort of avid forget-fulness of her person, and they would talk openly before her of the ways she would die. And she did not seem to notice; that made it sorrowful and ridiculous, as if they were anticipating a doom that had fallen already a hundred years.

Yet I think Dusie cared for only one of them all, for Madame K—, and that was not liking, it was something else; she loved her as one loves the only reality. You can see, madame, how that would be strong, inexorable.

Clarissa knew how it was with Dusie, and so she followed Madame K— about, and sometimes touching her for no reason at all, saying I adore that woman! Then Madame K— would go away, and sitting in the music room would play a waltz slowly, too slow for dancing, except in the numbed intervals of sleep. And soon Dusie would be found standing beside her, frowning, preoccupied.

One night it was raining, and Dusie came into the café where I was drinking my coffee, and she came up to me and she said I must come with her, because Madame K— had gone to see her mother that night, and she was afraid to sleep alone. It was very late, it must have been midnight, but I got up, and went with her.

When we got into the big house, and up into the boudoir, she opened a bottle of sherry, and we drank a little, and talked, as we sat on either side of the bed and got out of our clothes, quickly and quietly. And when we were in bed, she began to speak, staring up at the canopy.

"Have you lived here always?" she said, and I said "No, I had lived in many places," and I told her some of the names of the places, Berlin and Holland and Russia and Poland. And she said "What was in that town?" And I said, "In that town there were beautiful men in shining black beards, and they had sledges and ships and were happy and cold all day, nevertheless one man there had a mother who stole ducks." And that made her laugh, and then she said, "And what was in the other town?" And I said, "In that town there were hundreds of starving dogs." And then she said, "What was the last place like?" And I said, "There were churches there, and the bells rang one way, and every time they rang one way, hundreds and hundreds of old women came through the town and went up the steps, holding their skirts in front, and when the bells rang another way, they all came down again, their skirts lapping the steps, and went away through the town." And she said, "Were there no young people there?" and I said, no, there were no young people there, and she said she would like to go there some day, and be quiet, she always wanted to be where there were old women and animals, and no new life. And I said I wanted to go to America because I was tired of old women and dogs, and she said, "What do you think you will find in America?" And I said, "*Joie de vie!*" And she said nothing at all, and I said, "Is it not so in America?" And she said "No, that was not the way it was." But when I said, "Tell me the way it is with her," she said she did not know. Always so it was with Dusie; at the critical moment she could not explain.

Presently I heard a key in the lock. Dusie started up, and, getting out of bed, said, "Don't come in here. Go to sleep." And went out, pulling the curtain behind her.

For a long time I heard nothing. I must have slept. Then I heard Clarissa's voice, not loud, but sharp, and clear and sweet, and Dusie's not at all. And I wondered then how is it that Clarissa had a key to the house of Madame, and I thought, she would steal it; it is the only way that she comes by anything. And I knew that there was evil in her visit, and the teaching of evil, and a thing to be done with the heart of Dusie, and I said to myself, "Will Dusie do it?," though I knew not what Dusie was to do, but I feared suddenly for Madame K— and then did not fear because of the way Dusie and Madame K— were with each other always.

After a long time I head what Clarissa was saying, because I was drowsy and unguarded.

And she said, "You do not look as if you would live long, not long, but I am thirty and I think for you, and you must think too, about the most terrible virtue, which is to be undefiled because one has no way for it; there are women like that, grown women; there should be an end…"

I must have slept then, for suddenly Dusie was shaking me roughly and quickly, and I awoke and I said "What is it?" And she said, "You must go into the other room and sleep." And I got up, looking for my shoes, and went into the big room and got into bed and forgot. There I dreamed, about soldiers and priests and a dog, and people crowding into a thick pack, and the bells ringing, and when I awoke it must have been eleven. The sun was shining in at the window, and the clock had been striking a long time.

I got up to go into Dusie's room to get my dress, and as I came near I heard her crying, and I went in quickly then and said, "What is it, are you ill?" And she stopped crying, and turned her face to the wall, and someone was turning the key in the lock again and this time it was Madame K— and then I saw Dusie's foot. It was all crushed, and lying helpless, and a trifle of blood ran from the bed to the door and lay upon the hinge. And Dusie said nothing. And Madame K— ran down upon the bed, and took the foot in her lap, and I thought, she will weep now, but she did not weep, she said, "You see how it is, she can think no evil for others, she can only hurt herself. You must go away now." And I went away.

Yes, even now the story had begun to fade with me; it is so in Paris; France eats her own history, *n'est-ce-pas,* madame?

A Duel Without Seconds

THE BARON AND BARONESS Otterly-Hansclever were two at dinner, each immured in a lonely little canopy of light flung by the candles at either end of the long table. The third course had been served, and the Baron had helped himself to three cutlets in place of his usual two; for, now that his dueling days were practically over, he had no need to keep free of fat. The Baroness sat in silence and thinking of the days that were no longer.

Silent and preoccupied they both were, while between them the long, hard expanse of mahogany mocked them with a false gaiety of silver and glass and with shadows of candlelight that danced along its bland surface like ghosts of the company whose laughter it once had known. There was silence too, in the room that brooded darkly over the lonely couple—silence heavy and complete save for the whisper of the butler's feet as he moved pallidly in the dimness beyond the high, brocaded chairs. But to the Baroness the very silence was loud with echoes of the past, and to her wistful eyes the fleeting shadows now seemed to take form, almost to assume the outlines of phantom guests crowding around the table in a staccato pattern of talk and color as vivid as in the days, not so long ago, when this same room had buzzed with conversation, had rung with laughter. So strong was the illusion that she half-turned her head toward the place on her right hand where the old Duke of Yarhoven, with his daughter, had been accustomed to sit—then to her left, where the bosoms, bright with medals, of famous generals and politicians had once swelled with confidence and gaiety. She sighed now as she recalled, one by one, those delightful friends of a happier day.... There had been the lanky Hoving twins, eager young sportswomen whose laughter rang across a drawing-room in a kind of prolonged, double echo like the baying of hounds, making everyone think of pink coats and crisp, autumn fields so that they all felt enormously cheerful, even the sundry officers suffering from malaria contracted while doing the right thing by the colonies. There had been actresses, statesmen, princes, even a king—and always, like the charming sentimental refrain running through an operetta, there had been that assortment of wistful little wives whose husbands had been sent out of their own country to do some kind of political injustice in another.

But those days were tragically over; and now the Baron and his Baroness were alone, and as lonely as dethroned royalty. The money which had once been so plentiful had diminished until now it hardly served to cover the pheasants with their appropriate dressing. Their riches were gone, their friends were gone; before them lay nothing but a thin and dreadful solitude. But while the Baroness grew hourly frailer and more despairing, her husband seemed unaffected by their misfortune. Indeed, looking at him now down the grim length of that deserted table, she reflected that he seemed to live entirely in the past; placid, pink, and stupid, he busied himself only with his history of dueling from the sixteenth century to his own time—when, he assured everyone who would listen, he had been no mean hand at the fine art himself. He carried a long and nasty scar across his right cheek to attest to his veracity, and although the story of that scar altered brilliantly from year to year, it gave him tremendous *cachet*.

When he had first met his future Baroness (she had been Gertie Platz, then, and sweetly gullible) he had assured her that it was but a month old, having been won in defense of her beauty and fair name; but scarcely had the glow in her heart begun to brighten into something akin to love for her valiant defender, when she overheard him telling the Duchess of Yarhoven that he had come by his scar one unfortunate night in Madrid when he had righted a wrong half a mile out of town. In the succeeding years (there had been twenty) he had changed the story as often as he could find anyone to tell it to; it was, variously, on a point of personal honor that he had been wounded, for the honor of the church, for the honor of his country, for the honor of a woman...but it was always a highly entertaining tale. In the early days, the Baroness had been thrilled. She winced and breathed faster as he drew out, in an illustrative gesture, his bloody rapier; she shuddered and paled, and murmured: "You are wonderful!" But,

God of custom, that was long ago! Now her nostrils quivered slightly and she thrust her head away.

As her friends deserted her, and her life narrowed to a barren path of debt and despair, this once great lady's smile had come to be, of late, a little iced; her infrequent laughter a trifle shrill. Lines appeared about her fine eyes, and her step was slower as she walked in her lonely garden and listened to her gardener talk of winter packing for the strawberries and the gentler flowers. Alas, she knew too well why her friends had left her; as vividly as though it had been carved by a bitter blade upon her mind and heart, she could trace the first indication of disaster to that dreadful evening five years ago, upon the occasion of their fifteenth anniversary ball, when the most deplorable, the most tragic event of her life had taken place.

The Baron, that night, had just been telling the pretty wife of General Koenig how he had come by his scar in Budapest, fighting beside the blue Danube in waltz time with an adversary who would not keep step, when one of the Hoving twins, with a long, resounding wail (the acoustics of the Baron's mansion being peculiarly perfect for rendering anguish) screamed that she had been robbed not only of her mother's emerald pendant but of her father's father's time-piece, as big as a turnip and wound with a key in the shape of a spade, which she valued not so much because it was her grandfather's as because it was worth a thousand British pounds, its equivalent in dollars, its twin in marks, and its replica in lire. To this day, the Baroness shuddered as she recalled the stark silence that had followed the announcement of this loss, then the excited hum of voices as the guests began hastily to compute the loss in various currencies. Uncomfortable pauses there had been, too, lips tightened with unspoken doubts, eyes that rested a little too long, a little too thoughtfully on other eyes.... All the curious, eager, yet reluctant suspicion that is so easily roused among friends dwelt like an evil fog in that brilliant room. The thing had been hushed up, of course, although neither pendant nor watch was ever found, and there the matter might have ended; but from that day the Baroness, her eyes shadowed with anxiety, noticed that at each of her parties that followed something of value was lost. Her drawing-room lacked spontaneity after that; fewer and fewer guests came, and always there was that nervous expectation of someone rising to proclaim the loss of a jewel, or—worse still—considerately hurrying away, murmuring something about having misplaced a cuff-link or a tie-pin, a bracelet or a ring. The servants were questioned, and several were dismissed under suspicion; but still the thefts continued, and the Baroness grew as thin as a leaf in the wind, and seldom, now, raised her tired eyes to the faces of those friends who were left to her. Soon, even the last of these drifted away, and the Baron and Baroness Otterly-Hansclever were alone; alone, and somehow, she felt, disgraced.

It occurred to her now, as she tasted a salad dressing that seemed almost utterly tasteless, that had she been a younger woman she would have wept, and opened her heart to her husband. But armored and inert as he was among his papers and notes on dueling, he, too, was lost to her. So she ate in silence, turning over and over in her mind the thought that had been ripening there like a dark and cruel seed, that their honor had gone unavenged. Not only had their guests been despoiled, but their own family plate had disappeared, piece by piece, and even her own little rope of pearls could not be found. Was there, she thought fiercely, no alternative, no future for the Otterly-Hansclevers but to sit supinely, while the dark hand of disgrace closed upon them and their friends, one by one, turned surely and dreadfully away?

Why did the Baron say nothing, do nothing? Was he so engrossed in the history of dueling that he had no time nor inclination to fight when it was needed? Well...of what avail was the delicate art of dueling against the grim, evanescent shadow that hovered over them? Their adversary was the phantom, Doubt; so would the battle be a ghostly one. And she alone could fight it. Her fingers tightened around the worn silver of her salad fork, and in her eyes a resolve grew until they seemed like liquid pools of fire in her tired face. Yes, she alone would avenge the honor of the Otterly-Hansclevers...and she would prove in the doing that faint blood was not her portion.

When the Baron had kissed her hand and excused himself for a long night among his papers, as was his wont, she mounted slowly to her apartments. The rooms waited emptily for her, for her own maid had been dismissed not long ago, since they could afford no servants except the old butler and the gardener; but she walked across the threshold as proudly as though trumpets went before her. A duty awaited her—one last gesture to accomplish in defence of the honorable name she had assumed in marriage; and it was a gesture which must be accomplished beautifully, exquisitely. She must die.

She knew how she would die, knew that it would be by her own pistol which her mother had given her on her wedding day "in case of burglars." A handle encrusted in diamonds it had, and a long, gleaming barrel. No one had ever seen it but her husband and herself, and they had laughingly locked it away in the secret drawer of an escritoire—for, as the Baron said, "With a master of the rapier, a duelist of international fame in the house, what need could we have of pistols?" Often, in the years that had followed, she had looked at it fondly and had locked it away again.

Tonight it would serve.

Slowly she lit the tall, twisted candles in their heavy sconces; one by one the tiny flames wavered, hesitated, then grew into small spires of light, pale and steady in the high shadows of the room. The Baroness drew the curtains.... So, she reflected, must her courage grow and crystalize until it burned without faltering, and then—as the flame of a candle is extinguished in a breath, so would she die, quickly and alone. Her heart beat faster as she moved toward the drawer in which she knew the pistol lay. Then she paused, a hand at her breast, a dreadful indecision surging within her. Was it, after all, the best thing to do? Would her husband, her friends, know how truly, by this act, she had kept her tryst with honor, had sacrificed herself to an ideal? Or would they merely think her melodramatic? Would it, perhaps, be better to go on living, sleeping, eating, trying to forget?…. No! To die was the only vindication—and to die magnificently, by candlelight, the diamonds in her pistol flashing a last challenge to the heartless world.

She moved to the escritoire, and put out her hand toward the fateful drawer. The words, "Death, honorable and alone" came to her in a half-whisper, but as she tried to say them, her breath caught in a little knot of pain at the base of her throat. She trembled…but she did not falter. She pulled out the drawer, and thrust in her hand.

For one instant she stood as if turned to stone. Then she gave a faint, inaudible cry. The pistol was gone.

The Letter That Was Never Mailed

ALL THAT WINTER, Berlin had talked of nothing but the charm, the ineffable grace and beauty of the little Viennese dancer, Vava Hajos. She had, at the beginning of the theatrical season, flashed upon the public in a whirl of tinted drapery as fleeting as a dying man's breath upon a mirror, through which her limbs shone with the cloudiness of a memory. Her head was a mass of exultant yellow hair, curling with a languid yet bright ferocity up from the nape of the neck, flaring above high arched brows. And the slow *rallentando* of her dance, that drew her feet across the stage as if they were held faintly captive by some fragrant, phantom web, had driven not only all of fashionable Berlin mad, but all the provincial solons and merchants who crowded into town that season.

As they streamed from the theatre where she was playing, the cold, frosted air glittered with their admiring comments. Her mouth, they cried, was as warm and scarlet as a poppy, the last dying flutter of her hand a triumph of expression and beauty. "No other hand," they insisted, "has ever waved farewell with quite that *largo*. And the utter harmony that dwells in every long line of her body...the shoulders, so small, yet seeming wide and flat, the firm, tiny cylinder of the torso, tapering into hips that melt with the felicity of sleep into the lower leg and ankle, which in turn divinely concludes in a foot from which her very life seems to spring!" As bright as birds, the poems of praise fluttered nightly into the air above the gesturing hands and high, excited shoulders of Vava's worshipping public.

Four of the richest, most noble and ardently covetous eyes of all that besought her were those of the two friends, the Baron Anzengruber and the Vicomte Virevaude. Their ambitions in regard to her were definitely elaborate, for each was wealthy enough to retard the rhythm of even that matchless dancer a little by the weighty tribute of pearls and square-cut emeralds. Their passion for her was nothing short of insane. They paced their respective *salons* in a lashing torment of ifs, buts and maybes that wore their shoe leather to wafers, and their emotions to a shrill of intensity of despair; for, added to their mutual love-sickness was the almost intolerably dramatic fact that these rival swains had been bosom friends since childhood. They had shot marbles together on the same baronial floor, they had been thrown from the same horse in the *Bois*—for their families had always visited each other every year. Achieving manhood, they had suffered mutual losses on the Bourse, and had speculated with mutual satisfaction in the better Rhine wines. They had learned each other's language together, the Baron giving *Freund* for the Vicomte's *ami*. They had hunted in Africa together, had shared fortune and adversity alike...and, when the years began to tell on them, they

had drunk glass for glass of healthful waters at their favorite spa. Their loyalty had become legend, their friendship a noble structure founded upon the rock of truth.

And now, Vava Hajos had come into their lives. And
where, before, they had marched companionably arm-
in-arm, they must now tread softly, being careful of each
other's toes; where all simplicity had dwelt, there was
born, now, a doubt, a question. Across the tranquil path
of their friendship the dread shadow of rivalry had fallen.
They loved the same woman.

Strictly speaking, the Vicomte had an advantage of
forty-eight hours over the Baron in the matter of Vava.
He had seen her first, and had broken down under the
acute enchantment of her beauty to the extent of five dozen
of those famous German roses that seem always to be wilt-
ing upon the stem for their country.

Drunk with love, the Vicomte had staggered home that
night to light ecstatic candles to Vava's loveliness. Pacing
his floor, he tried frantically to think of ways in which he
could make himself worthy of this little unknown, this
little dancing miscellany of gold and ivory and drifting
tulle whose magic was so accurate, so unutterably potent;
for there was something in the rhythmic break of Vava at
the hips that spoke of deeds done darkly and long ago,
before her father and mother had thought twice.

The Vicomte walked his rooms until the dawn. And,
on the following night, took the Baron to the theatre with
him, that he might look upon the exquisite girl. Skepti-
cally, the Baron went—but when he saw Vava, a dizziness

came upon him, and his heart pounded so wildly that he shook as though with laughter...but he was not laughing.

In the entr'acte, they sat in the *Zelten* over black coffee and cigars and talked of her, and their praise was wild, lyric, rococo. Afterward, they sat out the night together before the Baron's smouldering logs, and it was almost dawn before the Vicomte realized that his friend was not talking about Vava for friendship's sake, but because he was as enamoured as himself.

Then began a charming *tête-à-tête*. They acknowledged their mutual love, they clasped hands on it; they were at once exalted and profoundly miserable. It never occurred to either of them to give Vava herself a chance to choose between them, for that is the way of rich and titled gentlemen when the lady in question has only God to thank for her standing; such a battle of three is always fought by two. But what, they asked themselves and each other, was to be done about it?

They talked it over frankly. No sly, secret maneuvers should dim the fairness of their loyalty. They were comrades, brothers...they would face this thing together.

The Baron insisted that his friend, having seen Vava first, should have first advantage in approaching her. He himself, said the Baron, would take his chances. And when, after he had protested valiantly, the Vicomte was finally prevailed upon to agree, it turned out to be a very good thing indeed. For, on the following day, he received a telegram saying that his aged mother, having contracted a disease of the throat while spending a fortnight in Venice, had hurried back to her home in the south of France, and was even then lying at death's door. He planned to leave at once, and his few remaining hours in Berlin were devoted equally to anxiety for his mother and to a last desperate effort to solve the twin problems of his friendship and his love.

The Baron, longing to ease his friend's distress, swore that he would take not the faintest step toward winning Vava during his absence. The Vicomte, for his part, vowed to spend every hour of his journey in constant effort to forget Vava for his friend's sake. As the train pulled out of the station, the Vicomte leaned far out of the window, and said:

"Do nothing, I beg of you my dear friend, until you hear from me. If I write you, it will mean that I have conquered my own heart for your sake—that I have succeeded in forgetting her. If, on the other hand, you do not hear from me within two weeks, you must forget her. And I think," he added, his eyes clouding, "that you will receive that letter."

Once in the South, the Vicomte fretted and fumed. He loved his mother and dutifully held her hand, glad to see her improving; but inwardly he raged at the prolonged separation from Vava. As the days passed, he was further troubled by a sense of guilt, of disloyalty to his friendship for the Baron—for the two weeks had come to an end, and he had sent no letter…that magic word that was to mean love and happiness, life itself, to his friend. How base he was, how utterly unworthy! Tortured, he pictured the Baron waiting, stoic and incorruptible, at the gates of Paradise, proof against temptation until he should hear from his friend.

Why could he not bring himself to write that letter? Half a dozen times in the past two weeks he had tried, had taken up his pen to write: "She is yours, my dear Baron.... I give her to you." But each time, he had faltered and failed. He could not write the letter, he simply could not. He would not give her up. After fifty years of friendship, he had become a miser denying his dearest friend that which meant everything to him.... What sort of man was he? he asked himself savagely. Why could he not be happy in the happiness of those two? He had promised to try, he had almost promised to succeed—and now, he could not.

As the hour approached when he was to return to Berlin, his despair mounted to such tragedy that, desperately, he bethought himself a plan, a subterfuge. Would a little lie matter now, at the eleventh hour, if it was to save his friend? So many people lied like that, writing swift letters of pursuit after the phantoms of all the letters they should have written, and did not. "My dear!" they cried, in incredulous flourishes of the pen, "do you mean to say you never *got* the letter I wrote you a month ago? Why, I *wrote*...." It was a white lie, a pale, martyred imitation of a lie. Why should he not make use of it now, mailing the letter of inquiry so that it would reach the Baron on the morning of the day when he himself would arrive in Berlin?

Hurriedly he wrote: "My dear friend, is it possible that you have never received my letter…" and added, "I arrive in Berlin the evening of the twenty-fourth. You must come and see me without delay." He sealed it with a heavy seal and mailed it, feeling happy for the first time.

He arrived in Berlin in a flutter of excitement. His friend would be waiting for him at his flat, waiting before the fire; and then, by the proper application of melancholy, by a subtly placed sigh of regret, a tragic gesture of renunciation, he would so affect the Baron that that emotional creature would surely, he felt, agree—nay, would insist upon giving up Vava once more, upon thrusting her back into the arms of his friend the Vicomte. And the Vicomte would be doubly blessed, since, having gone through all the motions of sacrifice, he would not suffer the loss of any prestige in the eyes of his friend. It was a subtle plan, magnificent in its simplicity.

He shook the snow off his collar as he ran up the steps of his flat. Breathlessly he inquired if the Baron had called. No, he was told, no one had called. He went into the salon where they had last talked together, poured himself a brandy and soda and looked at his watch. It was still early—probably the Baron would not arrive before half past ten. There was even, he reflected, time to call on Vava…but no. There should be no flaw in his final gesture. He would see his friend first.

He picked up his mail—bills, a letter from his tailor about a fitting…then he saw a letter, addressed in the

Baron's handwriting and with a postmark four days old. Trembling and afraid, he tore it open.

"Has man ever been blessed with so noble, so generous a friend!" wrote the Baron. "Of course I received your letter—it came a week ago, just as you said. You are a sportsman, a hero, a gentleman…and Vava and I both embrace you."

The First of April

INTO ROME for the last thirty years had come, for the month of April, that distinguished Bavarian visitor the Baron Otto Lowenhaven to meet, in secret, the flower of Italy, the Contessa Mafalda Beonetti. To say that this long liaison was secret is merely indulgent, for every cabman in the city cracked his whip with a knowing smile almost before the lovers had clasped hands in the high and dark room of the *pensione* overlooking the Tiber which had seen their love in its flower, and in every succeeding phase of its growth.

For many years the beauty of the Contessa Mafalda Beonetti had been a song in the heart of all Italy. Some feline propensity in her father, some lanky Devon blood flowing in her mother's veins had made her both ungainly and magnificent, and the sirocco that swung across Italy had been, for Mafalda, the furnace that fused her qualities into so perfect an accord that she might have been her own conception of herself, so exactly was she what she would have approved.

At twenty she had married the Count Antoni Beonetti because it was quite the right thing to do; at twenty-one she had become the mistress of the Baron Otto Lowenhaven because it was quite the wrong thing to do. They found each other delightful.

Otto was a year her senior, and as frostily handsome as the perpetual Bavarian idealism indulged in by generations of romantic mothers could make him. He was tall and slender and blond. His cheeks were a flawless mingling of red and white. His curling hair rose up from a high arched brow in crisp tendrils, and his mustache swerved away from his nostrils in a daring upward line with swift felicity of a bird on the wing. When he murmured "*Ich Liebe dich!*" it was with the voice of one who recovers a treasure mislaid a thousand years, and there was in his background, to make him stand out yet more sharply on the heart, an unhappy but politically perfect marriage with a wailing Viennese, Helena von Spergen...a thin woman who carried her knowledge of the Baron's affair with the "Italian devil" so close to her sense of injustice that she had, in thirty weeping years, earned the nickname of "The Eye in a Thousand Handkerchiefs."

During the long years of his affair with Mafalda it had been plainly hinted to the Baron that she would undoubtedly ruin his political hopes; she was not liked in Bavaria. To these remarks he had turned a consistently deaf ear, but as he neared fifty, and saw his political ambitions still unfulfilled, he began himself to see that perhaps the affair had gone on long enough. His wife, embittered with jealously and indefatigable with frustration, had often told him so, although on these occasions she spoke drearily, and without much hope.

Now it was nearing the last days of March and the Baron was making arrangements for his annual April in Rome. Everyone, his wife included, knew just where he was going, and to whom; and she thought her time had come. Wrapped in her usual trailing muslin, carrying a lace handkerchief and acrid with purpose, she entered the library where the Baron sat pulling his hound's ear, warming himself before one of the season's last fires.

Moving upon him in long, sweeping steps, tall and haggard as a winter willow, pressing her lace to her mouth, she pointed out to him in just what way he had become ridiculous.

She said that to walk in beauty was one thing, but to walk with a withering woman was another. She observed that the very emeralds that he, as a young man, had clasped about Mafalda's throat were now lost in the folds of her chin, as her beauty was lost in the corroding immensity of age.

Helena leaned a little forward as she talked, her handkerchief held below her mouth, and she saw the Baron wince.

Once more she took the room in her long, pitiless stride, and in the half arc of her passage, offered time's deadly weapon hilt out, and the hilt was flattery.

"You," she said, "so handsome and in your prime... tied to an *old woman!*"

The Baron's color slowly faded. He himself had thought that his affair should end, but never before had he thought of Mafalda as an old woman. It was true. She was stout. She was fifty.

"I will wire her. I will tell her it is all over, it is farewell."

For the first time in thirty years Helena pressed her handkerchief to her heart.

"You will not go to Rome?"

"No," he said, "I will not go to Rome. I am going to Florence for a little while. I want to be alone."

At the small, inconspicuous hotel over the Arno where he had first met the Contessa, and to which they had sometimes come in winter, the Baron asked for a room for the night. Being Bavarian, he wanted to cry a little for a love that had endured so many years, a love that was about to end. He paced from the window to the door, thinking. His friends were right, his wife was right; it was high time that he, a man in his prime, a man superbly fifty-one, should become a model husband and citizen. His youth could not go on forever....

His meditations were snapped in two by a voice in the next room. It was the firm, excellently modulated voice of the Count Beonetti—Mafalda's husband.

"My dear Mafalda," he was saying, "you yourself have begun to realize, perhaps without conscious knowledge, that your affair with the Baron should cease; or why did you come here to Florence, to the very hotel where, I believe, you first made his acquaintance? You said, when you left Rome, that you wanted quiet, that you wanted to think—well, of what does a woman think when she returns to that city in which she was first thoughtless? I do not blame you for coming here—women always like to terminate a romance where they began it." He paused. "I have followed you here to urge you, in case it was sentiment and not determination, to conclude this affair, my dear. Ten, twenty-five years ago I would have made little objection to it—in fact I made none. The Baron, in his day, was a very charming fellow—and if you had to be unfaithful, he was exactly the man I should have chosen. But—" There was a longer pause… "that was twenty-five, twenty, ten years ago. Now, I *must* object. I let you make yourself scandalous, but I will not let you make yourself ridiculous. I cannot permit you to link my name, which you bear, with that of an old man—and the Baron, my dear, is not only an unsuccessful politician…he is short of breath."

The Baron, sitting stiffly in his chair (for, at the first word, he had found himself unable to stand), heard her crying. Then he heard her say:

"Yes, Antonio, you are right. I will wire him. I will tell him it is farewell,that it is over. But please go now, I want to be alone, alone a little while…." Her voice trailed off and the door was opened and closed softly. Then there was silence, but in that silence the Baron's heart was pounding like a madman's. They were right, both of them, his wife and Mafalda's husband. The Contessa and he were old, and after all they were both ridiculous. Suddenly he stood up. If he got to Rome quickly he could retrieve his wire, he could save Mafalda needless pain. She might of course never receive it, and yet the *pensione* knew where to forward the Contessa's mail….

On the road to Rome, in the early dawn, two motors going at as swift a pace as their chauffeurs could make them, passed each other. The Baron sat in the one behind and he kept urging the driver to go faster, faster. Once the Baron's car passed the new crimson racer, but the Baron, leaning heavily on his cane, did not turn his head. For a few moments his car held the lead, then it dropped back again.

Drawing up before the familiar *pensione,* the Baron, as briskly as his shortness of breath would permit, hurried up the steps and moved toward the desk. Old Beppo, a familiar figure, came forward. He bowed, as he had bowed a hundred times; smiled, as he had smiled a hundred times.

"A telegram!" gasped the Baron.

"As always Signor." Beppo slid into the Baron's hand an envelope addressed in his name. Beppo bowed again, waiting.

The telegram was not the one the Baron had come for. It was the one Mafalda had promised to send the night before.

"Yes, yes," the Baron said hurriedly, crumpling it in his hand, "but the other...addressed to..." He got no further.

"Si Signor, as always," Beppo smiled with happiness, "*she* is here; she came not a quarter of an hour ago. She has received it."

The Baron dropped his cane with a crash. He stooped to pick it up, his face as red as flame. Beppo stepped out from behind his desk.

"Strange, Signor, but she, too, wanted not her own

telegram, but yours. But alas, you see, Amedeo, he is our new boy, was alone here when she came in, and not knowing that it would be…quite all right, would not give it to her. Of course when I came in I scolded him roundly. I said 'Fool, it is the custom, to give to either of them always what he or she asks for!' But it was too late, she had gone out. But now that you have it, it is all satisfactory, yes?"

He was a little troubled. "I have your rooms all prepared, my first spring flowers are in all the vases. Will you go up?"

The Baron, leaning on his cane in a daze tried to pull himself together. "Where has she gone?" he managed to whisper. "Where has she gone?"

"Ah," said Beppo happily again, "she will not, she tells me, be gone long. She went toward the Piazza."

Frowning with anxiety, the Baron allowed himself to be conducted to the familiar rooms, cool and dark. He sat down. Beppo left him, seeing him abstracted. The Baron removed his handkerchief and wiped his forehead. How could he have known that Mafalda would come to Rome? Still, he might have known—women were like that. When everything was over, dead, they came back—as he had.

From afar he heard what he thought was the cruelty of a dream…the familiar step. The door opened. He turned—stood up. For one long moment they looked at each other. She was smiling, drawing off her gloves. Then, suddenly, she was in his arms.

"It was sweet of you," she said, and her deep, enchanting voice held that pause, "not to wire me this time. Just to trust me to *know* that you would come."

He took her hand and put it to his eyes. "It was divine of you Mafalda," for a second he could not speak…"not to wire me. At last it seems we know each other, trust each other…."

She unclasped her cloak. "Telegrams are so unnecessary, really Otto. We know, the world knows, that we will both be here always on the first of April. The first of April…always." She leaned forward, taking his hands.

The waiter appeared. "Did you ring, Signor?" he asked, knowing quite well that the Signor had not rung.

The Baron turned with a flourish. "Yes!" he thundered, "a bottle of your best, and *schnell!*"

The Perfect Murder

PROFESSOR ANATOL PROFAX was nevertheless deeply interested in dialectology. The effect of environment on the tongue had been his life work; he had even gone so far as to assert that the shape of the tongue made people move up or down town; if it were heavy, large and flat it usually took them to the country, if it were a light tripping member they generally found themselves in Paris. The professor thought that the cutting out of tongues might produce mystics. He was sorry he had no power to try the experiment.

By the time he had reached middle age Professor Profax had pretty well covered his field—no pains had been spared. He had tracked down figures of speech and preferred exclamations in all walks of life; he had conversed with the trained and untrained mind; the loquacious and the inarticulate had been tabulated. The inarticulate had proved particularly satisfactory; they were rather more racial than individual. In England they said "Right!," in Germany they said "Wrong," in France they said "Cow!," in America they said "So what?" These were bunch-indexed or clubbed under *The Inveterates*—it was his sister (now swatting out a thesis on the development of the mandible under vituperation) that got him down.

She was always saying: "My God, *can you believe it!*" He classed her as the *Excitable Spinster* type and let it go at that. On the other hand the scores he had chalked up on defective minors and senile neurotics had proved disappointing. The professor was not even slightly interested in the human whine of the permanently hooked; conversely, he thoroughly enjoyed the healthy alkahest of applied appelatives—they were responsible for the most delightful boggles. What he had yet to lay his hands on was someone who *defied classification.*

Crossing Third Avenue toward Fourteenth Street, Professor Profax pondered the key-words of fanatics, men like Swedenborg and his New Church, Blake and his Bush of Angels. He decided that these gentlemen were quite safe (he had underscored their writings); they had saved themselves by the simple expedient of Getting Out Of Reach.

He thought of his father, a hearty con-conformist who had achieved a quiet insecurity over the dead bodies of John Wesley and early Mormons; who had kicked out the family foot organ in favor of a turning lathe, and who was given to shouting (rather too loudly) "Terrain tumult—ha!"

Deep in the pride of these reflections the professor smiled. He little cared that his figure was followed by many a curious eye. He was indeed old-fashioned. His frock coat was voluminous. Like all creatures that hunt too long he looked hungry. His whole head which was of polished bone, bore a fine sharp nose, a lightly scored mouth and deep cavernous sockets. He carried a cane over a crooked elbow that tipped inward to hold a worn copy of his book *The Variations*; it was precious in itself, additionally so for the notes on its back pages, made during a trip through the Allegheny Mountains and the fastnesses of Tennessee. He had gone to check up on reactions to the World War. The hill folk had resented the intrusion with dippers smelling strongly of liquor; of the war itself they had only heard as far as prohibition. There was little labial communication. These went under the head *The Impulsive*.

He raised his eyes. A poster depicting the one True and Only Elephant Woman confronted him in bright green and red. He lowered his eyes thinking of Jane Austen; a good tart girl of a *sec* vintage propelled by decency springing to the lash of matrimony. Love—now there was an emotion that had a repetitive vocabulary if ever there was one. It consisted of "Do you love me? Do you *still* love me? You *used* to love me!" Usually this was answered with "Yeah, I love you. Uh huh, I still love you. *What?*" Out west it changed slightly, the interrogative was almost unanimously responded to by "Hell, no!" But one needn't go West. Take his own case, he had never married, yet he was a man of violent passions, wasn't he? He thought this over slowly. Certainly at some time in his life he must have curbed an emotion, crushed a desire, trampled a weakness. The kerchief in his coat tail fluttered, filled with the dying life of a September noon. Perhaps he was a man who was living on embers and an annuity; a man of worthy memoranda and no parts. Well, it could not be helped now, after all, his Mistress was *Sound,* that great band of sound that had escaped the human throat for over two thousand years. Could it be re-captured (as Marconi thought it might) what would come to the ear? No theories for or against; no words of praise or of blame, only a vast, terrible lamentation which would echo like the "Baum!" of the Malabar Caves. For after all what does man say when it comes right down to it? "I love, I fear, I hunger, I die." Like the cycles of Purgatory and Damnation.

Some years back the professor had thought of doing something about it. He had even tried, but it had been a bit of a failure for, as he recalled sadly, he had been one jigger too elated, had had a swizzle too much (a thing, he was not given to as a rule). This Holy Grail of the Past has eluded him, fool that he was, and had become only a dull longing which he had satisfied by calling in the local firemen and the Salvation Army. He had offered them libations of Montenegran rum (which he kept hid in the darkness of his Canterbury)...; he had even tried to explain himself; somehow he had got nowhere. The firemen had not made him happy; the little woman in the Booth bonnet had not saved him. He remembered that he had pressed a five dollar bill into the hand of the one to remove the other. It had all been a most frightful fluke. He had ended weeping in his den, pen in hand, trying to write a legible note on his blotter to President Wilson; the trend was to the effect that he considered *kumiss* preferable to bottled beer. He had to read it in the mirror the next morning, his head tied up in a towel. Somehow he had written it back-hand and upside down. In general he tried to think that he had had a religious experience, but he said nothing about it.

At this moment someone in flowing black bowled into him. He reeled a step, recovered his balance, recrooked his cane and took off his hat.

"Heavenly!" she said. She carried a muff; the strap of one of her satin shoes was loose, her long yellow hair swung back as she caught up her velvet train. "Heavenly!" she breathed.

"What?" said the professor, "I beg your pardon."

"Dying!" she said taking his arm. "I am shallow until you get used to me. If it were not so early I'd suggest tripes and a pint of bitters."

"Britain," he muttered, "that stern, that great country. How did *you* get here?"

"But it *is* too early."

"Are you the elephant girl?"

"Sometimes, sometimes I work on the trapeze, sometimes I'm a milliner, sometimes I'm hungry." She was thinking. "I'm so fond of the austerities—you know, Plato and all that. He said 'Seek the truth, and take the longest way,' didn't he?"

"I don't know."

"I just died," she said, "but I came back, I always do. I hate being safe so I let the bar go and I flew out, right out into you as a matter of fact—"

They had come to the park, and now she released his arm, leaning against the rim of the fountain bowl. "I'm devoted to coming back, it's so agonizing." She swung her foot in its loose shoe, looking at him with her bright honest eyes. "I'm an awful fool when I'm uncomfortable."

"Are you uncomfortable?" he inquired, facing her all in black. "I shall be." she paused, "You see, what is really wrong is that I'm not properly believed; people are wicked because they do not know that I am a *Trauma.*"

"I know."

"Do you! That's wonderful. Nobody trusts me. Only last night that beast of a sword swallower (yesterday was Sunday you remember) refused to swallow six of my kitchen knives, he said it would spoil him for the canticles!" She threw her arm out (a velvet band with a bright red rosette was on its wrist). "Imagine! Such perfidy, such incredible cowardice!" she sighed. "Man is a worm and won't risk discredit, and discredit is the *only* beauty. People don't believe me because they don't like my discredits. For instance, I love danger, yet if anyone put a hand on me I'd yell like murder. Perhaps you heard me yell a moment ago, perhaps you even thought, 'The girl is afraid.' How stupid you are."

"Wait a minute," said the professor, "*Did* you yell?"

Two large tears rolled down her cheeks. "Do *you* doubt me? You bet I yelled."

"Lob." muttered Professor Profax, "Toss, bowl or send forth with a slow or high pitched underhand motion—lob."

"Wrong." She steered him back across the street, pressing her face against a confectioner's window. "I'm vindictive because I have a *passionate* inferiority; most people have a *submissive* inferiority. It makes all the difference in the world. I am as aboveboard as the Devil. I'd like some caramels."

He bought her a bag of caramels. He was a queer lead color.

"For instance, I'm lovable and offensive. *Imagine that position!*"

"Do you play dominos?"

"No. I want to be married." She blinked her eyes, she was crying again. "You see how it is, it is always too late. I have never been married and yet I am a widow. Think of feeling like that! Oh!" she said, "it's the things I CAN'T STAND that drew people to me. It has made me muscular. If I could be hacked down without sentiment I'd be saved. It's the false pride in violence that I abominate. *Why should he be there?*"

"Who?" said the professor nervously.

"The villain." she was smiling.

The professor was beginning to feel that a great work (which he thought he had written) was now hardly readable. He thought grimly "Poor child, I'd like to support her." He drew himself up with a jerk "I'd like to have her on my hands, it's the only way I can get rid of her."

"Yes," she said, "we might as well get married—time will pass."

"How about coffee?" he suggested. She nodded. "Tired and vigorous," he said to himself, "What a girl."

She turned him toward Third Avenue. How the dickens did she know it was East not West that his rooms lay.

442

"Shall we get married today or later?"

"Later," the professor said. "Later will do." He walked slightly listing, she was hanging on his arm, she had forgotten the train of her velvet dress, it was sweeping through the dust, dragging cigarette butts and the stubs of theatre tickets.

"I love enemies," she said, "and Mozart." She turned her head from side to side looking about her near-sightedly. "Let's never make a malleable mistake, do you mind!" She was taller than he, it was odd. "I can't stand my friends," she said, "except for hours."

"Extraordinary," he muttered, "I don't know how to class you."

She drew back with a cry. "Class me! My god, people *love* me!"

She was a little blind in the darkness of the staircase. "People ADORE me—after a long time, after I have told them how beastly they are—weak and sinful—most cases are like that, lovely people. All my friends are common and priceless."

He opened the door and she entered by a series of backward leans, turning shoulder blade after shoulder into the room. He took her muff and laid it down among his guitars and dictionaries—why on earth a muff in September? She did not sit down, at the same time she did not look at anything. She said: "You can criticize people as much as you like if you tell them they are wonderful. Ever try it?"

"No."

"Try it." She pulled her dress about her feet. "I want

you to understand, from the beginning, that I am the purest abomination imaginable." She sat down on the trunk. "And my father says that I am so innocent and hard-pressed he's always expecting me to fall out of a book."

He fumbled with his hat, cane, notes. They all fell to the floor.

She sat like a school girl, her knees drawn up, her head bent.

"You're a sedentary. *I* take solitude standing up. I'm a little knock-kneed," she added honestly, "and I want to be good."

Professor Profax put the kettle on. "Would you mind," he said, his back to her, "falling in with yourself until I light the fire."

A stifled scream turned him. She had fallen face down among a pile of musical instruments, knocking over the Canterbury, sending sheet music fluttering into the air. She was pounding her fist among the scattered caramels. Her fist was full of them.

At that precise moment Professor Anatol Profax experienced something he had never experienced before. He felt cold, dedicated and gentle. His heart beat with a thin happy movement. He leaned over. With one firm precise gesture he drew his pen-knife across her throat.

He lifted the heavy leather lid of the trunk and put her in, piece by piece, the velvet of her gown held her. He laid the toppled head on top of the lace at the neck. She looked like the Scape-Goat, the Paschal Lamb. Suddenly the professor's strength went out of him: he lay down on the floor beside her. He did not know what to do; he had destroyed definition; by his own act he had ruined a great secret; he'd never be able to place her. He shook all over, and still shaking he rose to his knees, his hands out before him, the heel of each he placed on the corners of the lid and raised it.

She was not there.

He clattered out into the street waving for a cab. He did not notice that the vehicle answering his call was one of those hansoms now found nowhere except at the Plaza. He climbed in slamming the little door. "Anywhere!" he shouted to the driver and slumped into the corner. The horse started at the crack of the whip, jogging the leaning face of the professor which was pressed against the glass.

Then he saw the cab's twin. Breast to breast they moved out into the traffic. *She* was in the other. She too was leaning her face against the glass of the window, only her face was pressed against it as she had pressed it against the confectioner's! Her hair fell across her mouth, that great blasphemous mouth which smiled.

The professor tried to move. He tried to call. He was helpless, only his mind went on ticking. "It's the potentialities, not the accomplishment…if only I had gotten her name…fool! fool? What *was* her name!…Lost, lost… something extraordinary… I've let it slip right through my fingers…."

Behind the mists of the two sheets of glass they rode facing each other. A van came in between them. A traffic light separated them.

Behind the Heart

"Now it is of a little boy that I would tell you, Madame, and what he meant for just one week to a lady who had great consequence because her spirit had been level always, in spite of the cost, and for her it had been much, for she at forty had known life for almost forty years, which is not so with most people, n'est-ce pas, Madame? Twenty years are given to a child in the beginning on which to grow, and not to be very wise about sadness or happiness, so that the child can wander about a little, and look into the sky and at the ground, and wonder what is to be that has not yet any being, that he may come upon his fate with twenty years to find safety in. And I think with the boy it was this way, but with her it was different, her life was a fate with her always, and she was walking with it when she and the boy met.

"Truly, Madame, seldom in the world is it that I talk of boys, therefore you must know that this was a boy who was very special. He was very young, Madame, scarcely twenty, and I think he had lived only a little while, a year perhaps, perhaps two. He was a Southerner, so that what was bright and quick in him, often seemed strange, so bound about he was with quiet. And she, Madame, she was a Northerner, and introspection hurried her. It was in Paris, Madame, and in the autumn and in the time of rain. For weeks, days and nights for weeks it had been raining. It was raining under the trees, and on the Avenues, and over the houses and along the Seine, so that the water seemed too wet; and the buttresses of churches and the eaves of buildings were weeping steadily; clinging to the angles, endlessly sliding down went the rain. People sat in cafés with their coat collars up, for with the rain the cold came; and everyone was talking everywhere about danger in the weather and in some cafés there was talk of politics and rain, and love and rain, and rain and ruined crops, and in one café a few people talked of Hess, this lady, Madame, of whom I am speaking. And they said that it was a shame that Hess, who had come to Paris again for the first time in two years to rest and to look over her house and to be a little gay, should have, in her third week, to be taken ill.

"And it was true. Scarcely three weeks, and she was hurried under the knife, so that all her friends were very sorry as they drank. And some said she was very brave, and some said she was beautiful, and some that she was alone always, and some said she was dour, and that, in an amusing way, she took the joy out of life with her laugh. And some of them wondered if it would be necessary to forget her.

"And they went to see her, and one of them came with the boy, that was on the day that she was to go home, and she was not very strong yet, and she looked at the boy, and she put her hand out to him and she said: 'You will

447

come and you will stay with me until it is time.' And he said, 'I will come.'

"And that is how it was, Madame, that she came upon her week that was without fate as we understand it, and that is why I am telling it.

"Do I know, Madame, what it was about him that she liked? It was perhaps what anyone looking at him would have seen and liked, according to their nature. That was a curious thing about him, people who did not like him were not the right people; a sort of test he seemed to be of something in people that they had mislaid and would be glad to have again.

"He had light long legs, and he walked straight forward, straight like an Indian his feet went, his body held back. And it was touching and ridiculous because it was the walk of a father of a family in the child of the father, a structural miscalculation dismissed when he sat down, for when he sat down he was a child without a father, from his little behind up he was so small. His hands were long and thin, and when he held her hands they were very frail, as if he would not use them long, but when he said *à bientôt* to his friends, Madame, his grip was strong and certain. But his smile, Madame, that was the gentlest thing about him. His teeth were even and white, but it wasn't so much the teeth that mattered, it was the mouth. The upper lip was a lip on a lip, a slight inner line making it double, like the smile of animals when it is spring; and where most mouths follow the line of the bone, his ran outward and upward, regardless of the skull.

"His chin was long and oval, and his eyes were like her eyes, as if they were kinspeople, brother and sister, but some happening apart. His were soft, and shining and eager, and hers were gentle and humorous and satiric. Sometimes he rolled his eyes up, so that one wondered if he were doing it on purpose, or if something in him was trying to think of something, and at that moment they would come back again without the thought, smiling and gentle.

"She lay on her great white bed with many lace pillows and pillows of holy embroidery behind her, and I think, Madame, she was very happy and taken aback, for she had known many loves; love of men who were grim and foolish and confident; love of men who were wise and conceited and nice; and men who knew only what they wanted. Now she looked at a boy and knew that she loved him with a love from back of the heart, alien and strange.

"He sat beside her, chin on hand, looking at her long, and she knew what was between them would be as he wished.

"And they talked about many things . She tried to tell him about her life, but what was terrible and ugly and painful she made funny for his sake; made legend, and folk-lore, and story, made it *largo* with the sleep in her voice, because he could not know it. And he told her of himself, quickly, as if it were a dream that he was forgetting and must hurry with. And he said: 'You like to think of death, and I don't like to think of death, because I saw it once and could not cry!' And she said: 'Do I know why you could not cry?' And he said, 'You know.'

"Then one night he said, 'I love you,' and she turned about, 'And do you love me,' she said, and he came beside her and knelt down and put his hands on either cheek, his mouth on her mouth, softly, swiftly, with one forward movement of the tongue, like an animal who is eager and yet afraid of a new grass, and he got up quickly. She noticed then that his eyes lay in the side of his head, not as human eyes that are lost in profile, but as the eyes of beasts, standing out clear, bossy and blue, the lashes slanting straight, even and down.

"And then, Madame, she said, 'How do you love me?' And he said, 'I love you more than anyone, as I love sister and mother and someone else I loved once and who is gone.' And happiness went marching with a guard of consternation. 'Mother,' he said, 'is beautiful and thin, and though she is quiet, there is something in her she keeps speaking to: Hush, hush! for sister and me. Sister is beautiful and dark, and she sings deep down in her throat "Now I Lay Down My Heavy Load," with her head held back, like that, to find where it is to sing. And when she laughs, she laughs very hard, she has to sit down wherever she is for the laughter in her stomach, and she dances like mad, and when you are well we will dance together.'

"And then she said, 'Do you love me as a lover loves.' And he looked at her with those luminous apprehensive eyes, and went past her and he said, 'What you wish is yours.' And the moment she was happy, he leaned for-

ward and said, 'Are you happy?,' and she said 'Yes,' and
she was very nearly crying, 'And are you happy?,' she said
to him, and he said, 'Frightningly happy.' And then she
said, 'Come and sit beside me, and he came, then she
began: 'Now where is that little boy I reached out my hand
to and said, you will come with me and you will stay with
me until it is time.' His eyes were wide with a kind of
shadow of light. Her voice was far away, coming from a
great distance to him. 'We lose that other one,' she said.
'When we come to know each other it is that way always,
one comes and the other one goes away, one we lose for
one we cannot find. Where is that other little boy? He's
gone now and lost now—' His eyes were still looking at
her with the shadow of light in them, and then suddenly
he was laughing and crying all at once, with his eyes wide
open, and his shoulders raised and leaning sideways, and
she sat up toward him and put her arms around him as if
it must be quick, and she said, 'My sweet! My sweet!,'
and he was laughing and crying and saying, 'Always I must
remember that I believed you.' And his hands between
his legs pushed hard against the bed, and they knew that
she had reminded them of something.

"The next morning she came to his bed where he slept,
for he slept many long hours like a child, and she lay down
beside him and put her arms over his head on the pillow
and leaned to waken him, and his mouth, closed in sleep,
opened, and her teeth touched his teeth, and suddenly
he drew his legs up and turned sideways and said, 'I
dreamed of you all night, and before I dreamed, I lay here

DJUNA BARNES: COLLECTED STORIES

and I was you. My head was your head and my body was your body, and way down my legs were your legs, and on the left foot was your bracelet. I thought I was mad,' And he said, 'What is it that you are doing to me?' And she got up and went to the window, and she said, 'It is you who are doing it.'

"And presently he came in, in a long dressing gown, his eyes full of sleep, carrying the tray with the tea pot and the *brioches* and the pot of honey, and full of sleep he put crumbs and tea in his mouth, holding one of her hands with his hand. So, Madame, to still the pain at her heart she began making up a story and a plan that would never be.

'You are my little Groom,' she said, 'and we will go driving in the *Bois,* for that is certainly a thing one must do when one is in love, and you shall wear the long military cape, and we will drink cocktails at the Ritz bar, and we will go down the Seine in a boat, and then we will go to Vienna together, and we will drive through the city in an open carriage, and I shall hold your hand and we shall be very happy. And we will go down to Budapest by water, and you will wrap your cloak about you and everyone will think we are very handsome and mysterious, and you will know you have a friend.'

"His eyes were enormous and his mouth smiled with the smaller inner smile, and he said, 'How could I have known that I was to be married!'

"And later, Madame, when she could get up and really walk, they wandered in the Luxembourg gardens, and he held her arm, and she showed him the statue of the queen, holding a little queen in her hand, and he showed her one of three boys running; and they looked at all the flowers beaten down by the rain and at the trellises of grapes and pears, that, covered in paper bags, looked in the distance like unknown lilies. Walking under the high, dark trees, with no branches until they were way up, he said, 'How much of you is mine?,' and she answered, 'All that you wish.' And he said, 'I should like to be with you at Christmas,' and he said, 'Mine and nobody else's?' And she said, 'Yours is nobody else's.'

"And then they went back home, Madame, and they had tea by a bright fire, and he said, 'You do not hurt anymore, and I must go now.' And she knew that there was a magic in them that would be broken when he went out of the house. And she said, 'What will you do when I die.'

"And he said, 'One word beneath the name.'

"And she said, 'What word?'

"And he said, 'Lover.'

"And then he began preparing to go away. Watching him dress, her heart dropped down, endlessly down, dark down it went, and joy put out a hand to catch it, and it went on falling; and sorrow put out a hand, and falling, it went falling down as he brushed his hair, and powdered his neck so slow, so delicate, turning his head this way and that, and over his shoulder looking at her, and away slowly, and back again quickly, looking at her, his eyes looking at her softly and gently.

"And it had begun to rain again and it was dark all about the candle he brought to his packing, his books and his shirts and his handkerchiefs and he was hurrying with the lock on his valise because a friend was coming to help him carry it, and his hair fell forward, long and straight and swinging, and he said, 'I will come back in ten days, and we will go. And now I will write to you every day.' And she said, 'You do not have to go,' and he answered her in his little light voice, 'I am going now so I will know what it will be like when you go away forever.' And she was trembling in the dark, and she went away into the bedroom, and stood with her back to the wall, a crying tall figure in the dark, crying and standing still, and he seemed to know it though she made no sound, for he came in to her and he put his hands on her shoulders, the thin forearms against her breast, and he said, 'You are deeply good, and is everything well with you?' And she said, 'I am very gay.' Then he took his valise, and his books under his arm, and kissed her quickly and opened the door, and there was his friend coming up the stairs. She closed the door then, leaning against it."

Saturnalia

THE WEST INDIES had finally got Mr. Menus. He had shifted out of Beacon Street and the company of his aunt, Miss Kittridge, with firm religious views, political ambitions and a happy journalistic talent. He was now suffering *mañana*.

Ten years of Kingston saw him sub-editor of a wilted local newspaper, and the probable first candidate for burial.

In these years his aunt had been in Europe; the war got her back with, it must be admitted, a touch of nerves, or so her brothers had written him. They had taken her off the boat and clapped her into a sanitorium somewhere up in the mountains. She had stayed a week. He knew his aunt: taut, thin, silent. He grinned running his handkerchief around his collar. He hoped she would "make it" (she was coming to visit him)…make it and get away. All non-Jamaicans hope that someday someone will weather the tropics and manage to escape. He had never known any one who had, that is, not as they expected; there was always a little malaise, a touch of the sun, a leaning toward occultism, a desire for Valhalla, a spot in immutability; star gazing, tea-leaf reading. He was not sure that Kingston was exactly ideal for a woman who was slightly shattered. He put his faith in the curative charms of his garden.

The lizards puffing out their throats on the heat of the stone turned their cold eyes toward the sound of collective intoning of Latin on the other side of the garden wall, where the Ladies Seminary (a select school for the daughters of British officers and the well-to-do) was now in session. Every afternoon at five precisely the girls filed across the lawn, their heads erect under the weight of Milton, the Inferno, and the Common Prayer. Coming in to tea, they bowed them off at the gate. Mr. Menus hoped his aunt would like them.

Then there was old Colonel Edgeback who had bought a tangerine grove, a rambling bungalow, a tobacco patch and a herd of asses. He gave his native women servants umbrellas and sewing machines to keep them happy, and for himself he kept an excellent cellar consisting of nothing but Scotch. He always spoke of returning to the incomparable Cotswolds. He never would and he knew it; but sipping his lemon squash, or downing a peg of brandy with his friends he liked to think of it. Then there were Lieutenants Astry and Clopbottom and their wives, and, unfortunately, a child apiece. One played the guitar, the other carried about a fly in a bottle and a game of "Go Fish." A liberal dotting of young ladies and common soldiers ended the list with the sane Mrs. Pengallis from the Dust Bowl as accompaniment. She had steel knitting needles.

Miss Kittridge arrived, her nephew behind with her

light Alice blue weekend case on which her initials stood
out sharp and bright. A black darted out of the obscurity
of the back garden and secured it. Miss Kittridge carried
a Liberty silk scarf and a volume of the letters of Madame
de Lafayette. She bowed to the peopled garden, and to
the group of South American girls who seemed like their
own shadow, as they leaned together under the clicking
of the lime leaves. Miss Kittridge's veil floated from a
honey colored chip hat on which a bird perched, over
the fine bone of her brow, its wings upraised; beneath its
breast, puffed out in a silent taxidermic warble, a diamond
pin shone in broken sparks. She sat down in the chair
her nephew pushed forward with the bumping motion
of an object propelled under low blood pressure. During
pauses in the conversation one could hear the dark sound
of dripping water striking a catafalque of stone—the tub
in the bathhouse.

The downy guitarist, suffering from uncertainty,
tangled himself in the strings of his instrument in his flurry
to do the honors. A string broke zooming upward smit-
ing a dying G. The sugar went into Miss Kittridge's lap.
"Thank you," she said in a voice made unreproachful with
introspection. "Thank you."

Without waiting for an introduction Mrs. Astry leaned
forward. "The little horror has brought his fly." She flicked
her lashes toward Master Clopbottom who, deep in his
angling, was oblivious to the buzzing of his captive.

"Has he?" said Miss Kittridge.

"Want to be introduced?" inquired a young lady sit-

ting on the grass at Miss Kittridge's left. She giggled looking at Mr. Menus who had forgotten the amenities. He
was always forgetting. "Mrs. Pengallis (Mr. P. is over there,
he doesn't count), Colonel Edgeback, Lieutenants Astry
and Clopbottom (and brats), Señorita Carminetta
Conchinella, Mrs. Beadle, Mr. Pepper...and you're Miss
Kittridge? Woops!" she said, catching her cup and saucer at the length of her gesticulating arm, "who cares!"

"Cecilia!" someone said, but it was a muted exclamation. It was so warm.

Lieutenant Astry offered thin bread and guava jelly.
"Hope you are used to inertia. How was Paris? Hear you
are just from Paris."

Miss Kittridge turned her handsome scant face toward
him. "Yes, Paris, but that was some weeks ago. I've been
up in the mountains since then...thaw just setting in, skis
coming up out of the snowbanks, toppling over, couldn't
hold...mud-week, slush to your axles. The mountain men
putting sodium bichloride into the culverts; cuts the ice."
She looked up into the sky. "Cuts like a knife." The pale
flesh trembled over the stride of her skeleton. "Sanitorium
you know," she said calmly and without embarrassment.
Everyone felt comforted and disabled.

The buzzing of the fly came to Miss Kittridge, and the
sound of leaves whirling on their stems. After *The Idiot*,
she thought, there should never have been another fly.
The horrible child suddenly yelled "Go fish!" Mr.
Pengallis, whose profile was darkened by the broad ribbon of his pince-nez, winced. At this moment Sir Basil

Underplush barged into the garden. He was an old and privileged friend who somehow managed to get back for a shooting in Scotland once in a while, but always came back to Jamaica and the overstuffed chair with purfled welt which Mr. Menus always trundled into the shade for him, along with the tea tray. Sir Basil had been engaged in the compilation of the exploits of his great great grandfather, who had served in India. He was quite pleased by it, but he was happier about having composed a pibroch of his own. He was said to be "hell on the pipes" in spite of shortness of breath and an addiction to *Three Feathers*. The natives considered him a sort of *buckra* or demon, because of his kilt and bare knees. He lumbered through the vanilla plants and waded to the chair.

"Dammit!" he said, easing himself down, "why not some other sort of thing altogether. Why animals, always animals?" He reached for the siphon. "Why not a buttered loaf say, floating before the eye; a vision of Fair Albion—why always animals?"

"Bad night?" inquired Mr. Menus timidly.

"Very. And always pink. Why pink? I must inquire why pink and why not something else entirely."

"Why buttered?" said Mrs. Pengallis clicking her needles.

Sir Basil regarded her. He was a heavy man, and he suffered to scale. "I use the word advisedly, Madame; I dislike a dry heel."

"Of bread?"

Mr. Pepper, a spidery little grocer's clerk, sneezed. He

had become neurotic looking at celery and now suffered war scare and eczema. He kept shuffling his hands as if they were a pack of cards. "Life is awful. I'm always uneasy…always."

Sir Basil grunted, a rich distilled grunt. "Try your ancestors, write them up, that will let you down. Try your hand at your grandfather; I presume you had one."

Mr. Pepper looked different. "I dare say, I don't know."

"Why *not* birds now?" Sir Basil continued, "why, since the beginning of man and the draught that cheers, always quadrupeds?" He spun his glass. "Why not the nightjar, the nighthawk, the nightingale? At worst the lapwing, the lark, but really why not the nightingale? I prefer the nightingale."

"*Why* did that bird have to go up so high?" demanded Mrs. Pengallis. "All that way up just to come down with Shelley in his mouth?"

"Beak!" snapped Sir Basil. "Beak for godsake!"

Mrs. Astry leaned toward Miss Kittridge. "We call him the bee-hive," she whispered. "Has the entire alphabet swarming after his name, all his orders and distinctions you know, Knight of the Bath and Garter and Professor Emeritus and what-not."

"It is all right once you get used to the heat and the flying batallions," Mr. Menus said to his aunt. He bobbed his head toward the militia. "We have billiards after supper, and the natives sing their wahoo, and the ladies do a bit of sewing. The heat nearly takes care of everything… rancor and folly, ambition and damnation."

Miss Kittridge said "I hear that a lot of expatriots are farming upstate, and raising cows. They are very happy and proud about it. They all give parties, and milk the cows into cocktail glasses."

Señorita Carminetta Conchinella rocked her little behind on her black mantilla. "Americans find God and Life very difficult, is it not so little father?" she turned to Mr. Menus her dark soft eyes. "I walk in your parks, even in your New York Zoo, and all the young people are talking psychiatry and Zen, and about diseases and nerves; the old people of cures and of healings, and of Mortal Mind, and they are all very comfortable and well-to-do and unhappy. Now in my country you go to God softly, a rose in your teeth, no?, to prevent yourself from asking Him for favors...that is nice, it is good, it rests Him too...but Americans, you go wringing your hands...when you are not tired, or too hot. It is good when it is too hot, it is like wisdom, it kicks off the top of the head."

A thin light smile flickered along the lids of Miss Kittridge's eyes. "Yes, I know, I have traveled; every country is afraid in a different way." She paused. "When I came back to America I found people behaving very oddly—all looking for something, beating the old gods up into hundreds of new forms, trying to find something...."

"Lost the taw, that's what," said Mrs. Beadle breathing loudly, "put off playing the game so long they don't know where to begin...it's bringing sanitoriums and isms up like mushrooms."

The head mistress arrived, a line of young ladies behind her in correct posture, all walking sedately, all sitting down capably, all smiling, simultaneously bending over their cups.

"Have a drink," the Colonel said to everyone in particular. "Thank you, I will," said Mr. Pengallis turning the anxiety of his face from the young horror. "Just a spot." "No thank you," ran in chorus down the garden. "Later perhaps," said Miss Kittridge.

"Woops!" said the young girl, for a second go unbuckling her legs. "Talking about nuts, I've as nutty a set of friends and relations as ever jumped over the moon if it comes to that. Want a list of 'em?" She placed her cup and saucer on the grass beside her and seizing her left thumb with her right hand began bending her fingers counting. "Aunt: a New Thoughtest. Mother: old opinion, a By God I Am! Sister: crazy about a neo-Greek quick-lunch counter Yogi who says he *knows* what Europe is thinking. Dad: in for a nifty number whirled up in a jubbah who has the Devil by the tail; and," she added, "Brother's up in Dannamara, for stealing a cow."

Mrs. Beadle threw her hands straight up in the air. "That's the best of it you know. That young man may yet live to see the end of the world."

"Something to be said for the Public School and the private fox," said Sir Basil turning his glass. "We British sweat it out."

"My grandmother knew Annie Besant," Miss Kittridge said in a lost sort of voice, "before she raised up that new Messiah; but she's dead, my grandmother I mean, and he got away to the hills, so all the mandolins are quiet now, and nothing suffers levitation." She turned looking into the insect troubled air. "I liked it better when Rasputin couldn't be killed; I liked it better when Romulus and Remus fed on a wolf upside down; I liked it better when the Romans changed clothes with each other; when the Arabs, observing Ramadan, threw their collection of grandfather clocks into the ravine with the offering of the rams horns."

"Advancement," said Lieutenant Clopbottom. "Advancement can't be helped."

Mr. Menus rubbed the cake crumbs into the alpaca of his knees. "Yes, I guess so, but you must have an income absolutely solid if you are going to be different. You can't be different unless you have money to fall back on. But with it you can be face down in the gutter and be said to be standing on your own feet, if you know what I mean." He looked worried.

"I liked it better before they started swinging Shakespeare and mugging Bach," Miss Kittridge said sliding her hands across her pocketbook. "I liked it better when the horse had hands. I saw one of them in a British Museum. Made me think of Beethoven, I don't know why. It's nice to be able to think of everything all at once. They used to, in the old countries."

"Fancy," exclaimed the Colonel, "a horse with hands! That horse might be playing a minuet on the piano this minute!"

"He might indeed," said Miss Kittridge.

"You know what I think," the young girl on the grass said. "I think all this brooding is clapping taboo on people, I do, honestly."

Miss Kittridge said, "That's what my brothers thought. They have never traveled, they stay put (all but my nephew here, of course); it keeps them in business. It doesn't pay to travel, you get to know things they don't like hearing about."

"I'm afraid, Miss Kittridge, you are not keeping up with the times," Sir Basil said, a gleam in his eye.

"Oh, the catkin, and the welkin, and the bonny blue getout!" wailed Master Astry, his guitar on his knee, his face heaving.

Mrs. Pengallis said, clashing her needles, "He's muddling through; he'd be in a cage if his parents didn't have money."

"Liberal educations," the Colonel said emptying his glass, "are madness and evil and all that—"

Mrs. Beadle bounded from her chair shouting "Out! Out! Devil!" Then she sat back quite calmly.

Everyone jumped except Mr. Menus. "Don't be alarmed," he said to his aunt, "she's only casting out Devils of course...She does it personally at least once a day."

"They save string in France," murmured Miss Kittridge, "and in Venice they sing 'La Forza del Destino.' At the sanitorium up in the Catskills they asked me if I knit." She was smiling. "I used to *plow*."

"I take it," said Sir Basil easing himself in his plush chair, "your doctor was not handsome."

"He liked the work," she said. "He told me the American mind was more profitable each day. He said if his house were only big enough he could shoot down seventy-five profitable minds a week. I think he is going to add a wing. One of the nurses thinks about writing a column for the papers to take the place of 'Advice to the Lovelorn.' She's going to call it 'What are You Thinking?' Everytime there's another blitzkrieg the head doctor rubs his hands and says to the waitress, 'Lay another place at the table.'"

Mrs. Beadle clicked furiously. "I'll stick to religion, thank you. It must be disgusting slapping your spirit down like that all in one bang."

"Breaking down is one of the American's destinations," Mr. Menus said glancing away to the hills.

"I'll stick to confession plain," Mrs. Beadle went on. "Thank you. It unties you slowly, year by year. The other business makes people very sick and proud, as if they had laid a volcano," she sniffed.

A faint low wailing sound came from the back garden where the smoke of the open coke fire rose in a thin wavering line. Mr. Menus said "Just Jinny Lou hankering after her race and yams."

"I'll stick to the church," Mrs. Beadle repeated. "I do love a church, a bride going in, a corpse coming out."

Mrs. Astry sighed. "Well, we do have to hold on to something."

The Colonel waved his glass. "They used to hold onto my ancestors at both ends, getting them up to bed after the stirrup-cup, the flowing bowl, the night-cap, the bid-ye-farewell my merry gentlemen. Sprightly old gentlemen of the golden age, slightly sprung from coming bang down on the brush."

The young girl on the grass ripped out, "My sister used to be a wallop at badminton, now she goes into a linen closet to concentrate."

"*Con declarar se eximió del tormento*" murmured Carminetta Conchinella. "Everything is bearable to Americans only if they have a name for it."

"I liked it better in the days when the nunneries were full of monkeys who jibbered too much, and parrots who had too much to say."

Mrs. Pengallis snorted. "And now it's the adolescent who enjoys all this sort of thing…they dart into the psychiatrist's office like wasps."

Mr. Menus stirred uneasily. Baskets of tangerines and prawns and twisted wet wash sailed along the height of the garden wall on the heads of negresses, hands on their hips, palm down. It was almost dark and the South Americans were leaving silently, barely distinguishable one from the other among the resting leaves. They turned their faces toward the gate and, turning them away, disappeared. From somewhere came the sound of dripping water and of singing, the last crow of a dying cock. "Have to kill them straight over the spit," Mr. Menus said comfortably, "it's the heat, and butter comes in tins." He said, turning a worried face to his aunt, "Hope you can stand butter in tins."

"I can," she said, "I've been many places and none of them safe for centuries. I haven't been safe since I began to use my imagination." She paused. "Up there the doctors said 'give us the middle classes any time, they tell you the damnedest things—right out.'"

"That's the way to fix 'em" said Mrs. Pengallis. She turned toward Miss Kittridge. "Did you have coordination?"

"Oh, yes, a dashing country doctor, striped trousers, not quite the right fit, and a bowler hat, and he carried a little black bag. I had to touch the tip of my nose with my eyes shut, and walk a straight line with my feet close together, and bend backward without falling."

"And did you make it?"

"Oh, dear me yes, perfectly. He went out of the room then, but he was back almost immediately; he'd forgotten my reflexes, my knees. I told him they worked—you hit them you know, with the side of the hand or a little mallet. I told him they moved very well, but he hit one anyway."

"What happened?" said Mrs. Beadle.

Miss Kittridge arose. She turned her face toward Mrs. Beadle. "I kicked his hat off," she said.

The Hatmaker

THE ENORMOUS FLOOR was beautifully waxed. The four posted bed was hung with massive folds of burgundy velvet; the bed proper a cascade of laces. Louis Quinze chairs, Empire sofas, dolls, crazy jades, heavy Buddhas, and Roman busts filled the place. Her admirers, women who loved her because she made them handsome, and accomplished gentlemen who loved her because she made them apprehensive, kept the room as full of flowers as a chamber visited by death. All in all it was a sort of *Schönbrunn.* Black May, Madam's maid, devoted and simple, would stand in the middle of the thing gasping: "My God, she is spoiled!"

The girls, apprentices, helpers, designers, never failed to bring Madame something from "Sidneytown" after a night out—nuts and ginger-root and little elephants. The girls usually got into trouble drinking rot-gut and smoking cigars in saloons where they learned what a man looks like when he gets his throat cut, and all the time without stop, the music playing like crazy. Stumbling and blind they would come back bringing gifts, and work the day through, blue and trembling with chills (Madame made them work late into the night no matter how they felt) telling their stories, breaking down, screaming "Slave-driver!" at her, twitching in her arms.

Madame, in her high soft voice with its long slurring "*e*" would say: "Eet is life, eet is beauteeful to be alive, everything ees love" (God knows where she got her accent). Laying the girls' heads and shoulders down on the table, she would suddenly cry: "Work! Work!" striking the table top with her strong thin fist, and jangling her rings, and the girls would work with a rising dangerous tension.

In the year nineteen hundred and thirty-two Madame was worth half a million dollars. The gain was partly from market speculations. As she could not write a letter that was understandable, being incapable of employing a negative in any sentence; as she could do nothing at all with figures, except frighten herself, she engaged a secretary, a Miss Swann. Every Saturday night Miss Swann told her, to a penny, exactly where she stood. Lying in her bed like a beautiful animal (in point lace) Miss Swann standing above her, Madame would fold her diamond-laden fingers—the nails stained with hatters dye—and listen. The sums pleased her.

It was not long before she became very intimate with Miss Swann. Miss Swann knew everything about her. She knew Madame's childhood among the Allegheny mountain folk, all about the hotel and her father and how Madame had been annoyed when papa had appeared in his shirt sleeves; she knew how Madame had always wanted to make hats, even when she was too small to reach the beer tap. She knew all about Madame's lovers, and the deviltry they had made her property. There wasn't a thing on the coast that Madame did not know about; and Miss Swann also knew, before Madame was herself aware of it, that the "depression" was wearing on her, making her nervous and extremely irritable.

That autumn, without the least warning, Madame—who had a habit of making unexpected moves—signed her shop over to her sisters. She had made up her mind to travel. Miss Swann could not account for it. Madame had never shown the slightest interest in any nation, she did not particularly like to travel, never read the papers, knew nothing of history; however, one of Madame's admirers had told Madame that she resembled Récamier, was a little like the Gioconda and had Early Italian bones; Miss Swann came to the conclusion that Madame was going to make sure.

The same day that Madame signed over her shop she bought a great black racing car, arranged for her cabin, Miss Swann's cabin and their passports. She could not do without Miss Swann; without her there was no keeping track of her life; she herself could only think of it as something important and threatened. Life was changing, times were hurrying her, life was no longer something that she had been used to always, but with Miss Swann, with her capable mathematical mind, life was saved for her, Miss Swann gave it back to her every time she spoke.

With twenty trunks, ten hat boxes, four fur coats and

Miss Swann, Madame sailed for Le Havre. She kissed her sisters and cried and said that everything was love, and that she might go to India to find out more about the spirit. She left Black May to look after her bedroom, the only part of the shop that she had not signed over.

She had never thought to ask Miss Swann if she spoke French. She was a little resentful to find that she did, resentful and relieved, it would make everything so much simpler.

Miss Swann stopped the car on the Avenue de l'Opéra, went into a shop and came back with a book for Madame to read, Miss Swann said it was essential to get the flavor of a people. The book was Proust's *À la recherche du temps perdu.* Madame tried to read it a few days later, but gave it up, she had never been able to read anything long, it would do if Miss Swann read it.

Madame hurried through a number of galleries and historic buildings; she did not seem to see what she was looking at. After an hour or so of "culture," she would demand the Ritz bar, Fouquet's or Sherry's. Sitting with Miss Swann she watched the faultlessly disarranged Englishmen who frequented the bars at that hour, small eager twittering Frenchmen who never seemed tired of talking, and other Americans who seemed to think Paris was America without restrictions. Madame was not happy, she drank too much champagne.

Miss Swann seemed to be having a wonderful time, she knew about everybody and everything. She hurried Madame from place to place telling her about people, all famous, marvelous and deathless. It wearied Madame, she had high words and cried. One afternoon looking down on the great coffin in Les Invalides she became nervous, so many people were jostling and pushing. She took hold of Miss Swann's arm so sharply that Miss Swann started. "What for, that, why?" she said.

"Napoleon" Miss Swann whispered, she decided to save his record until they were out of the place.

The drive back to the Crillon was taken in silence. For two days Madame saw no one. Cross-legged she sat on the floor and with her scissors slashed the fine even stitches of her fitch, refashioning the costly garment. She had remarked to Miss Swann that she thought of altering the coat herself. Miss Swann said that she thought it extremely risky.

The evening of the second day she took Miss Swann to the Boeuf-sur-les-Toit. When their drinks arrived she said she had decided to go on to Florence and Rome. She flirted with a man at the next table as she talked. She smiled at him as she asked Miss Swann if she could speak Italian also. The gentleman smiled back as Miss Swann answered "Hardly." Madame was quite gay and a little tight. Quite early, at about ten fifteen, the gentleman left. At eleven Miss Swann (who was maid as well as secretary since leaving California) undressed her mistress, and redressed her in a double white chiffon evening gown, because Madame insisted on it. When she had bought the gown, a few days earlier, she had remarked that she wanted to be buried in it. With long blind strokes like one drowning, she swam into bed. Miss Swann turned out all the lights but one; as she did so she heard the thin driving hand of Madame striking the taffeta coverlet, and the slurring voice, sharp and high crying "I *will* be adored!"

The next afternoon, on their way to arrange for their trip to Italy, Madame demanded the wheel. She drove though the intricacies of the Place de la Concorde without looking, half way across she struck a French car, sending it bounding onto the *trottoire* unhurt. Getting out she found that she had smashed her front lights. With something tearing at her vitals she left Miss Swann with the car and went into the Madeleine, kneeling down on the cold floor. "I am a wicked woman," she said looking vaguely up into the pillared and empty space. Her eyes wandered, Miss Swann was standing a little way off. "Go away," Madame said. Miss Swann moved away. Putting her hand one into the other Madame tried to stop being nervous, she tried to pray. "Me," she said, "Me. Me." She gave it up.

Florence, Rome, were so full of ruins, all about something so long ago, people about whom there was no longer any argument, for or against, that Madame could not concentrate. Africa was no better. Blida, El Kantara, Tangier, Fez, she became frightened. The Arabs could not die, not even the ones dying by the great gates, only foreigners could die, you knew that immediately.

She made another decision, she would hunt wild pig at the foot of the Atlas. Miss Swann said that it was a fairly dangerous sport. They went on horseback, a Berber accompanying them. Miss Swann rode almost as well as the wild Berber beside her. Madame rode straight and badly, holding way back in the saddle as if she were falling, her long wing-like coiffeur came down and away, spreading pins among the bush. When Miss Swann turned to encourage her, Madame did not look like anything she remembered. Looking back at Madame, Miss Swann noticed that she had high spots of color in her cheeks, and was breathing fast and short as the beaters got the beast up. The only thing that was changeless was the bold savage face of the Berber, wide open to the acts of nature, murderous, beautiful and complete.

Madame left Morocco soon after. Up to the last minute she thought of going on to Spain; an encounter with a beggar at the gates of the Grand Socco changed her mind. She had stopped to drop a few *hassani* in his hand, the first coin slipped though his fingers—unheard of for an Arab—and he murmured something, not changing the piercing upward thrust of his bearded chin. "What is he saying?" she asked Miss Swann. Miss Swann said that he was not begging, but praying.

Experiencing a sensation of having died without permission, Madame put the other coins back into her purse. "I have a God too," she said sharply. "He is a little man with wings like a chicken." Madame turned straight about and took ship for home.

Her sisters cried when she arrived, excused themselves for not meeting the boat, they were so busy, kissed her and told her about their husbands—all three had married while Madame was away—they could hardly wait to show the young men to her. Madame would have liked to dine with her sisters alone—but there the three husbands were. One was a doctor, and talked, when anyone would listen to him, about obstetrics. The second was jolly and lame and kept a pet shop. His specialty was parrots; he said he liked birds because they raised such hell when they found they were captured. The third was obviously a "marriage of money." He had several too large diamonds on his fingers, and his heavy tie was drawn through another. He never drank coffee at night.

Everyone ate a great deal and talked very fast, but they forgot to ask Madame any details of her trip. They told her that the N.R.A was cutting down profits, because the girls were not allowed to work late; not only that, but apprentices now had to be paid, which, of course, wiped out the old tradition. They added that the country was in a "state," that she would find it much worse than when she left, and that people were even more depressed than they were at that time. They forgot to ask her what she was going to do now that she was back.

A day or two later Miss Swann had the disagreeable job of telling Madame that she had lost a good bit in the market. Why she had gone into it without advice she couldn't imagine. Madame stared, she could not speak. She went up into her great bedroom at about tea time and went directly to bed. Black May was the only thing that had not changed; she had all the candles burning and she had arranged flowers by the bed. Madame dismissed her for the night, and lay there tossing and turning; she could not sleep. She got up toward midnight, the lace of her gown caught as she reached for the light, and a Dresden doll fell to the floor with a crash. Madame knelt to save it, to put the pieces together, but seeing them irreparably scattered, she grew cold, and leaning to ring for Miss Swann, kicked the fragments, half doubled over and trembling.

Miss Swann, hurriedly wrapped in her dressing gown, came in answer. "I can't sleep," Madame said. She looked around. "My God," she said, "Where is everything, where are my needles, my felts? I thought I'd go down into the work room and make up some designs. I have not worked for such a long time. I don't care for the new rules, the N.R.A. can't prevent me from working if I want to. I wanted you to lend me your head, seeing there are no helpers about at this hour." She knew it sounded idiotic, but she did not care. Naturally the felts had been used long ago. She snatched up a hat that she had bought in Paris, an expensive creation that, somehow, had never pleased her, pulling it apart.

They went into the empty work room. Madame set a kettle on to boil. Miss Swann was sleepy, but she sat erect while Madame turned and twisted the hat on her head. It was going all wrong. Miss Swann suggested that Madame was probably too tired, why not wait until tomorrow, there was plenty of time.

"There is no time," Madame said, "No time at all!" As she spoke she snatched up the scissors and slashed into the hat without looking at what she was doing. Miss Swann, trying to avert the damage, said quickly, "Oh you've ruined it! Here, give it to me, let me try."

Raising her head Miss Swann saw the furious slanting eyes of Madame staring at her from the wall mirror, the scissors in her hand. She had the ruined hat on, and Miss Swann could not help laughing, partly from nervousness; then she stuck the scissors in.

*

The girl who swept out the shop, stumbled over the body of Miss Swann at seven in the morning. The butt of the scissors were turning brown where they stuck out of her breast.

Black May confessed to the killing. When questioned by the police she would say little, except that she had lost her temper, because Miss Swann was always so "superior" and anyway her nerves were gone, what with the depression and everyone going about in a state. When the police quizzed her on the habits of Madame, Black May said they were all right, except that Madame was "rotten spoiled."

When she was pressed to explain what she meant by "rotten spoiled" she said: "Self spoiled, like men are self made." Nothing very interesting came out.

While waiting sentence, Black May was allowed to have a hat box that had arrived for her at the jail. In it was a hat that Madame had made before she sailed. She thanked her servant. Black May had admired it.

DJUNA BARNES

Long seen as a legendary figure by her admirers, Djuna Barnes has increasingly come to be recognized over the past few decades as a major American author. She is best known for her fictional masterwork, *Nightwood,* an anatomy; but she also wrote other works of fiction, *A Book* (reprinted as *A Night Among the Horses* and later, with new stories and substantial revisions, as *Spillway*) and *Ryder.* She also published an almanac, *Ladies Almanack,* and a drama, *The Antiphon.* Sun & Moon Press has published a selection of her early stories as *Smoke and Other Early Stories,* selected her theatrical interviews in *Interviews,* and brought together several of her writings on New York City in *New York.* Other plays planned are *Biography of Julie von Bartmann; Ann Portuguise;* and a new edition of *The Antiphon.*

With Eugene O'Neill and Edna St. Vincent Millay, Barnes was an early member of the Provincetown Players. Later, in the 1920s, she lived in Paris, where her wit and brilliant writing won her close friendships with T.S. Eliot, James Joyce, Peggy Guggenheim, and other well-known American expatriates. When she returned to the United States, she wrote for *The Theater Guild Magazine.* She died in New York in 1982.

SUN & MOON CLASSICS

PIERRE ALFERI [France]
Natural Gaits 95 (1-55713-231-3, $10.95)
The Familiar Path of the Fighting Fish [in preparation]

DAVID ANTIN [USA]
Death in Venice: Three Novellas [in preparation]
Selected Poems: 1963–1973 10 (1-55713-058-2, $13.95)

ECE AYHAN [Turkey]
A Blind Cat AND *Orthodoxies* [in preparation]

DJUNA BARNES [USA]
Ann Portuguise [in preperation]
The Antiphon [in preparation]
At the Roots of the Stars: The Short Plays 53 (1-55713-160-0, $12.95)
Biography of Julie von Bartmann [in preparation]
The Book of Repulsive Women 59 (1-55713-173-2, $6.95)
Collected Stories (1-55713-226-7, $24.95)
Interviews 86 (0-940650-37-1, $12.95)
New York 5 (0-940650-99-1, $12.95)
Smoke and Other Early Stories 2 (1-55713-014-0, $9.95)

CHARLES BERNSTEIN [USA]
Content's Dream: Essays 1975–1984 49 (0-940650-56-8, $14.95)
Dark City 48 (1-55713-162-7, $11.95)
Republics of Reality: 1975–1995 [in preparation]
Rough Trades 14 (1-55713-080-9, $10.95)

JENS BJØRNEBOE [Norway]
The Bird Lovers 43 (1-55713-146-5, $9.95)
Semmelweis [in preparation]

ANDRÉ DU BOUCHET [France]
The Indwelling [in preparation]
Today the Day [in preparation]
Where Heat Looms [in preparation]

ANDRÉ BRETON [France]
Arcanum 17 51 (1-55713-170-8, $12.95)
Earthlight 26 (1-55713-095-7, $12.95)

DAVID BROMIGE [b. England/Canada]
The Harbormaster of Hong Kong 32 (1-55713-027-2, $10.95)
My Poetry [in preparation]

MARY BUTTS [England]
Scenes from the Life of Cleopatra 72 (1-55713-140-6, $13.95)

OLIVIER CADIOT [France]
Art Poétique [in preparation]

PAUL CELAN [b. Bukovina/France]
Breathturn 74 (1-55713-218-6, $12.95)

LOUIS-FERDINAND CÉLINE [France]
Dances without Music, without Dancers, without Anything
   [in preparation]

CLARK COOLIDGE [USA]
The Crystal Text 99 (1-55713-230-5, $11.95)
Own Face 39 (1-55713-120-1, $10.95)
The Rova Improvisations 34 (1-55713-149-X, $11.95)
Solution Passage: Poems 1978–1981 [in preparation]
This Time We Are One/City in Regard [in preparation]

ROSITA COPIOLI [Italy]
The Blazing Lights of the Sun [in preparation]

RENÉ CREVEL [France]
Are You Crazy? [in preparation]
Babylon [in preparation]
Difficult Death [in preparation]

MILO DE ANGELIS [Italy]
Finite Intuition: Selected Poetry and Prose 65 (1-55713-068-X, $11.95)

HENRI DELUY [France]
Carnal Love [in preparation]

RAY DIPALMA [USA]
The Advance on Messmer [in preparation]
Numbers and Tempers: Selected Early Poems 24
   (1-55713-099-X, $11.95)

HEIMITO VON DODERER [Austria]
The Demons 13 (1-55713-030-2, $29.95)
Every Man a Murderer 66 (1-55713-183-X, $14.95)
The Merovingians [in preparation]

JOSÉ DONOSO [Chile]
Hell Has No Limits 101 (1-55713-187-2, $10.95)

ARKADII DRAGOMOSCHENKO [Russia]
Description 9 (1-55713-075-2, $11.95)
Phosphor [in preparation]
Xenia 29 (1-55713-107-4, $12.95)

JOSÉ MARIA DE EÇA DE QUEIROZ [Portugal]
The City and the Mountains [in preparation]
The Mandarins [in preparation]

LARRY EIGNER [USA]
readiness / enough / depends / on [in preparation]

RAYMOND FEDERMAN [b. France/USA]
Smiles on Washington Square 60 (1-55713-181-3, $10.95)
The Twofold Vibration [in preparation]

RONALD FIRBANK [England]
Santal 58 (1-55713-174-0, $7.95)

DOMINIQUE FOURCADE [France]
Click-Rose [in preparation]
Xbo 35 (1-55713-067-1, $9.95)

SIGMUND FREUD [Austria]
Delusion and Dream in Wilhelm Jensen's GRADIVA 38
  (1-55713-139-2, $11.95)

MAURICE GILLIAMS [Belgium/Flanders]
Elias, or The Struggle with the Nightingales 79 (1-55713-206-2, $12.95)

LILIANE GIRAUDON [France]
Fur 114 (1-55713-222-4, $12.95)
Pallaksch, Pallaksch 61 (1-55713-191-0, $12.95)

ALFREDO GIULIANI [Italy]
Ed. *I Novissimi: Poetry for the Sixties* 55
  (1-55713-137-6, $14.95)
Verse and Nonverse [in preparation]

TED GREENWALD [USA]
Going into School that Day [in preparation]
Licorice Chronicles [in preparation]

OSMAN LINS [Brazil]
Nine, Novena 104 (1-55713-229-1, $12.95)

NATHANIEL MACKEY [USA]
Bedouin Hornbook [in preparation]

JACKSON MAC LOW [USA]
Barnesbook [in preparation]
From Pearl Harbor Day to FDR's Birthday 126
  (0-940650-19-3, $10.95)
Pieces O' Six 17 (1-55713-060-4, $11.95)
Two Plays [in preparation]

CLARENCE MAJOR [USA]
Painted Turtle: Woman with Guitar (1-55713-085-x, $11.95)

F. T. MARINETTI [Italy]
Let's Murder the Moonshine: Selected Writings 12
  (1-55713-101-5, $13.95)
The Untameables 28 (1-55713-044-7, $10.95)

HARRY MATHEWS [USA]
Selected Declarations of Dependence (1-55713-234-8, $10.95)

FRIEDRIKE MAYRÖCKER [Austria]
with each clouded peak [in preparation]

DOUGLAS MESSERLI [USA]
After [in preparation]
Ed. *50: A Celebration of Sun & Moon Classics* 50
  (1-55713-132-5, $13.95)
Ed. *From the Other Side of the Century: A New American
  Poetry 1960–1990* 47 (1-55713-131-7, $29.95)
Ed. [with Mac Wellman] *From the Other Side of the
  Century II: A New American Drama 1960–1995* [in preparation]
River to Rivet: A Poetic Trilogy [in preparation]

DAVID MILLER [England]
The River of Marah [in preparation]

CHRISTOPHER MORLEY [USA]
Thunder on the Left 68 (1-55713-190-2, $12.95)

AMELIA ROSSELLI [Italy]
War Variations [in preparation]

JEROME ROTHENBERG [USA]
Gematria 45 (1-55713-097-3, $11.95)

SEVERO SARDUY [Cuba]
From Cuba with a Song 52 (1-55713-158-9, $10.95)

ALBERTO SAVINIO [Italy]
Selected Stories [in preparation]

LESLIE SCALAPINO [USA]
Defoe 46 (1-55713-163-5, $14.95)

ARTHUR SCHNITZLER [Austria]
Dream Story 6 (1-55713-081-7, $11.95)
Lieutenant Gustl 37 (1-55713-176-7, $9.95)

GILBERT SORRENTINO [USA]
The Orangery 91 (1-55713-225-9, $10.95)

ADRIANO SPATOLA [Italy]
Collected Poetry [in preparation]

GERTRUDE STEIN [USA]
How to Write 83 (1-55713-204-6, $12.95)
Mrs. Reynolds 1 (1-55713-016-7, $13.95)
Stanzas in Meditation 44 (1-55713-169-4, $11.95)
Tender Buttons 8 (1-55713-093-0, $9.95)
To Do [in preparation]
Winning His Way and Other Poems [in preparation]

GIUSEPPE STEINER [Italy]
Drawn States of Mind 63 (1-55713-171-6, $8.95)

ROBERT STEINER [USA]
Bathers [in preparation]
The Catastrophe [in preparation]

JOHN STEPPLING [USA]
Sea of Cortez and Other Plays [in preparation]

STIJN STREUVELS [Belgium/Flanders]
The Flaxfield 3 1-55713-050-7, $11.95)

ITALO SVEVO [Italy]
As a Man Grows Older 25 (1-55713-128-7, $12.95)

JOHN TAGGART [USA]
Crosses [in preparation]
Loop 150 (1-55713-012-4, $11.95)

FIONA TEMPLETON [Scotland]
Delirium of Dreams [in preparation]

SUSANA THÉNON [Argentina]
distancias / distances 40 (1-55713-153-8, $10.95)

JALAL TOUFIC [Lebanon]
Over-Sensitivity [in preparation]

TCHICAYA U TAM'SI [The Congo]
The Belly [in preparation]

PAUL VAN OSTAIJEN [Belgium/Flanders]
The First Book of Schmoll [in preparation]

CARL VAN VECHTEN [USA]
Parties 31 (1-55713-029-9, $13.95)
Peter Whiffle [in preparation]

TARJEI VESAAS [Norway]
The Great Cycle [in preparation]
The Ice Palace 16 (1-55713-094-9, $11.95)

KEITH WALDROP [USA]
The House Seen from Nowhere [in preparation]
Light While There Is Light: An American History 33
  (1-55713-136-8, $13.95)

WENDY WALKER [USA]
The Sea-Rabbit or, The Artist of Life 57 (1-55713-001-9, $12.95)
The Secret Service 20 (1-55713-084-1, $13.95)
Stories Out of Omarie 58 (1-55713-172-4, $12.95)

BARRETT WATTEN [USA]
Frame (1971–1991) [in preparation]

MAC WELLMAN [USA]
The Land Beyond the Forest: Dracula AND *Swoop* 112
(1-55713-228-3, $12.95)
The Land of Fog and Whistles: Selected Plays [in preparation]
Two Plays: A Murder of Crows AND *The Hyacinth Macaw* 62
(1-55713-197-X, $11.95)

JOHN WIENERS [USA]
The Journal of John Wieners / is to be called [in preparation]

ÉMILE ZOLA [France]
The Belly of Paris (1-55713-066-3, $14.95)

*

Individuals order from:
Sun & Moon Press
6026 Wilshire Boulevard
Los Angeles, California 90036
213-857-1115

Libraries and Bookstores in the United States and Canada
should order from:
Consortium Book Sales & Distribution
1045 Westgate Drive, Suite 90
Saint Paul, Minnesota 55114-1065
800-283-3572
FAX 612-221-0124

Libraries and Bookstores in the United Kingdom and on the Continent
should order from:
Password Books Ltd.
23 New Mount Street
Manchester M4 4DE, ENGLAND
0161 953 4009
INTERNATIONAL +44 61 953-4009
0161 953 4090